Be nice to the man.

Carol G. Wells

Sometimes, biting the hand that misdeeds you is the right thing to do.
Carol G. Wells
2012

Also By Carol G. Wells

Right Brain Sex

Naked Ghosts: Intimate Stories From The Files Of A Sex Therapist

Cupid's Poison Arrow: A Monograph

Sex And The Divorced Woman: A Workbook (with Orin Solloway, PhD)

For more information on these books visit Carol's website: benicetotheman.com

Dedication

To my clients, whose heartbreaking life stories have taught me about the enigmatic human mind and its convoluted path to character formation.

And

To the innocent children who have little control over their life story.

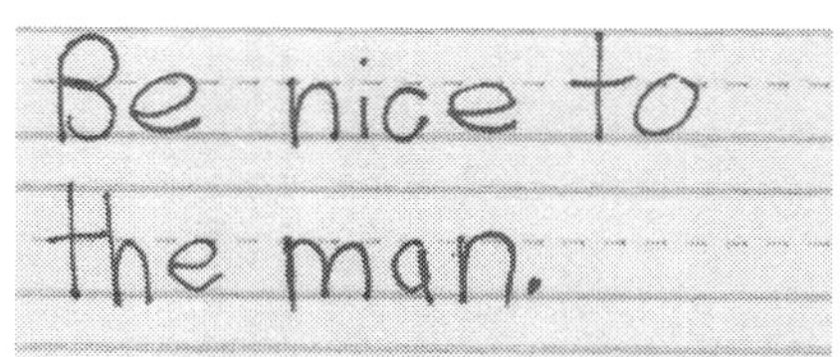

ISBN 978-1478210467

Also available in eBook publication

Printed in the United States of America

Acknowledgements

Deepest appreciation to:

Jan Ma'luf, my encouraging, faithful, and patient editor
Duke Pekin, my legal advisor and instructive literary critic
Orin Sollowy, word doctor extraordinaire
Betty Clement and Marsha Holland, my steadfast supporters
Greg Wells, cover design
Scott Parish, back cover and web design
Dick Parish, the best life partner a woman could possibly imagine

and

Riley Austin, age 6, cover & spine typeface

Dear carol,
thanks for letting me help
w th your book, I had fun
work ng w th you. hope
you l ked the drawings.
Love Riley

PAPETERIE
www.papeteriebaby.com

BE NICE TO THE MAN

PROLOGUE

Billionaire Bradley Cunningham had been misrepresenting himself for so long it had become second nature. Now, as he sat in the courtroom waiting for the jury to be seated, he forced himself to look straight ahead with the neutral, attentive facial mask required of him as a defendant. It was a task that should have been easily accomplished for a man whose whole life had been a sham. Underneath the feigned posture, however, Cunningham's mind was fighting with an obsessive, tortured thought: the fickle hand of fate had finally caught up with him. No one, not even his wife, knew that he had been consumed for months by the irony. He was on trial for something he didn't do and *not* on trial for the crimes he had persistently committed for decades. Secretly, he worried if his years of practiced deception would help him when he needed it most.

Normally, a deliberate and calculating man, he was convinced he had acted on simple human instinct that dark, foggy morning. He had slammed on the brakes when the crumpled form on the road appeared out of nowhere; the alternative would have been to run over it. The enigma, what tormented him every day, what had turned his life into purgatory, was why he had foolishly gotten out of the car to check on what turned out to be a lifeless body. He'd only bent over the body, not even checked for a pulse, before rational prudence returned, hurrying him back to his car. His judgement had lapsed for only moments, mere seconds of time that could end with his serving a prison sentence for killing an already dead person.

What happened next was more than foolish. Without looking to see if anyone was around, he backed his car up and then rapidly accelerated forward, his tires screeching as he maneuvered the car around the body. Then he made it worse by running the damn red light at the next intersection, unknowingly activating the camera flash. Leaving the scene and running a red light were actions any juror would attribute to guilt, not innocence. He hadn't even bothered to place an anonymous call to 911, a behavior that would have lessened the apparent callousness of his act and could be used by his attorney to persuade the jury of the truth.

As it was, he had a guaranteed option to assure his innocence and there was the irony. If he chose that option, it would lead to a fate worse than a guilty verdict on a hit and run.

DAY ONE

The anticipation in the jam-packed courtroom was palpable, the cacophony turning to an eerie, expectant silence only when demanded by the entrance of the judge, a once obscure man whose name was now well-known as a result of his association with the highest profile trial in recent memory.

Shifting in her seat so she could tug her skirt down over still shapely legs, the jury consultant for the defense, in a pissy mood from hot-flash disrupted sleep, almost missed the wide-eyed look of distress on the face of juror Seven as the group filed in. Now alert, the consultant followed the eyes of the young woman as they locked onto the defendant, then blinked rapidly in disbelief as if seeing a ghost. Whatever emotion was churning inside Seven, the consultant watched as it caused her to suddenly stop forward momentum, resulting in a pileup of remaining jurors, like cars in a freeway accident. The silence in the courtroom turned into murmurs of quiet laughter. The judge rapped his gavel, the noise bringing Seven out of her dazed state. Mumbling an apology, juror Seven moved her eyes away from the defendant and started forward again.

The consultant took note of how easily the judge passed over the momentary disruption, apparently choosing to assign it little importance. Months of speculative media limelight had preceded the trial, so it was no surprise to the consultant that the judge was as focused as *The Little Train That Could*: be damned any bump in the road, this trial was going uphill. The consultant, Dr. Erin Halloway, was certain, however, that this seemingly minor incident was a signal of something pivotal, something consequential that would come back to bite someone in the ass—the question, of course, was who and which side.

Halloway easily remembered the woman from the jury selection process or voir dire; she had strongly argued against her being impaneled. Her annoyance from too little sleep was now compounded by renewed anger at being overruled in the voir dire by her current employer, RJ Holland, the lead defense attorney.

Juror Seven appeared to be a mousy, fragile woman, a woman who, on the surface, could be easily influenced. To an experienced observer like Halloway, however, the woman was unpredictable and a perfect example of the dangers of *judging a book by its cover.* From the beginning Erin had sensed that juror Seven was not what she appeared to be. The pileup accident the woman had just caused in the jury box convinced Erin she had been right. Something about the woman was amiss.

Halloway had a unique set of skills, originating from tragedy but inventively, then masterfully, honed into a sought-after talent. A vicious virus at age ten had almost taken her life but instead had taken most of her hearing. Like many with hearing loss, she had learned to read lips, but Halloway had cleverly added a new expertise to her repertoire. With advance degrees in both linguistics and neuropsychology, she was an absolute master at observing and interpreting body language, a veritable Sherlock Holmes in an in-vitro field called kinesics.

In her late twenties Halloway received a cochlear implant which allowed her to recover most of her hearing. Still, in her world, the adage *Actions Speak Louder Than Words* ruled. Even though most experts touted listening skills as the most important of human relational qualities, she knew that the language centers of the brain could be consciously manipulated, allowing the voiced words to merrily dance on the grave of truth. The areas of the brain that were responsible for behavior, on the other hand, were not as accessible to consciousness and, therefore, not as vulnerable to deceit. Mannerisms and body posture were habitual and very difficult to alter. If you paid close attention, the way people gestured with their hands when they talked, for example, was as identifying as fingerprints. When the game of truth was being played, observational skills trumped listening skills.

Halloway was the highest paid jury consultant in the business. She was hired by defense attorneys to help select jurors likely favorable to their case and to carefully watch all the jurors during the trial in order to interpret and predict their voting behavior. When the attorneys didn't listen to her advice, they usually suffered dearly. Still, the arrogance of even higher paid defense attorneys was like Mount Everest: only the most elite of ego-climbers could place a flag on top. It wasn't the first time she had been overruled in a voir dire, but RJ Holland, the legendary defense counselor leading this team, was beyond just arrogance. The asshole was also a misogynist, a T & A man whose laser eyes were always zooming in on women's bodies. She had personally felt the red dots on her own breasts when he faced her, on her ass whenever she walked away. She almost quit when he had overruled her on Seven, only staying silent by reminding herself that if she quit over arrogant misogyny in the legal profession, she'd still encounter the incognito woman debaser in some other profession—and likely would be paid a lot less.

Erin looked down at her computer screen, reviewing the stats on juror Seven: white female, age twenty-eight, never married, no siblings, community college education, lab technician in a water treatment plant, never been on a jury before, no religious affiliation. Then she reviewed her observational notes: barely audible voice, poor eye contact, nail-biter, tentative speech, fidgety, slouchy posture, horrendous haircut, ill-fitting clothes, lack of any make-up. The notes on her unattractive appearance caused Erin to look up and restudy the woman, noticing now as she had in the voir dire that she wasn't genetically unattractive. Instead, she had the exterior frame of a slender, attractive, potentially sexy picture with her beautiful skin, large eyes, and excellent facial bone structure. Experience suggested to Erin that the woman's choice to deliberately muddy the lovely art inside the frame indicated repeated, unpleasant or even traumatic experiences with men, something the doctor knew a lot about.

Halloway's buds of sexuality had sprouted early under four major influences: the nurturing sun of the women's liberation movement, the shielding leaves of an older, protective sister, the choking weeds of a noticeable disability, and the lack of watering from her oxymoron of a mother: voluptuous but puritanical. Thankfully, the power of the first and second influences had given her the strength to stand upright despite the destructive tendencies of the last two influences.

Boys, so often cruel to an early budding young girl, dished out an even heavier dose of taunting to a girl with a disability. The teasing crescendoed when she reached full puberty and her mother's Delilah-coded DNA turned her into a sculptured goddess. By age thirteen Erin had the sexually mature body which turned hapless, hormonal boys into taunting bullies. Already an excellent lip reader in her teen years, the dishonoring words *prick tease* were easy to discern. Only years later did Erin learn how common it was for males of all ages to turn their powerful, sometimes tormenting sexual feelings into resentment toward what they saw as the causal object. This male behavior, the Adam and Eve Syndrome as Erin called it, turned the innocent female into the evil temptress while the male became the blameless victim, conveniently absolving himself of any responsibility for controlling his powerful urges. It didn't surprise Erin that this projection of resentment toward women was responsible for most rape and domestic violence.

Sighing over the never-ending plight of the female gender, Erin glanced at Mr. Big Shot defense counsel with his perfectly styled silver hair, his custom tailored Armani suit (adeptly covering his indulgent gut), and his too prominent nose held high in the air. Using her poker face to mask her unpleasant thoughts, she concluded that underneath his ersatz veneer is a presumptuous man, a man who naturally discounts women, particularly unattractive ones, a man who can only see the timid surface of juror Seven. The overbearing defense attorney had insisted on keeping Seven because he saw her as no threat to him or to his famous defendant. What the pompous lawyer hadn't factored in was the possible boiling anger, the volcanic below-the-surface fury, of a woman fractured by male resentment.

Jurors were imperfect human beings and their complicated, unconscious emotions motivated them in unpredictable ways. Jurors would have to be completely aware of every personal emotion a trial might invoke to even have a chance of being truly impartial. If Erin's suspicions about juror Seven was right, this might be the first time in her life the outwardly mousy woman would be given a chance to express her repressed anger at men. Halloway felt sure that RJ Holland was so stuck in puberty, so trapped in the victim role of Adam, so caught up in seeing women as sexual objects, that he had shot himself in the foot with this one juror.

Halloway turned her eyes back toward juror Seven and was astonished by what she saw. The woman was now sitting up straight with her shoulders back; on her face was the unmistakable expression of disdain. Alarmed, Erin was now convinced that juror Seven's meteoric transformation confirmed her earlier speculation: that while the defendant was ostensibly on trial for a hit and run, the underground trial would be about sexual fury.

Both hands glued to the bottom of her chair in an attempt to control her trembling body and, still preoccupied by her embarrassing entrance, Jane Nichols, juror Seven, hadn't heard a word that had been spoken in the courtroom since she first set eyes on the defendant, eyes now determined to avoid him. What an idiot she'd been to cause a Charlie Chaplin scene by stopping in her tracks, making everyone laugh at her for the clown-like behavior. She hated when she crumbled like this. God! What a joke it was for her to think that she, plain, anxiety-ridden Jane, could handle this kind of pressure.

She recalled how she had been so excited at the thought of being away from the routine of the lab where she worked that she forced herself to step out of her self-inflicted casket and go for it. She'd only been slightly nervous when they called her name and herded her with the others into a smaller room for questioning by the lawyers. When they brought the defendant in the room, however, her nerves had shot into orbit. Something about the imposing man had instantly given her the creeps, goose bumps jumping out all over her body. When it was her turn for questioning, she managed to keep it together by not looking at the defendant and by repeatedly telling herself that whatever negative reaction she was having to the defendant was just the usual anxiety she had in unfamiliar situations.

When she arrived home from jury selection, she excitedly told her roommate, Sydney, "I can't believe it, but I've been selected for the jury!"

Sydney shook her head, cautioning, "I still don't think it's a good idea. It sounds stressful and you know how stress triggers your insecurities."

Sydney was her best friend, in truth her only friend; it was rare for Jane to disregard what Sydney suggested. "I know, I know. I almost lost it today, but then I managed to keep it together and...well, I just need to do this," Jane replied.

"Need?"

"Yes, it's time I stopped being afraid of everything new."

"Hmm. Okay, so what's the trial about?"

"It's a hit and run. The defendant is some mucky-muck or something and he gives me the creeps."

"My God, Jane! You're telling me you've been selected to be on the jury in the Cunningham trial?"

"That's right. How did you know?"

"It's been all over the news for months."

"Yeah, well you know how I don't pay any attention to the news."

"Jane, trust me. This is a terrible idea. Cunningham is a very high profile man and the trial is going to be a very big deal.

The stress will get to you. I think you should admit having anxiety attacks and excuse yourself."

"Nope. I'm twenty-eight years old and I've never done one exciting thing in my life. I'm not going to back out of this opportunity."

"Better take a paper bag with you then."

"Oh, shut up, Syd. I'm going to be okay."

Jane went to bed that night feeling excited about the challenge ahead of her. But then she had the dreaded nightmare, the one where a little girl is shoved into a closet and the door is slammed shut. She awoke in a terrifying state, as she always did, at the chilling sound of the slammed door. It had taken her more than an hour to calm down and go back to sleep. When she awoke the next morning she was riddled with regret for thinking she could stand up to the stress of being on a jury. She'd paced the house wondering if she should quit, but hating the thought that she would give in to such chicken shit behavior.

She backed out of the driveway, then stopped before she got to the street, sitting in the car imagining herself telling the judge about her stupid anxiety attacks. Just the thought of revealing what a wimp she was caused a tightness in her chest. Maybe Syd was right and she should quit now. But damn it, quitting was what she always did. She took a deep breath and backed into the street, heading toward the courthouse. She'd gone only a block when she pulled over to the curb. *Could she make it through the whole trial without another moronic incident?* She closed her eyes and said out loud, "I'm twenty-eight years old and I've never done one exciting thing in my life."

It was only when the bailiff moved the group toward the courtroom, that she felt sure she had made the right decision. So, what?...it had taken maybe three-seconds in the courtroom, a single glance at the defendant, to set off her anxiety again. The only way to get out of this now would be to admit to being an unstable person. An alternate would take her place, an act that would end up in the newspapers and the whole world would know she was a royal fuck-up. Could she lose her job for being an emotional cripple? If the city fired her, she would never get another job like the one she had, one where she was mostly alone in the lab and rarely had to deal with the scrutinizing eyes of other people. As usual Sydney was right. Pitiful Jane was never going to make it through the weeks of a criminal trial—not unless she could get a grip and pull herself together right now.

Bringing herself back to the present, she glanced at the juror next to her, wondering if he had noticed her meltdown. She breathed a sigh of relief as she saw he was focused on what was going on in the courtroom.

That's it! Breathe! That's what Sydney would be telling her to do. Breathe.

She let go of her chair and took five deep breaths, finally feeling the tightness in her chest ease, the trembling calm, the chastising thoughts release, and the awareness of the courtroom proceedings return. The prosecuting attorney, a slim, clean-cut, nice-looking man, if a bit of a pretty-boy, Jane mused, was currently talking. *Probably Gay,* she decided.

She had no idea how much she had missed but her courage to see this through had returned, so much so that she let her eyes settle on the object of her disintegration: the defendant. This time she felt a penetrating, quiet coolness bordering on...what? Was contempt too strong a word? Maybe, but something about this man was churning up some very unpleasant feelings, feelings she knew an impartial juror should not be having on the very first day of the trial. All the more reason, she thought, to pay close attention to the proceedings. The pretty-boy was still talking and she knew she had to get back in the game if she wanted to be a player.

The prosecutor, Saul Greene, was on a life-changing mission. He was acutely aware of how fortunate he was to have this important case, a case that could leapfrog him to prominence. He was also acutely aware that there was not a millimeter of wiggle room for error; a simple misjudgment could ruin his career.

So, he had been meticulous in validating every bit of evidence and making sure the incriminating main witness was reliable and could withstand the skillful, cannibalistic questioning of the piranha defense attorney. You didn't bring felony criminal charges against one of the wealthiest and most beloved philanthropists in the city without doing your homework. And you certainly didn't take on a crackerjack defense attorney like RJ Holland if you didn't have all your ducks in a row.

Landing this case had forced him to begin a new chapter in his life. Fourteen months ago his partner of seven years, the soft spot of his life, had dumped him for another man, uprooting his world in a way he could never have predicted. During the seven years he had been with Richard, he had lived in a *don't ask/don't tell* world, assuming his colleagues guessed he was gay, but allowing him to skirt any direct scrutiny. Until Richard's betrayal shattered his world, he had a reputation as a hardworking, detail-oriented, dependable prosecutor. His lover's back-stabbing, however, had torn the tensile core right out of Saul's spine.

Whenever Saul thought of the humiliating, pathetic, obsessive scenes he'd created in an attempt to get Richard back, he cringed. The deplorable begging, the repeated telephone calls followed by hang ups, and the time he followed Richard and his new lover to a restaurant where he caused a predictable scene scripted for a B movie—all embarrassing memories he wished he could erase. It turned out that all his pleading and scheming had accomplished nothing but further blows to his self-esteem, each pitiable act leaving him in a devastating funk and a stifling depression that drained him of ambition. Despite the humiliation, despite the months of therapy, he was unable to let go of thoughts of Richard. His reaction to the rejection was a textbook case of lovesickness, a sickness that clung to him as if he was a charged ion in a magnetic field.

After months of poor work performance, he wasn't a bit surprised when the dreaded call to the DA's office came. Shaky, but resolved he had no one to blame but himself, he held his head high as he walked toward his boss's office. However, so devoid of sleep that he was zombie-like, his plan to *take it like a man* had crumbled and he broke down in front of her, divulging his secret personal hell as if in a confessional. He was expecting a reprimand, so her priestly response stunned him. Instead of a scolding, she had shown empathy, even admitting having been through the same experience a decade earlier.

"I plead guilty to once having been a basket case myself as a result of being cheated on. I can still remember recoiling when my friends told me I needed to give it time. You know, the trite 'time heals all wounds' crap. So, anyway, I was engaged to be married..."

She shook her head, "Wow! If I hadn't caught him cheating on me then, I'd likely be a divorced mom with kids to support. The thing is, the guy is still a philanderer, a jerk who can't keep it in his pants... Oh, God! It's been ten years and I can still rant like a nut case."

She slapped her hand on her desk, saying, "Sorry, Saul, I didn't call you in here to talk about me. I called you in to tell you that I know you're capable of great things. It's time for you to pull Cupid's poison arrow out of your heart and get on with it." She picked up a file from her desk and stood up. Walking around her desk to stand in front of him, she said, "I'm going out on a limb here." Extending the file in front of her she continued, "I'm assigning you the Cunningham case and I don't want you to disappoint me."

Saul was stunned, too flabbergasted to do anything but take the file from her and mumble something about not letting her down. His legs shook as he walked down the hall toward his office. *The* Cunningham case? Even in his living dead state, he'd been aware of the beehive of activity in the office around the case. He entered his office, closed the door behind him, and took a seat at his desk. With his head in his hands, he lectured himself on the need to get past his self pity and man-up to the challenge. After several soul-searching minutes, he'd lifted his head, opened the file, and began reading.

The notability of the case and the career opportunities it presented, along with his gratefulness at not having a homophobic boss, had finally done the trick, motivating him to rally. The case had given him a reason to get up every day and fight for something. It was a fight that he knew deep down was also a battle to return to his old self, to prove to his understanding boss that her belief in him was not the wrong decision. Although there was never a day he didn't think about Richard, the unrelenting emptiness, the pain in his chest, and the wretched despondency had receded to the background as he worked the case. This was a case worth all that was at stake: a life had been lost, a senseless death of a young woman whose only transgression was crossing the street in the dark of the early morning.

After months of due diligence, all the evidence continued to point to a celebrated, revered man. Saul knew he would not only be up against one of the best defense attorneys money could buy, but also up against a disbelieving public. He was determined, however, to be sure the idolized Bradley Cunningham did not use his moneyed power to walk away from his cowardly actions.

RJ Holland, short in stature but oversized in ego, began his opening statements with the same modus operandi he greeted each day: confident he would succeed. It was the same m.o. in which he sold flowers on the corner at age thirteen, cheap shoes at age seventeen, expensive suits at age twenty, luxury cars at age twenty-three, and high-end real estate at age thirty. During the years he spent his days selling shoes, clothing, cars and houses, RJ spent his nights in college and then law school. At age thirty-three he began selling his legal abilities and, as with all the other things he sold, he excelled. Within two years, his reputation alone became his salesman.

RJ's father had eked out a living as a short-order cook in a chain coffee shop. His mother had made paltry contributions by waiting tables in the same coffee shop while raising four boys. RJ was the youngest and the only one to have escaped the downward pull of a low income upbringing. He had obtained a higher education by sheer determination. However, he remained unschooled, completely clueless to the insecurity and fear driving his determination.

RJ Holland was frequently described as arrogant, overbearing, self-aggrandizing, and hubristic. His two ex-wives, both required to sign airtight prenuptial agreements, added the accusation *cheap bastard* to the list. His two teenage daughters (only to each other of course), snidely referred to him as ATM because the multimillionaire refused to dispense more than one twenty dollar bill a week in allowance. Exactly what the initials RJ stood for was a closely guarded secret. Behind his back his colleagues called him Reverend Jove, Jove being the mythical god of thunder, the patron deity of ancient Rome who ruled over laws and social order. Critical accusations aside, it was rare for anyone to underestimate RJ Holland's achievements. This was not an accidental development on RJ's part. Public accolades were what he lived for, the underlying motivation that made up the essence of his character.

Having intractable defenses against self-awareness, RJ operated on an unconscious level, oblivious to his obsessive need to prove himself to others. He masterfully compensated for his insecurity with an annoying, booming bravado. Since he was in denial about his own shortcomings, he found it impossible to allow the slightest weakness in others, lest the empathy should penetrate his own stone wall. He lived by the conviction that if he, given his humble background, could pull himself up by his bootstraps, so could anyone else: no exceptions, no matter the unfortunate circumstances.

Anyone who knew him would dismissively laugh at the inconceivable notion that the great RJ Holland was a closeted self-doubter who compensated for the doubt by overachieving; anyone, that is, except Erin Halloway. His unnecessarily firm handshake had flashed the first warning light to Erin: *Thou doest protest too much,* her built-in defense mechanism meter flashed. In thirty-seconds she had read RJ's body language: a vigilant, predatory body constantly on alert, constantly watching for weakness in others, ever ready to pounce on the vulnerable. His excessively loud voice dared anyone to interrupt while the vaingloriousness with which he spoke threatened to impale anyone who dared to contradict. The less intrepid individual was forced to acquiesce, giving RJ the stage he so enthusiastically embraced. To top off this unappealing package was his dismissive tendency toward the female gender. He "graciously" smiled as he talked down to women, ignored them altogether, or undressed the attractive ones with his eyes.

Even as the discovery material began to fill RJ's office with incriminating evidence against Cunningham, he never faltered in his belief that he could *sell* the jury a not guilty verdict. Having a narcissistic personality, a Utopian neurosis for a defense attorney (one nurtured by years of *closing the sale)*, RJ believed he could put a square peg in a round hole. In his mind, evidence was never the issue in any trial.

By the time attorneys finished with the voir dire, what was left were plastic jurors, individuals waiting to be molded by the most skillful artisan, the attorney best at shaping, even twisting, the truth in the minds of the jurors to fit the verdict he or she wanted. RJ never doubted that he was the best sculptor in the business. So, the eyewitness who claimed to have seen his client standing over the victim, the photo-camera that captured Cunningham's car running a red light near the scene, and the front end damage to Cunningham's car did nothing to dampen his assurance that he would sway the jury his way.

Like everyone in the courtroom, RJ's attention had been momentarily drawn to the traffic accident in the jury box. He had not seen what caused it, had missed juror Seven's wide-eyed look of alarm, and had immediately gone back to his notes on his opening statement after the juror had mumbled her apology.

Dismissive as he was of non-threatening people, RJ had not paid attention to *which* juror had caused the incident; memories of Dr. Halloway's strong exceptions to juror Seven now unaccessible to his consciousness, long put out of his mind since the moment he had overruled her in the voir dire.

The defendant, deep in his own tormented thoughts, completely dismissed the incident caused by juror Seven. Bradley Cunningham was a brilliant man, albeit in the limited fields of physics and engineering. However, he had honed one other expertise: the ability to feign the social pleasantries required to maintain his double life. His adept social skills had resulted in his being a well-liked man with a reputation as a generous philanthropist. Underneath the illusion, however, was a completely different person. Covered-up by his perfected social persona, Bradley was a shallow, selfish man whose risky, underground life absorbed and controlled him.

Cunningham had made his money as an engineer, the inventor then manufacturer of a part for an airplane, a simple part really, but one that had changed the entire industry. He had sold his company for just over a billion dollars right before his sixtieth birthday, turning his public face toward the children's foundation his wife had started.

Although he had no children of his own, Cunningham paraded himself as a true lover of children. In his late twenties he had married a pious woman, a woman he thought perfect for him, a woman he knew couldn't have children, but a woman he was steadfastly convinced was the perfect lifelong companion for him. He had not been wrong; they were coming up on their thirty-seventh anniversary. Through all the years, his wife, Rose, had made very few demands upon him, rarely challenging his decisions, accepting his demanding schedule and frequent late night obligations without complaint or interrogation. Rose filled her time with shopping, luncheons with her girlfriends, the entertaining required of an executive's spouse, her large, close-knit family, church related activities, and, in the last five years, the children's foundation.

Rose had been at his side from the moment of his arrest. She often reassured him by saying, "God would never fail to be there for an innocent person." This morning she was sitting right behind him in the courtroom, looking pert and perfect in her demure, powder blue, silk Michael Kors outfit and expensively styled shoulder length blonde hair. Her assured demeanor was fortified by belief in her husband and confidence that God would get them through the unfairness of her husband's simple mistake of judgment.

All day Erin remained troubled by the abrupt change in juror Seven. She couldn't remember seeing a juror make such a dramatic change. The woman's body language had gone from quivering prey to alert predator in a matter of thirty seconds. Yes, jurors did change their body language as trials moved forward, their body language changing according to their moods and thoughts. Even in criminal trials where the stakes were high but the days dragged on, a juror's body could read bored. Yawns, nodding off, constantly shifting in a seat, copious note-taking (maybe doodling)—anything just to stay awake were all common. Sometimes a juror's body read overload, a slightly different body language than bored. The difference, if one bothered to take note, was the vacant, sometimes regretful expression in their eyes. If you paid close attention, as Erin did, you could tell when a juror had made up his or her mind about guilt or innocence by the way the juror looked at the defendant. With over twenty different muscles in the face, a trained, observant person could read "verdict" emotions: sympathy for not guilty, contempt for guilty.

As the jury filed out of the courtroom at the end of the day, Erin continued to scrutinize Seven. The dramatic personality change in the woman, a change that began shortly after Greene, the prosecutor, began his opening statement, remained steady throughout the rest of the day. Erin knew she had to tell RJ what she had observed. She dreaded the interaction because she predicted it would end in a confrontation. RJ was bound to resist admitting he might have been wrong on this juror. Still, it had to be done. So, once the jury was out of the room, Erin stood, closed her laptop and reluctantly made her way to RJ, leaning to whisper in his ear, "I need to meet with the team right now. We've got a big problem on our hands."

RJ, continuing to put away his notes and not even bothering to look her way, grumbled, "What are you talking about? There were no surprises; it went just as I thought it would today."

Still leaning over, Erin groused right back, "Something is very wrong with Jane Nichols, juror Seven. We need to know more about her. I insist on meeting with the team now, RJ, and I especially need to talk with Toby."

RJ finally turned in his seat to look at her, his eyes first on her chest before moving to her face. "Seven? I didn't notice anything going on with Seven and I've already made plans for tonight."

Erin straightened. She glared at RJ, thinking, well, of course, you didn't notice anything about Seven but you certainly managed to notice my breasts. Barely holding it together she curtly responded, "This is not a good place to talk. It's imperative we all get together right now. I'll call Toby and then I'll be waiting in the conference room back at your office."

She turned around and literally marched out of the room. As she marched, she began to have second thoughts about her behavior. She grimaced to herself, thinking, well, shit...I was maybe a little over the top back there. Now I have him on the defensive, not the best strategy when starting a debate with the Reverend Jove. She slowed her pace, whispering to herself, *I'd better get a grip on my dislike for the man before it becomes my Waterloo.* As she pulled out her specially adapted cell phone from her purse, she glanced back. RJ was still at the defense table speaking with his two assisting attorneys and thumbing in her direction. She continued on until she was out in the hallway where she was able to talk on her phone. Using the speed dial, she called Toby Parish, their investigator. Toby picked up after two rings.

"Hey, Toby, it's Erin Halloway. We just finished for the day but we have a problem with one of the jurors and need more information on her. We'll be meeting in the conference room shortly. Can you get over there ASAP?"

Erin was sure she heard a slight snort before Toby answered, "I'll bet you a beer it is Seven."

Erin was first taken aback by his apparent clairvoyance, but then remembered Toby had been in the room when the debate over Seven had taken place. Angered, Erin carped, "Well, damn you, Toby. If you thought something was amiss on Seven, why did you keep your trap shut?"

"No point bucking the Reverend."

"My God, is *everyone* afraid of that man?"

There were a few seconds of silence before Toby languidly replied, "Didn't say I was afraid...just know when to pick my battles is all."

Realizing that the last thing she needed at this point was to piss off Toby, she backpedaled, saying, "Guess you're smarter than I am because I stupidly keep taking him on."

"No need to play me, doc. I know the man has an ego larger than an elephant, but he's the one who writes the checks. Anyway, I'm in my car now, probably take me twenty, twenty-five to get there."

Erin closed her phone, feeling foolish at being caught trying to maneuver Toby. She now realized she had been so focused on RJ's annoying nature she had not paid enough attention to Toby Parish. She had underestimated Toby's ability to read between the lines and been called out for it.

RJ and his two associates were thirty feet away, walking directly toward her. Anticipating a confrontation that would likely get her nowhere, Erin took a deep breath, hoping she could pull off a retreat that would appease "the man who writes the checks."

RJ, now five feet away, used his eyes to scan up and down her body as he approached. Erin assumed a mildly repentant posture, letting her shoulders and head drop slightly before saying, “Sorry about that back in the courtroom.”

RJ said nothing for a few seconds while he bore a hole through her with his steely eyes, finally replying, “Now, what is it about Seven that’s got your panties all in a wad?”

Erin’s instinct was to slap him in the face. Instead, she willed herself to keep her contrite posture in place as she spoke, “I saw some very unsettling behavior in her, behavior that indicates she has strong negative feelings toward Cunningham.”

“Explain negative,” RJ grunted.

Erin was hoping not to have this conversation in the hallway of the courthouse but she thought, *pick your battles*, so she replied, “I’m referring to negative transference, a situation where one transfers their past negative emotions onto someone in the present. Ms. Nichols’ reactions today made me believe that Cunningham reminds her of a man, or possibly men, in her past with whom she had some very unpleasant experiences. Obviously, this would bias her toward a guilty verdict. I think we need more background on her experiences with men. So, I thought Toby should do some digging around.”

“Was that who you called?”

“Yes. He’s agreed to meet us in the conference room back at the office.”

Three-seconds of silence passed before RJ shook his head no, saying, “Not *us*, sweetcakes, just you. First, I have to go back in the courtroom and get Cunningham so I can bulldoze the way through the mob of reporters outside and then, like I said, I already have plans. What I’ll do is authorize two hours of Toby’s time. If he finds something, call me, otherwise, give it a rest.”

Erin was surprised at his concession and relieved that she would not have to have more confrontational interactions with the man. However, remembering what Toby had said, she replied,

"You'll probably have to give him a call. I don't think he'll do the work on my say-so."

"Then get him on the phone."

Erin hit her speed dial, Toby answered immediately. "It's Erin again, Toby. Hold on for RJ, please."

RJ took the phone. "You got two hours, my friend," RJ said, before handing the phone back to Erin. Then RJ turned and headed back toward the courtroom, his two shadowing associates following in his footsteps.

Erin spoke into the phone, "So, Toby, it looks like it is just going to be the two of us. What do you suggest?"

"The internet, where else? Since the data bases are at my office, I'll meet you there. You'll need directions, right?"

Jane Nichols left the courthouse in an optimistic mood. Driving home she reviewed the day. After her initial debacle, she had glued herself back together and managed to act like a normal person—well, almost. There were still the puzzling angry feelings she was having toward the defendant. Jane had long ago acknowledged her discomfort with men and had dealt with it by mostly avoiding them altogether. She was sure the defendant reminded her of some *specific* man she didn't like, but no one person came immediately to mind, so she began going over the few men she could remember even letting into her life.

Currently, that would be her boss, not a likely candidate, she decided. She got along just fine with him. She had been at the same job for ten years and he had been her boss the entire time. Neither one of them was comfortable interacting with other people and the kind of isolating work they did accommodated that fact. Their lab duties allowed them to stay to themselves most of the day, each following their specific daily routine of testing water samples, a routine that rarely varied. In many ways he was just like her, quiet, shy, introverted—a nonentity really. No, the defendant was nothing at all like her boss.

Her mind traveled next to experiences with boys during her elementary and high school years. Unlike her friend Sydney, who was a beauty, Jane had always been homely, had always fit the Plain Jane tag the boys had given to her. She had been a wallflower and mostly ignored by boys, which had suited her just fine. She couldn't remember any bad experience with any one of them during her adolescence. Besides, she decided, the defendant was a man, not a boy. It just didn't seem possible that the defendant could remind her of a boy.

There was a boyfriend in her early twenties, someone she sat next to in a night class at the community college. She laughed to herself since calling him a boyfriend was a major stretch; they had only three dates. She never paid attention to boys, hadn't noticed this one either, so she was caught off guard when he asked her out. His interest in her had been flattering, a very unfamiliar feeling to Jane. The flattery had been enough of a confidence builder to overcome her trepidation. She didn't remember much about the first two dates but the last date was etched in her memory because he tried to take it further than kissing, tried to touch her breasts. The minute he touched her she had one of her embarrassing panic attacks and they ended up in the emergency room. After that fiasco, he disappeared like a magician's assistant, but in this case he didn't mysteriously appear again. She had felt nothing but relief when he avoided her in class. Picturing the non-boyfriend in her mind, she saw a small, wiry boy, a nerdy type who was the complete opposite of the defendant.

After the disaster with the boy from her class, she didn't have another date until two years later when she met another boy (a man really) in a bicycle group she had joined. Long distance bicycle riding had become her passion right after she graduated high school. For years she had ridden solo, but loneliness had eventually crept in. Hopeful she could make a like-minded female friend to ride with, she decided to try riding with a group. What happened was unexpected. On the first group ride a nice-looking man, close to thirty-years-old she guessed, initiated a conversation with her. On the next group ride he again approached her. They talked briefly and then they rode the fifty mile route mostly side by side. After the third group ride, he came right out and asked her to dinner. Hesitant, but ever optimistic that she could be like other women, she accepted, making the huge mistake of letting him pick her up at the house.

The date had been hellish. The man had talked about himself the entire evening, never once asking a single question about her. Then, immediately after dinner he drove her home. He walked her to the door and before she could get her key out, he made a forceful sexual move, pinning her to the door with his body as he leaned over and mashed his lips against hers. Instinctively, she bit him. He yelled in pain, pulled back, and slapped her hard on the face before saying, "You savage bitch! You're nothing but a cock-tease." He started toward her again, his hands reaching out for her shoulders to push her back against the door. Something inside her snapped and she kneed him in the groin. While he was bent over in pain, she managed to get inside the house and lock the door. The man beat on the door, yelled profanities at her for a few minutes, but eventually limped back to his car and drove off. Fearful of facing him again, she never returned to the group ride.

Jane concentrated on the image of the defendant, trying to find something about the distinguished older man that could possibly remind her of the younger bike-riding jerk that had attacked her. She came up blank.

So she thought about the only older man she knew: her adoptive father. He was a man who lived in the shadows of his controlling, domineering wife. Her adoptive father had been more like a robot: he went to work, came home, went to his workshop in the garage, ate dinner in silence, watched TV, went to bed. (*Wow! Sounds pathetic and just like my life!*) It was painfully clear to Jane that it was her mother who was the one who wanted to adopt a child. Her father had not been unkind, just indifferent. Jane didn't feel negative toward him, unless you could count feeling sorry for him as a negative. He was really a nobody, nothing at all like the powerful, big shot defendant. She firmly ruled him out as a possibility.

Well, it certainly couldn't be her natural father, a man she never met and knew nothing about.

As she pulled up in the drive of the small duplex she and Sydney rented, Jane was sure that her friend would be able to help her figure out the puzzle. Sydney was her advisor, the person she went to when she was uncertain, inexperienced, intimidated, doubtful, all the many times she found herself lacking confidence. She and Syd were opposite in so many ways; it never ceased to amaze her that the woman remained her steadfast friend. They had become friends when Jane was seven, shortly after she came to live with her adoptive parents.

Jane remembered nothing about the death of her real mother or of the months after her death, months in which she was apparently *in the system*. The only thing she knew about her real mother was what her adoptive mother was willing to tell her; her mother had died suddenly of an illness when Jane was six and Jane had no other family. The little that Jane could recall in the early days of living with her new parents was fogged by one distinct emotion: fear. She clearly remembered the anxiety of going to a new school, a fear which eventually progressed into a full blown phobia. Her new mother was not sympathetic, dragging Jane to school despite her cowering tears. "You'll get over it once you make some friends," her mother repeatedly said.

One day when her mother again pushed her out of the car and drove off after saying those insincere words, a little girl materialized out of nowhere. Standing next to the sobbing Jane, the girl said, "Hi, my name's Sydney. I heard what your mom said and I'll be your friend." Then she took Jane's hand and walked with her to the school building. Jane immediately found herself mesmerized by her new friend's outgoing, sassy manner—everything Jane wasn't. Her mother had been right after all; Jane's phobia did disappear when she made a friend. To this day she never understood what made Sydney take her under her wing. She decided long ago, however, that she never wanted to question it. She was just thankful for having found such a protective friend.

As the two friends matured, their very different personalities took them in divergent directions. Males were drawn to Sydney like a magnet and she had so many boyfriends Jane couldn't keep them straight. Despite their different social paths they remained the closest of friends. Immediately after high school they moved in together and remained roommates ever since. While Jane went to work in the lab, Sydney...well, she chose a line of work that Jane could never wrap her mind around. Sydney's choice of work, the kind of work that consisted of profitable relations with men, was one Jane found unimaginable. However, Jane's deep gratitude and loyalty kept her tied to Sydney despite her friend's choice to make a living using men—which was the way Sydney described her occupation.

It was a little after four-thirty when Jane opened the front door and peered into the small living room of the duplex, hoping Syd was awake so she could talk to her about her day. Disappointed when she didn't find her friend awake, she tiptoed inside, immediately taking off her shoes to keep from waking Sydney, whose day usually started in the late afternoon. Sydney would not be pleased if Jane woke her up. Jane picked up the various clothes strewn around the living room, carefully folding them and placing them on the couch. It was a rote task, one she did almost daily and without irritation because she believed it was little price to pay for all that Syd did for her. Next she went into the tiny kitchen to make coffee, not a chore but a simple favor she often did for her roommate. Just as the coffee finished dripping, Sydney strolled out of the bedroom. She did a cat stretch with her lithe, provocative body, and sniffed the air saying, "Now, that's a smell worth getting up for."

Jane brought her a mug of coffee, handed it to her, and they both took a seat on the couch. Jane remained silent and expectant, hoping Sydney would be the one to ask her about her day. Letting her do the asking was a practice Jane had developed over the years as a way of being sure that she had Sydney's full attention. Talking to Syd when she was preoccupied tended to result in short, vague, responses that ended with Jane feeling insignificant, always followed by feelings of deep sadness.

Today Sydney did not disappoint her. "So, tell me about your big day," she said, as she took a sip of her coffee before pulling her stunning legs up under her.

"It started off badly, just like you expected. But then I took some deep breaths like you always tell me and I managed to get my nerves under control for the rest of the day."

"Cool."

"However, there's something that concerns me."

Sydney blew on the mug before taking a sip, then asked,"What's that?"

"The defendant, something about him...." Jane stood up and began pacing.

Sydney took another sip of her coffee, waiting for about fifteen-seconds before saying, "Come on, spit it out, girl."

Oh, no, she's getting impatient, thought Jane, her heart accelerating. Jane also hated it when Sydney lost patience with her. "Okay, okay, so here's the thing. I'm just now realizing I'm not supposed to be talking about the trial. The judge warned us several times."

Sydney gave a scornful chuckle. "That's bullshit, Jane. Jurors are human, they all talk about the trial."

"You think?"

"Of course. They all say they are not supposed to before doing it anyway. It's human nature. People need to talk about something as important as being a juror, especially on a criminal trial and especially considering the man who is on trial. Few people can keep that kind of stress to themselves."

"You really think most jurors talk even when they've been told not to?"

"Absolutely. Unless they get sequestered, of course. Do you think I'm going to blab to the judge about what you tell me?"

"No! No! Of course not."

"So, talk to me. You were telling me something about the defendant."

Jane was now in the process of further demolishing a fragment of a fingernail when Sydney snapped at her, "Stop biting your nails!"

"Oh, right," Jane said, as she sat back down, placing her hand under her butt. "So, okay, when I first saw the man before the trial, it was like I was hit with a blast of bad vibes. Then last night I had one of my closet nightmares."

"The one where the little girl gets locked in?"

"Right. Well, today when I looked at the man, I literally stopped in my tracks, causing the man behind me to walk into me. Everyone in the courtroom laughed. I felt like such a fool but I did the breathing thing and got myself under control. So, anyway, what I was feeling was so weird...it's like I've had a really bad run-in with him at some point. But, you know, I've thought and thought about it and I'm pretty sure I've never met him. I mean where would I meet a wealthy, famous man like that?"

"Maybe he reminds you of someone."

"Yeah, I thought of that. While I was driving home I went over every man in my life that I can remember, which, as you well know, I can count on one hand. There is no one I can remember ever knowing who reminds me of this man."

"Well, then, maybe he's an archetype."

"What the heck is an archetype?"

"It's an embodiment, a stereotype—you know, maybe he just represents the *type* of man you find repugnant."

"Well, if that's the case, then I'm in trouble. I mean it's only day one and I took an oath to be impartial."

"Fuck the oath, Jane. Taking an oath in court to be impartial is a convenient social deception. There is no such thing as an impartial juror. Every person in that jury box comes with baggage. How can they not? Just think about it. You said the *man* behind you bumped into you. Okay, so he's a man. You think his being *male* has nothing to do with how he views the evidence that is going to be presented?"

"I guess not. But the jury is made up of an equal number of men and women."

"That's not the point. What I'm saying is that each person in that jury box is influenced by their own biography, by the way their own history intersects that biography."

"You're losing me."

"Okay, here's a hypothetical example. Let's just say, Mrs. X, juror number twelve, is married to a factory worker and has five kids. It's tough to raise five kids on a factory worker's salary but they're responsible, hard working people and manage to get by. So, here's comes the history part. There is a recession, the plant closes down and Mr. X gets his walking papers. Now it's no longer difficult to get by, it becomes impossible to get by. So, maybe they lose their house and the family has nowhere to live. You with me?"

"Yeah. I think so."

"Okay, so, what I'm saying is that Mrs. X would view the evidence against the defendant, a manufacturing mogul, a man who made millions on the backs of men like her husband, in one way before the recession and another way after the recession. It's just human nature that your personal experiences influence the way you see things."

"Okay, now I see what you're saying. Well, if no juror is truly impartial, then there is no reason for me to quit, right?"

"Right. Besides, it is still really early in the game. As the trial continues, you might remember some man with whom you did have a bad experience."

"So, then what?"

"Then you can match the bad vibes with the right person and not the defendant."

Erin was thankful she had a GPS in her car. Being lost in this part of town was a scary thought, as was being separated from her brand new BMW 335is. When the voice on the GPS said, "You've reached your final destination," she appealed to the God Of Parking to find her a space close to Toby's office so she wouldn't be walking alone for very long. She liked and trusted Toby, knew he was a good investigator, knew he commanded, like herself, a deservedly high price, all of which made her question why he chose to have an office in such a low-rent part of town.

There was considerable activity in the area and, unfortunately, no immediate parking space in front of the address Toby had given her. She was forced to circle the block, unnervingly taking note of the liquor store on one side of Toby's office and the large bail bondsman's sign on the other side. On her second go-round, a car pulled out from a space in front of the liquor store and Erin hesitantly pulled into the space. She sat in the car for a few minutes observing the kaleidoscope of people coming and going, looking for any sign of someone paying attention to her expensive car. Finally, deciding she was acting like an overprotective parent, she got out of the car. As she locked it, however, she couldn't help patting it on the hood and whispering, "I love you, baby. Please don't leave me."

Toby, dressed in a colorful polo shirt and black chinos, like every other time Erin had seen him, opened the door before she had a chance to knock. He ushered her in with a slight bow. In one hand he had a highball glass half filled with an amber fluid which he held up, clinking the ice as he asked, "Happy hour. Care to join me?"

"Absolutely. Any chance you happen to have Tito's?"

The two-hundred-fifty pound, six-foot-five former defensive tackle bowed even more deeply, saying, "So sorry, Madam, but I left the Tito's back at my chateau, sitting next to the ten-year-old Bordeaux."

Erin grinned at the formidable black man, "Okay, okay, I get it. I'll settle for the house vodka...on the rocks, please." They walked past a tiny reception area with a single desk and into another small room, also with a single desk. While he poured her drink, Erin scanned the utilitarian, tidy office, a room that seemed very undersized and understated for the large man. He handed her the vodka, saying, "I'll be glad to answer your question."

"Question...what question?"

"Come on, Doc. Walk the talk. Your body language says you want to know why, at my rates, I'm in this crummy location."

Erin, flushed at getting caught in her own game, wondering if had been watching her while she sat in her car scrutinizing all the people. She put her hands up in a surrendering gesture, saying, " Guilty as charged. By the way, it's no fun being ensnared by my own trap."

Toby gave a big belly laugh then took a swig of his drink. "I was raised in this neighborhood. It was good enough for me then so it's good enough for me now. Besides, many of my valuable contacts reside in its underbelly and being close by makes it easier to tickle that tummy for information."

This man is such an enigma, thought Erin. He is an industrial-strength, gristly, no-nonsense, street-smart man who is also intuitive, witty, kindhearted and, regrettably, a man she had underestimated.

"So, given my exorbitant rates," he continued, "we best get down to business so we have something to show the Reverend." He pulled a barstool up next to an unusually high desk, apparently custom made for the large man, where a computer screen was filled with a page of data. He sat in an extra large chair and then patted the stool, saying, "Sit."

Erin took a seat on the stool and examined the data that was on the screen. "These are birth records, right?"

"Right. And what I found is that there is no record of a Jane Nichols born on the date in the city she listed on her juror form."

"Whoa! That's curious."

"Yes, it is. Since they get the jury pool from drivers' licenses and voting registrations, it could mean she's been married...though she checked single, not divorced, on her marital status. Another option is that she was legally adopted and took the name of her new parents."

Erin sat back in her chair, thinking. "Adopted, huh? The form doesn't ask if you've been adopted, does it?"

"No, it doesn't. But I can."

"You can?"

Toby began typing on the keyboard. "I'm accessing that data base right now."

"Just like that, huh? Amazing."

"And necessary. How else could I find people who don't want to be found?" Toby worked the keyboard for another minute before saying, "Okay, here it is. Jane Nichols was born..." Toby leaned into the screen, shaking his head, " Yeah, I'm reading this right. She was born *Bane* Romer, birth mother was Tamara Romer."

"Did you say B as in boy?"

Toby pointed to the screen, "Look for yourself."

Erin leaned in toward the screen. "Bane? What an awful thing to do to a kid. What kind of person would give her child a name that means a nuisance or a curse? Maybe it was a good thing she was adopted. Can you find out more about the birth parents?"

"I'll see what I can do." This time it took Toby longer but he finally brought up a page on the screen. "It says here that Jane's mother, Tamara Romer, died when she was only twenty-two, no parents or siblings listed here for Tamara. No husband listed either. Tamara's daughter, Bane, was put in Child Protective Services when she was six and then went into foster care with a coupled named Sara and James Nichols. The Nichols officially adopted her when she was seven. Apparently they're the ones who changed her name to Jane."

"Thank God for small favors. But I thought adoption records were sealed?"

Toby gave her a mischievous smile. "Supposed to be."

Erin just shook her head. "So, does it say how the mother died?"

"Nope. Adoption files won't have that. But maybe the hospital records will." Toby began typing again.

"Now *this* can't possibly be legal?"

"You want legal, go get a court order. You want the information now, keep your butt on the chair and your mouth shut."

Erin did a zipping motion across her mouth and sat back in her chair. It took a while before Toby swiveled the screen toward her.

"Nothing in the hospital records but I did find something in the death records," he said.

Erin leaned into the monitor, taking time to read, then saying, "Drug overdose, huh? A child can certainly crimp the style of a drug addict. I guess I now have an explanation for the name Bane."

Toby swung the screen back toward himself and as he started typing again, he said, "Druggies usually have police records." After another couple of minutes he said, "Bingo! Tamara was arrested for prostitution when she was sixteen. Looks like she was ordered into the Child Protective system after her first arrest. Then nothing until she was arrested again at eighteen for soliciting, but she was released on special circumstances rather than put in jail."

Erin said, "Which likely means she was living on the streets, either an orphan or, more likely, a runaway. Since she died at twenty-two and her child was six at the time, it means at the time of her first arrest she would have already been pregnant...or already have given birth to Jane...I *refuse* to call her Bane. What does the system do with a minor who is pregnant or has a child?"

"State funded residential treatment. When they turn eighteen, the systems spits them out, supposedly with a job and social service follow-up. However, at eighteen they're of legal age and the state can't force them to cooperate. So, unless they get caught doing something illegal, way too many times they often just drift into oblivion."

Erin stood up and began pacing in the small room. "Well, damn, Toby. Our problematic juror was born to a drug-addicted, teenage prostitute, who died at twenty-two. Can you imagine what a nightmare of a life that would be for a small child? It's even possible Jane was an addict when she was born. Let me tell you, no one escapes something like that without some scars. Hell, we don't even know if Jane saw her mother having sex with her Johns. However, having an irresponsible druggie for a mother and later being adopted is not grounds for dismissal. That is, unless we can proved she lied on her juror form."

"Let me ask you this. What makes you so sure her lousy background is bad for our client?"

"I detected what I believed to be some negative transference for Cunningham. This morning I saw shock in her eyes when she first saw him, as if she knew him from somewhere. Then later I detected an expression of contempt which stayed with her until the end of court. Now that I know her background, my current hypothesis is that Cunningham represents the Johns in her mother's life. He's a powerful figure, a man who gets his way and uses people. Jane, being a small, helpless child would need to see the men, not the drugs, as controlling her mother—*forcing* her to do ugly things. It's survival instincts that keep a child from believing a parent could be so weak, so...defective."

"Obviously, you don't think The Reverend can work his magic on her, negating this transference thing."

"What I think is that RJ is just another powerful, controlling man to Jane, the kind of man Jane unconsciously blames for her mother's death. So, no...I think his persuasive, domineering personality will backfire this time."

"Well, I'll be the first in line to buy a ticket to the fireworks when you tell the Reverend that."

"How about we flip a coin to determine who has the pleasure of telling him?"

Toby dubiously eyed Erin for a few seconds before opening his desk drawer and pulling out a silver dollar. "Okay, heads up, you get to tell him."

"Hold on a minute. Let me see that coin."

"What? You think I would cheat you?"

"I've learned my lesson, Toby. I'm done with underestimating you. Let me see that coin."

He flipped the coin toward Erin. Erin caught it and looked at both sides, "Just as I thought."

"Can't blame a guy for trying. Besides, this negative transference stuff is your bailiwick. No way I'm trying to explain that to RJ."

"I thought you said you weren't afraid of him."

"Come on, doc, that manipulation won't work with me. And, hey...I thought you said you were done with underestimating me."

"Can't blame a gal for trying." Flipping open her cell phone, Erin said, "It's not going to get any easier so I best get this over with."

Rose Cunningham held on tightly to her husband's arm as RJ acted as front guard. The three *Specials-Of-The-Day* on the media's menu had to fight their way through the crowd of hungry sharks waiting to sink their teeth into the vulnerable meat. RJ, stopping for several minutes on the courthouse steps to talk to the press, enjoyed himself immensely as he spouted his usual bravado. Rose, even though an experienced media maven, remained half hidden behind her husband as they moved toward the waiting limo.

Once inside the car, Rose leaned into her husband and asked, "How do you think it went today?"

Distractedly, Bradley answered, "Fine, I guess."

Rose, ever attentive to her husband's tone, had immediately noticed his usual conviction was missing. "You don't seem your usual confident self. Is there something you're not telling me, sweetie?"

Without looking at her, Bradley replied, "Huh?"

Rose's instincts told her something wasn't right. "Oh, I was just wondering why you seem so distracted. It worries me. That's all."

Cunningham tightened, his body becoming rigid with anger, his voice threateningly loud. "You've never questioned me before so why are you questioning me now?"

Rose immediately cowered, shrinking back in her seat. "I'm so sorry...it was just something in the tone of your voice. You just didn't sound your usual confident self is all."

Bradley snapped, "I said everything will be fine and I meant it so give it a rest, will you?"

Rose grew quiet. Wounded by her husband's uncharacteristically sharp tone of voice, she had to fight back tears. As she nursed her hurt feelings, her thoughts were drawn to months earlier, when the whole mess had come crashing into their lives.

Bradley had chosen not to tell her about the incident when it happened; the first she knew about it was when he had been arrested. Later, when she had finally gotten up the courage to ask him why he hadn't told her about that night, his answer had been all about protecting her: "I didn't call 911 because I knew the woman was already dead and I couldn't do anything to help at that point. I didn't want the publicity to halo the children's foundation and I didn't want to upset you by telling you about something that couldn't be changed."

She remembered thinking back then that she had to make a decision: believe and stand by him or let suspicion ruin the life they had built together. She had sought God's countenance and believed with all her heart that His answer was for her to stand by her man, a strong, benevolent man whom she was convinced had truth in his heart. But now, smarting from his uncharacteristic outburst of anger, she found herself questioning whether he had really been protecting her and the foundation. Maybe he had only been protecting himself when he left the scene that night without telling anyone. Her body shivered with the thought he might not be telling her the whole story.

Just then Bradley broke the silence, apologizing, “I’m sorry I raised my voice. You didn’t deserve that. You’ve been nothing but an angel about this whole ugly mess. I couldn’t do this without you and I hope you know how much I love you.”

Rose melted, doubts about her husband disappearing from her thoughts, doubts that were immediately replaced by feelings of gratitude for having been blessed with such a wonderful, loving man. “I love you too, Bradley. And I know we’re in the protective hands of God, so we’ll get through this I’m sure.”

Bradley, taking her hand, squeezed it gently, saying with conviction, “Yes, I’m sure God is watching over us.”

To himself Bradley was saying, *Piss on His watching...the fucking Asshole has finally decided to punish me.*

It had been years since Saul Greene had been in a single’s bar. But the day had gone well and he felt like celebrating, choosing to do so, as a test, in the very bar where he first met Richard. As he entered the bar he felt upbeat, bordering on confident, a definite milestone in his bad case of lovesickness. Today he had convincingly and with aplomb (even if he did say so himself) presented his case against Cunningham.

The only glitch he could see was juror Seven. He was having trouble reading her. She’d seemed nervous and distracted when he first started his opening statement, but later she appeared assured and coolheaded, almost a different person. He wasn’t sure what to think about her, but there was nothing to be done about it tonight. Tonight he wanted to celebrate, to feel good for a change, to interact with some untroubled people who knew nothing about his pathetic behavior this last year. It was still early in the evening and there were maybe a dozen people in the bar so Saul decided he would buy them all a round of drinks.

As the crowd grew, he became engaged in conversation with a group of men. One of the men, a dapper computer expert of some sort, charmed Saul with his outrageously wicked sense of humor. It was the exact medicine Saul needed at the exact right time. Six months ago, he realized, he would have found the man offensive, comparing him, as he did everyone back then, to the intense, restrained Richard. The rowdy man displayed obvious interest in him but made no crass overtures; the discretion was quite alluring to Saul. However, Saul remained undemonstrative, reminding himself that he was just starting a trial that would occupy him for weeks and he still had notes to go over tonight in preparation for tomorrow. Petitioning his rational left brain, he forced himself to leave after sharing two drinks with the group. As he stood up to leave, the charming computer whiz slipped Saul a piece of paper with his phone number.

Speaking to the crowd of shouting reporters had whipped-up RJ's adrenaline, an exhilarating high that set the stage perfectly for the evening to come. RJ was having his first date with the stunning Caroline Perkins, a hostess he had met when he was having dinner with his investment advisor a few days ago. With well-seasoned charm, he had flirted with her and received the expected phone number slipped into his pocket.

RJ Holland had always known that he was not designed to be limited to one woman. However, he had once believed that marriage would enhance his professional and social standing, a belief he long ago discarded as foolish. The fact that he had twice yielded to the social pressure of the ridiculous monogamy contract remained a silent embarrassment. Never again would he make *that* mistake. For years now his relationships with women consisted of short spurts of time spent with vulnerable women like Caroline, gorgeous, vacuous, women who *thought* they could trap a wealthy man just because they were so beddable. These kinds of women had become items on RJ's appetizer menu; never again would they be a main course for him. In the midst of a trial as important as this, a Caroline-type woman became indispensable sustenance for him, fodder for his ego and his libido—just what he needed to energize him for his performance in the courtroom.

His driver had just pulled his Mercedes in front of the restaurant when his cell phone rang. "Shit," RJ said under his breath when he looked at the caller ID indicating it was the ever annoying Dr. Halloway. Bringing her onboard had been a cautionary decision made only because the evidence against Cunningham had been strong. He had not worked with her before but her pristine reputation had caused him to hire her, a decision he began to regret the moment he shook hands with the doctor and felt her eerily, penetrating eyes, eyes that seem to see through to his core. He immediately put her in his *pushy pussy* category, the kind of woman a man needed to be wary of. Sighing, he open his phone to take the unwanted call, unconsciously licking his lips as he silently admitted that for a woman her age her body was sensational. "Dr. Halloway, I presume?"

Erin sucked in her distain and replied, "Sorry, RJ. I know you had plans tonight but I think what Toby discovered about juror Seven is important—and disturbing."

"Disturbing how?"

"Well, it's a bit complicated..."

"Just net it out, doctor. I'm about to go into an important meeting."

Halloway paused, rolling her eyes while thinking to herself, *what did I expect from this asshole.* Unable to constrain herself, she blurted, "Okay, then, have it your way. I think Jane Nichols is going to annihilate you."

RJ looked at his watch. He was already five minutes late and didn't want to let his deliciously *hot appetizer* get cold. As he opened the car door he said, "Annihilate me? Certainly you jest, doctor?"

Erin, having promised herself before making the call, to hold her temper, promptly betrayed that promise, “You’re the one with the penis, puny as it is, so I’d be a fool to get in a pissing contest with you, RJ. If you don’t want to hear what you’re paying me to say, that’s up to you. But I’m going to enjoy seeing you taken down by an apparently mousy woman who is really a closet vampire waiting to get her teeth into Cunningham.”

RJ was dumbfounded—and fuming. No woman had ever talked back to him with such bold impudence. The puny penis remark was eventually going to cost the bitch. Now, however, he just wanted to be rid of her. So he restrained himself, saying, “Save me the melodrama, doctor. Just messenger the information Toby found over to the Blue Fin and I’ll take a look at it later tonight. We can talk about it in the morn....” The phone went dead, the dial tone leaving the astonished RJ further infuriated. “Fuck you, bitch,” he screamed into the dead phone. “You’ve gone and spoiled my appetite.”

Erin, chagrined, shook her head and looked up at the large, grinning black man standing by her side. “That went well,” she said.

Toby replied with pursed lips, “Hmm. I didn’t know you were *that* acquainted with the Reverend’s penis.”

Erin had to laugh. “I’m not, thank God. I guess I really lost it.” She gave Toby a sheepish smile, “I hung up on him.”

“No shit?”

“No shit. Oh, man, is that puny penis remark going to cost me.”

“Damn! I sure wish I could have seen the look on the great Reverend Jove’s face when you let go of that one.”

“Me too, especially since he’ll probably fire me in the morning and I won’t have the satisfaction.”

“Unemployed due to sexual harassment against the Reverend Jove? That would be the ultimate irony.”

Erin had to smile. Toby's satirical humor was charming. "You got that right. Still, as the expression goes, "What *was* I thinking?"

"Not thinking, just reacting."

"No excuse. I'm supposed to be a professional." Erin looked up at Toby again, saying, "You know, a wise man once told me that one should know 'which battles to pick.' I'm certain I just picked one I can't win."

"The same wise man now thinks the best strategy is to 'not cry over spilt milk.' How about another drink instead?"

Erin looked at her empty glass. "Tempting, but I think not. For now I still have a job and we've got work to do. Mr. Puny Penis wants a summary of everything you found on Jane Nichols messengered to him at the Blue Fin."

After her talk with Sydney about jurors being imperfect humans, Jane's optimism about staying the course returned, leaving her feeling energetic. Even the long day in court didn't dampen her energy for a bike ride. It was on her racing bike that Jane felt her most confident, her strong legs pushing her speed into the thirty-mile-per-hour range on the bike path beside the riverbed. She loved passing the other riders and would always respond to an informal challenge by another skilled rider. She especially enjoyed surprising the frequently cocky male challenger with a very close race, sometimes vexing him even more by winning. Today, she passed a male rider who immediately responded by ramping up his speed. They pedaled, mostly side by side, for twenty-five miles until they reached a narrow bridge that took the path across the riverbed. Jane slowed down, expecting the other cyclist to pass first across the bridge. Instead, he stopped and used his bicycle to block the entrance, forcing Jane to stop.

Although she couldn't see his eyes behind his sunglasses, Jane knew he was ogling her. Men never paid attention to her except when she was dressed in her lycra bike shorts and wearing her sunglasses and helmet. She wore the tight shorts because they made cycling more efficient and comfortable, not because she wanted to attract attention. She anticipated what was coming and already knew how she would answer.

"There's a beer joint about two miles ahead, just off the path. Want to cool down with a cold one?" he asked.

Behind his shades it was difficult to tell his age, maybe mid thirties, she guessed. Like most hard-core riders he was on the thin side with a tanned body, muscular thighs and ropy calves. Dark, curly hair peeked out from underneath his helmet. She found him attractive but was not tempted. "I don't drink," she replied.

She could tell he was taken aback, probably used to women succumbing to his charm. "Oh," he replied, his interest obviously waning. "Well, I'm sure they have coffee or sodas."

"Thanks, but no thanks," she said, trying to sound a bit more friendly. "I need to get back."

"Maybe another time, then?"

She knew he was giving her an opening but she thought, *what's the point? He'll just reject me down the road when he makes a sexual move and I have a panic attack.* In an attempt to be cordial, she replied, "Maybe. I'm sure we'll meet again on the path." Before he could ask for her phone number, she turned her bike around and headed back toward her home. As she pedaled furiously down the path she groused to herself, *being a dateless, virginal freak at twenty-eight sucks, but not as badly as going to pieces in front of a sexually aroused man.*

Thirty minutes later Jane put her bike in the shed, the feeling of being a mutant still clinging to her like the sweat on her body. Encounters with men always left her yearning, reminding her of how much she wanted to be normal, to date like other young women, to be held, to feel what other women felt around a man. Instead, she was damaged goods, freaking out when a man tried to touch her.

She walked toward the duplex, hopeful Sydney was home so she could talk to her. Sydney was always able to calm her down. However, her roommate's schedule was erratic, her comings and going so completely unpredictable that it made living with her difficult at times. Jane was disappointed to find the duplex quiet, Sydney obviously out for the evening. She took a shower, fixed herself a salad for dinner, and watched a movie on TV in an attempt to distract herself from her self-flagellating thoughts. The strategy didn't help much; she couldn't let go of her longing to be a normal woman. At ten-thirty she headed for bed, thankful the bike ride had physically exhausted her.

At four A.M. she was awakened by her own screams. She bolted upright in bed, her heart racing, her breath coming in gulps. Within moments Sydney was beside her, stroking her hand, reassuring her, "It's okay, Jane. It's just another nightmare. What was it this time?"

"The closet dream again," Jane choked. "The awful man...he shoved me in and locked the door. I screamed and screamed but no one would come. My God, Sydney, it always seems so real."

"Well, it's not real, Jane. It's just a nightmare like all the others. It's your claustrophobia coming out in a dream."

Tears streaming down her face, Jane said, "God, I hate being so afraid all the time. It's why I really wanted to be on this jury, to do something that normal people do."

" Look, it's important for you to go back to sleep so you'll be sharp for tomorrow when you go back to court."

"You really think I can do it?"

"Yes, I do. I was wrong when I said you shouldn't push yourself."

"Okay, thanks. I don't think I could do this without you, Syd."

DAY TWO

Ruminating was a worthless pastime as far as RJ Holland was concerned. He'd always believed that moving forward was an essential component to success and that people who lost precious sleep chewing on unchangeable events were idiots. Last night, however, he had joined the ranks of the idiots: unable to sleep because he was plagued most of the night by angry thoughts about the Halloway woman. That the ballsy bitch had ruined his dinner and bankrupted his seduction plans with her insulting accusation about his penis was unforgivable. To make matters worse, she had had the gall to hang up on him. So, instead of enjoying his flirting with the voluptuous Caroline, he had been distracted by revenge fantasies. When the messenger showed up with the file on juror Seven, he gave up on the evening, arranging to meet with Caroline again on Saturday night.

He couldn't remember anyone, not even a man, talking back to him the way Erin Halloway had, much less hanging-up on him. Toby must have been in the room when she had made the remark about his penis. The fact that she had insulted him in front of someone else was beyond embarrassing. The woman deserved to be put in her place. However, he didn't think he could simply fire her. It was well known in the legal field that she had been instrumental in saving some heavyweight defendants. He had been the one to insist to Cunningham that she would be invaluable, worth the expense. He would have to contrive a reason to fire her. He'd spent sleepless hours trying to fabricate reasons to get rid of her, but nothing made sense.

As much as it galled him to admit it, apparently she had been right about juror Seven. The information sent to him indicated something was amiss. Finally around three a.m. he came to the conclusion that, while the information was disturbing, it was not ruinous. He would need to keep an eye on Seven, maybe tweak his plans somewhat to win her trust. If he wasn't so furious with the doctor, he would have consulted her on how to handle the juror. No way was he going to seek the advice from a woman who dared to insult his sexuality. No, he would figure a way to handle juror Seven on his own. He wasn't sure yet how he would get his retribution from the doctor, but he did know he wasn't going to let her forget just whom she had dared to insult. The last he could remember was looking at the clock as it blinked four-ten.

The shrill of the phone woke him at six. He grabbed it on the second ring and growled, "I don't care who you are this better be good."

"That good of a night, huh?" the deep voice responded.

An aura, the eerie quiet before the hot-flash storm, jerked Erin out of a deep slumber. The hot flashes started when she was forty-eight and remained a tenacious enemy for the last six years. With a mother who died from breast cancer and a sister having recently survived chemotherapy for the same disease, hormone therapy was not a choice she wanted to risk. Some nights she would be awakened four or five times by the flush of heat and the awful sweating.

Imprisoned in the prescient period, the symptomless time before the flush of heat (which felt like boiling water had been injected into her aorta), Erin prepared for the inevitable blaze that was to follow. She turned on the bedside fan aimed at her face and neck, punched the pillow, and closed her eyes, trying to talk herself out of becoming angry; she learned long ago that anger only succeeded in arousing her even more. This morning, however, her troubled mind could not shake off the frustration.

As she sat up in bed, she thought, *These hot flashes are the bane of my existence.*

The instant the word *bane* enter her mind, a free fall of associations began Rolodexing through her brain. Bane made her think of poor Jane and the girl's miserable childhood. The word miserable led to thoughts of the offensive RJ and, inevitably, to the most unwanted thought of all: her regrettable sexual redress of the man. Now wide awake, she turned over on her back mulling over her stupidity. *I told RJ Holland he had a puny penis. What was I thinking? I'm sure to be out of a job and likely out of a career when he retaliates.* By four-thirty she succumbed to the philosophical decision that life is nothing if not lessons learned the hard way.

Resigned to her fate for having lost her cool with this odious man, she fell into a restless sleep. Two hours later her alarm went off. She hit the snooze bar, hopeful she could catch a little more sleep. Again, her conscious mind was overruled. The resignation she had adopted a few hours ago had disappeared along with the darkness. Her reflective *lessons-learned-the-hard-way* were now a distant memory, taken over by her renewed regrets for her unprofessional behavior. Finally deciding she had no option but to face the consequences of her behavior, she threw back the covers and headed to the bathroom.

After an inspirational self-lecture in the shower and two cups of very strong black coffee, Erin had a plan. No matter what RJ said or did, she would not smart-mouth the man, but she wouldn't cower or apologize either. He was a royal-class jerk, a narcissistic woman-hater and she would not play victim to his abuse. If he fired her, so be it. She went to her closet to select something to wear for the showdown. She considered several outfits before deciding that, for the sheer vindictiveness of it, she would wear her steel blue, sheath dress rather than her usual business suit. She chose the dress because it showed off her ample breasts, narrow waist, slim hips, and shapely legs. She mischievously smiled to herself; today she would purposely be a prick tease, albeit for a man with a *puny* prick. Then: *Thank God I have no idea what the size of his penis is.* Being chummy with RJ's thingy caused a repulsive shudder throughout her body.

The last penis Erin had intimately known belonged to a man she had deeply loved, a smart, witty, and gentle man who easily captured her heart. It was literally an accidental romance, a random meeting that started with a fight over a parallel parking incident. Erin had proudly managed to park her car between two others in front of the watch repair shop where she was picking up her cherished, two-generations-old watch. When she came out of the store, she was chagrined to find that a different car had parked so close behind her that she now had only a foot in front and back in which to maneuver her car out. Exasperated, she began the back and forth dance of trying to extricate her car. On the third backward move, she tapped the fender of the car behind her, a Volvo that still had its dealer plates. Suddenly, a man came running out of a store hurling expletives at her. Erin, who had been silently cursing the idiot driver who had blocked her in, rolled down the window and shouted back at the man, "It's your fault! You blocked me in."

"What are you talking about, lady? You have plenty of room to get out. You're going to pay for any damage." The man walked over to his fender to take a look.

Erin got out of her car and walked over next to the man. She pointed at the back of the car, "Look at how little room you gave me to get out!"

Suddenly, the man began laughing. Erin was totally confounded. "What's so funny?" she demanded.

"Me," he said. Bending down toward his bumper he said, "I don't see any damage. And I guess I did park a little close to your car."

Erin, struck silent by his honest declaration, now took note of the man. He was somewhere in his mid forties, she guessed, tall, with broad shoulders and an athletic build. He was wearing a short-sleeved shirt that showed off his muscular arms. He had a full head of dark, curly hair worn sightly long, a significant nose, and enticing brown eyes that were now crinkled in humor. Unconsciously, Erin's eyes glanced toward his left hand, looking for a wedding ring. Weeks later, in postcoital bliss, she would confess to the man that it was the absence of the ring that likely resulted in her joining him in the laugh.

His name, unbelievably, was Aaron, their two names never failing to be the butt of jokes. Besides sharing the same sounding name, they also shared a common past and present. Both had been married and divorced before the age of thirty and both were childless. Both had demanding careers, jobs that required intuitive sensitivity to people. Aaron was the CFO of a ninety-partner law firm, a job Erin first believed no sane person would take. But Aaron was no ordinary man. He was confident without being arrogant, commanding without being overbearing, generous without being a pushover, honorable without being obsequious. And he was a man who genuinely respected women without needing to compete. Sensitive to the gender issues so important to her, how could a woman like Erin not love Aaron?

They had three amazing years together, Erin the happiest she had ever been in her life and even thinking a second marriage might be in her future after all. Their happiness, sadly, was brief. Toward the end of the third year, it was discovered Aaron had drawn a short genetic straw. He was diagnosed with the merciless disease called ALS, also know as Lou Gherig's disease. The three agonizing years it had taken Aaron to die a wretched, increasingly paralyzing death, had slowly strangled Erin's heart, leaving her feeling lifeless for future romance.

Now four years since Aaron's death, and despite a few ventures, no man had been able to resuscitate her numb heart. Erin, forever the self-examiner, was aware that her unbridled irritation at men like RJ was fueled by the lingering anger she had over Aaron's death. She couldn't help being incensed at the unfairness of losing such a worthy man while such narcissistic ones marched on. As futile and unproductive as these thoughts were, Erin continued to let interactions with self-absorbed men open her still-healing wounds. She knew she should be smarter, more immune to the egotistic, bullying behavior. Yet, here she was acting like a preschooler by name-calling and blaming the perceived bully for some injustice that had happened to her years ago. The puny penis remark had been impulsive and childish. As she drove to RJ's law office she vowed to act like a grown-up, reminding herself that RJ was neither responsible for Aaron's illness nor for her lingering grief. This morning she would, with adult composure, take her nasty-tasting medicine for acting like such a child.

At eight o'clock, Erin, her head held high despite feeling foolish in her alluring outfit, walked into the conference room to face her providence. RJ and his two associates were already there, papers spread out across the table in front of them. However, Erin was surprised to see Toby leaning up against one wall. RJ didn't bother acknowledging her. Instead, he looked over at Toby and said, "Good work, Toby. I like to know what I'm up against." Still without acknowledging Erin, RJ headed for the door, saying to his assistants on his way out, "Bring those files with you to court."

One of the assistants gathered up the papers, put them in his briefcase and then, like the Tweedledee and Tweedledum act the two so often imitated, they left together. Erin looked over at the ever self-controlled Toby, asking, "What gives?"

"After you left last night, I started thinking about our juror's situation. All we could find out about the cause of her mother's death was that it was a drug overdose. There were no details on Jane in the police reports, nothing in Protective Services about the circumstances surrounding the death, about where the child was when her mother died. Like you said last night, it's a gaping hole in her biography. It bothered me so I did some further investigating."

"What kind of investigating?"

"I knocked on some doors, talked to some people who were around back then."

"You did that late last night?"

Toby smiled, "The people I needed to talk with are usually asleep during the day."

"Okay, but you're talking twenty-two years ago. What could you possibly find out all these years later?"

"I found someone who knew Tamara back then. I guess you would politely call her a colleague. This colleague was the one who found Jane. Turns out Tamara's death was a memorable event, the kind of thing you don't forget."

"Tell me!"

"The whole thing is worse, much worse than we suspected. Apparently, Tamara died in the rathole apartment she was living in. It was three days before Jane was found." Toby shook his head sadly. "Jane was found locked in a tiny closet. Apparently the only thing that saved the child was the smell of her mother's dead body. Her friend noticed the awful smell when she went to investigate why she hadn't seen Tamara in days."

Erin grabbed on to a chair, "Oh, my God. What if it was her mother who locked her in while she was with a John? Then she overdosed before she could let her out." Erin plopped down in the chair, putting her head in her hands, "It's unimaginable to me what that would do to a child."

"Right. Like you said, it leaves scars. Problem is it doesn't prove she can't be impartial. Truth is, we still don't have anything we can use as grounds for removal. A traumatic childhood doesn't count for a thing in a hit and run felony case."

Erin was quiet for a while, finally looking up at Toby. "You rescued my ass, didn't you? You wanted to find something RJ couldn't disregard, something so juicy he would overlook my...*verbal indiscretion* of last night. You must have called him very early this morning, wanting to beat me here so I could avoid getting my ass chewed out." Erin got up from her chair and walked over to Toby, intending to give him a kiss on the cheek.

Standing next to him she realized that even if she stood on her toes she couldn't reach his cheek. Instead, she said, "I'll be glad to pay you for your time last night, Toby."

Toby grinned, then said, "You know, if I was a cop, you could get arrested for making that offer...especially in *that* outfit."

Erin had to laugh. "You know what I mean. You did this on your own dime and you did it for me. And thanks for noticing the outfit."

"Look, doc, you don't owe me a thing. Just hearing someone tell The Reverend he has a puny pecker was worth the time I spent."

Erin gave Toby an indignant look. "Let's set the record straight. I did *not* say he had a puny pecker, I said he had a puny penis. And I do owe you, Toby. How about I treat you to a dinner at the Blue Fin?"

"The Blue Fin, huh? Well, that should cost you several hours of my time, so I'll take you up on that offer."

Day two of the trial was as packed as the first day, everyone eager to hear the evidence the prosecution had against the highly regarded Cunningham. No one was disappointed when the first thing the prosecuting attorney did was to call his eye witness, Manny Islas, a twenty-five-year-old Hispanic male. The young man had been in the process of dropping off stacks of newspapers for delivery when he claimed his attention had been caught by the sound of a car screeching to a stop in the middle of the road.

Saul Greene decided to put Mr. Islas on the stand at the starting gate to set the stage for Cunningham's guilt by letting the jury hear first hand exactly what the witness had seen: a car coming to a stop, a man getting out, the same man leaning over something in the road and then hurrying back to his car, a late model Mercedes. According to Mr. Islas, the man then backed up his car, swerved around whatever was in the road and sped away. Mr. Islas had been able to get the first three letters of the license plate of the Mercedes, which, Saul pointed out, matched the defendant's plate. When Mr. Islas was asked if the man he saw that morning was in the courtroom, the witness pointed to Cunningham.

Saul frequently observed the jury as Manny gave his testimony and was satisfied that his witness had given the needed impression: an honest, hardworking young man (fortunately a legal citizen), doing his civic duty by giving a detailed description of the awful events he had witnessed. All the jurors, except Seven, had appeared attentive, focused, and vigilant throughout his witness's testimony. Seven bothered him, however. She had been fidgety and unfocused throughout the testimony. After he was finished questioning Mr. Islas, Saul walked back to his table and made a note to recheck juror Seven's form. Her behavior was making him uncomfortable and he didn't want any surprises when it came to jurors.

On cross, RJ made sure to clarify three points to the jury: Mr. Islas had not noticed the body in the road, had not actually *seen* the defendant hit the woman with his car, and had no knowledge of how long the victim had been lying in the street.

Throughout the witness's testimony, RJ kept a close eye on juror Seven. Her unceasing, penetrating stare at Cunningham forced him to admit that the woman was probably as unstable as the doctor had warned. RJ wasn't sure if he could be in the same room with Halloway without losing his temper, but after today he knew he would need to hear what she had to say. He scribbled a note to one of his assistants: *Get Halloway and Parish back in the conference room at the end of the day.*

By five-thirty, Erin, Toby, Tweedledee and Dum were in the conference room waiting for RJ. Toby, in his usual position, leaned up against the wall rather than attempting to fit his long legs under what was for him a dwarf sized table. Erin was sitting with her computer open, going over her notes on Jane Nichols. The two Tweedles were also sitting with open computers in front of them.

At five-thirty-five, Erin glanced up at Toby, rolling her eyes in exasperation: *He's making us wait so he can make the grand entrance.* Toby gave a barely perceptible nod in agreement. At five-forty-five, RJ hurried into the room, loudly slapping his briefcase down on the table. The Tweedles sat up at attention. Erin, absorbed in her reading, was startled; enough adrenaline poured into her blood stream to make her heart skip a beat. She caught her breath, angrily concluding: *it had taken RJ only seconds to establish himself as the asshole alpha male in the room.* However, having made a promise to herself to behave, Erin took great effort to calmly close her laptop and give RJ her full attention.

"As you all know," RJ began, "Toby did some crackerjack investigating last night regarding juror Seven." Then facing Erin, he added, "It seems the woman's troubled background is certainly cause for concern. But since we don't have solid grounds for dismissal at this point, our only option is to anticipate how her troubled background might effect her attitude toward our client. You're on, Dr. Halloway."

Outwardly, Erin was giving the man her full attention while on the inside she was thinking, *how very clever of him to save face by giving all the credit to Toby.* Nevertheless, remaining faithful to her pledge she accepted the half-mast, white flag he was giving her. "I've been doing some research on Post Traumatic Stress Disorder, commonly called PTSD, which I believe Jane Nichols is likely to have, given the experience surrounding the death of her mother." Looking at RJ, Erin asked, "Should I read you what I've found?"

"As long as you keep it brief."

"While not the most scientific source, Wikipedia does keep it simple. So, I'll read you what they've written. *PTSD is a severe anxiety disorder that develops after exposure to any event that results in psychological trauma. The trauma is so overwhelming that it interferes with the individual's ability to cope. Symptoms include: re-experiencing the original trauma through flashbacks or nightmares, avoidance of stimuli associated with the trauma, and increased arousal—such as difficulty falling or staying asleep, anger, and hypervigilance."* Erin looked up from her screen. "It's these last two that I'm most worried about. Under that mousy exterior of hers, I think the woman is angry and I think she is angry at men, especially powerful ones."

Dum asked, "But we don't have information on who locked her in the closet. It could have been her mother, so why are you so sure she's angry at men?"

"Because young children intuitively understand that they can't afford to be angry at their parents, especially their mothers. It's instinctual, built into the survival genes. Being young and relatively helpless makes them vulnerable—we don't bite the hand that feeds us—even if it is feeding us venom. The human psyche is emotionally complex, however. While children may not allow themselves conscious anger toward a parent, it doesn't mean there *is no* anger...."

"What's any of this have to do with Cunningham?" RJ interrupted.

Swallowing her impatience at the interruption, Erin continued. "Since a child's survival instinct doesn't allow her to be angry with her mother, she projects it outward. In Jane's case, even though her mother is soliciting the men, in her mind it's the men who are to blame. It's men that she doesn't trust. I'd place money on the fact that Jane has problematic relationships with men or that she avoids them all together...."

"Net out the relevance to our situation," RJ snapped.

Again, Erin swallowed a nasty comeback. "Bottom line? Being on the jury might be the first time Jane can use this buried anger to punish a man."

The room became very silent. Finally Dum spoke again. "But she's an adult now. Are you saying this anger from childhood is still operating unconsciously? Or is she aware she's doing this?"

"Good question. It's definitely not rational behavior so I'm sure most of her anger remains unconscious. There is still much we don't know about Jane—such as just how much she remembers about her childhood experiences and whether she's ever been treated for the traumatic experience surrounding her mother's death. Knowing this would help me determine more about what to expect from her."

RJ looked over at Toby. "Get on that, will you, Toby?"

Toby knitted his brow. "Psychotherapy info is protected, more secure than other medical info, but I'll see what I can find."

"If she's had effective therapy she would have been helped to recall the event," added Erin. "In PTSD, reliving the event in a safe, secure environment is the best way to dispel the stored hurt and mitigate the destructive behavior. She would be much less of a threat to us if she's had treatment."

"What about this hypervigilance stuff you said you were worried about?" asked RJ.

"Right. Hypervigilance is a constant state of awareness where an individual is always on alert for threats that reproduce the original trauma. Any high pressure situations exacerbate the hypervigilance."

"Like maybe being on a jury in the biggest criminal trial in years?" mocked Toby.

"Exactly. I've been watching Jane closely and I've seen two very distinctive demeanors. The first one, of course is anxiousness. But it's the second one, contemptuousness, that bothers me the most."

This last statement got RJ's attention. "Contempt? I've been watching her too. I didn't see anything like contempt."

"It was the contempt I picked up yesterday that first alerted me. At first, when she was entering the courtroom and then stopped—it was when she looked at Cunningham—right after that she became extremely anxious. Then, shortly after Saul began his opening statement, she changed demeanor. It was almost as if she was a different person. For the remainder of both opening statements she looked as if she couldn't wait to pronounce our client guilty. It was this demeanor that alarmed me. Then today she was back to being anxious and avoided looking at Cunningham."

RJ began pacing the room. "All right, so we likely have one juror who has a bias against powerful men. But if she has this PTSD shit, she can't possibly be a persuasive person. Isn't it more likely she would be afraid of speaking up during deliberation, afraid of calling attention to herself?"

"There seems to be two ways to go with this PTSD. One is to cower and the other is to get violent. Normally females choose the first, men the second. But sometimes, women can be passive aggressive...."

"Tell me something I don't know," RJ interrupted.

"In any event," Erin continued, "at this point we have a very unpredictable person, a person constantly on alert for threats to her physical and mental safety. Being anxious is what you would expect of a PTSD victim. It's the contempt that I'm worried about. I need to observe her more to see if I notice any more negative emotions. One thing is for sure, we should *not* underestimate her shy exterior."

Pounding the table RJ bellowed, "Damn it! I do not want a mistrial just because one fucked-up juror is prejudiced against men." Picking up his briefcase he stormed out of the room. Predictably, the Tweedles followed right behind him.

Erin stood, putting her laptop in the case. "It occurred to me, Toby, that we don't have much information on Jane's adoptive parents. Her life with them could make a big difference. If she was lucky, they got her into therapy soon after adopting her."

"I'll do some snooping around but I've got to be careful. Questioning anyone who knows the juror could easily be considered jury tampering."

"Do be careful then."

"Always that. So, Erin, I sure could go for a happy hour boost. You up for it?"

"I don't know. I didn't get much sleep last night. Even one drink is likely to put me out. I spent most of the early morning thinking I wasn't going to have a job today after the way I mouthed off to the Reverend yesterday."

"Well, then, let's celebrate your *not* being canned."

"One drink. Then I'm going home for a long soak in my hot tub followed by an Ambien."

Toby raised his eyebrows, "Hot tub, huh?"

At the same time the defense was considering what to do about Jane Nichols, the prosecution team was in Saul Greene's office reviewing the information they had on Nichols, information that came from the standard juror questionnaire. At the beginning of the jury selection process, Saul noted the nervousness of juror Seven. Jury selection, on criminal trials especially, can be daunting and many potential jurors get nervous during the voir dire. He did not want to use one of his preemptory challenges on an otherwise neutral witness and, finding no other cause to strike her, let her go through. He was more than aware that removing a seated juror was very difficult and could only be done for misconduct or illness. Being a nervous Nelly didn't count for anything when it came to dismissal. In the end, the team decided they would simply have to watch the woman carefully, remaining watchful for any behavior that might offer irrefutable grounds for replacing her with an alternate.

After the team meeting broke up, Saul was invited to join two of the other single attorneys for drinks and dinner, an offer he was tempted to accept but ended up declining. Seated in his car, he began casting aspersions on himself, wondering if he declined out of fear. As he thought about that possibility he could feel a familiar knot forming in his stomach. Now he knew he declined because he anticipated the gut wrenching isolation he always felt whenever he tried attending any social event without Richard. He guessed he was just not quite ready for a social debut with people he knew from work.

He had intended to drive home but found himself instead parked a block down the street from last night's bar. Part of him wanted *a chance* meeting with the raucous man he had spent time with last night, but another part was dubious of any relationship, especially with a flamboyant man who seemed comfortable and open with his sexual orientation. Saul had always been the quiet, private type. Years ago, in his twenties, he had tried a few casual relationships but they left him feeling empty. The *conquest high,* common to many gay men, was not at all enticing to him. Apparently he had monogamy in his bones; another reason he had been hit so hard by Richard's betrayal.

He was puzzled by why he was so beguiled by the outgoing stranger from last night as well as disconcerted by his impulse to drive to the bar hoping to see him again. It was out of character for him. Besides, how likely was it that the man would be in the same bar two nights in a row anyway? He pictured himself walking into the bar, trying not to be obvious about searching for the man. The image left him feeling foolish and shook him out of his ambivalence, causing him to start the engine and head home.

Last night's dream, nightmare really, had shaken Jane to the core. Although she couldn't remember the details of her childhood dreams, she did remember having nightmares for weeks after coming to live with her new parents. She still flushed with embarrassment whenever the memory of her bed wetting came to mind. The infuriated look on her new mother's face was etched into her mind. Fortunately, the bed-wetting stopped shortly after meeting Sydney; the nightmares becoming less and less frequent as well. She only had nightmares now when she was under stress.

Controlling stress had become a way of life for Jane. The routine job with very limited interactions with others and a sport activity she could do on her own left her without much challenge. She didn't participate in any organizations, didn't have any friends other than Sydney, didn't date; all of it was the way she eliminated stress. She knew last night's nightmare was caused by her decision to break out of her self-imposed coffin. Sheltered, plain

Jane had decided to be a juror in a criminal trial! So, she had no one to blame but herself for introducing the stress. She would hate to admit defeat by removing herself from the jury.

As she drove to the courthouse this morning, she'd repeated the affirmations she had given herself yesterday. Affirmations were something she had read about in one of her self-help books on the relationship between stress and self-esteem; positive thoughts led to a positive attitude, or so the book promised. By the time she was at the courthouse she was feeling capable of handling the challenge. However, the minute she walked into the jury box her resolve began a downward spiral, picking up momentum like a roller coaster. Driving home she wept at her failure to keep her composure during the trial.

She had been a total wreck all day, barely able to pay attention to what was happening. She was sure it was the defendant who was causing her to come unglued. She only managed to make it through the day by not looking at him. Something about the man was bugging her, giving her a creepy-crawly feeling; even from thirty feet away she felt sullied, wanting all day to get home and take a shower. She was aware of how irrational her feelings were, conceding by the time she arrived home that she could not remain impartial. The only conscientious thing to do was to remove herself from the jury.

Entering the duplex, the first thing Jane did was look for signs of Sydney. The small living area and galley kitchen were as she left them this morning, tidy. Sydney was obviously not around. Disappointed, she put her coat and purse away and hurried into the bathroom to take a shower. Afterwards, still in her robe, she sat down on the sofa to relax, but within moments found herself again ruminating over the situation she had gotten herself into, the anxiety swelling the more she chewed herself out for being such a fool. She squelched an impulse to fix herself a drink, sure that the lack of control she felt from alcohol would only make her more of a basket case. Instead she began pacing, anxiety burgeoning in her chest, heart pounding, breath becoming rapid and shallow, nausea gripping at her gut. She hurried to her purse and dug around for her cell phone. It had been years since she had had a full blown anxiety attack requiring medical attention. With the last one, she had been about to call 911 when Sydney rescued her at the last minute by making her breathe into a paper bag.

Paper bag! She hurried into the kitchen and rummaged around for a bag when Sydney was suddenly beside her.

"Another panic attack, huh?"

Jane, eyes the size of saucers and gulping for air, could only shake her head yes.

Sydney took the bag from her, opened it, held it up to Jane's mouth, squeezing the opening tight around her mouth. "Slow it down, girlfriend. Take deep breaths. Breath in for five counts...one one thousand, two one thousand, three one thousand, four one thousand, five one thousand. Now let it out slowly. Good. Okay, now do it again, five, deep, slow, breaths." After the fourth deep breath, Jane was beginning to feel the panic subside, her breath coming more easily, her pulse slowing down. Eventually Sydney took the bag away, asking, "Better?"

"Yes, better. I'm so glad you showed up."

"You remembered the paper bag trick."

"Yes, from the last time you saved me."

Sydney took a wine glass down from the cabinet. "So, what happened to cause you to panic?" As she asked, she went to the refrigerator, opened the door, and took out a bottle of wine, pouring herself a glass.

"I'm sure it's the defendant, Cunningham. The man is giving me the creeps. I couldn't even look at him today. I just don't understand why I'm having such a negative reaction to him."

"Come sit with me," Sydney said. "Let's talk about it. Maybe we can figure it out."

Sydney took her glass of wine with her as she walked into the living area, taking a seat on the sofa, patting the seat next to her. "Sit down, Jane. We'll figure this thing out."

Jane took a seat next to her. "It has to be that he reminds me of someone, but I just can't think who that might be."

Sydney took a sip of her wine, saying, "Maybe he reminds you of somebody you knew before you were adopted. You've told me many times that you don't have any memories of your life before you came to live with your adoptive parents. So, it's possible he reminds you of someone you knew but can't remember you knew."

"Maybe," Jane said, as she began chewing on one nail. Sydney glared at her. "Okay, I'm sorry. I know how you hate it when I bite my nails."

"Maybe you need to be hypnotized."

Jane sat up, blurting out, "What?"

"Relax. It's just a suggestion. I've read that hypnosis is great for recalling memories."

"I'm not so sure I want to remember."

"Look, Jane, you've been saying that ever since I met you. You know you'll always be plagued by anxiety attacks until you remember what happened to you before you were adopted."

"Maybe, but being hypnotized while I'm sitting on a jury doesn't seem right. For now I have to decide what to do about this jury situation. I mean, how can I can stay on the jury when I get weak-kneed and panicky at the sight of the defendant?"

"I guess you're right. Though, if you take yourself off the jury, I'd like you to promise me you will get some professional help. Remember, you decided against my advice to try this and now you want out. You'll never have a normal life if you don't get some help with your anxiety."

Jane started to tear up. "Okay, I promise to get help. It was stupid of me to think I could do this."

Sydney took another sip of her wine, saying, "I'm going to get you some names of some therapists who specialize in anxiety."

"How would you know about therapists?"

"I don't know them personally, but I have a client...."

"You always have a client who knows somebody, don't you?" Jane demanded.

Sydney laughed. "You're right. In my line of work I know many people who would be glad to do me favors."

"You don't mean people, Sydney, you mean men."

"We're not going there, Jane," said Sydney as she rose from the sofa. Looking down at Jane, she continued, "We're very different, you and I. Our friendship works because we accept those differences." She walked into the kitchen, opened the refrigerator and poured more wine into her glass.

Jane remained sitting, a sulky look on her face. Sydney came back into the living room, stood and looked down at her roommate. "Pouting is so childish, Jane. You're twenty-eight years old; it's way past time you start acting like an adult."

"That's why I wanted to be on this jury. To prove to myself I could act like an adult. But look at me. I'm falling apart just like always."

"You need to get some professional help, Jane. And that means facing up to your memories. Do it—or continue to be an emotional cripple," said Sydney as she crossed the living room on her way to her own bedroom.

Jane watched her go, feeling both scared and intimidated. Tomorrow she would have to be brave enough to talk to the judge and face the humiliation that was sure to follow. Then she would need to tackle her fear of going to see a therapist, an act she had avoided for over a decade. But she promised Sydney she would do it, so she would just have to face her fears.

That night she again dreamed of being locked in a closet. Only this time someone heard her screams and came to open the door. Looking down at her, debauchery in his eyes, was a man she recognized—a much younger Bradley Cunningham. He reached out to pick her up, but she bit down hard on one of his hands. She tasted the metallic bitterness of the blood. Shouting obscenities, Cunningham slapped her hard on the side of the head, knocking her to the floor. Then he slammed the closet door; she heard the dreaded sound of a lock clicking. She was sobbing and kicking at the closet door when she awoke from the terrifying dream, breathless, drenched in sweat, and her heart racing.

She didn't know if she had screamed out loud, but Sydney was not by her side. She got out of bed and tiptoed into Sydney's room. Her bed was empty. Without Sydney she knew she would need to get her rapid breathing under control by herself to avoid a full blown panic attack. She walked into the living room, sat on the couch and began focusing on her breathing, counting each breath the way Sydney had earlier. Within ten very deep breaths, she could feel the panic subsiding, her heart rate slowing until she finally felt her control return. Once her panic had diminished, she was able to recall the scary, visceral nightmare.

NO! Gasping, she jerked herself straight up.

My God, I don't think it's a dream at all. I think it's a memory. I think it was Bradley Cunningham who locked me in the closet when I was a child.

Jane began pacing the room, deep in deliberation, her fear now replaced by something very unfamiliar: anger. The anger slowly grew into a completely unprecedented state, a warrior-like, gutsy, defiant composure. She decided she wasn't going to quit, not now, not when she thought that Bradley Cunningham didn't just *remind* her of someone; he was the someone...the someone who was responsible for so terrifying her that he had scarred her for life.

In the early hours of the morning, with his wife sleeping upstairs, a despondent Bradley Cunningham was sitting behind his immense, roll-top, collector's item desk in his private study holding up a glass of twenty-year old Benriach single malt scotch. He was staring at the amber liquid, unnerved, his attorney's assurances slipping through his brain like a wet bar of soap. He mulled over how, for the first time in his adult life, his money, resources and own expert duplicity might not be enough to save him. It galled him that he felt helpless to control these recent virgin feelings of doubt. It was also the first time he dared to admit to himself that his whole life he had been helpless to control the impulses that had put him in this depressing situation.

He downed the entire glass of scotch in one gulp, set the glass carefully on a coaster, stood up, walked over to the office door, and turned the lock. Then he walked over to a picture on the wall, opened it like a door, and began turning the dials to the wall safe. When it unlocked, he opened it and took out the hard drive inside. He moved back to his desk, connected the firewire from his computer to the drive and turned on the computer. Once he was looking at the open screen, he typed in a password, clicked an icon, and waited for the drive to load. When it was loaded, he stared at the screen for several seconds, his hand poised over the delete key. His breathing became rapid and his hand shook as he considered destroying the years of carefully catalogued corruption. In front of him was decades of furtive sinfulness which could send him to prison for much longer than a hit and run. His hand continued to hover over the delete key as he pondered the years of compilation and the enormity of what a simple touch would be doing.

If RJ was able to prevail, this action would be pointless and years of coveted, satiating material would be discarded because he was feeling spooked. Yes! The unassailable Bradley Cunningham had been reduced to feeling abject fear.

This admission caused him to withdraw his hovering hand from the keyboard. Instead he poured himself another stiff drink, again downing the liquid in one swallow. In minutes he could feel the tension ease up. What was wrong with him? After all the chances he had taken, after all the years of being fearless, why lose his bravado now? It's way too early to crap out he thought. "I can weather this," he said out loud. He unhooked the hard drive from his computer and returned it to the safe.

DAY THREE

On day three the prosecution put into official courtroom evidence the time-stamped photo image of Cunningham's car running a red light, placing his car near the scene of the dead body. Although it was damaging, the evidence was still circumstantial, which meant an inference is required to connect it to a conclusion of fact. As the State's accuser, Saul was charged with persuading twelve jurors to conclude guilt based upon a chain of inferences that ruled out any other alternative. The State was the underdog because it was up against the *beyond a reasonable doubt* requirement.

The defense's strategy, on the other hand, was simply to introduce doubt. RJ wasn't trying to deny his client was at the scene. His strategy was to persuade the jury that his client was only guilty of bad judgement for leaving the scene and for not calling 911, not laudable behavior but not criminal behavior.

Both sides knew the most contentious evidence was still to come. The prosecution had found front fender damage to Cunningham's car and was prepared to put an expert witness on the stand to claim the damage could have come from a collision with a person. The defense would claim the damage was from a previous fender bender caused when Rose Cunningham was driving and would put their expert on the stand to corroborate their claim. RJ was adamant, however, about not putting Rose on the stand to testify that she had damaged the car. Putting Rose on the stand would leave her vulnerable to the prosecution on cross and RJ had no intention of letting Rose be questioned.

With the legal system perpetually overloaded, cases that made it to trial had to have factual evidence of guilt, or at least enough credible circumstantial evidence of guilt to justify the spending of taxpayers' dollars. Whether direct or circumstantial, however, the evidence ended up before the twelve individuals sitting in the jury box, individuals sanctioned with the power to ponder the evidence and to determine a verdict. By day three of

The People v. Cunningham, it was clear to *both* sides that juror Seven had slipped through the selection process without the diligent examination she deserved. They both feared the unpredictability of Seven, possibly causing the remaining jurors to behave in aberrant ways.

At the lunch break, both the defense and the prosecution called their teams together to deliberate on the strange behavior of juror Seven. Day one she had appeared nervous...only to quickly become derisive. Day two she had been tightly wound, jittery, unfocused, eyes darting everywhere except toward the defendant. Now, on the morning of day three, she was a chameleon of a different color altogether: attentive, resolute, implacable, with eyes fixated on the defendant. Both sides were perplexed. Who the hell was this woman? More critically, what, if anything, should or could be done about her?

Reasons for removing a juror included a variety of behaviors from the mundane (inability to concentrate or sleeping during the trial) to more serious matters such as absence, lateness, family emergencies, or illness. Misconduct was the most egregious cause for removal and included contact with the defendant, communication with outsiders, bringing information not part of the evidence into the jury room, or dishonesty in the voir dire process.

Both sides had gone over the list of reasons to dismiss and both sides had come to the same conclusion: justifiable behavior for removal was lacking. On opposite sides of the case and in separate conferences rooms, both prosecution and defense believed the judge would throw them out of chambers if they came to him with a request for dismissal based on a description of her chameleon-like behavior.

As concerned as the prosecution was about the atypical behavior of juror Seven, the team was uncertain about whether the behavior of Seven would be favorable or unfavorable to their case. By the end of the lunch hour, they decided their best strategy was to keep a careful eye on her.

The defense team, however, was being influenced by Erin's unrelenting insistence that Jane Nichols was a woman biased against their client. She wanted Toby to dig up more information about the woman, hopeful they might find some legitimate reason to dismiss her. Toby was instructed to further investigate her background. The team would then meet again at the end of the day to see what Toby had discovered.

Driving home at the end of day three, Jane Nichols was feeling calm and resolute. Thinking about what Sydney said about recalling past memories, she stopped at the library and checked out two books on hypnosis before heading home. Opening the door to the duplex, she found it as it was this morning, uncluttered, an indication that Sydney had not been out late last night. She put her ear to the bedroom door and listened for the Nintendo sounds of Syd's one addiction, *Final Fantasy*, a video game obsession Jane would never understand. When Syd was involved with the game's fictional world of magic, warriors, and elemental orbs, she was lost to the real world. Syd had tried to explain the game to Jane but the many characters, continents, and races of people with unpronounceable names left her cold. Jane softly opened the door to the bedroom, peeked in, and was surprised to find the bed made, but no Sydney.

She was disappointed her friend was not there because today had been a milestone for Jane and she wanted to share the watershed with her friend. She had made it through the entire day without any signs of anxiety and even had found herself feeling a burgeoning strength, a courage far more solid than anything she had known. She closed the door to Syd's bedroom and headed to the kitchen, making herself a cup of green tea and taking it to the couch where she settled down to do some reading. After about an hour, she looked up to find Sydney coming in the door.

"What are you reading?" Sydney asked, as she dropped her purse on the table.

"Hypnosis stuff."

"Really?"

"Really."

"Something must have happened today. Tell me," Sydney said as she sat down next to Jane.

"Well, I guess it started last night. I woke up with the same nightmare of being locked in a closet, but instead of waking up at this point I continued dreaming. This time the closet door was opened and a threatening man tried to grab me." Jane stopped talking and took a very deep breath.

"And?" Sydney asked.

"The man in my dreams was Bradley Cunningham...much younger but I'm sure it was him. I woke up at this point and it felt very much to me like a memory, not a dream at all."

"Whoa, Jane. Sounds to me like you're fusing your dream anxiety with your daytime anxiety."

"That would make sense, but, you know, I don't think that's it."

"Hmm. You're sure?"

"Remember, you said I might have met the defendant before but just couldn't remember when or where. Well, last night I'm sure I did remember."

"But I was suggesting you might have met someone *like* him. I mean, how likely is it you're on a jury with a man you know from your past? And then to have him be the one to open the closet...well, that's just too crazy."

"I know. It would be very unlikely that I've had some past contact with Cunningham. Still, I can't shake this feeling that I somehow know him. And there's something else."

"What?"

"The part in the dream about the closet...well, I think it has something to do with my mother's death."

"That's just bizarre, Jane."

"I know it sounds crazy but I think the scary closet thing and my mother's death are somehow related." Turning to Sydney,

Jane said, "So, I want to be hypnotized to see if I can remember exactly what happened when my mother died."

"Damn, Jane! You've never wanted to know before. I mean right now doesn't seem like a good time. Maybe after the trial."

"I don't want to wait. I don't know why but I'm not as afraid as I have been. I think it has something to do with last night's memory and with being on the jury." Jane took Sydney's hand, asking, "So, will you hypnotize me?"

Sydney jerked her hand away. "Me? That's ridiculous, Jane. I don't know a thing about hypnosis."

Jane picked up one of the books, handing it to Sydney. "It's not that difficult. Anyway, if it doesn't work nothing bad is going to happen."

Sydney took the book but set it down on the table beside the sofa. "It doesn't sound like a good idea. You need to go to a professional."

"I can't do that now. I'm on a jury. If they found out, I would be disqualified."

"If you're so sure you've met this man, then maybe you should take yourself off the jury."

"I'm not going to do that. I could be wrong, could be making this all up and then what would I have accomplished besides quitting yet again. But if Bradley Cunningham is the same man who hurt me or my mother, I want to know." Jane pointed to the second book, saying, "It says here that my best chance of remembering is by being in a high anxiety situation similar to the original trauma. If Cunningham had anything to do with my mother's death or my being locked in a closet, seeing him in the courtroom every day is the best way for me to remember. Besides, if he did something to me, maybe I want to do something back to him."

"I can't believe you just said that. It's so *unJane*-like."

"I know. But I said *maybe*. I won't know how I'll feel until I know for sure if I've had some awful experience with this man. So, will you do it?"

Sydney got up and began pacing. " Gosh, I don't know. What exactly is it I have to do?"

Jane reached across the sofa and picked up the book on the table, opening it to a page she had marked. "Just read these words to me. Use a relaxing voice. Then ask me some questions about my closet memory. If it doesn't work, it doesn't work."

"How will I know if it is working?"

"Two ways. First, you'll ask me to do something simple like floating my hand to see if I follow your command. Also, when you ask me questions, I'll be able to remember vivid details, stuff that would be hard to know if I wasn't really there."

"What if you start to freak out on me?"

Jane laughed. "Like I haven't done that before?"

Sydney nodded, "I guess you're right. Seeing you freak out would not be a first. So, when do you want to do this?"

"How about right now?"

Sydney was quiet for a few moments then sat back down and looked at the open page Jane had given her, scanning the words. "Okay, I'll give it a try, but first I have to get something." She stood up, walked into the kitchen, got a paper bag and returned to the couch, holding it up. "First aid. So, do you lie down or what?"

"Yeah, I'll be on the couch." Pointing to the side chair she said, "You sit there."

Jane stretched out on the sofa while Sydney sat in the chair. Sydney asked, "You're sure you're ready for this?"

"I can't believe I'm doing this but yeah, I'm ready."

"I can't believe we're both doing this," replied Sydney and then she began reading. "Close your eyes. Now imagine you're on an elevator at the tenth floor. You're going down. I'm going to count backwards from ten and with each count I want you to take a very deep breath and let it out slowly, letting your body relax as you descend. Okay?"

"Yes."

"Okay, you're on the tenth floor of an elevator going down. I want you to take a deep breath and let it out slowly, feeling your body relax as you descend. Good. Now you're on the ninth floor, another deep breath, now let it out slowly and feel your body go down into a deeper relaxation as you further descend. Good. You're now on the eighth floor, another deep breath and as you slowly let it out your body will feel yourself go down into a deeper state of relaxation. Very good. Okay, now you're on the seventh floor. Another very deep breath. Good. Let it out slowly and feel yourself descend to a lower level of relaxation. Now you're at level six, take a deep breath and let it out slowly as you go further down into a relaxed state..."

When Sydney had finished reading, she looked over at Jane. She was breathing deeply. She returned to the book, again reading, "Can you hear me, Jane?"

Jane gave a barely audible, "Yes."

"Okay, I want you to pay close attention to your left hand. You'll notice it's feeling very light, light as a feather, a feather that wants to float gently up in the air." Sydney looked over at Jane, her left hand was slowly lifting up in the air. "Are you with me, Jane?"

"Yes, I'm here. My left hand feels strange, like a balloon is pulling it up."

"Okay, you can let your hand relax now."

Jane's hand flopped back to her side. Sydney raised her eyebrows in wonder, her mouth open in disbelief. Then she returned her attention to the book. "Okay, I'm going to ask you some questions now."

It was late afternoon on day three and the defense team was gathered in the conference room waiting for Toby to show. The tension between Erin and RJ had abated only marginally. The room was eerily quiet for an end-of-court day. RJ had his laptop open, his eyes glued to the screen, obvious to even a non-expert that he was avoiding eye contact with Erin. Erin had managed to make a quick stop for a double espresso and was now savoring the lingering taste and the slight caffeine buzz, deep in thought about the ramifications of a perpetual conflict between her and RJ. Never wanting to appear idle in front of RJ, the Tweedles also had laptops open, either intensely involved in something of importance—or pretending to be.

RJ, finally looking up from his computer, checked his watch for the third time before he cursed, "Damn it. He said he would be here ten minutes ago." He looked over at Dum, barking, "Get him on the phone. Find out where he is."

Dum was taking out his phone just as Toby rushed into the room. "Sorry, guys." He shook in head in disgust, "Traffic is a mess...makes me insane...."

RJ cut him off, snapping, "I'm not paying you for a traffic report. What did you find out about Seven?"

Toby stiffened, clearly not pleased with having been cut off and spoken to so rudely. The tension in the room escalated. Erin was closely watching Toby, wondering if he was going to be able to *pick his battle* now that he was the target of the demeaning Reverend Jove. Toby took several steps toward RJ, towering over the man, not saying a word, just glaring down at him.

RJ, realizing he had reprimanded someone he couldn't intimidate, quickly retreated, saying, "Sorry, Toby. Rough day. Please, what were you able to find out?"

Erin didn't fail to notice that Toby merited an apology. Hell would freeze over before RJ apologized to her.

Toby walked over to his usual position, leaning against the wall. "So, here's the skinny: literal dead end on Jane's adoptive parents, who were older when they adopted her. Her adoptive mother died four years ago and her adoptive father is currently institutionalized at an Alzheimer facility. Apparently his brain is fried. However, by pulling a few favors I was able to find out something about her birth family. As you know, the adoption records gave us Jane's birth surname. From there I originally hit a wall. Well, today I pushed through the wall. A long shot, really, considering how many years ago it was. Anyway, I called my contact at juvie and asked her to see if a file on Tamara Romer still existed and I got lucky. Turns out Tamara, after her first arrest, made a phone call to a sister who was living in another state. Which means, naturally, that Jane has an aunt."

Erin's eyes widened, "You said *ha*s. How do you know she's still alive?"

Toby grinned slyly, replying, "I called the number my friend gave me, asked for the woman by name. She identified herself and asked why I was calling. When I tried to sell her cable service she hung up on me."

RJ drummed his fingers on the table. "So, big deal. Jane has an aunt. This information doesn't get us ahead of the game. We can't approach the aunt directly about Jane or we'll be sliding the slippery slope surrounding jury tampering."

"Nice alliteration," Erin said, without thinking. RJ glared at her in return.

Well, damn Erin thought. *No more double espressos for me when I'm around the Reverend!*

Quickly sensing a need for a diversion, Toby hurried on, "I've thought about the jury tampering issue. I have a colleague in the city where the aunt lives. I could ask her to do some very quiet nosing around."

Relieved at having been rescued yet again, Erin smiled at Toby, saying, "It seems you have contacts everywhere." Toby smiled back and was about to answer when RJ, eyes darting back and forth between Erin and Toby, interrupted, "We're conducting business here, you two can get a room later."

Erin felt herself turn beet red, the first time ever she wished she was having a hot flash instead of the embarrassment she was feeling. She didn't dare look at Toby but she knew he would be saved by the color of his skin. Yet again the Reverend had slung insults, only this time he had included Toby. Nonplussed, she was unable to speak.

Toby, however, didn't miss a beat. Raising his eyebrows at Erin, he deadpanned, "Good suggestion." Then he pushed off against the wall and walked over to RJ, staring down at him, saying, "Since we'll be working up a sweat, you'll be paying, I presume." The room went silent for a flash, before a muffled snicker leaked out from Tweedle Dee. Erin, determined not to further dig her own grave, starred straight ahead, willing herself to remain mute, repeating the silent mantra, *shut-up, don't laugh, shut-up, don't laugh.*

Toby, without giving RJ an opportunity to respond, added, "No, I'm guessing not. Listen up RJ, you want me to put my friend on the case, let me know." Then he stormed out of the room.

RJ immediately began shutting down his laptop, sliding it inside its travel case. "I'm going to watch the woman one more day before I decide if we need to take any further action." Turning to his two associates, he curtly said. "You guys are dismissed for the day." He then walked out of the room, heading to his office down the hall.

Erin slumped back in her chair, letting out a big sign, relieved that this time she had managed to keep from inflaming the situation.

Dee and Dum were closing-up shop as well. Dee completely took Erin by surprise when he leaned over and spoke conspiratorially to her, saying, "Nobody told me I should have bought disability insurance before I started this job. I'm only twenty-eight but my blood pressure has gone up twenty points since I started working for him. I'll probably have a stroke before I'm thirty." Dum shook his head in exasperation, then drew his hand across his mouth in a zipping motion.

At that moment Erin's cell phone signaled her that she had a text message. She pulled her phone out of her purse, glancing at the screen; it was from Toby: *Room 555 in 15?* She smiled, knowing 555 was also known as The Triple Nickel, a classy restaurant and bar that was located a few miles from RJ's office at 555 Broadway. Toby Parish, she mused, was getting curiouser, and curiouser; she texted back: *15 it is.*

Erin was sure that at this time of the evening she would not find a spot anywhere near the restaurant so she decided to use the valet. After turning her precious new baby over to the valet, she began searching for Toby in the crowd of people milling around outside the restaurant waiting to be seated. Toby, with his six-five frame, should have been an easy target to spot but Erin couldn't find him. Just as she was beginning to think she might have misunderstood his text, a very alluring middle-aged woman approached her, asking if she was Dr. Halloway. When Erin hesitantly said yes, the woman replied, "Your party is already inside. May I show you to your table?"

The two of them maneuvered their way through the crowd, a few of whom eyed Erin with disdain. The woman, who Erin had finally concluded was the hostess, showed her to a booth in the corner of the bar where Toby was already seated. He stood as she approached, bowing slightly, saying, "Glad you could join me."

Nodding at the retreating hostess, Erin said, "I see you found *room* at Room 555. Another one of your contacts?"

"Yes, having useful contacts are everything in my line of work."

Sliding into the seat opposite him, Erin shook her head in wonder. "Literally, Toby, you're a man of many colors—and I mean that in the best possible way."

"Thank you. When you're my color and size stereotypes abound. Some of my greatest pleasures in life have come from foiling people's assumptions."

"Then I've provided you with some amusing entertainment, I guess."

Toby grinned, "Yes, you have at that."

Erin was taken aback. "Oh, well, at least you're honest."

"Always that." Toby pointed to a martini glass on the table. "By the way, I took the liberty of ordering you a Tito's, very dry."

"Thank you for remembering." Erin picked up the glass, took a sip, gently twirled it in her hand, then said, "So, tell me, what further assumptions about you should I avoid?"

"Well, for starters, don't assume just because I'm having fun baffling you, I don't find you amazingly fetching, intellectually captivating, and valiantly intrepid."

Erin flushed. "Damn you, Toby. I haven't felt this unnerved in years."

With a sly smile, Toby replied, "I hope that's a good thing."

Erin sat back in the booth, taking another sip of her drink, thinking. Then she scooted forward on the bench, leaned in toward Toby and said, "Well, now that I've had a moment to recover, let me say in return that I find you remarkably sagacious, incredibly prepossessing, and...totally beguiling."

"Damn it, doc, you one-upped me. You got me with sagacious." He took out his iPhone and began tapping on it, finally looking up at Erin. "Whew! Says sagacious means wise; so, that's a compliment, right?"

"Definitely a compliment. Only a truly sagacious person could have handled RJ the way you did today."

"Well, I don't take the man too seriously. He reminds me of a couple of quarterbacks I used to know. Men who don't just want to be the quarterback, but *need* to be the quarterback...you know, to be calling all the plays and receiving all the accolades because deep down inside they are insecure. RJ's smart but he's also insecure and he deals with it by trying to intimidate others.

"I couldn't agree more, but somehow knowing this doesn't help me keep my cool around him."

"Probably a gender thing."

Erin narrowed her eyes at him, "What do you mean?"

"I mean, having been a defensive tackle, powerful men don't intimate me, but let a woman dis me the way RJ did today...well, I'd probably lose it. I might even cry."

"Yeah, sure. I'll believe that when I see it."

"You might just see it right now if you don't agree to stay and have dinner with me."

"Well, I'd like to have dinner with you. On the other hand, I'd *love* to see you cry so maybe I should say no to dinner."

"Okay, I lied. I won't cry if you leave. Now will you have dinner with me?"

"Yes, I will."

A text message was also waiting for Saul Greene at the end of day three. His boss wanted to meet for an update on the case. District Attorney Alisa Lorenza was an exception to the rule in the ladder-climbing legal world: an apolitical, no-nonsense, competent, open-minded woman who didn't pretend to have all the answers and didn't mind admitting she was wrong. As Saul headed for her office, he reflected yet again on how fortunate he was to be working under her; he would never have been given this opportunity if she wasn't fair-minded and willing to give him a chance to redeem himself.

The DA's door was open and as he approached, Alisa looked up from her desk, giving him a signal to enter. As he did, she came out from behind her desk and took one of the two chairs that were opposite her desk, indicating he should sit in the other. It didn't go unnoticed by Saul that Alisa had purposely eliminated the desk as a symbol of power.

As soon as they were seated, Alisa began, "From what I've heard, you're holding up well under the stress of this high-profile case."

"I'll be frank, Alisa, you saved me from myself by giving me this case."

"I may have opened the door, but you're the one who had the courage to walk through it. So, what's this I hear about juror Seven?"

"We don't know what to think about this woman because she did a one-eighty on us. Day one she looked like she would crumble under the strain, today she was a monolith with a stone face that said, 'Give me everything you got.' We have nothing on her that we can use to disqualify her or a solid reason to put an investigator on her. And I'm not sure if we want to; she may be on our side, but it's difficult to tell."

"Forget hard evidence, Saul, what does your gut tell you?"

"My gut tells me she has something in her background that makes her dislike Cunningham, which would, of course, work in our favor. Except that with Dr. Halloway on the defense team, I'm sure they have come to the same conclusion. As you know, they also have Toby Parish, one of the best investigators in the business."

"You think the Reverend would risk jury tampering charges by sending Toby out to investigate?"

"The Reverend is consumed with winning and I think he has the scruples of a politician. In other words, he would do it if he thought he wouldn't get caught—and I think Toby is good enough to keep anyone from finding out."

"I tend to agree with you. So, what do you want to do at this point?"

"I need one more day. Tomorrow is going to be the most difficult day for us. I'm putting our CSI expert on to talk about the damage we found on Cunningham's car. We already know RJ is going to tear into the guy. I want to assign someone on our team to watch Seven like a hawk. I'm thinking maybe Karen Pekin might be the best person. What do you think?"

"Yeah, I think you're right. She's got great intuition. Have Karen text me right before you put our guy on the stand. If I can get away, I'd like to be in court to see what Seven is all about."

Saul left Alisa's office with mixed emotions: encouraged that she had agreed with his take on the situation, disquieted that she might be in court watching him. Not wanting to leave any room for surprises, he decided he would go directly home to review his notes for the next day's witness. He would stay at it until he was confident he had not overlooked anything.

Three hours later Saul felt as prepared as he was going to get, realizing that the more he rehearsed, the more wired he was becoming. It was times like this that he most missed Richard, times when he needed someone to talk with, to discuss his thinking on a case, to get an outside opinion from someone who really cared, someone whose perspective he trusted.

He picked up his cell phone, scrolling through his contacts to see if there was anyone he could call, any former friend he hadn't shunned beyond restitution as he had moped his way through life without Richard. Just as he was about to the end of the alphabet, his phone beeped, indicating he had a text message. When he read it, his chest constricted and his breath became compressed, as if a huge boulder was sitting on it. The message was from Richard: *meet for a drink tonight*?

The message was so unexpected, so clairvoyant that Saul felt dizzy; his heart pounding with a mixture of trepidation and excitement at the thought of seeing Richard again. Every rational brain cell in his head told him to ignore the summons, while every emotive, impassioned brain cell compelled his fingers to text back a yes. If he went with his sensible brain and ignored the message, he would maintain his pride and the stingy progress he had made toward a new life. But he would never know what Richard wanted. If he sided with his emotions and met with Richard, he knew his brain would be reacquainted with the attachment drug, a drug his therapist had told him was as powerful as cocaine, the drug responsible for his months of misery. His therapist had warned him that any contact with Richard would be like an alcoholic having one drink: his brain chemistry would be reignited like fireworks, leaving him wanting more and wiping out any gains he had made.

Until Richard had abandoned him, Saul had never truly understood the power of drug addiction. He had always thought it was a matter of will power, of choosing constructive behavior over self-destructive behavior. However, after going through the painful chemical withdraw of loss, the idea of will power seemed laughable. All these months later and the temptation to see Richard was tugging at him like an undertow. He wished he had a *lovesickness* sponsor like they do in AA, someone he could call to rescue him from the temptation. He paced, trying to think of someone he could call. He momentarily considered his sympathetic boss but immediately ruled her out. In the midst of the most important trial of his life, she didn't need to know how pathetically weak he was feeling. Then, quite suddenly, an image of a face flashed in his mind: the attractive man at the bar, the computer hotshot with the outrageous sense of humor who had given him his phone number.

Where had he put it? Maybe the pocket of the suit he had been wearing? He hurried into the bedroom, opened the closet door and searched the jacket pocket of the suit he had worn the first day of court. When his hand found the piece of paper, he felt a huge sense of relief. He pulled the paper out and unfolded it. Scribbled on it was the name, Allan, and a phone number. Saul quickly dialed before he had second thoughts, before even thinking about what he would say, before considering what he would do if Allan didn't answer. After two rings it went to voice mail. Saul hung up; he needed an immediate life-preserver and an unanswered distress call would only escalate his panic. Maybe, Saul thought, I could just text Richard back and ask him what he wants. That way I wouldn't have to see him. As he lifted his phone to type a text, it rang, startling him. *Shit! What if it was it Richard?* Hesitantly, he looked at the screen, relieved when the caller ID didn't indicate Richard. Instead it was the last number he had dialed. He took a breath and answered, "This is Saul Greene."

Silence for a few seconds, then,"This is Allan Feldman. I think you just called me."

More awkward silence before Saul replied, "Yes, I did. I don't know if you remember me..."

"Sure I remember you. From the other night at the Speak Easy bar."

"Right. Umm...I know it's last minute but I was wondering if you wanted to meet for a drink. Tonight...now, I mean."

"Well, sure, sounds like a good plan to me. You sound a little bummed, though. Something happen with your case? I mean I've been following it in the newspapers."

"No, it's not the case. It's something else. I just need some upbeat company right now."

"Want to meet at the Speak Easy?"

"No, anywhere but."

"How about my place, then? I promise to be a gentleman, no unwanted moves."

Saul, suddenly skittish, replied, "Maybe this isn't such a good idea after all...wait...that sounds all wrong. I mean it has nothing to do with you or your place...it's just that I won't be such good company."

" Uh oh, something tells me you just had a lover's quarrel."

"No, that's been over with for eighteen months, six days, twelve hours, but then who's counting, right?"

"Dumped, huh?"

"Like garbage. Thing is, the jerk just texted me a few minutes ago. Wants to meet tonight."

"I see. You're tempted but afraid you'll get addicted again?"

"You sound like the therapist I went to."

"Doctor Fabricant, I bet."

"How did you know?"

"Hey, he was my therapist too. How many gay therapists are there that specialize in treating romantic disasters?"

"So, I take it you've been a dumpee as well?"

"Right. Better to have loved and lost...yada, yada, yada."

"Well, I've been kind of pathetic and I think my months of despondency have alienated all my friends."

"So it's time you made a new friend. Come on over. We'll get acquainted."

Saul didn't answer for a few seconds, then said, "You know, it's late and I'm feeling better now that we've talked. How about we meet tomorrow after work instead?"

"You sure you'll be able to hold out?"

"Yeah. Just telling someone how tempted I was seems to help. It also helps to have something to look forward to."

"Me, as well. Okay. So where and when shall we meet?"

"My schedule is always a little unpredictable. Should be around six, but how about I call you when I can get free?"

"Sure."

After hanging up, Saul felt a small twinge of excitement, the idea of a possible new friend (maybe lover) boosting his spirits, giving him just the grit he needed to ignore Richard's text. At the very moment he was feeling buoyed, his phone rang. He had a uneasy premonition that it would be Richard and he was right. Just glancing at the caller ID started his heart racing, his brain immediately going into temptation mode again. His finger hovered over the answer key. *Damn it! Was he ever going to get over the man?* He closed his eyes, letting an image of Richard in bed with his new lover flow into his mind. *He's a jerk and I deserve better*, he said out loud as he tossed the phone on the sofa, letting it go to voice mail. Then he got ready for bed, joined an online game of scrabble on his phone, and, before going to sleep, erased Richard's voice message without listening to it.

Day three had been more of the same for Cunningham: a day that required him to wear the dispassionate facial mask while the prosecution crucified him. Instructed to maintain frequent eye contact with the jurors, Cunningham, less self-absorbed than on days one and two, had not missed the penetrating stare, the raised chin, and the slightly upthrusted lip in one corner of juror Seven's mouth. The woman was blatantly sneering at him.

At the end of the day he said something to RJ about Seven. As always, RJ assured him they had everything under control and that he was aware of juror Seven's behavior. Cunningham, however, was not calmed by RJ's assertions. The sneer was troublesome, but there was also something else about the woman that was disconcerting, something gnawing at him. In the car on the way home, he decided it must be that she reminded him of someone he knew, maybe someone he didn't like. For several minutes he was thinking about who it might be and was deep in thought when he finally realized Rose was talking to him.

"I'm sorry, dear. What were you asking me?"

"About the car. I know RJ doesn't want to put me on the stand, but I think I should tell the jury I was the one driving when the car was damaged."

Cunningham was in no mood for debating issues they had gone over many times. RJ had patiently explained to Rose on numerous occasions why she should not be put on the stand. Forcing himself to remain calm, Cunningham firmly said, "We've been over this many times. You will not be testifying. RJ says his experts will be able to discredit whomever they put on the stand."

In a petulant voice, Rose, continued,"But it's true that I was driving...."

Cunningham exploded, shouting at the top of his lungs, "Enough! You're not testifying and you're never to mention it again. Do you understand me?"

Rose's eyes immediately began to tear. "Yes. But it's not necessary to shout at me."

Cunningham knew he should apologize, but something stubborn in him pushed him further into his anger. He bellowed,

"It is necessary when you repeatedly ignore what you've been told to do."

Rose shrunk back, tears now flowing easily. Her husband rarely yelled at her so she was at a loss for any verbal response. She pulled a tissue from her purse and wiped at her eyes. She felt she had been brave, holding up under the strain all these months, but her husband's explosion had caused the whole awful mess to feel overwhelming. The urge to talk to Father Clement suddenly and forcefully came over her.

Meekly she asked, "Could Damon drop me off at the church and pick me up later?"

Cunningham cringed. He abhorred her weak need for God's counsel, her need to run to a *higher power* whenever she felt life's small struggles tugging at her. He had always done what it took to swallow his scorn, to be the perfect, indulgent husband, knowing that her attachment to the church had given him the freedom he needed to live his double life. This very moment, however, he was in no mood to be circumspect. He looked over at his wife, thinking, *she is such an anemic, hollow, sexless woman and, yes, I married her for these very reasons but right now I just can't continue with the charade.* He found himself with the impulse to slap her. His hand, seeming to have a mind of its own, raised up to strike, but somehow, at the last minute, his survival instinct automatically kicked in. Instead, he let his hand fall gently on her knee, saying, "Of course." He leaned forward in his seat and told his driver to take them to St. Michaels.

Alone in the car, Cunningham was ruminating on his close call. He had almost hit his wife, the wife he so desperately needed to juggle the surreptitious aspects of his life, the adoring wife who would give him Brownie points in the eyes of the jury. He almost thanked God for whatever had saved him from his impulsive behavior, then quietly scoffed, realizing how hypocritical it would be for him to evoke God's name. For Bradley Cunningham, beseeching God would surely mean going straight to hell.

When Rose returned home from the church, she went straight to her separate bedroom without saying a word to her husband who was in his study with the door closed, an explicit signal he was not to be disturbed.

DAY FOUR

It was after midnight and Sydney was sitting by herself on the couch, completely unnerved. The Syd who was known for her unflinching, ballsy approach to whatever life tossed her way had been thrown totally asunder by the hypnosis session. Jane's recall of the events surrounding her mother's death was macabre: horrifying to hear and gut- wrenching to imagine in the detail that Jane revealed. A six-year-old child locked in a closet while her mother lay dying on the floor right outside the closet...well, it was a tale that made your heart break, even a jaded heart like Sydney's. Jane's recollection of the trauma, however, explained a lot about Jane's self-effacing, easily frightened, anxious personality.

Sydney was also an adopted child, one of the reasons she and Jane had bonded so strongly. The day she met Jane had been her first one at the new elementary school. Meeting Jane that day had been serendipitous, two lost souls finding each other in a sea of what felt like unfriendly sharks. Jane was like a jellyfish, though, with a soft underbelly through which life's tribulations easily penetrated her vulnerable spirit. Sydney, on the other hand, was like a shellfish, a child who had developed a hard shell, impenetrable to life's abrasions. Yet, here Sydney sat with Jane's memories of the long-ago trauma having penetrated that seemingly impervious shell. As Sydney listened to Jane's memories come flooding back, she found herself furious at the injustice of it: cruelty, exploitation, and atrocities that terribly victimized an innocent six-year-old child and vandalized Jane's ability to cope with the world.

During the hypnosis session, Jane had sobbed, cried, pleaded in a child's voice—as if it were happening to her in the moment rather than twenty-two years ago, unnerving Sydney in a way she never remembered. Yet, somehow her instincts told her to let the disturbing scene play out, to let Jane have her exorcism in the hope that her demons would be expelled.

So, she had done nothing to stop her when Jane described in choking sobs her memories of that night: *the thrill of her mother unexpectedly dressing her in a new, beautiful pink dress...the delight quickly changing to dread when her mother let a man come into the tiny apartment where they lived...the man handing her mother some money, money, that even at six years of age, Jane knew would be used to buy the white powder her mother would later put in a needle and stick into her own arm. Then her mother, before leaving the apartment, sternly telling Jane to be nice to the man and do whatever he told Jane to do. With her mother gone, the dread quickly turning to fear, the man sitting on the sofa, motioning her to come close, patting his lap, telling her to be nice and come sit. Jane, frightened but also strangely willful, refusing to move...the man's spooky smile turning to an ugly frown as she kept shaking her head no...the man standing, angrily coming toward her, picking her up...Jane crying, kicking, screaming...the man holding her so tight she couldn't breathe. Then the man walking with her to the closet, opening the door, shoving her inside, slamming the door, yelling at her that she could come out when she was ready to do what she was told. The darkness so frightening...the panic overwhelming, the crying so desperate...until there were no tears left. Then the closet door opening, the man reaching down to pick her up, Jane biting down hard on the man's hand, tasting blood and something soft...the man yelling and jerking back as he screamed awful words. Then the man suddenly slapping her, sending her sprawling to the floor...the closet door slamming, the lock turning...the slamming of the front door...then nothing but the silence, the darkness, and the terror.*

Drained of all energy after the hypnosis session, Jane had fallen asleep. She woke two hours later with the memories still intense and the two women talked for an hour more about what Jane had remembered. Jane had maintained the eerie conviction that the man from her memories was the very same man on trial, Bradley Cunningham.

"Well, you don't have any proof it's him," Sydney reminded Jane. "You only have recalled images of a man, images that could be coming from a fusion of the stress of being a juror and the deluge of painful memories."

"Still, I feel I'm right. I think the man in my memories is Cunningham."

"If you're that convinced, you should remove yourself from the jury, don't you think?"

"Well, that's a fair question. But the truth is I'm not ready to do that yet. I want to know for sure."

Sydney began pacing the room. "Okay, so here's an idea. If you bit the man as hard as you described, he would likely carry a scar."

Jane got excited. "Oh, God, Syd! Maybe you're right. But I don't think I would be able to see it from the jury box."

Now Sydney got excited. "I've got an idea."

Retrieving her laptop from the bedroom she scrolled through her client list, searching for the name of the person she thought might help them find definitive proof.

"Here it is," she exclaimed.

"Here's what?" Jane asked.

"The name of the photojournalist I know. I'm going to ask him to get us a picture of Cunningham's hand."

Sydney opened her cell phone to make a call but Jane reached out to stop her, asking,"Isn't it too late to make a call?"

"Maybe, guess we'll find out."

She dialed his cell phone and when she got his voice mail, left a prearranged, coded message. Within minutes her call was returned, an agreement secured, and the first step of the plan ready to be put into operation. After Sydney put down the phone, she looked at Jane with raised eyebrows, saying, "You wanted to know for sure, so are you ready to become a Light Warrior?"

Feeling a strange mixture of fear and excitement, the kind of feeling that comes from illicit ventures, Jane responded: "I'm really nervous but I'm not willing to quit. Does that mean I'm ready to be a Warrior?"

"You're in the game anyway—and that means you must face the challenges thrown at you by the enemy."

Rose was definitely not herself on the morning before the fourth day of the trial. She had not spoken a word to Bradley at breakfast, nor had she eaten anything. Last night and this morning she had begun to question her earlier commitment to stand by him *no matter what.* As they were being driven to the courthouse, she stared out the window, lost in anxious thought. Her hurt feelings from yesterday were still fresh in her mind, as was the gnawing trepidation that she was expected to give her husband devoted looks throughout the day. A few minutes before arriving at the courthouse, Bradley took her hand. Rose knew it was a gesture of truce on his part and, deciding she wanted no part of a confrontation, didn't withdraw her hand. However, she refused to look at him. Instead she continued to stare out the window, her mind still in deep turmoil.

For the first time in her thirty-five-year marriage, she wondered if she really knew her husband.

Last night Father Clement had cancelled his previous plans so he could receive her. Rose knew that he would because she was well aware that her devotion to the church, via her deep pockets, meant deferential treatment. For the first time ever, however, his once comforting words felt like platitudes. He had said what he always said, "A wife's role is to be by her husband's side." Then, of course, he had added, "And know that God will always be standing next to you whenever you need His support." These words had always given her guidance in the past, but last night they had felt inauthentic, even vacuous. She had no idea what was happening to her; she only knew that something was changing. Try as she might she could not quell a pivotal question in her mind: *why had Bradley refused to tell her what he had been doing in that seedy part of town so early in the morning?*

When she first asked Bradley that question all those months ago, he had changed the subject. Weeks later she had brought it up again and he snapped at her, saying, "It isn't important to the case." Back then she knew that couldn't be right, but she had been too intimidated to object. Then like all problematic things in her marriage, she had put it out of her mind. In the last few days, however, that very question seemed to be in the forefront of Saul Greene's mind. He had hammered away at that issue in his opening statement, leaving Rose with a grain of uncertainty. She had tried to put it out of her mind, but Bradley's anger yesterday had stirred up her misgivings. Today, Rose was sure Greene would again be casting suspicion on the redoubtable Bradley Cunningham's presence in a known red-light district. Rose, still staring out the car window, swallowed hard, thinking about the possibility of her husband's being with a prostitute, a thought she had never before allowed to enter her head.

Tears came into her eyes as she forced herself to acknowledge something once unthinkable. All those years of avoiding any marital conflict had really been a tactical maneuver to protect herself. For thirty-five years she had kept a secret from everyone but her husband, a secret impossible to hide from a husband. It was such a shameful secret that even Father Clement was denied confessional access. The shame had caused her to commit a sin, to lie to her family and a few close friends. She had told them that she couldn't have children. Her highly religious family, believing these were private matters, had never asked for further details. The few friends Rose had told knew to respect her privacy. No one but her husband knew the truth.

Within a few weeks of meeting Bradley Cunningham, Rose was hopelessly in love, wishing desperately that he would ask her to marry him, but fearful that he couldn't accept her determination to comply with the church's dogma of virginity until marriage. However, Bradley had been a saint, respecting her beliefs in First Corinthians: that marriage is the cure for sexual immorality. She was thrilled beyond imagination when he proposed.

Shortly after Bradley proposed, she had gone for her very first pelvic exam and discovered her shameful condition. The exam had been extremely painful and humiliating. She was horrified to learn that the doctor was unable to perform the exam because he was unable to insert the speculum. Afterwards, the doctor took her into his private office, awkwardly mumbling to her about something called vaginismus, a condition in which the vaginal muscles involuntarily contract preventing vaginal penetration. The doctor, obviously uncomfortable, had quickly scribbled the name of a specialized therapist on his prescription pad and sent Rose on her way.

Fearful that Bradley would never marry damaged goods, she had not said a word to him about what the doctor had told her. So, in secret, she had gone for two visits to a sexual therapist, quitting abruptly when the therapist told her two things: her condition was psychological in origin, most likely stemming from her religious beliefs, beliefs that had created a deep, unconscious fear of sex, and that she would need Bradley to be involved if the problem was to be solved. Hearing the therapist say these two unacceptable things had ended with her feeling hopeless for a solution. For weeks she had anticipated his abandonment if he found out and she prayed for guidance, asking God to help her find the courage to tell him. As the time approached to send out wedding invitations, however, she yielded to the knowledge that God would disapprove if she entered a marriage with such a sin of omission.

So, she had swallowed her pride and tearfully told Bradley she couldn't marry him. When he refused to accept her decision unless she told him why, she had finally confessed her problem. She was astounded by his unflagging devotion. "I love you, Rose, and want to be your husband. I'm confident we'll work out the sexual problem after we get married," he had proclaimed.

The disgraceful truth was what they had "worked out" was a silent, perverted complicity. All these years she had convinced herself that Bradley was a saint, loving her despite her pitiful asexuality. Now, however, she had come to see another alternative: seeing him as a savior had been convenient; it had allowed her to avoid confronting her sexual fears. Rose wasn't infertile, she was a still a virgin, a married woman living for thirty-five years in an unconsummated marriage.

And Bradley's part of the complicity? Just as the car pulled to the curb in front of the courthouse, she finally turned toward her husband. Her heart thudded as she wondered, *what shameful secret is he hiding from me?*

The crowds outside the courthouse had not diminished on day four. The hoards of reporters, microphones extended like pointed pistols, encircled the Cunningham's car when it stopped in front, all shouting questions at once at the famous defendant. Instructed to say absolutely nothing to the vultures, the couple, escorted by security guards, pushed their way through the crowd and up the courthouse steps.

Benjamin Coe, press pass around his neck, easily blended into the crowd of reporters all wanting a piece of the prominent couple. Granted, he had to be aggressive to get close enough to get the pictures he wanted, but being a consummate pro, he had shoved his way into the inner circle, his 16.2 megapixel digital Nikon D7000 snapping six frames a second. In a melee like this, Ben was confident not a single person noticed where he was aiming his lens. Within five minutes he was back in his car and downloading the photos to his computer. Heading to the closest Starbucks, he ordered a tall latte, sat down at a table, drank his coffee and emailed the pictures to Sydney.

Ben had been more than willing to make the trade that Sydney had offered. She was one skillful, sexy woman who never disappointed, never made any demands on him, never complained about being too tired after a day with the kids, or that he didn't help her out enough around the house. Syd performed pleasurable acts his wife refused to do. Not only that but Syd's focus remained on him the entire time, making sure he was satisfied. The best part was that he didn't have to put up with his wife's whining and her constant complaint that he was selfish and unconcerned about her pleasure. An evening with Sydney was worth every fucking (ha! ha!) dollar. Not only did he get wild, absurd, unbelievable sex, but without Sydney to satisfy him, he would likely be cheating on his wife with a troublesome woman, one who would expect him to leave his wife. That would mean having to pay alimony. As far as Ben was concerned, the cost-benefit ratio worked in his favor.

Ben had been reading about the high-profile Cunningham trial so Syd's request had piqued his curiosity. He had asked her, "What's up with a photo of a hand?" All Syd was willing to say was, "It's like the two of us...a need to know situation and one best kept to yourself." He was aware of the implication in her voice, a quid pro quo: *I keep your secret you keep mine.* "Not a problem," he replied, since the truth was he didn't really care why she wanted a photo of a hand. He was a freelancer and in his business there were many unusual requests. As long as he got paid, he did what was asked of him and did it well. Still, for Sydney to be asking for close-ups of the left hand of a prominent man on trial for a felony was curious indeed.

Was Bradley Cunningham one of her clients? Now that would be very interesting indeed.

Day four and Jane Nichols is solid as a rock, observed Erin. There was none of her former jumpiness. Instead, she was focused on the defendant again, the penetrating stare, narrowed eyes, tight mouth all remaining fairly constant, changing only when she moved her focus to Saul Greene or to a witness. Erin knew that it was typical human behavior to make quick judgements about another person, usually within thirty seconds of seeing them. If this wasn't true, she wouldn't have a career as a jury consultant. These opinions were usually based solely on physical appearance and mannerisms—and likely some unknown, odorless chemical that humans emitted. It didn't surprise Erin that a juror, in this case Seven, was having a strong reaction to Cunningham. What did surprise her, however, was Seven's dramatic transformation: the woman vacillated between Nervous Nelly and Jaded Jane, leaving Erin to wonder which personality she would bring into the deliberation room.

At the beginning of the day Erin wasn't sure what she would recommend to RJ regarding Jane Nichols. She knew he would be expecting her observations at the end of today's proceedings...whether he listened was another question altogether. Likely, he would have been mulling over Toby's offer to investigate Seven. Erin was very aware of the potential problems of an investigative decision in either direction: investigate and risk jury tampering or do nothing and risk a mistrial if Nichols held firmly to a guilty vote during deliberation.

Erin watched Jane carefully as the prosecution put its expert witness on the stand to talk about the damage to the car. Saul had the witness on the stand for hours, presenting visuals of the damage and explaining in detail how it was possible for the damage to have been made by slamming into a human being. Jane had been attentive to the witness but stole repeated looks at Cunningham, always with a hard stare.

RJ had, of course, done his homework and, on cross examination, he grilled the witness for a solid hour about the word *possible*, leaving the jury, Erin noted, with the clear understanding that the witness was stating an opinion and could not provide direct evidence. Jane was alert to the testimony, but it was evident to Erin that Jane found RJ's bullying tactics very distasteful, furrowing her brow when he tried to intimidate the witness. Not good, thought Erin. It's not good for Cunningham and not good for me: I'm going to be the one to have to tell RJ that his menacing strategy is backfiring with Seven. She cringed at the thought. The man is still simmering over the puny penis mess and now I have to tell him he is being too antagonistic for Seven. Erin decided she would have to give some considerable thought to how she would diplomatically approach RJ; she had no interest in further confrontations with the man. His hitting-below-the-belt sexual innuendo about her and Toby getting a room was enough quid pro quo.

Another unsettling observation Erin made had to do with Rose Cunningham. Unlike other days in which Rose had looked devotedly upon her husband, today Rose seemed to be in her own world and Erin noted that it hadn't slipped Seven's notice the way it did the other jurors. Erin assumed the couple had an unresolved spat, never a good development in a trial and just one more unpleasant topic to add to the agenda when she spoke with RJ. The stress of any kind of trial often brought couples to the brink, challenging the framework of their relationship. With high profile trials where the media was involved, the daily stress created a vortex of harassment and additional misery. Most made it through the acute stage required by the trial, only to collapse in the weeks, months, or years following such an ordeal when the adrenaline that had served as the glue disappeared. Then a disagreement over the squeezing of the toothpaste tube would become enough reason to get divorced.

Neither Saul nor RJ on cross, each for his own reasons, had asked the expert witness about blood or clothing fibers found on the car. Given the discovery rules that apply pretrial, which require each side to inform the other of a potential witness, Saul's next witness was not a surprise to RJ. After the break for lunch, Saul called the Cunningham's driver to the stand, getting him to admit that he had washed the car in question the day after the accident. Erin anticipated the jury would have a strong reaction to this testimony and was not surprised when they all, including Seven, looked suspiciously at Cunningham. On cross, however, RJ was easily able to counterpoint by having the driver tell the jury that he washed that car on the same day every week. So, by the end of the day four it was still an impasse, neither side having won a clear victory.

His mind shifting between worry over juror Seven's distressing stare and his wife's stony face in the ride over, Cunningham was finding it increasingly difficult to maintain the mask of neutrality. Of course it had been a terrible mistake to have lost his temper with Rose. However, all their years of marriage had taught him that she was quick to forgive. He had never known her to be a pouter or grudge-keeper. So, he was surprised by her behavior at breakfast and in the drive to court. During breakfast she had not said a word, and then in the car she stared off into the distance, refusing to look at him. For the first time in his life, his wife's behavior was frightening him, an unfamiliar and very disturbing emotion. Was the stress of the accusations causing their unspoken tradeoff of thirty-five years to unravel? And could it possibly be happening just when having a loving wife by his side was more important than ever? If she abandoned him now it would be disastrous to the outcome of the trial. He vowed to make it up to her at the lunch break. Maybe later some new diamond earrings would get him back in her good graces.

What to do about juror Seven was a more challenging problem, something that could not be solved by throwing diamonds around. The woman was casting daggers at him, of that he was sure. The fact that he had no control over her was infuriating. Relinquishing control was an entirely aberrant experience for Cunningham. Turning over the decisions regarding the trial to RJ, despite the lawyer's reputation as a winner, had also been problematic from the start. He couldn't serve as his own counsel and, of course, he needed a forceful, confident man to defend the lies the prosecution was professing. However, the arrogance of the lawyer, the *I'm-right-you're-wrong* indisputable attitude, was butting up against his own authoritative character and eroding his restraint. Yesterday, when he had made it clear to RJ that Seven was a problem and had been treated offhandedly yet again, Cunningham felt something snap. Most likely, that was the reason he had stupidly taken it out on Rose.

As the prosecution's expert witness droned on, Cunningham found himself becoming increasingly indignant at the way things were going. His mind began to conjecture, plotting what he could do about the irritating, homely, woman in jury seat seven. An idea of a way to deal with her began percolating and just before the break for lunch, Cunningham's game plan was completely brewed. First, though, he would have to apologize to Rose and ease her back into a familiar role where she would be an asset.

The judge called for a recess and the humanity in the courtroom immediately became a blur of motion. Cunningham turned around so he could face his wife, immediately noting that she was still in a brooding mood. "Are you all right, honey? You haven't been yourself at all today."

Rose finally looked into his eyes, saying, "No, I'm not all right. In fact, I don't think I can make it through the rest of the day. I have a bad headache and I'd like to go home."

"A headache? You hardly ever get headaches."

"Are you questioning me? Because if you are, I think you need to remember I'm not the one on trial."

Cunningham was stunned. Never had Rose spoken to him in such a confrontational manner. However, he knew better than to let his temper flare, not now when he needed her and not in the courtroom where he was always meat for the media sharks. The best he could muster was a staid, "Okay, if you think you need to leave, then I guess you should. Damon can't drive you, though, because he's expected to testify after the break."

"I'll take a taxi then."

He walked around the defense table and sat down next to her intending to whisper reassuring words in her ear, but she slid away from him. Cunningham was confounded. *What the hell is wrong with this woman?* He hoped no one had seen her pull away from him. There were still people in the room and that meant reporters could be among them. Rose was teary-eyed and he knew he had to be very careful. Despite the indignity he had just suffered, he spoke as gently as he could muster, "I'm guessing you're still angry about last evening and you have a right to be. I was wrong to snap at you. I'd like to make it up to you. Maybe later, after today's session is over, I can take you out for dinner. I'll be sure Damon loses the media idiots and we can go to De Leon's, one of your favorites."

Rose looked at him, her eyes blinking rapidly as she tried to hold back the tears. *Was he being sincere or just putting on a self-serving, appeasing act?* She didn't know and didn't care; she just wanted to be alone. Realizing that relenting was the only way she could exit with any grace, she gave him a weak smile, saying, "Maybe, I'll see how I'm feeling when you get home."

Then she stood up and began walking out of the courtroom, Cunningham hurrying after her so he could be by her side as they left the room. He felt her stiffen as he took her arm, another first from a woman he had only known as passive. He experienced a mixture of anger and fear in his chest at her surprising response. He refused to let go, though, aware that it was necessary to present a unified front as they exited the building. RJ, his entourage of Dee & Dum by his side, was waiting for them in the hallway. Erin was just walking up to join them when the Cunninghams reached the group. Leaning into RJ, Bradley whispered, "Rose is not feeling well. I'm sending her home."

Rose's red eyes were apparent but they elicited no sympathy from RJ. Turning to Rose, he practically barked, "You're aware, I'm sure, that leaving now will create a storm of negative speculation from the hounds out front."

Rose, never having had a violent thought in her life, suddenly felt like punching the snake of a man in the face. What came out of her mouth seemed to be coming from a complete stranger, "Go to hell, Mr. Holland. I'm going home."

The group was dumbfounded, no one saying a word at first. Then Erin stepped up to her, softly saying, "I noticed you weren't yourself today. It's probably a good idea for you to go home and get some rest."

"Good idea or not," Rose replied, "I'm going." Not even sure if her legs would hold her up, Rose started toward the exit. Cunningham caught up with his wife, again taking hold of her arm. This time she didn't tighten-up. RJ gave Erin a cold stare before scrambling to catch up with the couple as they exited the building. As always, the media was swarming like buzzards and the three of them had to run the gauntlet; this time RJ refused to answer any questions. Cunningham was relieved that Rose kept her head down, preventing the press from seeing the distress on her face.

Taxis were lined up outside. Cunningham put Rose into one and watched her drive away. The irritating noise of the press shouting questions at him sounded like crickets in heat. He turned around to face them, now prepared to preempt the inevitable speculation. He held up his hand, waiting for the shouting to stop. When the group finally quieted he said, "My wife has a migraine, she's going home to rest." The mass surged forward, microphones extended as they hurled further questions at him. Cunningham, with RJ by his side, pushed through the crowd, heading for the car that RJ always kept ready for the lunch break.

To avoid the press and to ensure any courtroom strategy remained secret, RJ and his clients usually lunched in the conference room at his well-appointed office, which included a nicely equipped kitchen and, during trials, a private chef. Today they were dining on ginger-carrot soup and lemon dill salmon on a bed of warmed spinach. RJ was a stickler about prohibiting any alcohol while there was an ongoing trial, so sparkling mineral water was served. Cunningham, however, had more pressing matters on his mind than food. He ate only several spoonfuls of the soup and when the salmon was served, he took a few bites before announcing to RJ that he was worried about Rose and wanted to call to see how she was feeling. He pushed his chair back, left the conference room, and entered the men's bathroom.

He had sold his business but had not lost his contacts, his great wealth making most of his past resources still available to him. His chief of security had been paid generously, had been given an obscene pension when the business was sold, and would gladly do what Cunningham had in mind for him. He took out his phone, checked under the stalls to be sure he was alone, and scrolled through his contact list, tapping on the name and number of his former head of security.

The phone rang five times before going to voice mail. "Hey, DeBeck. It's Bradley Cunningham. I need you to do something for me ASAP. Please text me with a time when you're available to talk. As I'm sure you're aware, I'm in court this afternoon, so I'll call you back when I can get to my phone." The minute he ended the call, he was feeling more in control, his mood uplifted with the knowledge that he would no longer allow himself to be a victim, a role he despised, a role that no powerful person would ever embrace no matter what the circumstances. Where juror Seven was concerned, he would not leave his fate to an egotistical attorney no matter how many cases the man had won.

He returned to the conference room with a renewed appetite. As he entered the room, RJ asked, "How's she doing?"

"Huh?"

"Rose. How's she feeling?"

"Oh! Yeah. She says she still feels like she had a bomb go off in her head."

"Too bad. It's best if she stays by your...."

Causing a loud scraping noise as he pulled out his chair, Cunningham interrupted, saying, "Give it a rest, RJ. She's perfectly aware of what's best. She wouldn't leave my side unless it was absolutely necessary." He then picked up his fork and began eating the remains of his Salmon. After a bite, he cheerfully said, "This is quite delicious, even cold."

RJ stiffened. He picked up his glass of sparkling water, thinking he would like to dump it on his arrogant client's head.

Instead, he took a sip, forcing himself to say nothing in response. He ate the last bite of salmon, wiped his face with the cloth napkin, stood up and headed for the door. With his back toward his client, he coldly said, "I'll be in my office when you're ready to leave."

Cunningham smiled to himself. *Good. I pissed him off and let him know I won't be pushed around.*

Bradley enjoyed the remaining food on his plate, not concerned in the slightest that his retort to RJ would affect his defense. He knew RJ won cases to glorify himself. The man was way too concerned with his winning record to be revengeful.

Knowing he should check on Rose, Cunningham looked at his watch, deciding she would be home by now. Just as he opened his phone to call, it signaled him that he had a text message from Debeck. Cunningham stood up and closed the door to the room before returning the call.

Debeck answered on the first ring, saying, "Hey, Bradley, good to hear from you. Damn shame about the trial. Been reading about it in the paper and it sounds to me like they sandbagged you. Gotta be hell what you're going through. Anything I can do to help, I'd be glad to do it."

"Well, there is something you can help me with. I don't have much time so I'll get right to it. Hold on a sec," he said, as he walked to the door, opened it and looked out in the hall for any listening ears. He re-closed the door to the conference room before quietly saying, "So, it seems we've got a problem with one of the jurors...better if you're in the dark about specifics."

"Gotcha. What do you want me to do?"

"We need to have this particular juror replaced by an alternate. That would only happen if she got sick or had to go to the hospital...nothing too serious, you know, just something that would cause her to be unavailable for a couple of days."

"I think I can arrange that. When are we talking about?"

"Soon. This afternoon if possible."

"I can do that. I can be at the courthouse at the end of today's session. Tell me what she looks like, so I will know who to shadow."

"Tallish, around five seven, five eight, maybe. She's got dirty blonde, short hair with a really bad cut...like she does it herself or something. She's somewhere in her late twenties and always dresses in loose fitting clothes. Hard to tell her weight because of the dumb-ass clothing but I'm guessing around one twenty-five, on the slim side. Today she's wearing what looks like the kind of dress the polygamists make their women wear. You know, long to her ankles, hangs on her so you can't tell what kind of figure she has. It's a dark navy color and she's wearing it over a white long sleeved blouse with a high neck. Couldn't see what kind of shoes she's wearing because of the jury box."

"Not to worry. With that description, I'll be able to find her."

Cunningham cleared his throat before saying, "I'm sure you know to take every precaution. Because you used to work for me, it will be easy for authorities to associate you with me. If that happens we could end up cell mates."

"You know, Bradley, I'd take a bullet for you. However, I will not go to jail for you. Accordingly, I won't take any action unless I'm positive there are no eyes on me."

"When it's done, text me the letter 'X'and I'll know to look for a new face in the jury box tomorrow."

"I'm on it."

Cunningham closed his phone, leaning back in his chair. It felt so damn good to be taking action instead of letting the misconceived events of the last year determine his future. He had been turning his fate over to RJ for way too long. Abdicating his power had turned him into a hollow shell of a person, a person he could no longer tolerate. That's why he had yelled at Rose. He had been angry at himself and taken it out on her. None of what happened was her fault and he needed to repair the damage.

He tapped on his phone to call her but it immediately went to voice mail. She must have turned off her phone, maybe sleeping, he thought. He left a message, "Hey, honey, it's me. Just calling to see how you're doing. I'll call again later. Don't forget I'm taking you out tonight. You've been a trooper and I had no right to lose my temper. Get some rest and I'll see you after court."

Toby, in his usual holding-up-the-wall position, was waiting for Erin in the hallway outside the courtroom at the end of the day. *Was he imagining it or did her eyes light up when she saw him?*

As she approached him, he pushed off against the wall saying, "I was able to find some more information on Nichols' aunt. Unfortunately, it's worse than we thought."

"God! I didn't think it could get much worse. So, I guess RJ gave you the dispensation to use your out-of-state contact."

Toby gave Erin a sly smile. "Dispensation, huh?"

"Sorry, it means..."

"I know what it means. And no, his Holiness did not give me permission."

"Okay, then please explain."

"Sure, but let's get out of here. Courthouse walls have ears. How about we walk?"

"If we're walking, you'll have to talk fast. I'm wearing these damn high heels and believe me, they ain't made for walk'n."

Erin turned and headed for the exit. Toby followed a few steps behind, silently admiring just how bootylicious she looked in the high heels, and thinking that surely such a sexy but ridiculous invention had to come from the mind of a horny male. However, if women didn't want to look sexy, why the heck did they wear them? When he had lagged behind as long as he could without being noticed, he stepped up his pace until he was next to her. Erin looked up at him and said, "Taking in the scenery?"

Toby held up his hands in surrender. "I plead guilty...as reluctant as I am to do so inside a courthouse."

"Well, at least you didn't deny your sexist behavior. Anyway, I just remembered I have some sensible shoes in my car. Let's go to my car so I can get them."

"Hey, don't do a sexist pig any favors. I'm not deserving."

"Right. You aren't deserving, but I am. I've been in these absurd shoes all day. High heels are a long-lingering professional expectation and the one concession I'm willing to make to the imperiled, male dominant culture of the Western world."

"You're very sexy when you talk like that, you know?"

"Oh, shut-up, Toby. You're making fun of me."

"Honestly not, Erin. I'm not accustomed to hanging around women who use words like dispensation and imperiled. It's a turn on to be in the company of an intelligent woman who has a remarkable command of the English language."

Erin stopped walking and looked up at the bear of a man beside her, now also standing still. She probed his face for signs of mockery. Finding only sincerity, she said, "Thank you, Toby. I promise I'll peruse my thesaurus tonight so I can further dazzle you."

Erin started walking again and Toby followed, saying, "See, there you go again. How's a man supposed to hold himself back when you promise to *peruse* a *thesaurus* for him?"

"You are such a flirt, you know that?"

"I've been accused of worse. By the way, what is a thesaurus?"

Figuring Toby was still playing with her, she quickly responded, "It's a dinosaur who has a remarkable command of the English language."

They were now standing outside on the courthouse steps and Toby started laughing, which caused Erin to laugh, which caused Toby to laugh even harder, which caused Erin to laugh so hard she started to cry. Finally, Erin caught her breath, saying,

"Oh my God this feels so good. I haven't laughed like this in way too long. This trial has been so stressful...read, RJ."

"Yeah, well that RJ is in a league of his own all right."

"Okay, big guy, enough stress relief. Sad to say, it's time to get back to business. So, what is it that you've done behind RJ's back regarding Jane Nichols and her aunt?"

"In my defense, I will first put forth that I did not consult, nor did I ask any investigator to check out Jane Nichols' aunt. Which means I did not go behind the Reverend's back."

"You didn't?"

"No, I did not. Turns out I didn't have to. I simply did a Goggle search and found a plethora of information in just a few minutes."

Erin giggled. "Plethora? Now who's been into the thesaurus?"

They had reached her car and Erin opened the back door, taking a seat with her legs out the door. She removed her high heels, tossed them behind her, and then reached for a gym bag on the seat. Rummaging inside the bag, she pulled out a pair of sneakers, asking, "So, what exactly is it you found out?"

"I'm glad you're sitting down."

Erin, holding the sneakers in her hands, looked up at Toby with intense interest. "You've got my attention."

Standing above her with one arm resting on the frame of the open door, Toby grimaced before saying, "In the newspaper archives I found a whole series of stories on Jane's aunt. It seems twenty-two years ago the aunt had more than her fifteen minutes of fame. Well, infamy is more like it. At the age of sixteen, she was convicted of stabbing her own father to death."

Erin, incredulous, dropped the shoes. "Oh my God! I can't believe how Jane's backstory keeps getting worse."

"Yes, except that with Jane's having been adopted, it's likely she doesn't know anything about the aunt or the manslaughter conviction."

"Manslaughter? That would means there were extenuating circumstances surrounding the murder. Hmm, I think I have an idea what they might be but I'll let you tell me anyway."

"Yes, I'd certainly say there were unusual circumstances. According to the newspapers, Jane's aunt testified that her father had sexually abused both of his daughters. Jane's mother, that would be Tamara, was the older of the two girls. According to the story, Tamara ran away from home when she was sixteen and it was after she fled the house that her father started raping his younger daughter."

Erin interjected, "Let me guess. Tamara, ran away because her father got her pregnant, something so shameful she probably felt she couldn't tell anyone. That would explain Tamara naming the child Bane, the child being the bane of her existence—a child parented by her own father. So, the next part of the saga, I'm conjecturing here, is that when Tamara got arrested and called her younger sister, she must have told her about having a baby parented by their father."

"Of course we can't be sure but it would seem so, because the timing is right. It was soon after that phone call that the younger sister stabbed her father, likely the next time he tried to rape her. She was fifteen when she killed him, sixteen when she was convicted. She served some time as a juvenile but was released shortly after she turned eighteen."

"I think I already know the answer but I'll ask anyway. Where was the mother of the two girls in all of this tragedy?"

"She remained loyal to her husband. She even testified that her youngest daughter was lying about the rapes."

Erin picked up the dropped shoes and finished putting on her sneakers while she spoke. "A mother living in the same house with a husband who is raping his own daughters and somehow she doesn't know anything about it? Unbelievable, huh?"

"Well, it doesn't make any sense to me."

"The only explanation for such egregious behavior is denial. Denial, my friend, is probably the most powerful and potentially destructive of all the psychological defense mechanisms. Intellectually, I get denial because it is an effective way to keep from absorbing unconscionable behavior. The alternative, in a situation like this one, would have been for the mother of the girls to acknowledge what a heinous man she married and get herself and her girls the hell out. However, being single with two young children to take care of isn't easy, so instead, her self-protective mind just refuses to recognize the indefensible behavior."

"She just buried her head in the sand, huh?"

"Right. She protected herself instead of her kids. You know, even though I know all of this textbook mumbo jumbo, when I meet this kind of destructive denial in the real world, it just seems so damn inconceivable." Erin shook her head in disbelief. "Let's walk while I try to digest all this."

They walked in silence for a while, Toby finally breaking the quiet by saying, "This situation, well not the murder part, but a father getting a daughter pregnant happens more than our society wants to acknowledge. I guess you could call it collective denial."

"Interesting observation. Still, it's vile, nauseating, and so very, very sad. So, let's see. In summary, our juror Seven was sired by her grandfather, raised until she was six by a drug-addicted mother, locked in a closet while her mother lay dying on the other side, put in an institution for a while, then finally adopted by elderly parents we know little about."

"Yeah," Toby said. "Add it all up and the package makes for a very unstable person."

"You got that right," said Erin. "It's not likely that our Jane Nichols survived all this with an intact ego. Still, there is nothing on the surface that we can use to remove her. The information we have about her horrible background doesn't prove she lied on the jury questionnaire. Since she was so young when her mother died, she's not likely to be cognizant of the circumstances. If she's not aware of it, we can't say she lied during the voir dire. We can't go to the judge with a complaint that we don't like the way she looks at the defendant, a charge that would get us thrown out of chambers. She's not delusional—that we know of—or acting crazy in any overt way."

"Makes you wonder how many people with unstable egos are sitting in jury boxes around the world as we speak."

"Well, as a jury consultant, I can tell you there are many volatile people who end up sitting on a jury, but this story takes the cake."

They walked in silence for a while before Erin asked, "You're going to tell the Reverend what you found out, right?"

"Only if you're there to hold my hand."

"Hey, as I remember, you said you weren't afraid of the man."

"I'm not. It was just a ploy, apparently a failed one, to get you to hold my hand."

Erin smiled at him, saying, "I'm sure you get this all the time, but underneath all that muscle and brawn there is a tender soul."

"Aw shucks, Erin, you're making me blush."

Erin looked up at large black man, smiling. "I think you're toying with me, but I'll never know."

Daniel Debeck, who had been nicknamed Bunky as a baby, was anything but the sweet, endearing, and well-behaved child implied by the name. Daniel wasn't the cutest newborn so his mother had tried to counteract the reprecussions by naming him after the adorable, very popular 1940s' cartoon character, *Bunky,* the creation of a man named Billy Debeck.

While Daniel had never been a winsome baby, he might have had a chance to be a good kid had he not been knocked around by an alcoholic father, a man who scapegoated his not-much-to-look-at child for all that went wrong in his own life. The unattractive, flat nose that Dan had been born with got considerably uglier after his father broke it several times during the many "I'll teach you a lesson" poundings. Dan survived by developing a thick skin and a cold, hard view of life, a view that eventually allowed him to even the score with his father. At fifteen he fought back, breaking his father's alcoholic bulbous, vein-covered nose in return and assuring the end of any future beatings.

The adult Daniel Debeck knew he had never been a looker and made sure that well-behaved was a word not likely be used to describe him. In fact, Debeck was a man so turbulent he had eventually been thrown off the police force for unnecessary brutality. He was on the force for years, building a reputation as a bully but getting away with it until he pulled what is known in the profession as an *alley court,* an incident where an officer takes it upon himself to beat a person in custody, usually while handcuffed, before the suspect arrives at the station house. The alley court incident ended badly for Debeck. By his late thirties he was out of a job, newly divorced, and embroiled in a police brutality law suit. The divorce papers came with a restraining order demanding he keep away from his ex-wife.

As many former police officers do, Dan went into the security business. He rapidly became known as a tough guy, an intimidating man who would get the job done; underhanded tactics were his forte. When Bradley Cunningham hired him as head of security for his rapidly growing empire, Debeck was forty; he knew he had moved up in the world, finally getting the break he deserved. Dan remained with Cunningham until the day the company was sold. The two very different men had always gotten along, a fact which puzzled almost everyone who knew them. Cunningham was a true *Bunky*, a gentleman to all who dealt with him, while Dan was a ruffian whose brusk manner made him a daunting, friendless man.

Since making friends had never been Dan's strong suit, why someone like Bradley Cunningham befriended him had always been a mystery. However, few things had gone Dan's way in life and if a mega-wealthy man chose to favor him, he didn't press his luck by questioning it. And if his former boss now needed a favor, Dan was more than happy to serve it up, no questions asked—which is how he found himself sitting in his car looking through binoculars at the hoards of people leaving the courthouse. The reporters were pushing and shoving to get a piece of his friend. *Idiots*, Dan thought. For a moment, he fantasized picking the vultures off with a rifle one by one.

It didn't take long for him to spot his target. The woman, looking like something from centuries past, was wearing an ill-fitting Puritan-like outfit. The dress hung on her as if she had just been released from a concentration camp and her haircut made her look as though someone had plugged her into an electrical outlet. He followed her with the binoculars as she headed for the parking garage. He didn't know her car and she would be lost to him while in the garage, which was why he had arrived early enough to choose this particular parking spot. With his high-powered lens, he would be able to watch the drivers as they left the garage. As planned, he sighted her as she exited the garage, made a left turn, and headed up the one-way street away from the courthouse. He waited for several cars to pass and then maneuvered his car in behind.

He followed several cars back as she stayed on the main artery that eventually connected with the freeway. The traffic was heavy at this time of day and the line of cars heading toward the freeway crept forward at a snail's pace. Dan checked himself out in the mirror to be sure his disguise was not askew: a fake nose and a ball cap with a pony tail coming out the back to cover his easily identifiable bald head.

He could see the woman's red Honda Civic as it slowly moved along with the other cars. As expected, she edged her Honda into the line of cars waiting to enter the freeway ramp, eventually easing into the steady stream of cars. The heavy traffic meant the cars were traveling about thirty-five miles an hour, a speed which made it easy for Dan to keep her in sight.

Stage one of his plan was going well, the Honda easily staying in his sight. Eventually the woman pulled into the drive of a duplex with a small but well-maintained front yard. Flowers spilled from multicolored containers thoughtfully spaced both in front of and on the small porch.

Dan continued past the duplex, going around the block, then parking his car down the street where he could observe the house with his field glasses. After parking, the first thing he did was pay attention to the layout of the neighborhood. It consisted of older, smaller houses and duplexes tightly squeezed together with a few driveways and fewer garages. This meant parking spaces were at a premium and drivers would rarely find a space in front of their own home. This was a lucky break for him; residents would not notice a strange car parked in front of their home.

He picked up his binoculars and observed the woman he had been following. She was still in the car, just sitting and staring out, as if in a trance. She was a strange-looking woman, he thought, with even stranger behavior; no wonder Bradley wanted to be rid of her. She continued to sit in the car for a full five minutes before finally getting out and going into her home. Dan didn't want to take the chance that he might miss her if she left the house, plus he needed the cover of darkness, so he was prepared to wait for several hours. Although it had been years since he had done a stakeout, he had not forgotten about the absolute boredom. An iPad, loaded with one of his favorite action movies, sat on the seat next to him. He intentionally picked a movie he had seen before so that he wouldn't become so engrossed he might miss the woman if she left the house. He looked around for observing eyes and when he didn't see anyone, he got out of the car and moved to the passenger side, lowering the seat's back to a more horizontal position, making him less visible and allowing a better view of the iPad on the dash.

Stuck in the slow traffic inching its way toward the freeway, Jane had plenty of time to think about day four in the courtroom. With a certainty that permeated her every sense, she felt the defendant was not the public face he pretended to be.

While she despised her constant fear and mistrust of people, wishing every day that she could be more normal, the same faculty that caused her to be wary of people had allowed a special antennae to evolve, a sort of sixth sense, an instinct that detected and interpreted the inner virtues of others. Initially, she had attributed her discomfort at seeing Bradley Cunningham to her general discomfort with men, and to the possibility that he reminded her of someone. With each day in the courtroom, however, she had become more convinced that the man, a man who presented a virtuous face to the public, was evil in his core. First her dreams, then her recalled memories indicated that Bradley Cunningham had done something terrible to her. If Sydney's photographer friend came through, she would know for sure by the end of the day.

Even if the photos proved her intuitions of personal harm wrong, she was still stuck with the conviction that the defendant was a sinister person, leaving her to face the fact that the impartiality she had sworn to uphold was a sham. With each mile she drove, she became more conflicted, acutely aware that she would have to take some action regardless of whether the defendant was the man who locked her in the closet. By the time she pulled into her driveway, the mental strife had escalated to an intolerable level; the thought of looking at the photos of Cunningham's hand sent a chill down her spine. She sat in the car, immobilized by fear of what she might discover. Last night, with Sydney by her side, she felt determined to know...but last night she and Sydney hadn't thought this out to its ultimate conclusion.

What was she going to do if Cunningham was the same man who locked her in the closet? As a juror she had the power to do him harm. Could she—and would she? And if she was wrong about his being her tormentor, would she remove herself from the jury?

Finally, she decided that sitting in the car was only increasing her anxiety. Instead, she would go for a bike ride, hopeful that the endorphin high of intense exercise would inject some courage back into her. She got out of the car and headed for the duplex, stopping for a short while to give some of her plants a little TLC before she went inside.

Dan stayed low, watching his movie and looking every several minutes through his binoculars at the target's house. About fifteen minutes into the movie he saw someone coming out of the front door. It was definitely a woman, decked out in black, clingy spandex easily showing off a curvaceous body with amazingly muscular legs. The woman was in the process of putting on a bicycle helmet. If it hadn't been for the awful haircut, he would never have realized it was the same woman from the courthouse, the one wearing the shapeless Puritan getup. "Well, I'll be damned," he said under his breath. He was so stunned he almost forgot his mission—until he saw her take a bicycle out of the storage shed. He could hardly believe his luck. Riding a bicycle, the woman would be a sitting duck. It would be so easy to follow her and just give her a little clip with his car. All he had to do was give her enough of a swipe to assure she would be laid up for several days, a much less risky plan than his original one to break-in and knock her around a bit.

The woman now had her helmet on and was snapping her shoes into the pedals of her bike, a sign which should have given Debeck his second clue (after the spandex) that she was a serious rider. However, Dan Debeck knew motorcycles, not bicycles. He started the car engine and fell in behind his target, following twenty-five yards behind her and still thinking the woman was going for a leisurely bicycle ride. It was too risky to try something in the residential area so he just kept following her, staying twenty-five to thirty yards back, as she maneuvered through the residential streets. At the first traffic light at the intersection of a main road, the uninitiated Dan realized his target had some skill on a bike. He watched in amazement as she managed, like a circus performer, to keep her feet on the peddles and somehow balance the bike while going nowhere until the light turned green.

Still, he thought, I'm in a car and she's on a bicycle; I've got the advantage. When the light changed, she took off—fast! *What the hell? This is no leisurely ride.* He was several cars back from the light and by the time he made a left turn through the intersection, the woman was becoming a tiny speck. He had to speed up and weave in and out of cars just to keep her in sight. With the woman now around fifty yards ahead of him, he looked down at his speedometer. His jaw dropped; she was going thirty-five miles an hour. *Was this Lance Armstrong in drag*?

He couldn't believe his luck when he realized she was turning onto a one way, busy street without traffic lights. She was riding on the shoulder so he could easily move alongside her and just give her a shove. Without traffic lights, the cars on the road were moving along at a fast clip, giving him an advantage: drivers would not likely see his shoving maneuver. He followed several cars behind the woman until he could jockey his car directly behind her, continually taking surveys of nearby cars. After several minutes of tailing her from a reasonable distance, he found his opportunity; there were no cars immediately behind him; it was time to make his move.

Jane, always alert when on her bicycle, had noticed the black car pull out behind her when she left the house. Using her helmet mirror she watched the car, noticing that a man was driving. Even though she had made several turns while in the residential area, he remained behind her, an observation that caused her to be concerned. When it came to cars driven by men, she knew to stay on guard. She had been harassed multiple times by men while she was riding. Some men just yelled out demeaning sexual comments, some just did the wolf-whistle thing, a few had thrown things at her, but twice she'd had the horrific experience of a man in the passenger seat of a car reaching out the window and pinching her on the butt as the car passed her. The first time it happened she had been so startled she almost lost control of her bike. After the second time she'd been grabbed, she vowed she would never let that happen again. So, her plan of action was ready should the man in the black car behind her attempt to touch her.

She glanced down at the computer on her bike, noting she was moving right along at twenty-five miles per hour. Then she again checked her mirror; the car was now several hundred feet behind her and approaching rapidly. Since they were on a one-way road, the solo driver could easily come alongside and reach her with his arm. The entrance to the bike path, which was blocked off to cars, was still a mile ahead and unavailable as a way to avoid the fast approaching car should the driver try something. She slowed down just enough to be able to handle the bike with one hand while she reached down and unclipped her bicycle pump from its frame. She sped up again and held the pump in her hand, letting it rest on the handle bars. In her mirror she could see that the car was now about thirty feet behind her and the male driver had his left arm hanging out the window. As the car moved alongside her, Jane watched in her mirror as the man's hand came up. Her survival instincts kicked in and without hesitating, she lifted her arm and swung the pump in an arc, coming down hard on the man's arm, an awful crunching sound causing her to grit her teeth. She braked and her hand automatically let go of the pump; the fast moving car passed her. She came to a stop and waited to see what the man was going to do about the surprise counterattack. If necessary she would just turn her bike around and ride the wrong way on the shoulder. She watched as the car braked, slowed, but did not stop. She breathed a sigh of relief when the man in the car accelerated, leaving her far behind.

Out of immediate danger, all the adrenaline that had pumped itself into Jane's blood during the incident was now causing a bad case of the shakes, leaving her in no condition to ride, especially on a busy street with cars going at such high speeds. She pulled further over onto the shoulder, got off her bike, carefully laying it down against the curb. Then she leaned over, put both hands on her knees, and gulped in air. A car came to a stop on the shoulder beside her. Startled, Jane jumped back, quickly scanning the area for her bike pump before noticing this was a different car. The window came down and a middle-aged man asked, “Are you okay? Do you need some help?”

“I’ll be okay in a few minutes,” Jane replied. “I just had a close call with a man in a car trying to grab my butt...but I wasn’t hurt, just shaken.”

“I’m a bike rider myself so I know about close calls with cars. Some drivers think they own the road and try to bully us off *their* road out of sheer meanness, I guess. Makes me plenty angry.”

“Yeah, I know.” Shaking her head, Jane said, “ Somehow, though, this one felt very personal. Anyway, I’ll be okay in a few minutes.”

“You have a cell phone with you in case you change your mind about needing help?”

“Yes, I do. And thank you for being concerned.”

“Hey, no problem. Just don’t let selfish jerks stop you from riding. That’s just what they want and they don’t deserve to win.” The window went up and the man eased his car back into the flow of traffic.

Jane searched around for her bike pump, finally seeing it on the shoulder of the road about twenty-five feet back from where she was. Her legs were still shaky as she walked along the shoulder toward the pump. On the walk back to her bike, however, she began to feel steadier. Arriving at her bike, she lifted it up, returned her bike pump to its holder, clipped her shoes into the pedals, and continued on toward the bike path. About two miles into her ride on the path, however, she finally accepted the fact that the lingering skittishness of the close-call with the driver was ruining her ride. Instead of reducing the stress over the trial, she was feeling more anxious than ever. She turned her bike around and headed home, vigilantly watching in her mirror for the black car.

Twenty minutes later Jane walked into the duplex. Sydney was sitting on the sofa, her laptop computer next to her. She took one look at Jane's face and said, "Uh, oh. You look pissed. What happened?"

"Some asshole old man tried to grab my butt."

"Oh, shit, Jane. I'm sorry. I know how you hate that."

"What's wrong with men like that? It's so damn juvenile...like they're still in grade school and pulling a girl's pigtail. It wasn't a harmless prank because the man could have killed me."

"It's anthropological, my dear, but I know that's not a consoling answer."

"No, it's not. Anthropological means that top dog thing, right? The male needing to dominate women through intimidation blah, blah. It's disgusting. Honestly, Syd, I don't know how you put up with men."

"Look, we've had this discussion many times. And I keep telling you there are many ways to stay above the fray by turning the tables on them."

"Well, trust me when I say I found a way today. I showed the asshole who was top dog."

"What do you mean?"

"When he reached out to grab me, I smacked his arm with my bike pump. I might even have broken it."

Sydney starting laughing. Jane eventually joined in until Sydney finally said, "Well, I guess that's one way to teach a would-be alpha dog who's boss."

"Right. I bet the jerk doesn't try that prank again."

More soberly, Sydney added, "Good thing he doesn't know where you live. Men who are desperate to prove their top dog status are usually quite revengeful, especially when they've been humiliated by what they think is the weaker gender."

Jane's eyes widened in alarm, "Oh my God, Sydney. I just remembered he was parked down the street when I left our house. I went right by him and he followed me. Do you think it's possible he saw where I live?"

"Well, shit, Jane. You didn't tell me that before. Where were you when he tried to grab you?"

"I was on Charles, about a mile from the entrance to the bike path."

"So he was behind you all the way from our street to Charles?"

"Yeah. Are you thinking he could have been waiting for me, intending to hurt me?"

"I'm thinking that a rich, powerful man is on trial for a criminal act and you're on the jury, despising the man at best and suspecting him of attempting to molest you at worst. Given these circumstances, he's definitely an *Elemental Fiend.* The forces of good and evil are in play in the Cunningham *Overworld*."

"Be serious, Syd. I live in the real world, not a video game, and you're suggesting my life may be in danger."

"The real world *is* a game, Jane. Human beings are all about self-preservation and status; it's just like in *Final Fantasy*. Winning battles in life is how you attain both. So, what we have to do is figure out a way to get you maximum *Hit Points* while bringing *Fiend's* points to zero. If we can do that, we eliminate the danger and win the battle."

"Please, you're scaring me with all this mumbo jumbo and I don't need to be any more scared than I already am."

Sydney stood up and began pacing, reprimanding Jane, "*Now* you're scared? Well, I'm tired of your whining. Who insisted on being on a jury? Who conveniently omitted on the form that they suffer from anxiety attacks? Who is it that has consistently refused to remove herself from the jury? Who pleaded to be hypnotized? And last night? Who okayed the plan to have my friend take the photographs? You can't have it both ways, Jane. If you're too scared, then quit...walk away, stay afraid for the rest of your life. Or shut up about being scared and grab your fear like you did your bicycle pump. Use your fear to fight your demons and..." she turned and grinned at Jane, "get some *Hit Points*."

Jane had been watching Sydney pace, her mouth agape with surprise at the challenging words. Sydney had never talked to her this way. Rather, she had always been supportive, letting Jane be who she was. Syd lived her own life, a very different life, making choices that Jane would never be able to make. It had always been this way from the very beginning, the very day all those years ago when Syd had said she would be her friend. Listening to Sydney lecture her, scold her really, Jane began to reach down deep into the newly explored internal place of determination, the place where she had gone when she made all the choices Syd was now throwing back at her. Jane straightened her back and said, "You're right. I've been a pathetic wimp all my life. It's time I learned to be a...what kind of warrior?"

"A *Light Warrior*."

"Okay. So what do I do next to become a *Light Warrior*?"

"You take a look at the photographs that Ben emailed me. You find out if the enemy is who we suspect."

"Oh shit! The bicycle scare made me forget all about the photographs. Have you looked at them yet?"

"No. I was waiting for you."

Jane glanced over at the laptop on the sofa, a twinge of fear launching a pain in the pit of her stomach. She looked toward Sydney for courage, only to find her best friend had assumed a warrior pose, brandishing a virtual sword.

Jane had to laugh. "Okay, then, time to find out if the demon of my nightmares is a figment of my anguished mind—or is the real demon I face every day in the courtroom."

"So, Jane," Sydney said, "before we take a look at the photographs, I think I should bring up two other possibilities we didn't think of last night."

"Yeah? What possibilities?"

"Well, the scar could have faded or he could have had plastic surgery to cover it up."

"Hmm. I guess I hadn't thought of that."

"Well, it's just something to consider if the photos don't prove anything."

"Well, I guess we'll have to deal with those possibilities if we don't find anything conclusive."

The two women moved over to the sofa, sitting down beside one another. Sydney opened her laptop and began tapping on the keys. The detailed first photo emerged onto the screen. Jane gasped when she saw a small circular scar visible in the exact spot where she dreamed she had bitten the man. "It is him! It has to be; it can't be a coincidence."

Sydney scrolled through several more photos, saying, "I agree. It can't be a coincidence."

The twinge of fear that had gripped Jane earlier now became a storm of immobilizing dread. She could feel the familiar state of pre-hyperventilation coming on, so she closed her eyes and took five deep breaths. The oppressive, nauseating fear began to lose its grip. Opening her eyes she continued to breath deep, slow breaths until she found herself able to talk. "Some, warrior, huh?" she said.

Sydney gave her a sly smile, saying, "How about warrior-in-training?"

Jane managed a small smile in return. "Okay, warrior-in-training. But I don't have much time to be schooled. Tomorrow, I need to be able to sit in the jury box without panicking."

"So, you've already made the decision not to quit?"

"Quitting wouldn't be what a *Light Warrior* would do. Besides, if I quit, I lose any possibility of seeing this evil man punished."

"Okay, let me ask you this. Are you willing to punish him for something he may *not* have done in the present to get even for something you know he did in the past?"

"I guess if you put it that way, I'm not sure. I do know that I'm helpless to punish him for what he did to me twenty-two years ago."

Sydney stood up and began to pace, saying, "Maybe not."

"What do you mean?"

"Well, if he was a pedofile twenty-two years ago, he's still a pedofile. A pedofile doesn't get cured. They never stop unless they get caught and are kept away from children."

"So you're saying he's still molesting little girls."

"I don't know about that. I just know he's still a pedofile. Maybe he's using pornography to satisfy his perversion. The internet has made that quite easy."

"The whole thing is so crazy...and so revolting. I mean, it's just too insane that I'm sitting on a jury where the defendant is the same man who tried to molest me all those years ago. He repulses me and yet I have to pretend that I'm impartial if I want to punish him. How crazy is that? And how am I going to be able to be in the courtroom with him tomorrow without falling apart?"

"Now you see just how much real life is like a game. You're in the middle of a major conflict involving serious danger and it's up to you to prevail. What you need is a weapon. Of course, it would have to be symbolic, a physical object you can keep with you at all times, something to touch so you'll stay grounded, to remind you of your warrior status."

"It has to be something I can take into the jury box, though."

"Right, right...."

"How about something I can wear around my neck, like jewelry?"

"Oh, that's perfect!" Sydney shouted.

"We'll have to find something that won't go off when I go through the metal detector."

"Oh, yeah, I forgot about that. Let's go look in my stash and see if we can find something that would work."

The two women hurried into Sydney's bedroom. Even though Jane had been in the room many times, she was always felt uncomfortable there, overwhelmed not only by the volume of clothing and accessories her friend owned, but also by the style of the clothes. The small closet was jammed-packed and Sydney had bought a portable rack to hold more outfits. Most of the clothing and lingerie were sexually alluring, clothes designed to draw attention to the shape of the body, which was something that Jane went to considerable effort to avoid. Costume jewelry was overflowing on the dresser, hanging from the end of the clothing rack, and even on the door knob to the closet. In the bottom of the closet were piles of high-heeled shoes and on top of the dresser, surrounded by all the jewelry, were three wigs, two long, flowing dark ones and a short, sassy blonde one. The clingy clothes, the jewelry, the shoes, the wigs were Syd's *working* clothes, the embellishments that so many men seemed to require of the women they paid for sexual pleasure.

As Jane had done for all the years they lived together, she shut her mind down, refusing to let the details about what her best friend did for a living come into focus. Instead, she concentrated on the task at hand, finding a talisman she could get through the metal detector. Jane attacked the pile of jewelry on the dresser while Sydney looked through the tangled mess of necklaces hanging on the end of the clothing rack.

It was Jane who picked up a leather tie with a large polished stone hanging from it. "I think I found it," she exclaimed, as she held up the pendant. "It's perfect. This won't set off the detector and the stone will make me think of something solid, something difficult to pierce."

Sydney walked over to her, taking the pendant from her, holding it up. "Wow! I forgot about this because I never wear it anymore. I got it on my seventeenth birthday after I ran away from home and worked the streets for a while. One of the veteran hookers gave it to me for the exact reason you need it. I think you've found the perfect amulet, Jane. I used it back then to help me feel strong." She gave a mirthful laugh, saying, "It's too powerful a symbol for the men I'm with now." Sydney fastened it around Jane's neck and then took her hand, pulling her toward the mirror. "Look," she said to Jane, "touch it and feel its rock-steady power. This will serve as your armor, protecting you from the forces of evil." Jane stood there, her hand on the stone, letting herself imagine the magical powers of the stone, powers that would give her the strength needed to face the ogre who had tried to molest her as a little girl.

Sydney stood next to Jane as they both looked into the mirror. Sydney said, "It's time for plain, wimpy Jane to get in touch with the other Jane, the strong woman inside who has what it takes to face the horror of what happened to you. I was wrong when I said you shouldn't take on the stress of being on a jury. As difficult as it has been and will be, it provides you with the opportunity to set yourself free from your past."

Jane could feel a tingling sensation starting in her legs and moving up through her body, a conscious awareness of positive energy that was sending a signal to her brain, a message telling her she was a capable, even formidable enemy. It was the first time she could remember feeling strong rather than afraid. She said, "I'm glad we thought of this, Syd. I think it's going to work. I'll touch it if I start to feel afraid and I'll be reminded of my inner strength."

"Okay, warrior-in-training, let's go back into the living room and make a plan of defense. The man in the black car is not likely done with you. He's lost some *Hit Points* and will be regrouping for another attack."

Jane's hand automatically reached up to the stone. "Do you think he'll come to the house?"

Sydney started back toward the living room, thinking out loud. "I'm betting his plan was to make the bike incident look like an accident so there would be no suspicion of the incident being tied to your jury duty. If he comes back to the house, then he would spoil the accident part." She sat down on the sofa. Jane took a seat next to her. “Still, we need to be prepared. I’m going to reschedule my appointment tonight. Two against one is better odds. We’ll put hornet spray by our beds and I’ll have the baseball bat ready just in case. You know what a light sleeper I am. He won’t get in this house without my knowing and we’ll be prepared.”

“I’m so thankful you’re here with me, Syd. Even with my new found determination, I couldn’t be doing any of this without you. You know, I’ve always thought your involvement with *Final Fantasy* was silly. Now I’m glad. You think ahead and are proactive where I’ve never done anything but react.”

“Not today, my friend. You were looking out for yourself on that bicycle and I’d say you were not only proactive but very brave. And speaking of being proactive, we need to consider your vulnerabilities.”

“What do you mean?”

“I mean, we need to think ahead. Think like the enemy. What behaviors put you at risk and what might be the man’s alternate plan of attack? We’ve got the house covered, so what else do we need to think about?”

Surprise was the first thing Debeck felt when the Puritan, wielding a weapon of some sort, whacked him on the arm, causing him to unthinkingly pull his arm back into the car. He immediately looked in the rear view mirror and saw she had slowed her bike down. His car was now way ahead of her when the surprise turned into fury. The area where she had hit him was now causing waves of pain. *God damn the Puritan cunt. Had she broken his arm?* He slowed the car down, trying to ignore the pain while he decided what to do. At least he knew where she lived and he could find her when he was ready for his retaliation. Right now, he decided, he better check out his forearm and see just how badly he was hurt. So, he drove on, watching the bitch in his side mirror. She was bent over as if she was going to throw up. Then a car pulled along side of her. He picked up his speed and left her behind to deal with later.

To Debeck, a man with a long history of violence, broken bones and pain were not a new experience. He drove himself to a strip mall where he could pull over and do something about his forearm. It was red and beginning to swell; he would need some ice right away. He noticed a Subway in the mall and parked his car out front. He went inside, ruefully saying to the woman behind the counter, "I've done something very stupid. It seems I closed the door on my arm. Would you have some ice I could use?"

The woman, a young girl really, did not seem the least bit sympathetic and eyed him suspiciously. Instant anger broke loose inside him, the same fury he always felt when women gave him that familiar look of distrust just because he wasn't a looker. He swallowed the urge to come around the counter and punch her, saying instead (as nicely as he could muster), "I'll be glad to pay for it."

The false pleasantry got the response he wanted; the girl quickly dropped her attitude, saying, "No need to pay." She gave him two plastic bags and he moved to the drink machine where he filled them with ice.

Debeck mustered a slight smirk, saying, "Thanks. You're very kind."

He returned to the car, putting the bag of ice on his forearm while he considered what he wanted to do. He didn't know a thing about the Puritan other than she looked and acted dykey and was some sort of crackerjack bicycle rider. He assumed that if Cunningham wanted her off the jury it was because he thought she was leaning toward a guilty plea. What would that tell him about her? Maybe she was a lesbo man-hater? Then he realized it was useless to speculate since he had no idea why Cunningham was concerned about her. He also had no idea if the woman would be clever enough to associate the failed attack with her jury duty. When it came down to it, he didn't know squat.

Injuring her, something that had originally seemed easy, had now become considerably more difficult simply because the bitch had unexpectedly fought back.

He took the ice off his arm and made a fist with his hand; pain shot up his arm. He felt confident it wasn't broken but he couldn't be sure about a possible hairline fracture. He needed to get the arm X-rayed, but first he needed to decide what to do about the woman. He put the ice back on the arm and returned to planning his next move. If she had associated the attack with being on the jury, she might be prepared, might have even have alerted the police. So, breaking into her house would be considerably risky, not to mention he would be one-armed. His biggest obstacle was how to make it look like an accident now that she had been attacked once. He slowly came to the realization that an accident that left her alive was the problem. Dead...well dead she couldn't suspect anything, couldn't alert anyone, leaving Cunningham in the clear; a dead juror can't vote a man guilty.

The bag of ice was melting and causing a sweaty mess so he tossed it out the window. Since admitting failure to Cunningham was not an option, he would have to come up with a plan that permanently eliminated the Puritan while still protecting Cunningham, which meant his attack had to be perceived as an accident. An idea struck him. Tomorrow morning she would be *driving* to the courthouse and Debeck would make sure she never arrived anywhere again. Right now he would take care of his arm. He started the engine and headed toward the nearest urgent care facility. He was sure he would have plenty of waiting time to come up with the next plan of attack.

Day four ended with no surprises for the prosecution. Saul Greene was satisfied that he was making a good case against the defendant and that RJ had yet to wipe his ass with his cross examinations. Tomorrow was going to be the important day, the day in which he would introduce to the jury the question of what Cunningham was doing in that part of town at such an early morning hour. He knew Cunningham had been playing his monthly poker game earlier that night. He had subpoenaed the poker group's six other members to testify as to where the game had taken place and when it had ended. Their testimony would confirm that Cunningham had left the game an hour earlier than the rest of the group, which meant he had an hour and half to account for between leaving the poker game and having his car photographed running the red light. He also knew that RJ would never put Cunningham on the stand. Saul's strategy was to get the jury to question why Cunningham wouldn't take the stand to explain the missing time. It wouldn't be evidence of anything, except that the defendant had been doing something in the early hours of the morning and was refusing to explain what that was. The defense was required to provide him with a list of witnesses. Saul had studied the list and concluded it would not be calling anyone who would explain the unaccounted-for time. Saul's game plan was to cast suspicion on Cunningham's character, tactics often used in criminal trials when the evidence was circumstantial, as it was in this case. It was the way the game was played, fair or not. After all, Saul was up against a legendary defense attorney, so it was essential that he remove the defendants's halo. The issue of Cunningham's character was pivotal to his winning his case.

Saul had put his concerns about juror Seven on hold. Today she had been steady, paying close attention, and staring directly at Cunningham with what looked like scorn. Feasibly, she was leaning more toward his camp, a very good sign. So, as he pulled his notes together at the end of the day, he allowed himself the luxury of looking forward to his date with Allan. Maybe his life was going to get back on track after all. He now saw the possibility of winning the biggest case of his life, finally getting over Richard, and focusing, instead, on the chance of forming a new romantic alliance.

His evening with Allan turned out to be as he hoped: the man was attractive, charming, entertaining, very fit and apparently highly talented in both the kitchen and the business world. He had gone to Allan's condo and as he sat at the kitchen bar watching Allan work, he sipped on a delicious pinot noir. Allan deftly "whipped up" a delectable dinner of salad and veal Parmigiana. He had made the production look so easy that Saul was amazed when he tasted the veal and discovered the delicious, complex flavors.

However, one thing troubled Saul: why Allan remained vague about the exact nature of his work. All the man would say was that he was a computer consultant; apparently a very successful one, given the lovely penthouse he owned. A two thousand square-foot, three-bedroom, three-bath condo with a huge sliding glass door that led to a front deck with a killer view of the city didn't come cheap. The largest of the bedrooms had been turned into an electronic sanctum, looking to Saul like a scene from a spy movie.

Saul ended the evening early, a vow he had made to himself before he arrived at Allan's. He knew he wasn't ready for anything more intimate and he wanted to be well-rested for the next day. As promised, Allan made no advances, but it was apparent to both men that there was a strong sexual attraction.

Mulling over this most promising opportunity, Saul fell into a deep sleep, waking the next morning rested and convinced he hadn't slept this well since Richard left. When his feet hit the floor, an overwhelming feeling of confidence captured him; today he was going to kick butt and take names.

The antique grandfather clock in Cunningham's study chimed eight times, reminding him yet again that he had still not received a text message from Debeck. Cunningham had expected to hear from him hours ago and was sure something had gone wrong. However, it was too risky to call his friend from either his home phone or his cell phone. The one call Cunningham had made earlier from his cell phone could be explained away but two calls would be much more difficult to cover, should it come to that. Now he was considering whether to drive to a pay phone or to just leave it alone. In the end he decided he trusted Debeck and if the man hadn't signaled him with a text then there must be a good reason.

The entire day had been a roller coaster ride. He had felt a high when he finally decided to take control of his fate and made the decision to intervene with Juror Seven. The last few hours of waiting to hear from Debeck, however, had plunged him down into despair. On top of that, Rose had refused to come out of her bedroom when he knocked on her door after he arrived home. The whole mess with Rose was a mystery to him. Okay, he granted, he had snapped at her, but he didn't believe that one short flair of temper could be responsible for the dramatic change she was exhibiting.

Just as he was exploring the enigma concerning his wife, she knocked on his study door, saying, "I'd like to speak with you for a moment. May I come in?"

Cunningham had an immediate rush of adrenaline as he found himself caught in the middle of an internal conflict. His study was his private domain, the place of the secret cache. Rose rarely came inside his study, but he didn't want to shut her out at the very time it was crucial to mend the rift he had created.

He walked over to the door and opened it, instinctively blocking the entrance as he said, "I'm so glad you want to talk. How about we go in the living room where we can sit on the sofa together?" Rose eyed him suspiciously, another first, thought Cunningham.

"Why do you always keep me out of your study?" she asked.

"I don't keep you out, Rose. I just thought we could sit together on the sofa where it is more comfortable."

"Yes, you *do* keep me out. It's just that I never questioned you before. In fact, I've never questioned you about anything before."

Cunningham mustered the control to speak in a calm voice, saying, "I simply don't know what's going on with you,

Rose. You're not your usual self. Tell me, what can I do to get back the Rose I know and love?"

"You can answer some questions for me."

Feeling a tightening knot in his stomach, he cautiously said, "Okay, but let's go into the living room where we can be comfortable."

He turned to close the door to his study and when he turned back to reach for his wife's hand, she was already headed for the living room. He remained standing a few moments, realizing the strange sensation in his stomach was caused by fear. Rose, a woman who had never been anything but compliant, was alarming him. The feeling was unfamiliar...never in all the years he had known Rose had he been afraid of her. He took a deep breath and followed her into the living area, anxiously wondering what questions she wanted to ask and what he would answer. When he reached their large living room, she was sitting forward on one of the wing side chairs with her legs crossed at the ankles and her hands in her lap. Her head was bowed. He took a seat on the sofa across from her and waited.

Eventually, she looked up but stared straight ahead rather than look at him. "I know this is out of character since I've never challenged you on anything. However, this trial has caused me to reflect on our life together and, in particular, my inability to confront or challenge you. I've always avoided conflict because I lacked the courage and now I find I don't respect myself for....

"That's not right, Rose. You have so much courage...."

"Don't interrupt me, please. I need to say this. I've been thinking about it for hours. So, here it is. I want to know what you were doing on Grover Street the morning of the hit and run. You were supposed to be playing poker, not driving around where prostitutes hang out."

"I promise you I was not having sex with a prostitute, if that's what this is all about."

"Then what were you doing there?"

"You've always trusted me, Rose. I don't know why you've suddenly decided you can't trust me now."

It was at this point that Rose turned and looked at him, saying, "See, you're doing it again—deflecting my question, just like you did months ago when I asked the same question. You're trying to make me feel guilty for asking when it's you who should feel bad. Stop avoiding the question and just tell me what you were doing on Grover."

The knot in Cunningham's stomach tightened unbearably, not because the question had caught him off guard but because he didn't have a plausible lie, not when RJ had asked the same question and not now, when he needed to give Rose an answer. He had thought about it so many times he was ragged, but he had not been able to fabricate an answer that made sense and telling the truth was tantamount to total self destruction. RJ had warned him it would be dangerous to his defense if he couldn't account for his time, but all he was willing to tell RJ was that it was a private matter.

Cunningham was deep in contemplation when Rose spoke, "You're not answering me."

Shaken from his own thoughts, Cunningham stood up and walked over to Rose. He bent down on one knee, taking her cold limp hand, saying, "I swear to you I was not having sex with a prostitute."

Tears began leaking from Rose's eyes. "Then I know what you were doing."

Cunningham's heart slammed into his chest. "You do?"

"Yes, I do. You're gay and you were with your lover. All these years...that's why you never complained about our celibacy. You have a gay lover." She jumped up, sobbing, "Oh, my God, what an ostrich I've been. I can't stand myself and I can't stand you. I simply can't face the crowds of people at the courthouse tomorrow. Heading for the stairs she said, "I'm going to stay with my parents for a while." Cunningham started after her but stopped himself, deciding it was better for now that she thought him gay rather than for her to know the truth.

He returned to his study, closing and locking the door. Sitting at his desk with his head in his hands, he felt the first twinge of suicidal thoughts since the whole nightmare began. The irony of his predicament felt like an iron chain around him, a chain too heavy to bear anymore. The benevolent veneer that he had successfully perpetrated for his entire adult life had been cracked by a single altruistic act and now his secret core was beginning to seep to the surface, threatening to expose the ugliness inside. He removed a key from its hiding place, opened the bottom drawer of his desk, and brought out a gun, placing it on his lap, thinking *I'm not going to prison over something I didn't do and I'll die before I tell the truth about what I've done.*

He had no idea how long he had sat with the gun in his lap, his trance finally interrupted by the sound of a noise on the stairs. He put the gun back in the drawer, locked it, and opened the door to his study. His wife was standing at the bottom of the stairs, suitcase in hand, and eyes red from crying.

He walked up to her, saying, "I don't want you to go."

"I can't live with lies any longer so I can't stay," she replied.

"I love you, Rose. And I'm not Gay. Having you by my side all these years has meant everything to me."

"I don't believe you. Having me by your side was a convenience, allowing you to fool the world into thinking you're normal. I'm just now realizing that I'm anything but normal, and there has to be an ugly reason why you've let me get away with being a virgin all these years. You know where you can find me if you decide you want to tell me the truth. Maybe then we can get the help we should have gotten thirty-five years ago." She headed for the door to the garage, leaving Bradley standing by the stairs, helpless to keep her.

His entire life was crumbling around him and he could feel the pressure building inside him; it was a different kind of pressure than what had been driving him to perversions for as long as he could remember; it felt like a rock crushing down on him. Ever since the police had knocked on his door, he had resisted acting on the usual pressure. But now it was building to a crescendo and he didn't know if he could resist much longer. Since his arrest he had not gone to his monthly poker game, the excuse he had used for years for being out late at night. He had always left the poker game early and had driven to the part of town where he knew he could relieve the compulsion, where he knew the right people to help him with the persistent longing that possessed him. But with the media following him like a hound dog, he had been unable to move about freely, essentially a prisoner to their relentless pursuit. He returned to his study, picked up a bottle of scotch and poured himself a double, downing it in one gulp. Immediately refilling the glass, he downed the second double shot as well. He returned to his desk, staring into space until the liquor began to take effect. Then he unlocked the drawer and again took out the gun, wondering, *how many shots of liquor would it take for the final shot?*

DAY FIVE

Debeck had correctly diagnosed the damage to his arm: not broken through and through but there was a hairline fracture. The doc had wanted to immobilize it with a cast but Debeck refused, not wanting to be limited in his motion. During his six hours wait at urgent care, Debeck had plenty of time to build his fury at the Puritan and to formulate a lethal plan of revenge. He now had several hours before it was time to execute the plan. A bit drowsy from the pain medication the doctor had given him, he returned to his car, lowered the seat-back, set his phone to wake him in three hours, and quickly fell asleep.

At four a.m. his phone beeped him awake. Still very groggy from the pain pill, he drove to a twenty-four hour convenience store and bought a double espresso and chocolate doughnut. He downed the caffeine and sugar in less than a minute, knowing that the two legal drugs would give him the jolt he needed. He took a leak as a precaution for the stakeout ahead and was feeling wired even before he reached his car. Then he headed toward the Puritan's home, making one stop at a convenience store for more coffee and a special gift he was planning to give to the red Honda's gas tank.

Cruising past Jane's house, the first thing he noticed was her car was no longer parked in the drive. *Now what the fuck was he going to do?* He drove around the streets for a while, searching for the car but couldn't spot the red Honda anywhere. The only plan he could come up with now was to wait and watch. He parked down the block from her duplex, donned his baseball cap with the ponytail, took out his field glasses and waited. He would have to improvise.

Just before seven o'clock, a woman came out of the Puritan's house. He checked around for possible witnesses and when he didn't see anyone, he picked up the binoculars and got a close-up look. The woman, wearing spiked heels and dressed in a classy business suit that showed off a knockout figure, had long dark hair that framed an attractive face. She carried a large, plain canvas shopping bag as she headed down the street and turned the corner at the end of the block. The woman must be the Puritan's roommate, thought Debeck. A second thought caused him to sit straight up. Hey! I bet the bitch *is* a dyke. The Puritan is the butch and that's her girlfriend who just left. That would explain the Puritan's sexless outfit and the aggressive attack on him. His theory allowed him a slight reprieve for having been thwarted by a she-male.

The neighborhood had begun to come alive and people were leaving for work, strolling past him as they walked to their cars, making use of the binoculars more precarious by the moment. To make matters worse, the pain pill had worn off and his arm hurt like hell. He had a momentary concern: *maybe I'm too old for this shit.* However, he refused to abandon his commitment to his former boss and instead downed another pain pill, continuing to watch the duplex, waiting for the dyke to leave for court. When eight-thirty came and went and the Puritan still hadn't come out of the house, Debeck guessed he had been foiled again. She must have spent the night somewhere else, which would account for the missing car. If that was the case, it would also mean she knew the assault yesterday was not an isolated event. He took out his phone, touched some numbers on the pad and waited. After more than ten rings his friend finally answered, saying, "This better be good, Bunky, buddy."

Debeck winced at the use of his banned nickname, but let it pass because he needed a favor from the only contact he still had on the police force. "Yeah, yeah, I'm gonna owe you, I know."

"You already owe me—something equivalent to the national debt."

"Hey! I'd rather fuck a horse than ask a favor of you, but a man's gotta do what a man's gotta do."

"So what kind of get-my-ass-fired favor do you want me to risk my pension for this time?"

"Need to know if a young female bicycle rider reported being harassed by a car yesterday afternoon on Charles Street near Washington."

"That's it?"

"Yeah, that's it."

"Hold on a moment, I'll check the computer."

After about a minute of silence, the man said, "Nothing on file."

"Okay, then, thanks."

"So, Bunky, be sure to buy some carrots. I hear horses like them after they do the nasty."

"And I'm sure that's firsthand knowledge not hearsay."

"Hey, Bunky buddy, don't you know that biting the hand that feeds you is never a good policy?"

"Thanks for that awe-inspiring, state-of-the-art advice."

"If you're done under-appreciating my assistance, Mr. Golden Parachute, I'm signing off because unlike you, I've got work to do protecting the oh-so-appreciative public."

"Always the wise guy, huh," Debeck said. "Check you later."

Debeck was relieved that the bitch hadn't called the police. Now he could go forth with his plan: make sure she was eliminated as a juror without raising suspicion. He was a day late but better late than never. He knew he should give Cunningham a call and fill him in on what happened, but he would have to do it from a pay phone; he didn't want a series of calls to Cunningham on his phone. Debeck checked his watch, noting that he might just be able to reach him before court started, provided he was lucky enough to find one of the increasingly extinct pay phones. When he finally did find one, it was after nine and Cunningham's phone went right to voice mail. Debeck left a brief message, saying only, "Calling from a pay phone. Project delayed one day."

The woman in the spiked heels and business suit boarded the bus, not bothering to look for a seat since she was getting off at the very next stop, only a mile ride. Exiting the bus she walked a block to her red Honda Civic, got in, and drove to the courthouse, this time choosing not to park in the lot provided for jurors but instead parking in a pay lot two blocks from the courthouse. After parking her car, the woman took the shopping bag out and headed for the Starbucks a half block from the lot. She bought a latte and took it with her to the bathroom where she took off the dark wig, business suit, and heels. She then put on a formfitting T-shirt and tight-fitting capris, slipping a loose pinafore dress over the outfit she had just put on. Without bothering to look in the mirror, she quickly ruffled her short blonde hair. Lastly, she fastened the talisman around her neck. She put the clothes she had just taken off into the shopping bag. Sliding into her usual Birkenstock sandals, she headed out the door, shopping bag and latte in hand. When she arrived at the courthouse, she checked the shopping bag and breezed through the metal detector without a problem. At the end of the day, she would retrieve the shopping bag, enter the restroom where she would simply slip off the loose-fitting dress, put the wig and heels back on, and, wearing the T-shirt and capris, walk to her car.

As Jane and Sydney had planned the night before, Jane used her bird-watching binoculars to check for suspicious cars before leaving the house the next morning. She spotted the black car parked down the street from her house, the same black car with, presumably, the same driver who yesterday tried to shove her off the road. Upon seeing the car through the binoculars, Jane felt the familiar rush of adrenaline that usually meant a panic attack was coming on. She controlled her breathing and concentrated on the plan that she and Sydney had concocted last night, a plan that predicted the black car with its driver would be back in the morning. Eventually, she could feel herself calm down enough to follow through on the strategy they had carefully plotted out. She dressed in the clothes they had picked out, putting on the comical wig and the ridiculous shoes and stuffing the change of clothes into the bag before leaving the house and walking to the corner. After she turned the corner she hid from sight and peeked around some bushes to see if the black car followed; the car stayed parked. Satisfied their plan was working, she continued on to the bus stop.

Waiting for the bus, she became aware that many of the men in the passing cars took notice of her, the same attention paid to her by the men (and even a few women) on the short bus ride. Admittedly, it was an empowering feeling, an unfamiliar but not unappealing feeling, she decided. Maybe the outfit and the wig wasn't as comical as she first thought, maybe it was, just as Sydney claimed, another weapon to be used by a *Warrior* in a brutish world.

As she entered the jury box, Jane intentionally avoided looking at Cunningham until after she was seated. She collected herself by touching her stone necklace and reviewing the words Sydney had thrown at her yesterday: "get in touch with the strong woman inside of you and free yourself from your past." When she thought she was ready, she looked over at Cunningham. He was staring right at her with a cold stare that made her heart race. Instinctively, her fear told her to look away, but she kept her hands on the necklace and eventually found the courage to stare right back. She silently repeated the mantra she and Sydney had rehearsed: *The roles are reversed. I'm a Light Warrior and I'm in control of his fate. My weapon is my courage.* The more she said it, the more she could feel her heart slow and her fear subside. The prosecutor was calling someone to the stand and she turned her attention to the witness.

For Erin, drained of energy from yet another night of interrupted sleep, day five was the most difficult yet. She had first been awakened at two in the morning with a hot flash, gone back to sleep only to be jolted awake at four with a night sweat lasting forty-five minutes, destroying any chance of going back to sleep. For a while she lay in bed, furious yet again at the irony: a *Mother* Nature who dared to perpetrate such a cruel fate on Sisters who lived past menopause. She knew that getting angry only made it worse and that she was certainly not alone in her struggle. These reminders, however, did nothing to lessen her frustration: she still felt she had the brain power and training to be great at her job, but lack of sleep definitely affected her ability to be sharp in the courtroom. It didn't seem fair to be forced to throw in the professional towel just because estrogen had so callously abandoned her.

At five a.m. she finally decided to get out of bed and begin the day, acutely aware that with the loss of sleep would come with some loss of perception during the trial. She headed for the kitchen for her first cup of coffee.

Seated in the courtroom, Erin silently thanked her best friend, caffeine, which had allowed her to notice the multiple transformations of Seven. She had observed Jane's going from skittishness to bravado in a matter of minutes, from refusing to look at Cunningham to staring right at him. Her facial features indicated determination, a willfulness of spirit that made her seem as if she had decided to finally face a long-suffering enemy. There was, however, something even more intriguing about Seven today. She was wearing a stone pendant of some sort and she was holding on to it as if it were a life-preserver. Curious, Erin thought.

Erin was sure Jane's reactions were caused by classic transference, a defense mechanism in which a person unconsciously redirects feelings from one person to a second person; the second person has some significant qualities or characteristics that are similar to the original person. Erin was also aware that some amount of transference goes on whenever new people meet each other. She was certain, however, that Jane had, from the very beginning of the trial, been exhibiting more than the normal transference to Cunningham. Clearly, the defendant must be reminding her of a very disliked person from her past. What was puzzlingly, though, was the vacillating nature of Jane's reactions: one moment she was fearful, the next minute scornful, and the next minute full of grit—none of which was good for Cunningham. Still, her various behaviors were not grounds for dismissal. Erin inwardly sighed at the conviction that the defense would be stuck with Seven despite her obvious, but unprovable, lack of impartiality. RJ could never go to the judge with Erin's conjecture about negative transference, although she inwardly laughed when she imagined the decidedly compos mentis Reverend Jove attempting to defend an unconscious psychological phenomena to the judge.

The thought of RJ making a fool of himself before the judge caused Erin to remember what happened late yesterday afternoon when the team had gathered in RJ's office to review the proceeding and to talk strategy. The meeting started with Toby reporting to RJ his appalling new findings: Jane's grandfather was also her father. At first RJ appeared confused, asking, "How is that possible?" Toby had glibly replied, "Easy, you just take a sick bastard of a father who sexually molests his own daughter without any protection." RJ, obviously embarrassed by his naiveté, tried to whitewash his reaction with indignation at the perversity of such behavior, ending with a ranting tantrum about his helplessness to remove the juror just because she was a "freak of nature." Toby, having caught the fire in Erin's eyes as she opened her mouth to respond to RJ's implication that it was somehow Jane's fault for the father's perversion, managed to give Erin a warning look before she spoke. Catching herself just in time, Erin quietly seethed at the man's cold-blooded, male chauvinism. Oh how she loathed the man! If it wasn't for Toby she would have blown her cool.

Erin now pleasantly mused on the thought that Toby seemed to be saving her from herself on a daily basis. The perplexing giant of a man was turning out to be an antidote for the toxic RJ, and the more time she spent with Toby the more he grew on her. Could he, she wondered, be a more permanent antidote for what was missing in her life? *Uh, oh, Don't even go there, she* reprimanded herself. Daydreaming about her future was dangerous business at any time, but especially right now when her business was to pay attention to the court proceedings.

Erin turned her attention back to the courtroom, this time focusing on the defendant. The trial was definitely taking its toll on Bradley Cunningham. His eyes were bloodshot, looking like he had gotten even less sleep than she had. At the moment Cunningham was focusing his menacing bloodshot eyes on Jane Nichols. Juror Seven remained unflinching, however, staring right back at the defendant. Cunningham's glowering stare made Erin remember how RJ had brushed Cunningham off yesterday when the defendant had mentioned his concern about juror Seven. Now, as Erin watched the staring contest, she was convinced that RJ's brushoff of Cunningham was a mistake which was now turning into a calamity.

She quickly scribbled a note to RJ, telling him Cunningham was giving Seven the evil eye. She passed the note forward to Dum, who glanced at it before passing it on to RJ. The defense attorney quickly read the note, looked at Cunningham, then touched him on the shoulder and whispered something in his ear. Erin watched as Cunningham's facial muscles tightened into strained indignation. Erin was also keeping an eye on Jane's reaction as RJ spoke to Cunningham. Was that a smirk on Seven's face? Had Jane taken satisfaction in what had just transpired, as if she had planned the whole scene? Could it be that Jane Nichols was intentionally playing Cunningham? Erin sat back in her seat, thinking over the confusing scene she had just witnessed. So far, there had been nothing predictable about Jane Nichols, a woman who was turning out to be the most puzzling juror Erin had ever evaluated.

Even though Cunningham had stopped staring at Seven, Erin noticed that his facial expression remained indignant, an expression that would do him the most harm at a time when he needed to look above suspicion. To make matters worse, the defendant's wife was no longer present in the courtroom. Rose's absence, Erin observed, had been noticed by every one of the twelve jurors whose eyes at one time or another had settled on the vacant seat. As to Rose, all Erin knew at this point was that she had not been feeling well yesterday. She felt sure there was more to the story than a headache, but without being privy to the details, she could only conjecture. All in all, day five was showing signs of being a harmful watershed for the defense, and it had only just begun.

Saul Greene was now calling the first poker playing witness to the stand and Erin forced herself back to the present, carefully scrutinizing all the jurors' reactions as they became party to the prosecutor's attempt to discredit Cunninghams's pristine character. She knew the yet-to-be explained reason for Cunningham's presence in the area of the hit and run was going to be a crucial bit of *non-evidence*: while being in that part of town *proved* nothing about guilt, it, nevertheless, screamed for an explanation, a fact the prosecution knew would be a vulnerable part of the defense. Greene had taken statements from all six members of the poker group and would probably put at least three of them on the stand. The statement, reluctantly given, established the fact that Cunningham had left the game early as he usually did. After the second poker player's testimony today, Erin could see that Greene's questioning of the players was having the intended effect; all twelve of the jurors showed signs of being unsettled, all twelve of the jurors had facial expressions that indicated misgivings. Erin felt sure they were asking themselves why Cunningham regularly left the games early and why he did so on the night in question. Why did he go to Grover Street, a part of town known for drugs and prostitution? As Erin carefully watched all the jurors, she was forced to conclude that their misgivings would cast doubt on Cunningham's character...just what the prosecution intended.

Cunningham, angrier than he could ever remember and feeling like shit from last night's fiasco, sat in the courtroom trying to absorb the reality of the unfolding events of the last few days. Without thinking, he reached up and rubbed the stabbing pain in his neck muscle. He had awakened around three this morning with his head twisted to one side on his desk. When he pushed himself away from the desk and stood up to go to bed, an awful pain shot up his neck; the pain felt like the gunshot he had been too spineless to fire. He tried to go back to sleep, but the pain in his neck made it impossible to get comfortable and his stomach churned from the huge amount of alcohol he had consumed. He lay in bed awake, his mind playing with various scenarios. What could have happened with Debeck that he hadn't called? What was he going to do about Rose?

Finally, at five a.m. he had given up on sleep and returned to his study where he unlocked his safe, removed the hard drive, connected it to his computer, and turned on the machine. A few keystrokes and, as they always did, the images on the screen began to release the steam from the pressure cooker his mind and body had become.

The release was only temporary, however, and early this morning the stress had started to rebuild. Still nauseated from last night's alcoholic indulgence, he was unable to eat anything or even get coffee down. Once at the courthouse, he had been forced to deal with the God-awful reporters hounding him about Rose's absence. He had sounded like a broken record, saying, "No comment," so many times he couldn't count. He knew her absence would be headlines tomorrow and there would be even more aggravation; the nettlesome reporters wouldn't be shy about their speculations. His celebrity status, once a sign of proud achievement, had been transformed by the trial into a prison cell; with the media following his every move, no action on his part had gone unnoticed by the public. The million dollars in bail he had paid to stay out of jail was a mockery; it was supposed to buy him freedom but it had resulted, instead, in his being placed in a virtual lockup.

Now, squirming in his seat due to a still lurching stomach, he was being subjected not only to the incriminating testimony of his poker buddies, but also to the glaring stare of Seven. The placid mask he was expected to wear while others decided his fate could not trump his angry mood. All the rage, resentment, and unfairness of his plight had invaded his stomach like the creature in the *Alien* horror movie.

If only Debeck had come through for him....

God damn Seven! She was truly an annoying, man-hating woman who should never have gotten past the selection process. He was beyond pissed at RJ. Why couldn't the man have listened to the jury consultant? After all, he was paying through the roof for her expertise. Because of juror Seven, he no longer trusted his famous defense attorney to save him by using his acclaimed powers of oration to counter the circumstantial evidence. He was positive juror Seven would be leading the crusade to crucify him and, using the circumstantial evidence, would persuade the others to follow suit.

As one by one his poker buddies gave their incriminating testimony, the defendant started to think that replacing Seven with an alternate might not be enough to clear him. What he needed now was a mistrial, which would buy him time and a whole new jury. Since he hadn't heard from Debeck, maybe it wasn't too late to take a different route.

Cunningham made a decision. Since RJ was so concerned about jury tampering and had refused to investigate Seven, he would take matters into his own hands. If he could locate Debeck, he would pay him to find something on Seven, something that would show prejudice, something that could be sprung during deliberations. The woman was such a man-hater there had to be something in her history. At the lunch break, he would have to find a pay phone and call Debeck. Thoughts of a new direction to take finally gave him some hope and just enough optimism to keep the demons at bay until lunch.

Immediately after the judge and jurors had left the courtroom for the lunch break, Cunningham checked his cell phone and found the brief message from Debeck indicating there had been a delay in the original plan. A *delay* meant that Debeck was still on the original course, so Cunningham knew he would have to contact him immediately if he wanted to change the plan. At the moment, however, RJ was by his side, waiting to escort him out of the courtroom and over to the office for their usual luncheon meeting.

He spoke quietly in RJ's ear, saying, "I'm going to skip out on lunch today. I want to go see Rose and see if I can change her mind."

Checking to be sure there was no one in hearing range, RJ pulled his client aside before replying, "It's a little late for that today. The damage is already done. Besides, I need to speak with you again about the now *infamous* unaccounted-for time, which is killing us." Cunningham started to speak but RJ interrupted, saying, "Look, Bradley, I want to remind you yet again that if what you're hiding is being with a prostitute...well, that's a forgivable crime compared to what you're being charged with here. You'll get past it and have your life back in a few months."

Cunningham felt his anger skyrocket to its earlier level. Barely able to contain his fury he said, between clinched teeth, "You also told me that if I was with a prostitute, I would have to produce her so she could testify." Cunningham took RJ by the shoulders and turned him so they were face to face. Then he hissed, "I want to remind you, *yet again*, I can't do that."

RJ stiffened and casually removed Cunningham's hands from his shoulders. Arching his eyebrows he asked, "Can't or won't?"

Cunningham didn't answer for a few seconds. Finally, he shrugged his shoulders saying, "Not a question worth answering because it doesn't matter. Either way it's not going to happen."

RJ shook his head in frustration. "You realize you're digging your own grave."

"What I realize is that I'm paying you a fortune. Originally, you told me you could get around the issue. Now you're telling me you can't. How am I supposed to trust you?"

"Ha! Trust me? I'm not the one hiding something. So don't talk to me about trust."

Cunningham started to snap back at RJ, but then realized he was wasting time. He should be using the time to speak with Debeck, not engaging in this foolish showdown. He glared at RJ, saying, "Get me through the media circus outside and then I'll see you back in court after lunch."

RJ shook his head in frustration but conceded to the man paying his fees. He turned and strode out of the courtroom. Cunningham followed behind as RJ pushed a path between the screaming reporters with their extended microphones.

"Where's Mrs. Cunningham?" one shouted.

"What were you doing on Grover Street?" several shouted at him simultaneously.

"Are you going to testify in your own defense?" shouted another.

To all of these questions, RJ repeated, "No comment," as he shoved his way through the crowd to the car waiting to take him the few blocks to his office.

Cunningham, to escape the reporters, rode with RJ to the office. He asked the driver to let him out after they entered the parking garage and were safely away from the press. On his way out the door he said to RJ, "I've got to speak with Rose. I'll see you back at court." He then exited the back entrance of the garage and began rapidly walking, searching for a pay phone. After walking three blocks and not finding a phone, he began to get panicky; he had to tell Debeck there was a change of plans and, having skipped dinner last night and breakfast this morning, he had to get something to eat or he might faint in the courtroom. He decided he couldn't wait to find a phone so he looked up Debeck's phone number in his own phone, memorized it, put his phone back in his pocket, took a twenty dollar bill from his wallet, and stopped a young woman on the street.

"Sorry to bother you," he said. "Do you have a cell phone I could use? My battery is dead and I have to make an urgent local call. It will just take a moment. I'll be glad to give you twenty dollars for your trouble."

Taken aback, the young woman didn't respond at first. She glanced at her watch and then at the obviously exhausted, anxious but neatly manicured man in the exquisitely expensive suit and decided, why not? "Sure," she said, taking her phone out of her purse and handing it to him.

Cunningham took the phone, stepped away and dialed Debeck, cursing under his breath when it went to voice mail. He left a brief cryptic message and hung up. He extended the twenty dollar bill to the woman, saying, "Thanks, you may have saved me big problems."

"No big deal," the woman said. "You really don't need to pay me."

"Please," Cunningham said. "You really have saved me." He thrust the money at her. "Please, take it."

Hesitantly, she took the money and put it in her purse along with her phone.

She was starting on her way, when Cunningham asked, "I'm not familiar with this area, do you know a place where I can get a really quick sandwich or some soup?"

"Yes, go back that way," she said, pointing in the direction he had just come from. "Go about a block, turn right and go about a half block. There's a wonderful deli called Cohen's...it's on the right side of the street. Big sign. Can't miss it."

"Thanks. You've saved me again."

"You're welcome," said the woman as she walked away.

Cunningham started walking toward the deli, hoping he could make it before he passed out from the nutritional weakness now overtaking him.

After leaving the voice mail on Cunningham's phone, Debeck had decided to get some sleep so he could tail the Puritan again at the end of the day. He drove home and went immediately to the kitchen to swallow another pain pill. He then went into his bedroom and set his phone alarm to wake him at two, plenty of time to arrive at the courthouse for a stakeout. He fell asleep immediately after hitting the bed, still in the clothes he had worn for more than twenty-four hours. He was so exhausted and drugged he didn't hear his cell phone ring at twelve-thirty-four, nor did he hear the alarm go off at two.

Having slept through his alarm, he awoke at three-forty-five with a start, looked at the clock and did a jack-in-the-box out of bed. *Shit! No time to eat, no time to change clothes.* Wearing the same wrinkled, smelly clothes, he thrust the bottle of pain pills into his pocket and ran to his car. Still in somewhat of a haze from the drug, and worried he might miss the Puritan as she left the building, he forgot to grab his cell phone, leaving it, with a blinking message signal, on the nightstand by his bed.

He wasn't as lucky today as he had been yesterday in finding a good parking space from which to watch the courthouse. He had to drive around the block three times before a car pulled out and he could snatch the space. This morning he had shoved his ball cap disguise under his seat and he took it out now and slipped the cap on his head. He was just pulling the binoculars out of the case, when the courthouse began spitting out humans. Through the binocs, he carefully watched the exit where he had spotted the Puritan yesterday, but he couldn't see any woman remotely resembling her. After a while Cunningham, along with his defense attorney, came into view as they pushed their way through the throngs of reporters with extended microphones. Figuring he had somehow missed the Puritan, he turned his glasses on the parking garage, watching for the red Honda. Ten minutes passed and several red cars came out, none of which were the Honda Civic he was looking for. After twenty-five minutes, cars were no longer exiting from the garage.

Well, shit. What the hell's going on? Could he have screwed up again?

Now his plan to arrange a car accident would have to be revamped. At least he could find her again now that he knew where she lived. Right now he would get something to eat, then after dark he would go to her home and stage the break-in he had originally planned.

After eating a hamburger at a coffee shop, he drove to the chop shop where he had originally "borrowed" the car he was driving. As a precaution, he exchanged it for another car and transferred his gym bag with his tools to the different car. He would have to park down the street to observe her house and he didn't want any observant neighbors to see the same car parked on the street.

He drove by the Puritan's house at about eight. This time, at least, the red Honda was parked in the drive. He pulled over to the curb in a different spot and took out the binoculars. It was then that it occurred to him that he hadn't checked his phone for messages. He reached in his pocket...aw, man! He'd left the Goddamn phone on his nightstand. He was furious at his stupidity, but it wasn't worth risking the hour and a half round trip drive to retrieve it. Leaving the area to find a land line to call his phone for messages could mean missing the Puritan if she decided to spend the night somewhere else, as she must have done last night.

His arm was throbbing again, so he swallowed another pain pill and lowered himself down in the seat, settling in for a couple of hours of watching and waiting.

It didn't quite work the way he planned, however. After about thirty minutes the pain pill kicked in...and so did the drowsiness. Waking at midnight and confused about where he was, he automatically wrenched himself up in the seat, pulling a muscle in his lower back. A searing pain shot down the back of his left leg.

Jesus! That hurts. I'm too Goddamn old for this stakeout shit.

He pushed the seat as far back as it would go and tried to stretch out his legs to relieve the pain, but he couldn't get the position he needed. In terrible agony, he was forced to open the door and get out. He did several toe raises in an attempt to relieve the shooting pain and when that didn't work, he tried bending at the waist and twisting his spine from side to side. Still in misery, he tried walking, limping really, around the car several times. The pain was unrelenting. He was bending over trying to touch his toes, hoping to stretch his hamstrings when a female voice startled him.

"Sorry to intrude, but I've been watching you and I can tell you're hurting."

Debeck instinctively straightened and looked in the direction of the voice. A tall, skinny woman of indeterminate age was standing a few feet from the car. By her side was a large, leashed dog. " Sit, Daisy," she commanded to her dog, who did exactly that.

He immediately knew he had made a mistake by directly looking at the woman so he bent over again, mumbling, "Yeah, a cramp or something."

"I'm a Yoga teacher and I think I can help you. Where is it hurting?"

Not wanting to bring attention to himself any more than he already had, he knew the last thing he needed was to have a conversation with the woman. Being rude, however, would only make him more memorable, so he answered, "Pain shooting down the back of my leg."

"That's what I thought," she said. "You need to stretch the piriformis muscle. It sits right on top of the sciatic nerve which runs down the back of your leg."

"Yeah?"

"Which side is the pain on?"

"Left."

"Okay, then. Put both hands on the car for balance and bend your knees."

Putting any kind of weight on his injured arm, which was now throbbing again, was not a possibility, so he put the uninjured arm on the car and bent his aging knees as far as they would go.

"Now, standing on your right leg, cross the left leg over the right at the knee."

Debeck, never one for exercise of any kind other than muscle building, decided the woman was out of her mind if she thought he could stand on one leg and cross the other over his knee. Still, the pain had intensified and she seemed to know about muscles so he tried it, finding that he could just barely get the left leg crossed over the right.

"Now squat down as far as you can," she instructed.

Easy for you to say, he thought, as he lowered himself down a few more inches. His left hip felt like it was being pulled out of the socket, but the pain running down the back of his left leg began to ease, eventually going away after about fifteen-seconds.

"Is it better yet?" she asked.

Still trying to avoid looking directly at her, he said, "Yeah, it is. It's much better."

"Well, good,then.That piriformis muscle is a troublemaker, tight on just about everyone. You know, you should get in a regular Yoga class. It would really help you stay flexible."

"Thanks," he mumbled. S*ure thing, lady, I'm gonna sign up for a Yoga class first thing in the morning.*

"No, problem. Trust me, Yoga is the best thing you can do for yourself." She reached down and patted the dog on the head, saying, "Come on, Daisy, let's get back home." The well-behaved dog stood up and the two of them headed down the street in the opposite direction from the Puritan's house, leaving Debeck in a quandary.

What next? Now I've got a witness to my being in the neighborhood. *How else could I screw up this simple mission?*

He decided the best thing to do was to follow the dog lady to see where she lived. If he was lucky, she would be blocks away on a different street and not likely to make any connections between him and the Puritan. Besides, he had an unidentifiable car and his baseball cap on, so maybe it would be okay. Worried that the pain in his leg might return, he was hesitant to get back in the cramped car, so when the dog lady was a block ahead, he started walking after her, warily at first but speeding up once he was convinced the pain wasn't going to return. Fortunately, at the end of the block she turned left. Staying about fifty yards behind her, he continued to follow her for two more streets before she turned right, away from the Puritan's house. Good enough, he thought, and headed back for his car.

There he retrieved his binoculars and took a look at the Puritan's house. Everything seemed quiet. The red Honda was still parked in the drive, causing him to think that at least one thing was going his way and that he was way overdue to get this fucked-up mission completed. He got back in the car, started it up, and drove around the block, intending to park closer to the Puritan's house so he could make a quick getaway. His plan vanished when he discovered there were no parking spaces anywhere near the house. He had to drive around the block again, ending up in the only open space, right back where he had started. He would now be forced to walk down to the Puritan's house and scope it out, looking for a path to a quick, camouflaged escape route.

After parking, he opened the trunk and rummaged through the gym bag, pulling out a black nylon jacket, a black knit cap, a pair of black leather gloves, a stun gun, some tools to pick a lock, and a tire iron. He replaced his baseball cap with the knit cap and put the black jacket and gloves on, putting the baseball cap and the binoculars back in the bag and the stun gun in his jacket pocket. He closed the trunk, and, after looking around for any obvious witnesses, crossed the street to be on the opposite side of the Puritan's house. He began walking toward the house, carrying the tire iron low beside his leg. Staying in the shadows across the street from the house for a few minutes, he scoped out the street lighting, looking for the best possible exit route where he wouldn't be seen leaving. Fortunately, there was no street light in front of the Puritan's house. He thought he saw an escape avenue between her house and the next door neighbor's. Wanting to be sure it went through to the next street, he crossed over to check it out. Slowly, he walked alongside the chain link fence between the two houses, careful not to make any noise. Toward the back, he came upon two trash cans that would present a problem in a quick getaway. He set the tire iron down and quietly lifted each of the trash cans out of the way, creating a clear path to the alley. He picked up the tire iron and walked toward the alley, looking around for a few minutes until he decided on the best route to get back to the car. When he was comfortable with his escape, he walked back along the side of the house the way he had come. He saw two windows he thought belonged to bedrooms. By standing on his toes, he was just tall enough to peek in the first window and see a sleeping person in a bed. Moving to the next window, he spotted a lump in that bed as well. As suspected, one of these sleepers would be the roommate. Of course, he didn't know which one was the Puritan and which the roommate, thus the stun gun.

Debeck silently moved to the rear of the house. The inconsequential backyard contained a small deck scattered with more planted pots and a bistro table with two chairs. Two steps up to the deck led to a back door. Soundlessly, he stepped up on the deck, gently laying the tire iron on the table so he could remove the picks from his pocket. Within thirty-seconds he had the door open. He picked up the tire iron with his good arm and entered the house, finding himself in the kitchen. Standing still, he listened for any activity. When he heard nothing but silence, he cautiously moved forward toward the side of the house where he had spotted the sleeping forms. From the doorway of the first bedroom, he could see a sleeping figure covered to the neck. Long dark hair spilling out on the pillow told him it was the roommate. He would put her out of commission and then move on to the Puritan.

Taking the stun gun out of his pocket, he moved, cross-country style to prevent any sound, toward the bed until he was right over the sleeping body. His hand with the stun gun was hovering above the figure when he suddenly heard a noise behind him. Instinctively, he turned his head toward the sound, raising the tire iron in defense. A flash of light directed right at his face was immediately followed by a jet of cool, liquid spray. Debeck automatically dropped the tire iron, its landing making a loud clanging sound on the hardwood floor. His hands flew up to his face as he felt the burning first in his eyes, then in his throat and chest. *Aw, shit. Pepper spray!* His eyes were now feeling as if they were on fire and his chest as if it would explode. He blindly reached out for the bed and sat down, pleading, "Jesus!...my eyes are on fire...you gotta help me!"

"Sure," a calm female voice said. "I've already got 911 on the line." Then he heard the voice say, "There's a man in trouble, I think he's having a heart attack. No, he's out on the street...yes, on the street...Barrister Street, the two-thousand block near the corner of Aspen. He's on the ground, clutching his heart. Come quickly, please."

Debeck, with both his chest and eyes feeling like an inferno, was as helpless as he'd ever been in his life. A flash of himself as a small child terrified and helpless when his father had gone on one of his violent rampages entered his memory. A calm, female voice beside him said, "I'm going to walk you out into the street so the EMT's can find you." Then he felt two hands on his body, assisting him up from the bed. Blinded, disabled, and powerless, he let himself be shepherded forward until the voice said, "Okay, there are three steps here. Take them slowly."

Debeck somehow managed to get down the steps, allowing the woman to steer him for what seemed like a very long distance. Then the voice said, "You'd better sit down. There's a curb here." He felt for the curb with his foot and when he found it, he let himself be helped to a sitting position. He was still bent over with his head in his hands, the burning pain in his eyes so intense he wondered, despite his knowledge of pepper spray, if he would ever see again. Sirens echoed in the distance, giving him hope.

Then a voice close to his ear said, "When they get here, you need to tell them you've been sprayed with hornet spray. You'll need an antidote."

"Hornet spray? What antidote?" Knowing nothing about hornet spray, his fears of permanent blindness were magnified tenfold. "You Goddamn, bitch. If you've blinded me, I'll come after you and you'll wish you were never born!"

"I think not, asshole. I have a picture of you in my bedroom with that tire iron and stun gun in your hand. You just lost all your hit points so you're out of the game." Then Debeck heard retreating footsteps.

Hit points? *What the hell is the bitch talking about?*

The sirens were now getting louder so Debeck stood up and waved his hands, screaming out, "Over here, over here." Within moments he heard the ambulance drive up, stop, doors open, hurried footsteps and a male voice say, "We're here to help. What's the problem, sir?"

Debeck screamed, "I'm not having a heart attack! I've been sprayed in the face with hornet spray...I can't see and I can't breath...I need the antidote!"

"Okay, sir, take it easy. We'll take you to the emergency room and they can take care of you. We're going to put you on a stretcher and into the ambulance, okay?"

"The pain is awful...can you give me something? Am I going to be blinded forever?"

"No, sir. You're going to be uncomfortable for a while, but you'll be okay in a few days. Here, let us help you onto the stretcher."

Once inside the ambulance, Debeck allowed himself his first enraged, apoplectic thought since he'd been sprayed in the face. He'd been outsmarted, outplayed by the Puritan bitch and her roommate. They had been one step ahead of him the entire time.

The sirens brought the neighbors from their houses to watch the commotion. They gathered in small groups to speculate on what was happening. The owner of the home on whose curb Debeck had been deposited was puffed up with the news that he had heard the man screaming about hornet spray. After the ambulance left, all the neighbors, intrigued by the mysterious crisis, buzzed with the energy of eager-to-know humans. They speculated for an additional ten minutes before returning to their homes.

After leaving Debeck sitting on the curb down the street from her duplex, Sydney, having retreated to a hiding position behind some shrubs, watched the scene play out in front of her. Since Jane intended to stay on the jury, they decided it would be wise to avoid being identified in any way with the intruder. She and Jane debated about which one of them should confront the man if he came back to the house. Jane claimed she didn't think she had the courage, while Sydney maintained it was exactly the sort of action she needed to take to develop courage. Secretly, however, Sydney was excited about the opportunity to acquire hit points by taking on the opposition. When Jane got cold feet at the last minute, Sydney had no trouble stepping in and had no qualms about using the hornet spray against an unscrupulous scoundrel who obviously intended to do some serious damage to Jane. Sydney did not doubt Cunningham had put the man up to the attack. A man without conscience who could use children for his own sexual pleasure was an exploitive reprobate and a man who would not hesitate to destroy another human being.

Sydney knew that if the intruder wanted emergency room treatment, he would have to give out his name and provide some identification. However, she had no doubt the wealthy Cunningham possessed immense resources and could easily replace the injured man.

Knowing there would be new battles ahead, Sydney, still waiting for the crowd to disperse, began to review what Jane had told her earlier. According to Jane, the testimony from

Cunningham's poker playing buddies seemed very damaging. Jane believed the other jurors, like her, had to be seriously questioning what Cunningham had been doing on Grover Street. After hearing this new information, Sydney surmised Cunningham was likely to be running dangerously scared, maybe even desperate. Sydney, a woman who had firsthand knowledge about desperate, sexually perverted men, smiled to herself; her unorthodox sexual backdrop would prove useful in the strategy she was beginning to formulate.

Given her childhood history, Sydney's personal experience with the back-alleys of the sexual underworld was not that unusual. She had no memory of her natural parents. The woman who adopted her had been a shell of a person, an anemic, selfish woman who needed to believe that she could love a child, but whose insecurities made her incapable of providing nurturing love. The man Sydney knew as her father could be summed up in one word: apathetic. With these two people as her lifelines to emotional attachment, it naturally followed that what Sydney most remembered about her younger years was a feeling of being untethered, floating freely in a forbidding, often threatening world with no one to ground her. Like so many adolescent girls who feel the pain of being unattached and unloved, Sydney sought love and belonging in the back seats of cars where, for a few moments at least, she felt desired.

It would take a few years of lingering emptiness after each boy's sexual hunger was satisfied before Sydney would mature enough to realize that adolescent male sexual needs had nothing to do with love. She left home the day she turned eighteen. By that age she was quite familiar and very bored with the sexual needs of boys; she moved on to men where she could at least get money in return for the ceaseless emptiness.

Blessed with a natural beauty, a voluptuous body, and, fortunately, brains, Sydney remained at the lower end of the sex trade business for only one year. In that year, however, she made street contacts in the trade. She continued to nurture many of those contacts today, allowing her to obtain information about potential clients, the high-paying Johns she now serviced. Women who use their bodies to earn a living know they are taking risks and one way to minimize those risks is by sharing the names of dangerous, debasing, and violent men. Sydney decided that she would impose upon her long-held contacts, asking them to help her with her scheme to sabotage Cunningham before he could do harm to Jane.

She emerged from her hiding place only after all the curious neighbors had gone back into their houses. Furtively avoiding any of the street lights, she walked back to her duplex.

Jane opened the door the second Sydney was on the porch. "I'm so glad you're back. I thought those nosey neighbors would never leave!"

"Come on, let's get back into the house. I don't want anyone to see us."

Once inside, Jane said, "It went exactly like you said it would. You predicted he would come in the back and go to the first bedroom. The pillows and wig really fooled him, didn't they? And I got the picture of him with my camera just like you suggested."

Sydney laughed, "Don't you just love what a baby he was, whining 'help me, help me.' It gave me so much pleasure to turn the tables on that thug and give him a dose of his own medicine."

"I don't think I could have done it, Syd. I mean, I know I should have had the courage to do it, but I guess I'm not ready yet."

"Well, you have the grit to stay on the jury and somewhere, deep inside you, you must have a spunky side, the side that made you bite Cunningham when he intended to molest you. Just think about that. You were only a child and you took a chunk out of him. All you need to do now is keep on fighting. Believe me...you'll get in touch with your intrepid self. Just keep reminding yourself you are a Light Warrior."

Instinctively, Jane reached up to touch her pendant, saying, “While you were out there waiting, I couldn’t help but wonder if all of this...you know...my deciding to be on a jury and the defendant being the man from my past...if it all wasn’t preordained. You know, some higher power taking care of me, getting me to face my fears. Although I’m not there yet, or I would have been the one spraying that man in the face.”

“Believe in a higher power if you want, Jane, but I’m betting on you. Like I said, you already have the strength inside you. Okay, so maybe the universe has provided you an opportunity to find that strength, but I don’t think it comes from a higher power. I think it comes from the long buried, forgotten, gutsy you. It’s just a matter of digging it up and using it.”

“You know, Syd, you’re always there for me, always cheering me on. Who would I be without you?”

“Don’t do that, Jane. Stop giving me the credit. Remember, I was the one who said you shouldn’t sit on the jury. You challenged yourself despite my warning, so don’t go giving me credit for what you decided to do.”

“I guess. But I probably would have quit if it hadn’t been for you.”

“Okay, so we’re *Light Warriors* together, which means we have to plan our next strategy and I have an idea about what that should be.”

When Cunningham didn’t hear back from Debeck by ten p.m, the intolerable feeling of helplessness had caused him to take risky action. Rather than drink himself into a stupor as he foolishly had done last night, he chanced being tailed by a zealous media hound and left the house to find a pay phone. His call to Debeck had gone immediately to voice mail. Feeling sure that Debeck would never intentionally leave him in the lurch, the unanswered call left Cunningham with a combination of outrage and trepidation; something had gone very wrong and he was left only with his imagination to figure out what that might be.

After hanging up the pay phone, he drove around for a while to be sure he wasn't being followed. Not knowing what else to do, he took the even riskier action of driving to Debeck's house. He sat in the car for some time, debating about getting out until his distress finally won out. Throwing caution to the wind, he went to the front door and rang the bell. He walked around the house when no one answered the door. His efforts to see in the windows were thwarted by the darkness inside. Then he tried the back door. Finding it locked, the overwrought Cunningham had no options left. The one man he felt confident enough to ask for help had evaporated and Cunningham now found himself without a plan of attack.

Unsure of what he should do, he returned to his car where he sat, mulling over the alien feeling of helplessness he was having. His lifelong obsession was always intensified by stress and his need for the perverted sex that had been his consuming passion was building inside him like steam in a pressure cooker. For a few seconds he considered driving over to Grover Street where the nightmare had all started. This extraordinarily risky action was stopped only by the realization that his very public trial had rid him of all anonymity. His sources of drug-addicted mothers, so desperate for a fix they were willing to trade their daughters for drugs, lived in a single-minded world of self-preservation; television and newspapers were rarely a part of their life. Unfortunately, his face and name had been so front and center in the media for the last few months that even a resolute drug addict may have seen him on television. So, as wretched as he felt, Cunningham realized that recognition by one of his sources was just too big a chance to take.

For a man accustomed to dominance and power, where a solution was always within reach of a telephone, not being able to take corrective action was driving Cunningham mad. Spoiled and pampered from birth, Bradley had never wanted for anything. His single mother, an ascending star in the fashion design world, had not planned on a pregnancy and quickly decided (when informed of the unexpected news) that a child need not be a hurdle. Even before her child was born, she had hired a mature, experienced, full-time nanny to ensure that her child received all the attention a child could ever want.

Until he was six, Bradley had been raised by this nanny, an obedient, devoted, but humorless woman. When she quit to take care of an ailing mother, a new nanny was quickly put in place, a younger, livelier woman with a bubbly personality. The second nanny, Maribel, was more playful but also more easily distracted, especially with telephone calls from her large, extended family. Maribel had many nieces and nephews and, on occasion, would babysit the youngest of the nieces at the Cunningham's house.

One day when Bradley was eight years old and Maribel was on the phone, the niece, an adorable two-and-a-half-year-old, pushed open the slightly ajar bathroom door and wandered inside just as Bradley was finishing taking a pee. She toddled over to him, staring at his exposed penis. Bradley thought this was comical so when the toddler reached out to touch his penis, he didn't stop her. He wasn't prepared, however, for the amazingly delightful sensation that jolted through his body. He stood there transfixed as she fondled it, babbling on about her baby brother's *ninus*. Suddenly, he heard Maribel calling out the toddler's name.

Bradley, old enough to know he shouldn't be letting the little girl play with his penis, was instantly afraid that he might get caught and be scolded for the forbidden behavior. His heart accelerated and his brain automatically pumped adrenaline into his body at the fear of discovery. Riveted in place, however, by the pleasurable sensations, pleasure now exceedingly heightened by the adrenaline, he continued to let the toddler touch him, holding up a finger to his lips to shush the girl.

The hapless eight-year-old boy, mentally wedged between intense gratification and intense fear was in the midst of the perfect chemical storm to create a deviance: innocently, and very unfortunately, giving neural birth to what would become a lifelong perversion.

As Maribel's voice grew louder and closer, Bradley finally removed the little girl's hand, quickly zipped up his pants and whispered to the girl, "It's our secret game. Don't tell anyone, understand?" The toddler nodded with excitement and then turned and ran to the door, calling out her aunt's name. Maribel opened the bathroom door, drawing in a breath as she saw Bradley in the bathroom, now washing his hands. She eyed him suspiciously but said nothing. Instead, she took her niece's hand and walked her out of the bathroom.

At only eight years of age, Bradley was clueless that what had just transpired would eventually grow into enslavement. How could such a young child possibly know that this innocent sexual act with its addictive combination of pleasure and fear would ensure an obsession—would forever scar his young, vulnerable sexuality and reset its normal course of neural development? How could an eight-year-old anticipate that this faultless but highly erotic act would redirect the objects of his sexual desires? How could the young Bradley Cunningham, who never before had been a sly, sneaky child, foresee that he would grow into a lifelong, cunning predator? How could he have predicted that he would, from this moment forward, hope every day that the toddler would be there when he got home from school?

Yet this is exactly what happened to the still forming brain of young Bradley. With the wiring in his brain reset on a destructive path, Bradley became a plotting schemer, finding devious ways to repeat the erotic scene with the unwitting little girl he brought into his "secret game just between the two of us." His conniving game was replicated many more times in the next two years, ending only when the little girl became old enough for preschool and no longer needed to be watched by her aunt. Bradley's ten-year-old mind slowly let the exciting game fade from awareness. However, when his adolescent hormones kicked in a few years later, the normal heterosexual teen dating and sex play left him uninterested and sexually unaroused. Instead, the need to replicate the earlier arousing mixture of fear and eroticism came roaring back.

Compelled by a power greater than reason, Bradley, at only fifteen years of age, found himself returning to his con artist ways, hunting for unwitting little girls he could find to bring into his "secret game of doctor." He was surprised at how easy it was to find several young neighborhood girls whom he could bring into his games. However, the older he became, the more difficult it was to find young girls for his game without raising suspicion. So, with plenty of money available to him, a seventeen-year-old Bradley began to pay for his sexual pleasures.

Almost five decades had passed and Bradley had been able to keep his strategy of *paying to play* under the radar until months ago when he foolishly stopped his car to check on a body in the road.

It was now approaching two a.m. and Cunningham was still anxiously sitting in his car outside Debeck's home. He was beyond furious, reliving in his mind every detail that had gone against him the last twenty-four hours. First, Rose had walked out on him. Then, the one man he thought he could depend on, had left only a single cryptic phone message before disappearing without a trace. Next up: his own friends had been forced to testify against him. Even though he knew it was coming, listening to his poker buddies had been more difficult to hear than he had imagined; he hadn't needed Dr. Halloway's expertise to tell him the jury had been negatively swayed by their testimony. To make matters worse, Juror Seven, who had been giving him that steely stare in the morning, had not hidden her smugness when the last of his buddies stepped down from the stand. Then, at the lunch break, RJ nipped at his butt yet again. Having nothing to counter with on cross examination of his poker friends, RJ had been livid about Bradley's stubborn refusal to explain the missing hour and a half. With all this on his plate, he also had to factor in the annoying media; they would have a field day with the incriminating testimony of his friends; tomorrow's headlines were sure to suck him even further down the drain.

Cunningham, powerless and feeling defeated, was about to start the car and head back home when a taxi drove up and parked ten feet behind him. He automatically scooted down far enough so he couldn't be seen but could watch what was happening in his rearview and side mirrors. The taxi driver got out of the car, opened the back door, and guided a man out. Cunningham could see that the man had bandages over his eyes. The taxi driver led the man up the walk to Debeck's house and that's when Cunningham concluded it must be Debeck. The realization caused a sinking feeling in the pit of his stomach. His earlier fear that something terrible had gone wrong was now proving correct. *God damn! Could things really be getting worse than they already were?* Cunningham started to get out of the car to help Debeck into his house, but then realized it wouldn't be a good idea for him to be seen by the driver. Waiting until the driver helped Debeck inside the house and drove off, he got out of his car, walked to the front door, and rang the bell.

From behind the closed door Debeck yelled, "What? I didn't give you a big enough tip?"

Bradley didn't want to bring attention to himself by yelling loudly enough to be heard through the door so he just rang the doorbell again. He heard a crashing sound and some cursing before the door opened and Debeck screamed, "What the fuck do you want?"

Quietly, Cunningham said, "Stop yelling, Debeck. It's me, Bradley. Let me in before someone sees us."

Debeck stepped aside. "Come in, but you're not going to like what I have to say."

Cunningham stepped inside, closing the door behind him. "What the hell happened to you," he hissed? "I've been going crazy with worry."

"As you should," Debeck replied. "Right now I need to sit down." He turned back toward the living room, shuffling along, hands out in front as he continued, “You sent me after a she-devil. As you can tell, the devil won.”

Cunningham caught up to him, taking his elbow while escorting the bandaged man into the living room and onto a sofa. After Debeck was seated, Cunningham asked, “I don’t understand. When did this happen?”

“I lost track of time...earlier, some hours ago. The bitch sprayed me in the face with hornet spray while I was in her home.”

“Well, shit! Obviously, you didn’t get my message calling off our original plan.”

Exasperated, Debeck slumped in his seat, his bandaged head now in his hands. “You’re fucking shitting me, Bradley. You changed your mind?”

“Yes, earlier today and I called you immediately.”

“Well, I didn’t get your message because I fell asleep from the drugs I had to take to kill the pain from the fractured arm the bitch gave me yesterday. Then I accidentally left my phone at home this afternoon because I was late getting to the courthouse.” Debeck shook his head. “And now you’re telling me everything I’ve been through was for shit.”

“Fractured arm? What the hell, Debeck? Start from the beginning, okay?”

“Right. So, yesterday, I followed the bitch to her home. I thought I got lucky because she went for a bike ride but when I tried to shove her off the road, she hit my arm with some kind of weapon...spent hours in the ER. Then, I overslept this afternoon so I hurried to the courthouse and got there just in time...but couldn’t spot her leaving. Tonight I broke into her house. That’s when the bitch sprayed me in the face with the God damn hornet spray and then called 911. I just got home from the ER *again*.”

Cunningham, mouth agape, was speechless. He finally managed to ask, “911? Shit. Does this mean the police got involved?”

Debeck gave a big sigh, then reached out with his hand, feeling for the sofa's arm before slowly lowering himself to a reclining position. "I'm going to be okay in a few days. Turns out I won't be permanently blinded, but thanks for asking."

"Sorry, pal. Forgive me if I've been a tad self-absorbed...given I may be going to prison soon."

"Yeah, yeah...I can see...nix that...I get it that you've been worried. However, I checked and she didn't report the incident on the bicycle. Unless the lunatic decides to call the police tonight, you should be clear. But I'm pretty sure she won't be telling anyone. After she hit me with the spray, she anonymously called 911 and intentionally walked me down the street from her house. The ambulance took me to the ER and they asked a lot of questions for which I gave them a lot of bullshit. But since the cops never showed up they finally had to let me go. I'm thinking she doesn't want the police involved...you know, like she's making sure she isn't taken off the jury."

"God damn it. For the life of me I can't figure out this whacky woman. All day today she glared at me like I did something personal to her. I don't remember ever seeing this woman before but maybe...well, when I called you this afternoon, I wanted to ask you to nose around, maybe dig up something my lawyer could use to get her off the jury and put in an alternate. That's why I called you at the lunch break."

"Man...it's crap about my phone. I could have saved myself the pain and aggravation if I had just gotten your message. After she fractured my arm, I was so doped up on pain pills I wasn't thinking straight."

"I gotta ask, Debeck. How could a wimpy woman like this one fracture *your* arm?"

Debeck, beginning to fade, shook his head, saying drowsily, "Good question. It seemed like a simple plan. Just drive by, give her a little push, put her in the hospital like you asked. I reached out to shove her...man, I think it was some kind of pipe she used to whack my arm."

Cunningham began pacing, saying, "It's all so insane. I'm on trial for something I didn't do and there is some unhinged woman on the jury who's taking it personally and seems determined to make sure I'm convicted. I need your help to find out how I can get rid of her. Thank God it's the weekend. It will give us two days to figure out what we should do."

Debeck, now considerably more sluggish from the pain medication, mumbled, "No good for a couple of days...Yoga maybe..."

"Yoga? What the hell?" Cunningham walked over to the sofa, knelt down, and shook Debeck. "Don't fade on me yet. You're talking nonsense."

Debeck, eyes now slits, said, "Can't help...."

Cunningham shook him. "Look, I'm going to send over a nurse to stay with you until you can see." Debeck didn't answer. Cunningham shook him again. "Are you listening to me?"

Debeck muttered, "Yeah. Nurse." Then he passed out.

DAYS SIX AND SEVEN

Before going to bed Friday night, Erin decided she deserved to sleep in and skip her usual Saturday eight a.m. aerobics class, promising herself she would go to the gym later and do both the cardio machines and the weights. She took a sleeping pill and although she was awakened during the night by the usual hot flashes, she went back to sleep and did not open her eyes until almost nine. It was glorious sleep, the best she'd had since she reluctantly agreed to work with the maddening RJ. For a change, she lingered in bed, daydreaming.

The leisurely morning was just what she needed to reenergize, especially since tonight she would be taking Toby out for the promised dinner at the Blue Fin. This blossoming relationship had caught her completely off-guard. No way could she have predicted a black, former NFL player turned private investigator might occupy even a moment of her romantic thoughts. Yet here she was enlivened, maybe even a little intoxicated, with fantasies about the evening ahead of her. She thought about what she might wear, deciding it needed to be elegantly sexy, alluring but tasteful, classy but definitely not professional. She took a mental inventory of her closet, trying to picture her choices and came to the conclusion that it had been so long since she had dated, she couldn't remember if she had anything that fit her criteria.

She finally got out of bed and padded into the kitchen for coffee. Using the kitchen counter as a bar, she did a few stretching exercises while the coffee brewed, taking deep breaths and enjoying the aroma of the coffee as it dripped into the glass carafe. Pouring herself a large mug, she returned to the bedroom and inspected her closet, a closet filled mostly with business suits, casual wear, and workout clothes. She found three cocktail dresses from her years with Aaron when she had attended corporate parties. She took them out of the closet and hung them on the back of her bedroom door. As she stepped back to appraise them, she was unexpectedly flooded with memories of Aaron. Tears formed in her eyes and she walked over to her bedside table to get a tissue, chastising herself: *Don't go there. You've spent too many years living in the past...time to move forward.* She wiped her eyes, took a deep breath and returned to studying the dresses, immediately deciding they were filled with too many memories and were way overplayed for tonight—but just right for a trip to the thrift store which was on the way to the gym and was only a couple of miles from Nordstrom. The thought of shopping for something other than a professional outfit brought her mood back around to her earlier Prince Charming fantasies. Toby Parish intrigued her, the first man to do so in many years and she was way overdue for some romantic adventure.

However, before feeding this new spirit of potential romance with a shopping spree, she wanted to get some reading out of the way. Returning to the kitchen, she made a piece of whole wheat toast and refreshed her coffee, both of which she carried into her office. She stood in front of her bookcase searching for her *DSM-IV*, the Diagnostic and Statistical Manual of Mental Disorders, a manual widely used by professionals for diagnosing mental disorders. It was a book put together by psychiatrists and psychologists that gave labels to a specific group of behaviors. For the most part, Erin didn't like labeling people as abnormal, but she had to admit that at times labels were a professional shortcut that could be helpful. She hefted the tome down to her desk and looked in the Table of Contents for the topic, Schizoid Personality Disorder. In one hand she munched on her toast while the other flipped through the pages for the section she wanted.

All week long, Jane Nichols had grown into an increasing enigma for Erin. From the get-go, she had thought Seven was a woman with some troubling psychological problems. Now with the traumatic childhood history that Toby discovered and the increasingly strange behavior that Seven had been exhibiting during the trial, Erin felt it was likely Jane had one of the labels in the book.

When she came to the section on the label, Schizoid Personality Disorder, she looked at the behavioral criteria for the condition.

1. *Neither desires nor enjoys close relationships, including being part of a family*
2. *Almost always chooses solitary activities*
3. *Has little, if any, interest in having sexual experiences with another person*
4. *Takes pleasure in few, if any, activities*
5. *Lacks close friends or confidants other than first-degree relatives*
6. *Appears indifferent to the praise or criticism of others*
7. *Shows emotional coldness, detachment, or flattened affect*

Erin knew that the jury system, with a voir dire questionnaire intended to determine one's ability to be impartial, was not designed to detect serious psychological problems; a fact that made an astute jury consultant invaluable. During the voir dire, lawyers had the right to ask a potential juror questions about their views on a variety of issues they thought would tell them something about the prospective juror's beliefs. However, asking direct questions about one's mental health...well, that had to be done surreptitiously. It took a trained person to make correct inferences from answers to camouflaged questions.

The DSM IV described behaviors that were not elicited on a cursory juror questionnaire or by questions allowed to be asked by attorneys. These were behaviors that could not be confirmed without further investigation, the kind of snooping that could get the defense in trouble for jury tampering if it were discovered after a juror was impaneled. As Erin reread the list of behaviors in her manual, she felt sure, even if she couldn't prove it, that Jane

Nichols was a Schizoid Personality type, especially since this type was usually the result of severe childhood trauma involving issues of intimacy and attachment.

The regrettable thing about a person who has a Schizoid personality is that the person doesn't act mad-as-a-hatter-crazy, the kind of crazy that gets people's attention. They go unnoticed, ending up as a parent, spouse, coworker, or neighbor. Superficial relationships in the person's life usually don't reveal the disturbed behavior boiling under the surface. However, anyone trying to form a longer-term intimate attachment with a schizoid personality type would find the experience similar to trying to cut through an overdone steak: they would have to work tirelessly to get through its tough, outer surface only to discover inside an unyielding, dispassionate, flavorless inner center. Still, some Schizoid types did marry, become parents, coworkers, and, unfortunately, jurors.

Slapping the book closed, Erin regrettably acknowledged that unless Jane Nichols started acting outwardly bonkers, she would be staying on the jury. During deliberations a Schizoid Personality type could be quietly unyielding, likely causing the remaining jurors to pull out their hair. As Erin returned the book to the shelf, she said aloud, "Too bad, Reverend, you should have listened to me."

Erin returned to the kitchen for a bowl of oatmeal before dressing for the day. She packed her bag for the gym and gathered up the three dresses to take to the thrift store. After dropping off the clothes, she did an hour and a half workout at the gym, took a shower, and then drove over to Nordstrom where she ate a light lunch in their restaurant and shopped in the store's sale racks. Although she could afford the outrageous prices, Erin enjoyed finding bargains, treasures others had deemed unworthy. She found a gem, an eggplant colored, short-sleeved, fitted knit sheath that was belted at the waist and hung mid calf, a perfect length for her leather boots. It was trimmed in leather at the neck and sleeves and fit her like a glove, showing off her curves but without being excessively clingy. The bonus was she already owned the perfect blazer to wear over the dress. She headed for home feeling she couldn't have asked for a better day.

Or so she thought. Before she could even hang up her new purchase, her cell phone rang. She tossed the dress on the bed and dug her phone out of her purse. Looking at the caller ID, her stomach lurched in anticipation of something gone wrong. She answered the call by saying, "Please don't tell me I bought a new dress for nothing."

"You bought a new dress for me?"

"Yes, I did. Tell me, am I going to be wearing it?"

"Depends."

"On what?"

"On how sexy it is."

Erin could feel herself blush. *Had Toby been reading her mind?* "Hold on a minute...what exactly does that means?"

"I'm in need of a slutty woman to help me on tonight's assignment."

"And you think I fit the bill?"

"I guess that came out wrong. I meant it as a compliment because you have to have it to flaunt it."

"Thanks, I guess. So tell me, something about the word slutty makes me need to ask...is this assignment dangerous?"

"Well, not dangerous to life and limb, but it does involves talking to some unsavory characters."

Erin was quiet for a few moments before saying, "Let me guess. The Reverend Jove wants you to snoop around the Grover Street area and see if you can find out exactly what his client was doing there on the morning of the hit and run."

"I can see why you get paid the big bucks. You're very perceptive."

"I don't suppose the esteemed Mr. Cunningham has approved this."

"Not likely, but I didn't ask. RJ's paying my bill, regardless."

" I guess I'm not surprised RJ decided to take some action after yesterday's testimony. He had nothing to counter with on cross so he was left looking ineffectual. And I don't have to tell you how much he hates that. He was fuming when he left the courtroom. So, you haven't told me...exactly what am I supposed to do?"

"I'm playing the role of a pimp. You'd get to play the part of my 'ho."

"A whore? Hmm, how lucky can a girl get? Before I agree to *that*, you'd better tell me exactly what crazy plan you have in mind."

"Okay, here's the scoop. I'm the pimp and you're my whore. I put some makeup on you so it looks like you've been beat up. Then we go to Grover Street where I show Cunningham's picture around to the *other* working girls, asking if they know him. They're always more cooperative if they think there is an abusive man out trolling."

"Aren't I a little old for the part?"

"You'd be surprised. Lots of *mature* woman are still out there turning tricks."

Erin laughed, "Mature woman? Well, aren't you being politically correct. You realize, of course, I've never done anything like this in my life. I don't suppose RJ knows you're including me in this assignment?"

"I thought it was a need to know only situation."

"You realize, of course, if he found out, I would likely lose my job, maybe even my career."

"Yes, there's that. However, with the dress and makeup, I think it would be impossible to recognize you."

" I'd be insane to do this, you know."

"Trust me, Erin, given all the insane things I've done in my life, this one is tame."

"If this is tame then I guess your life is worlds apart from mine."

"Why not think of it as an opportunity to merge the two worlds."

"Hmm, I have to give you credit for being a consummate negotiator. So, if I were to say yes, what happens next?"

"I'm going to assume the dress you bought today wouldn't be described as slutty, right?"

"God I hope not!"

"So, we'll go shopping at the thrift store for an appropriate outfit and a wig. Next we get something to eat, then get you dressed and ready to experience first hand the other side of the tracks."

"I can't believe I'm saying this but it sounds fun...perilous but exciting. If I didn't trust you, I wouldn't do it."

"So, you're in?"

"What the hell...yes, I'm in."

"Okay, I'll pick you up in a half hour."

The moment Erin hung up, she began to have doubts. Nothing in her past had prepared her for taking such an outlandish risk. Her entire life had been spent doing due diligence, working towards goals, all to overcome the long ago handicap that had slapped her down. She was at the pinnacle of her career with a reputation to protect, and a few moments ago she had agreed to pretend she was a prostitute.

She walked into the bedroom and stood in front of the mirror, asking herself, *Have you lost your mind? Are you doing this just to please a man you have schoolgirl fantasies about and hardly know?* The face that stared back at her said, *Let loose for a change. You've always been such a prude. This man might just show you that life has a lot more to offer than just hard work. Besides, if you're even thinking about a relationship with this man, you will eventually have to merge two very different worlds.*

Erin turned around, picked up her new dress from the bed, and hung it in the closet. She started going through her alternative options for the evening. She was going on a date to a thrift shop instead of the Blue Fin so jeans seemed to be in order. She grabbed a pair of her most comfortable jeans and then a white, cotton, crew neck sweater and placed them on the bed, feeling chagrined as she reflected on the juvenile daydreams she had entertained until Toby called.

With her fairy-tale mood gone, she was confronted with the reality of a potential relationship with Toby. A dinner at a fancy restaurant with him would have been a one time, engaging evening. However, she should know better than to play with fantasies about coalescing two very different biographies, two backstories that had little in common. The two of them might work in the short run when the newness caused the excitement and passion to run high, but she knew it wasn't sustainable. Novelty and passion inevitably wane and two people need common values as a strong foundation if a relationship is to survive the storms of life.

She had agreed to go outside her comfort zone to please him. Was she being foolish? She reached for her phone to call Toby, began dialing his number, then threw the phone and herself on the bed. Staring at the ceiling, her mind rehashed her options: go with her intellect or go with imprudent indulgence. Her internal debate had not been settled when the doorbell rang. Glancing at the clock she realized he was right on time. She smiled to herself as she realized she was guilty of the psychological trick of subliminal decision by not making a decision. Toby was here and if she backtracked now, she would feel even more foolish. She hurried into the bathroom, ran a comb through her hair, opened the front door and moved aside to let the large man come in.

As he passed her, she said, "I'm not going to wimp out on you, but I can't say this is the smartest decision I've made in my life."

"There is more than one kind of smart," Toby replied. "I learned a lot while I was in college, but I really learned how much I didn't know when I started working the streets."

"Ah, so you're talking street smarts?"

"Yes, I am. I asked you to do this for several reasons. First, I'd enjoy your company, but I also think you could benefit from stepping out from behind the pages of textbooks...you know, get cozier with the people you're paid to analyze."

Erin didn't answer. Instead, she turned and walked into her living room. Toby followed, looking around at the eclectic choice of furnishings and art. "Wow!" he said. Your place is fascinating. You have a little bit of everything here. You probably did all this yourself, right?"

"Yes, I did and thank you. I enjoy too many different styles to be stuck with one theme."

"The colors all work together, though. So even if the styles are different it comes together through color."

"Thanks. I appreciate your astute perception," she said, as she conceded to herself that she had yet again underestimated the man. Maybe she was miscalculating the differences in their values. After all, what did she really know about him? Just now she learned he knew something about decorative style and color and had gone to college, the college part something she had unthinkingly (and prejudicially?) assumed he had not done. If she had given it some thought, she would have realized that most pro ball players begin their careers in college. "So, you're telling me you thought I could benefit from leaving my ivory tower."

"Yes, and I hope I haven't misjudged you here. I thought about that stepping-out-from-your-textbook statement by the way, and decided you were openminded enough for me to say it...that you wouldn't be insulted."

"I'm not at all insulted but to be honest, I can't say that I trust your motive."

Toby screwed up his mouth in a look of puzzlement, replying, “My motive? What does that mean?”

“I don’t know if you’ve intentionally done it, but you have created a situation of cognitive dissonance.” Seeing the baffled look on Toby’s face, Erin continued, “A situation where I’m forced to choose between conflicting principles. In this situation, if I want to think of myself as open-minded, and who wouldn’t, then I’m forced to make the choice you want me to make or, by default, I end up being defined as rigid rather than flexible.”

Toby laughed. “I’m not sure I understand what you just said, but I’m one hundred percent sure you just proved my point.” Shaking his head, he continued, “You live inside a textbook, Erin. Who the hell but academics talk like that?”

Erin was silent, walking over to her burnt orange and plum chaise lounge and taking a seat. She looked up at the giant of a man, saying, “You know, you’re right. Only *eggheads* talk like that.” She paused for a moment before continuing, “So, let me restate my dilemma in plain English. You’re saying if I stay in my academic shell, I’ll eventually get hardboiled. But what I’m saying is....if I crack the egg, I risk being fried.”

Toby started laughing, a gentle laugh that grew into a hearty laugh that expanded into a big belly laugh, the contagious, snowballing kind that infected Erin as well. Toby was laughing so hard he had to move over and hold on to a chair. When he finally got the laughing under control, he said, “You are so full of surprises. I just don’t know what to think of you.”

Erin, still with tears in her eyes, replied, “Well, ditto about you!”

Their eyes met and held for a few seconds, each feeling something pass between them that they didn’t want to disturb, yet didn’t feel at ease with either. It was Erin who broke the silence. She smiled slyly at Toby, saying, “I think we both just had a moment of cognitive dissonance.” Toby started laughing again.

Erin stood up, saying, "Okay, I guess I'm making the choice to be fried rather than boiled. At least that way I could end sunny-side up. So, tell me, what does a girl wear to go thrift store shopping?"

Toby laughed again, saying,"What you have on is just fine. But you will need to bring a pair of those CFM shoes like you had on the other day. The spike heeled shoes are standard fare."

"I don't know how long I can last in those shoes. Normally, I only wear them on days when I have to be in court where I'm sitting most of the day."

"I'll be sure to let you take some breaks, then."

Toby drove to a thrift store in a part of town where Erin had never been. As soon as she stepped inside, she felt assaulted by a foreign lifestyle, almost as if she was in another country. This store, nothing like the store where she had earlier dropped off her dresses, was much smaller, smelled unpleasantly musty, was crowded with people talking in a variety of languages, and was jam-packed with round racks of wrinkled, gaudy, cheap clothes. Everything about the place made her aware that she was purposely slumming. She felt embarrassed and even creepy, feelings that caused her to yet again question her motives. Was she here to expand her reality or was she just trying to please Toby?

Toby seemed to feel right at home and went over to a rack of clothes. He was now holding up something on a hanger; it was shiny, gold, small and quite ugly; exactly what the object could be mystified Erin. He had a serious look on his face when he said, "I think this would do the trick to turn some tricks."

Erin frowned, saying, "Very funny. What is it?"

"I'm not sure but it looks skimpy enough to turn heads."

She walked over to him and took the hanger out of his hand, turning the mystery object in several directions. "I can't tell whether it's a tube top or a skirt."

"You think it matters?"

Erin's head shot up, giving Toby a stunned look. His lips were tight, almost in a pout and she could tell he was trying hard not to smile.

"You're toying with me."

Now he had a large grin on his face, saying, "You're right. I am. You look so out of your element I thought you needed some help lightening up."

"Yeah, well you're right. I am out of my element." Holding the garment next to her body, Erin said, "I'm beginning to wonder if you're just a T & A man and this whole scheme is a just a ploy to see mine."

"Guilty as charged. I am definitely a T & A man."

"Damn you, Toby. You could at least be a little more defensive. That way I could get a better read on you."

"Read? Still don't trust me, huh?"

Erin narrowed her brows in thought, finally saying, "I think it's me I don't trust. I'm wondering if I'm playing along just to please you."

"And that's bad how?"

His question stopped her. All along she had presumed going along with his plan just to please him was unacceptable. Now, however, confronted with her assumption, she had to ask herself why. *Hadn't she bought a dress just to please him? So, was she being a hypocrite? It was all right to please him with a dress from Nordstrom's but not from a thrift shop.* She smiled up at him, replying, "Your question deserves a thoughtful answer...one best not answered while we're shopping for floozy clothes. Is it okay if we discuss this further at dinner?"

"Sure," Toby said.

Erin returned the shiny, gold undetermined piece of clothing back to the rack, saying, "I have my limits and this thingamajig crosses it."

She began looking through the rack of clothing in front of her, shaking her head in dismay at the sheer tackiness of what she was looking at. The clothes in front of her were the kind of items all teenage girls were wearing these days. Apparently, exposing a good deal of your body was the current rage. She thought the young girls were just asking for trouble by wearing these tawdry, come-hither fashions. A woman her age would look ludicrous not seductive in these clothes, unless, of course, she was intending to snare a concupiscent male. (*Ha! Toby would love that a word.*) The thought of Toby made her wonder where he was and she was about to look for him when he tapped her on the shoulder. She turned toward him; he was holding up two items, a coppery red, skimpy skirt and a pearl-white, stretch-lace, see-through blouse with a low-cut neckline.

"These looks about your size. What do you think," he asked?

"They looks like something a prostitute would wear."

"Perfect, huh?"

"I don't know...."

"Try it on."

"I'm not sure...."

"Come on, Rapunzel, let down your hair, decamp from your tower."

"Shit, Toby, you're really going to make me do this?"

Toby shoved the two hangers at her, turned her toward the dressing room, and gave her a little push, saying, "Go!"

Erin took a few steps in the direction Toby had pushed her and immediately stopped when she noticed that there were four women waiting in line to get into two bathroom size stalls with only a curtain for privacy. The women, all with several outfits in their hands, were chatting away with each other. No way I'm waiting for a chance to have a claustrophobic moment in a grungy cubbyhole, she thought. She headed back toward Toby, who was busy looking at a platinum, shoulder length wig.

"There's a line to get into the so-called dressing rooms."

"So, I'm not in a hurry."

Erin shoved the skirt toward Toby, saying, "Here, hold this." She scrounged around inside the blouse for a size, finally finding the faded label where she could barely make out the printed size eight. "This will do. I don't need to try it on. Give me the skirt." Erin exchanged the blouse for the skirt. The label was torn out so she held the skirt next to her body. It had some stretch to it. "I guess this will do as well. Let's get out of here."

Toby cocked his head, giving her a disgruntled look. He started to say something, then changed his mind. Instead, he held up the wig. "What do you think?"

Erin arched her eyebrows at Toby. "It's atrocious, but it looks the part. Let's go."

Toby tossed the wig back on the shelf, saying in an annoyed tone, "Why don't we blow off this ruse? Evidently, you're not going to have fun with this and your attitude is beginning to piss me off."

Toby's testy words gave Erin pause. She felt the heat rise in her neck as she realized he was right. *I am behaving like a spoiled, elitist child? Why can't I have fun instead of being such a pretentious curmudgeon?* The inner questions caused her to conclude: *My behavior is a defense—but against what?* The more she thought about it the more she realized that it was fear. She smiled to herself when she realized that she was afraid of exposing her own buried exhibitionistic fantasies.

"What?" asked Toby.

"I think I just figured out why I'm behaving like a colossal chump. "Come on," she said, as she picked up the wig. "Let's get in the check out line and we'll talk about it at dinner."

They ate at a local dive where Toby had promised the food was outstanding. He was right. Over a huge rack of ribs, the most delicious coleslaw Erin had ever had, and an ice cold beer, she explained to him why she had been behaving like a jackass. She told him about losing her hearing, about being teased as a result of her early sexual development, about her fight to prove herself by overachieving, about being afraid to be seen as using her femininity rather than her accomplishments to get ahead, about her conundrum over pleasing a man, and finally (embarrassingly) about her fear of her own exhibitionist fantasies.

Toby listened without interrupting, noticing the blush on Erin's face as she mentioned the fantasy. When she was done talking, he reached across the table and put his hand on hers, saying, "I'm certainly not an expert on women, but you seem to have nicely weathered all that history. You're one remarkable woman, Erin."

"Thank you, Toby."

"As for the exhibitionist fantasies, well, according to Shere Hite they're very common in women."

Surprised, Erin straightened up in her chair. "Shere Hite? I thought you said you were no expert on women?"

"So I read *The Hite Report on Female Sexuality*, that certainly doesn't qualify me as an expert."

"Out of a hundred men, how many do you think have read *The Hite Report*?

"Not many, but she's a sociologist and that was my major in college."

"Well, I'll be damned."

"What? I don't *look* like a sociology major?"

"That's a loaded question and you know it." Erin grinned sheepishly, saying, "You're not going to catch me admitting I'm stereotyping."

"No, I guess not." Toby glanced at his watch before saying, "Okay, so now that we both understand why you were such a grouch, do you think you can be a good sport? Because we have an appointment with a true expert on women."

"Hmm. Now you got me curious! Yes, I promise I'll go with the flow. So, tell me more about your mystery expert."

"Nope, I think not. You said you'd go with the flow. So, this joint we'll blow, make a stop for a show, then head to skid row."

Even though the restaurant was crowded and noisy, Erin's laughter received some inquisitive looks from the diners at the surrounding tables.

Back in the car, Erin began asking questions about the so-called expert on women. The only thing Toby would say was, "You'll have to wait and see" and "I'm testing your ability to go with the flow." Twenty minutes later they were in a residential area with older, smaller homes with tidy yards. Toby took out his cell phone and dialed a number, saying, "We're just around the corner." Then he hung up and a minute later parked in front of one of the houses. He said, "Okay. Grab your bag of haute couture and your CFM shoes. It's party time."

Erin, intrigued but also nervous about this mysterious adventure, ordered herself to do as she had promised: keep quiet and go with the flow. She grabbed the bag of thrift store clothes and shoved her high heeled shoes inside. Toby had come around the car to open the door and help her out. They walked up to the already opened door where a tall, slender woman with long red hair and generously applied make-up greeted them. She was wearing snug fitting shorts over lacy white tights, a long sleeved, high-neck, stretchy top that showed her well-endowed chest, and knee-high, four inch heeled boots. The woman opened the door for them, saying in a throaty voice, "Come in, please."

Erin hesitantly stepped inside, followed by Toby. The living room was small and sparsely furnished with one small sofa and one well-used lounge chair with a TV tray sitting beside it. The walls were bare except for a giant, flat screened TV against the wall opposite the lounge chair. The room was opened to a galley style kitchen.

Toby said to the woman, "I'd like you to meet the academician I told you about. This is Dr. Erin Halloway."

Hearing herself described this way, Erin immediately felt like some sort of experiment, even more so because the woman was obviously ogling her body. Remembering her promise, however, she extended her hand, saying, "Hi, Please call me Erin."

The woman took her hand, giving her a very firm handshake while saying in a very deep, male voice, "Nice to meet you Erin. I'm Mitchell." Then in the previous throaty but higher voice he said, "Or Michele, depending on what's called for."

Erin was stunned. She looked over at a grinning Toby who said, "Mitchell is undercover vice and an expert on how to dress like a hooker. He's going to help get you ready for the evening."

"Come," Mitchell said, as he turned and headed into the hallway. Erin, still taken aback, followed her he-she host down the hall into a small bedroom that had been turned into what looked like a theatre dressing room. A long rack of garish clothing was against one wall, a full length mirror hung on another wall. Against another wall was a beat-up, metal desk with a lightbulb encased mirror, serving as a dressing table. On top of the improvised dressing table were a variety of wigs, jewelry, and make-up trays. A well-used office chair was shoved up under the jury-rigged dressing table.

Mitchell said, "Welcome to my morphing room." Extending his hand toward the bag Erin was holding, he added, "Okay, let's see what you got."

With trepidation, Erin pliantly handed over the bag. Mitchell rolled the office chair out and dumped the bag on its seat. He lifted the platinum wig from the bag, frowning as he held it up. "All wrong," he said. Then he held up the short skirt, eyed Erin up and down again before saying, "Passable." Then he held up the see-through lace top, shaking his head affirmatively before saying, "Good choice." He handed the two items to Erin, saying, "There's a bathroom down the hall. Let's see how you look."

Erin looked over at Toby who was doing his best to look innocent of any duplicity. She shook her head in exasperation but took the clothing and headed down the hall. She surveyed the utilitarian bathroom, so small she could have fit two inside the Nordstrom's dressing room she had been in just that morning, a comparison which made her ruminate on how differently her evening was transpiring from her morning fantasies. She put the thrift store clothes on the only space she could find: the toilet seat. She undressed and temporarily had to pile her clothes on top of the others. She lifted out the formfitting, lacy blouse, realizing for the first time that it had a zipper in the back and an unpleasant musty smell. Wrinkling her nose, she halfway unzipped the blouse and shimmied into it, forced to leave it party open in the back because she couldn't reach the zipper. The shiny, copper-red miniskirt had a wide elastic band at the waist and was easy to step into and pull up. There was only a small medicine cabinet mirror in the bathroom so Erin had no idea how she looked, but she was confident it wasn't the look she had planned for her evening out with Toby. She slid into her high heels, took a deep breath, and warily walked back down the hall to the repurposed bedroom.

Erin noticed Toby's eyes widen when he saw but he quickly resumed a neutral face. Mitchell's eyes narrowed in scrutiny before saying in a commanding voice, "Turn around slowly."

Erin, feeling self-conscious, ignored the order, testily saying, "This ridiculous blouse has a damn zipper I can't reach."

There was an awkward moment before Toby walked over to her and said, "I'll get it." Erin swiveled so her back was to Toby. He zipped up the blouse and then stepped back.

Mitchell, unruffled by Erin's piqued mood, said, "Okay, now do a slow three-sixty and let me take a look."

Erin's initial instinct was to resist being directed and she opened her mouth to object, but closed it when she saw the reprimanding look on Toby's face. Okay, she thought, *as long as I'm playing the role I might as well ham it up*. She pictured Jamie

Lee Curtis in her black panties and bra in the movie, *True Lies,* and assumed a seductive posture as she did a slow pole-dance turn.

"Yeah, the outfit will do just fine," Mitchell said with a salacious male grin on his female face.

Erin glanced at Toby who did a zipping motion across his mouth before moving toward the wall, leaning against it with arms crossed in his usual waiting pose.

Mitchell pointed to the makeshift dresser, saying, "Sit. Now we'll do the hair and makeup." Erin took a seat in the chair and Mitchell picked up a brush from the dresser, brushing Erin's own straight, bobbed hair back from around her face before fitting the wig cap over her head. With the cap on, Erin thought she looked like a cancer patient on chemotherapy. Mitchell lifted an auburn, shoulder-length, wavy-haired wig from its stand on the makeshift dressing table and slipped it on Erin's head. She was astounded at the immediate transformation from a sickly woman to playful coquette. "Wow!" slipped out of Erin's mouth. "I don't look anything like myself."

Mitchell replied, "I know. We all live under the manipulative influence of visual typecasting but never realize it until we can see it reflected back in the mirror." Thumbing his finger toward Toby, Mitchell continued, "Your friend here will always be labeled threatening, for example, just because he's a big guy. Because I was slim for a guy, I walked around all my life with a label of effeminate. I always wanted to be a stage actor but, like *Tootsie*, I was never 'quite right for the part.' I worked out, put on some weight and still couldn't make a living as an actor. But, hey, look at me now. I'm using my acting skills on a different kind of stage where my typecast body is perfect for the part."

Erin mused, "In my work, I've always known that visual image is a form of communication. However, you're right about not being confronted with your own self-typecasting until you try to change it and see it reflected back." Pointing at her reflection in the mirror, Erin said, " Who *is* that I see? I've lived so long with my image of...what would you call it? Umm...professional, I guess. I mean, almost all my life I've wanted to be taken seriously so I intuitively knew I had to look formidable. That's certainly not what I see looking back at me now."

"Well, when I finish with you, you'll still look like a professional, but it will be quite a different profession from the one you're in now. You'll be in the world's oldest profession."

Mitchell swiveled Erin toward him and began deftly applying makeup from the various containers on the dressing table. Five minutes later he stepped back, turned her back toward the mirror and said, "Voilà!"

Erin stared at herself, not able to absorb the character looking back at her. "Toby, you were right," she said. "No one would recognize me. I don't even recognize me."

"Stand up," Mitchell said. "Come, look at yourself in the full-length mirror."

Erin, as if in a hypnotic state, did as she was told. Standing in front of the mirror, she seemed to slowly come out of her reverie. She kept shaking her head as she turned her back to the mirror several times, saying, "Unbelievable. I'm fifty and I look like a thirty-something hooker. Who would have thunk it?"

Toby pushed away from the wall, saying, "You must be in shock. You just let slip your real age."

"I didn't...did I?"

"You did."

"Well, damn. Given how I look and what I'm conniving to do, I guess I won't forget my fiftieth birthday."

"Wait a minute. It's your birthday today?" Toby asked.

"Not exactly, but close enough for me to associate this evening with the big five-0."

Toby held up his iPhone, asking, "All right if I take a few pictures for your scrapbook?"

"Wait! No. Photos make me nervous."

"Nervous? Are you thinking I might do something nefarious with the pictures...like blackmail, maybe?"

"No. Well, yes, maybe. I don't know. It just makes me nervous with all the stories you read about embarrassing photos showing up on the internet. How about you use my phone? Then I'll be in control of the pictures."

"Forget it," Toby said petulantly.

"My God, Toby, stop acting like such a baby. How about we get Mitchell here to dress you up like a female hooker and let me take photos of you with my phone?"

Her remarks caused Toby some pause. "Okay, okay. I see your point. Where's your phone?"

"In my purse. I'll get it." Erin walked over to her purse on the floor and dug out her cell phone. "Here," she said as she handed the phone to Toby. Erin hammed it up a little with some seductive posturing while Toby snapped a few shots.

"Okay, kids, playtime is over," Mitchell said. "According to Toby I still need to make you look like a John roughed you up. The fake bruising makeup will take a little longer."

Toby went back to holding up the wall while Erin sat at the dresser, facing Mitchell as he began applying various concoctions from his array of cosmetics. After many dabs of this and that, he turned Erin toward the mirror. "What do you think," he asked?

Erin was aghast. "Oh my God, Mitchell. You're good."

Toby pushed off against the wall and walked up behind Erin, bending down to see her reflection in the mirror. "She's right, Mitchell, you are good. She really looks like she's was worked over."

"Thanks. So, Toby, you gave me only a sketch of why you're involved in the ruse. How about some details?"

From his jacket pocket, Toby withdrew a newspaper article with a photo of Cunningham. "This man is Bradley Cunningham and he's on trial for a hit and run near Grover Street months ago."

"You're on the Cunningham case? I'm impressed."

"So you know who he is....any chance you've seen him hanging around Grover Street."

Mitchell took the photo and looked at it carefully. "No, I haven't seen him."

"Well, I want to know if any of the street girls, or maybe even the boys, have seen him around. As you know they probably wouldn't be willing to talk to me as a P.I. snooping around. They have a good communication network when it comes to the perverts, bullies, and rough Johns, and a network that is too tight for me to get away with pretending I'm a pimp from around here. So, I'm going to tell them I'm from Lincoln City. Erin's going to be with me when I show them the picture and I'm hoping they will open up when they see her."

"Hmm. It might work but let me remind you that they all carry cell phones these days. As you know, it's very territorial out there so you should count on at least a few of them calling their pimps, even if you claim to be from Lincoln."

"I realize that. That's why I've got Erin here. Since a pimp doesn't take kindly to anyone but himself roughing up his girls, I think if I run into one of the girls's handlers, they'll back off when they see Erin."

"Wait just a minute!" Erin exclaimed. "You *think* they'll back off?"

"Don't get all worked up, Erin. It's not likely there will be any trouble as long as they realize I'm not trying to worm in on their territory."

Erin looked over at Mitchell. "What do you think about his plan? Is it safe?"

"In theory, yes. But on the streets anything can happen so I won't tell you it's failsafe. I can't blow my cover so I won't be there to help if anything does goes wrong."

Erin shook her head, saying, "I don't know, Toby. Listening to you two talk...well, the whole thing now seems a bit risky to me."

Toby was silent for a few seconds before saying, "Maybe you're right, Erin. The thing is...risk is relative. In my world, I push the envelope every day and to me this scheme has very little risk in comparison to some of the chances I've taken. However, when I asked you to be a part of it, I should have considered your world, not mine. I guess I got too caught up in the sport of it. I realize now that I've kind of bullied you into it and I'm sorry about that."

"Well, you did come on a bit strong but you didn't hold a gun to my head. I mean I could have said no from the beginning. I guess there is a part of me that wants to do this, to step way out of my comfort zone. Wait, damn it! I'm getting into my analytical mode and if I go there, I'm sure to end up with the paralysis of analysis. I've done nothing all day except hedge my bets." Erin stood up and paced a few moments before saying," Okay, I've decided. Now that the river card is up, I've decided to go all in."

"All in? Incredulously, Toby asked, "You play Texas Hold 'Em?"

"I did." Erin gave Toby a sly smile, saying, "I put myself through college and graduate school playing poker, which is really a bluffing game. I'm good at reading faces and body language, remember?"

Shaking his head in amazement, Toby said, "Well I guess it's my turn to eat humble pie for stereotyping." Toby walked over to Erin and took her by the shoulders, turning her toward him and looking her in the eyes, asking, "You're sure about this?"

She stared right back at him, saying, "I'm sure."

"Okay then. Let's rock and roll."

Annabel Stephensen, holding a tray of food on her hip, knocked softly on the closed bedroom door of her daughter; Rose had been holed up inside for almost two days. When she didn't get an answer, she called out, "Rose, please, open the door. You have to eat something. Please, sweetie, I promise not to ask any more questions about you and Bradley...or the trial. Just let me bring you some food."

From behind the door, Rose said, "I'll open the door but you have to keep your promise. No questions."

"I promise, sweetie."

Rose, exhausted from crying and weak from hunger, dragged herself off the bed and opened the door. Her mother almost dropped the tray of food when she saw how bedraggled her normally flawless daughter appeared. "Oh! Rose, dear, whatever is bothering you, you know you can talk to me about it," Annabel pleaded.

Rose turned away saying, "You promised, mother."

"Okay, okay. Just eat something then. I brought your favorite, minestrone soup and a fruit salad," she said, as she put the tray on the bedside table.

"I'm not hungry."

"Please, just try eating a little of it. You've had almost nothing to eat since you arrived. You can't deal with whatever crisis is going on if your body is starved. Go! Sit on the bed and I'll put the tray on your lap."

Rose dragged herself back to bed, letting her mother prop several pillows behind her and put the tray of food on her lap. Annabel sat down beside her daughter and picked up the spoon. "I can do it, mother," snapped Rose. "Just back off."

Annabel was taken aback. Her daughter had never talked to her in that tone of voice. She put the spoon back in the soup and moved to the arm chair a few feet away, staying silent for fear of another ill-tempered outburst.

Rose took several spoonfuls of the soup. She looked over at her mom, saying, "It's good. You're right. I did need something to eat." She finished the bowl and began nibbling at the fruit salad. After several bites, she pushed the dish away, saying, "I'll try to finish it later."

"Are you feeling a little better?"

"Yes, mom. Thanks. I know you want to help but, please, I just can't talk about it right now."

"Well," said Annabel, softly, "If you won't talk to me maybe you could talk to Father Clement."

"Ha! A priest is the last person I need to talk with," Rose said bitterly.

"Rose! Whatever does that mean? He's always been a good listener and given sound advise."

"Sound advice? What a crock of shit."

"Rose! What in the world has gotten into you? I've never heard you talk like that."

"Exactly. And that's how I got into the mess I'm in."

Annabel stood up, saying, "Whatever is bothering you has turned you into someone I don't know and don't like. And your stubborn silence and awful language is making it impossible for me to help you."

"But you are helping me, mom. You brought me my favorite soup. And you're letting me stay here. That's exactly what I need from you right now."

"All right," Annabel said as she sat back down. " I'm glad I'm helping. But you're not going to stay shut up in this room, are you?"

"Mom!" Rose whined. "You promised no more questions."

Annabel stood again, saying huffily, "Well, then, have it your way. Go it alone. If you change your mind, I'll be glad to talk with you...try to help you. And Rose, I'm sorry, but I have to ask this one question. Since you turned off your cell phone, what do you want me to tell Bradley? He's been calling and it's not fair to make me keep putting him off."

"Just tell him the truth. Tell him I won't talk to you, so you have nothing to tell him."

Annabel gave a big sigh, shook her head in frustration and left the room.

Rose called after her, "Please shut the door, mother."

As soon as her mother was gone, Rose put the tray on the bedside table, lay down, and returned to her catastrophic thoughts about her future. She accepted that she had a very serious sexual problem. Now she needed to know for sure why Bradley had chosen to ignore her problem, never once challenging her in thirty-seven years of marriage. Her husband's refusal to answer her simple question about what he was doing that early morning, plus all the years of their celibacy, had led her to a devastating conclusion: her perfect marriage was a fantasy. Her long marital voyage had suddenly become a sinking ship, adrift on a vast, stormy ocean. Rose's only lifeboat was her parent's home, a smothering, scriptural lifeboat filled with rights and wrongs, blacks and whites, and certainly no room for the sin of homosexuality.

Could Bradley be lying to her about not being with a prostitute? She might be able to forgive him for being with another woman. After all, she had never given him sex. But what if the prostitute was a man? If Bradley was homosexual...well, she agreed with her parents on that one: it was an unacceptable sin. She couldn't go on living with a husband knowing he was an abomination of nature.

She curled herself further into her fetal position as she wondered if she was being hypocritical? If Bradley was an abomination of nature, what was she? If Bradley had never been arrested, if this trial had never happened, she would still be living in her pretend world, a world where she could stay happy by simply denying that living a nun's life inside a marriage was its own abomination of nature. The "if's" had not prevailed, however. Bradley had been arrested, the dominoes had fallen and she now realized she could never go back to a marriage based on pretense.

Rose's eyes traveled to the food tray sitting on the bedside table. She now saw that her mother had placed a small Bible on the tray, something her subconscious must have chosen not to notice when she was eating the soup. For as long as she could remember, a Bible had been a source of comfort for her. All the years she was growing up, her parents had quoted scripture to her as an explanation for what life dished up. She had many of the verses memorized. Sexual temptations? Thessalonians 4:3: *For this is the will of God, your sanctification: that you abstain from sexual immorality.* When she was older and in her Catholic girls school, the nuns quoted even more scripture. As an adult she had automatically taken up the practice, never once questioning her faith in the Biblical words to give her guidance.

She reached out and picked up the Bible, turning easily to Colossians 3:5*: Put to death, therefore, what is earthly in you: sexual immorality, impurity, passion, evil desire, and covetousness, which is idolatry.* Well, she certainly had taken those words literally; she had killed all passion, had done exactly what the scripture said: put to death what was earthly in her. Realizing the days of quoting scripture were gone, she slammed the Bible closed, dropping it in the trash can beside the dresser. Her mother would be appalled if she found the Bible in the trash. Well, so be it.

It had been easy to live by the Scriptures because what had life really thrown at her until now? As Bradley Cunningham's wife, her life had been charmed. Mrs. Bradley Cunningham had lived a dream life. She had been a pampered princess, wanting for nothing, and she had been able to give back to her church and the community.

These recent disturbing events, however, had caused her consciousness to doubt the sacred book as a source of answers to problems. This small kernel of acknowledgement—that instead of providing answers, The Bible, and her indisputable devotion to it, might be responsible for her current plight—was forcing her to *wake up and smell the coffee.*

All those years ago, the sex therapist had outright told her that her religiosity was at the root of her sexual problem. And what had she done about it? Buried her head in the sand, played the denial card, pretended it didn't exist because there was no scripture she could quote that would make it all go away.

However, if she wasn't by her husband's side on Monday when the defense started their case, Bradley would never forgive her. Should she risk all that she had when, in reality, she had no real proof of her suspicions? Had she acted in haste? Was it already too late to save her marriage?

She had been struggling with these circular thoughts for days, going round and round and ending with nothing but the same questions, questions which led her back to the beginning. She had to get off the merry-go-round, had to do something other than stay locked up in a room in her parent's house worrying herself sick with unanswered questions. She had to do something other than what she had been doing her whole married life; she had to break the cycle of denial.

She pushed herself up from the bed and walked on shaky legs over to the dresser, sitting down in front of the mirror. A ghastly sight stared back at her; no wonder her mother had gasped. She opened a couple of drawers until she found a hair brush and gave her matted hair a few strokes, a simple action that actually helped; the person staring back at her more resembled a neglected woman rather than a wild banshee.

She sat up straighter, looked in the mirror and made a decision. She was no longer going to be a religious robot, which likely meant a break with her parents and her church, a scary and untethered feeling, but one she would have to deal with later. Reliance on scripture, she now realized, conveniently provided simplistic Band-Aids to complicated issues, phony dependence on dogmatic words. How convenient! If the Bible had ownership of all wisdom, then she could avoid taking any personal responsibility for her life.

Well, she no longer wanted to hide behind God or her own denial, so she would have to do something very novel: she would have to think for herself. She squared her shoulders and, staring at herself in the mirror, asked out loud, "What would an intelligent, thinking, self-reliant woman do?" She was surprised when an answer immediately revealed itself: *stop making assumptions about Bradley's sexuality. If he won't tell you what you need to know, then find out for yourself.*

Okay...sound thinking, but how?

Again, she was shocked when an answer to her own questioning immediately produced a possible answer: you could hire a private investigator. Before she could ponder this far-reaching step, the word investigator led her to a new reflection, a memory of a long ago incident that she had conveniently put in the denial vault she had constructed in her mind. As the details of the incident flooded her brain, it became clear what action she could take. And she could do it on her own before she involved an investigator. It would take an act of duplicitous courage, one that would surely test her still shaky resolve, but she had just promised herself a new, take-responsibility-Rose and this would be an undeniable test.

Scared but determined, Rose decided she would follow through on her plan of action, her appetite returning almost immediately after making the decision. She gobbled the remaining fruit salad (could have eaten a giant hamburger!) and went to take a shower. Rose Cunningham, she decided, was returning to the world of the living, but without the cloak of religious irresponsibility that shrouded her life. In the shower she vigorously shampooed her hair, all the while singing out loud, *I'm washing that denial right out of my life.*

After gloating over their victory with the intruder, the two Light Warriors slept well and late, an extraordinary event for Jane whose usual Saturday started with a sunrise bicycle ride. During breakfast, Sydney told Jane her idea of what the next move should be for the Light Warriors—well, really only one Warrior.

Sydney thought she knew what Bradley Cunningham was doing in the Grover Street area in the hours before the hit and run accident, and she had a plan to prove that she was right. If Sydney was correct in her assumptions, her plan could possibly provide a solution to the ethical dilemma Jane found herself in: remaining on a jury in a case involving someone with whom she was sure she had personal and troubling experience. The plan involved dicey actions, actions that Jane could never pull off but were right up Sydney's alley.

"Grover Street was my old stomping grounds," Sydney claimed. "I still keep up with some of the girls I knew back then and I'm sure they will talk to me, especially when I tell them what I think Cunningham was doing that night."

Jane, who long ago learned how fruitless it was to argue with Sydney when she had made up her mind, kept her misgivings to herself. "Okay, but I insist you wear the amulet to ward off danger."

"I'll wear it for you, but I won't be in any danger," Sydney insisted. "Besides, I'm carrying my trusty wasp spray, an item in my line of work that's more of a backup than an American Express card—I never left home without it."

As usual, Sydney was booked as an *escort* for that evening, but since the girls she needed to talk with kept very late hours, her date for the evening would not be a problem. She would talk to her remaining Grover Street contacts after her escort commitment.

Along with the close-up photos of Cunningham's hand, her friend Ben had sent two close-up shots of the man from the waist up. Sydney made prints of both photos and put them in her large purse before leaving the house for the evening.

Sydney met her date for the evening at the bar of an upscale hotel. After a drink they headed upstairs; she emerged two hours later with fifteen hundred dollars in cash carefully stashed in her large purse.

Sometimes after a particularly profitable date, Sydney would head over to Grover Street where she staged a carefully rehearsed routine with the girls she still knew from the days she was on the streets. She would slowly drive around the area as a signal to the girls that she was in the neighborhood, park her car several blocks away, then head to a coffee shop. If any of the girls thought their pimps eyes weren't on their tails, they would drift over to the coffee shop where Sydney would give them a few extra bucks, money they didn't have to share with their handlers.

Sydney knew most of the money she gave them went up their noses or into their arms, but who was she to judge their plight? She felt lucky; somehow she'd been given the gift of foresight. The only reason she had been able to get off the streets was because she purposely resisted the temptation to blur her world, never once allowing an addicting illegal drug inside her body. She intuitively knew drugs led only to the down escalator and she was headed up. From the moment she left her pathetic, adopted home, she had a goal in mind: no pimp would be using her. No, it was going to be the other way around. She would use the biggest weakness men had, their little heads, to get ahead. Working the streets was a necessary step, but only a step.

Sydney and her girlfriends had their routine prearranged. They never arrived at the coffee shop all at once. They knew Sydney usually stayed about an hour and they also knew they couldn't have any pattern that could be detected by their pimps or another hooker who might report suspicious behavior in order to receive favors from their pimps, favors meaning more drugs. That night three of her friends came to the coffee shop. When Sydney showed the first two girls Cunningham's picture, both denied knowing the man. However, when she told them what she thought Cunningham was really after, both girls readily gave over the names and locations of some women who might fit the bill, warning Sydney she would be heading into dangerously malignant territory where the pimps were totally inhumane.

When she asked the third girl about Cunningham, however, she received some surprising information.

"Someone else showed me a picture of that man just before you showed up," she said.

Surprised, Sydney asked,"Tonight? Someone tonight showed you a picture of this man?"

"Yeah. A very large black man. He had his bitch with him. She'd been beat up and he wanted to know if I'd seen that man in the picture. I could tell the man was pissed about his bitch taking the beating and he seemed ready to do some damage."

Tapping the photo, Sydney asked, "And you're sure it was a picture of this same man?"

"Yeah, I'm sure."

"What did you tell him?"

"The truth. I haven't seen that man around here."

"Did they hang around or leave?"

"I thought they left, but on my way over here, I saw him asking some of the other girls, the ones that hang near the intersection of Chase."

After her friend left, Sydney thought about what she had been told. Who else would be nosing around Cunningham's tracks? She concluded it must be an investigator for the prosecution. He was likely using a fake bitch to try to gain incriminating information, strange action for a prosecution hound to be taking so late in the game. She smiled, murmuring to herself, "This hound is barking up the wrong tree."

She looked at her watch, noticed it was almost two, and waved to the familiar waitress. She wasn't sure how she would pull it off, but she wanted to get the phony black pimp to approach her about Cunningham. Nor was she sure what she would accomplish, but a Light Warrior would never pass up the opportunity to check out the competition.

She left her usual ten dollar tip for use of the table and hurried from the coffee shop, walking toward the area where the mysterious large black man had last been seen. She wanted to see the two people in action for herself. She knew she had to be careful, though. Not only was she over dressed for the area, but a new girl on these territorial streets was immediately noticed, possibly resulting in a phone call to a pimp.

Sydney began walking toward Chase. It was easy to spot the bogus couple, the enormous black man stood out like a giant

Sequoia in a forest of saplings. They were talking to a street woman Sydney didn't recognize and the woman was shaking her head no. Sydney quickly stepped back into a doorway, peeking around to see which direction the two would take. Luckily, they were heading her way so she busied herself by looking into her large purse as she stepped out of the doorway, timing her actions so she could bump into the woman dressed up as a bitch. Upon contact, the woman politely said, "Sorry, I didn't see you."

No bitch talks like that. Sydney scrutinized the pretend bitch as if she was new competition, snidely saying, "I haven't seen you before." She narrowed her eyes in suspicion. "What you doing around here?"

Protectively, Toby quickly stepped in front of Erin. He pulled some money from his pocket, making sure Sydney saw the folded stack of bills before he let his hand drop down beside him. "She's with me and I'm looking for someone," he said.

Sydney let her eyes linger on the money, saying, "Yeah? Who would that be?"

He reached into his pocket and withdrew a newspaper photo. "This man," he said. "He did a number on my bitch here and no one beats up on my girls. You seen him around here?"

"I know him, yeah."

The large man held up the stack of bills, asking, "What can you tell me about him?"

Before Sydney could answer, Erin stepped out from behind Toby, pointing at the pendant around Sydney's neck, asking, "Where did you get that?"

Surprised, Sydney's hand automatically went to the pendant. The black man reacted instantly, stepping back in front of Erin, again holding up the bills. "You were telling me something about this man."

Still shaken up by what the woman had asked, Sydney didn't answer for a few seconds. "He's the rich bastard, the one on trial for killing one of the girls. I've seen his picture in the paper."

Erin tugged on Toby's arm and tried to step back around him but he blocked her way, fearing her concern over the pendant would cause the informant to clam up. Toby tore off three twenties from his stack of money, holding them in front of the woman, asking, "Have you ever seen him around here looking for a date?"

Sydney eyed the money and was about to ask the man why he wanted to know, but then she saw a menacing-looking man with a shaved head covered in tattoos approaching them. The man's hand was in a bulging pocket and he was coming up behind the large black man. She gave a quick nod of her head to warn the black man before stepping back into the alcove where she had hidden a few minutes before.

Toby picked up the warning sign and slowly turned, forcing Erin around behind him.

The man stopped just a few feet from Toby, withdrawing his hand just enough so the barrel of a gun could be seen. "What's your business here?" he asked.

Toby held up the newspaper clipping, saying. "Looking for this man. He beat up on my bitch."

"We ain't seen you or your bitch around here. Why you looking here?"

"We're from Lincoln. Can't find the man there and thought he might frequent Grover Street."

Shaved-head glanced at the picture. "Grover Street ain't your business. Best you be moving along."

Toby hackles immediately rose; he didn't like being told what to do. However, the man had a gun and he had Erin to consider so he calmed himself before replying, "No problem. I ain't looking for trouble. Just don't tolerate my girls being treated badly is all."

The tattooed man nodded toward the doorway, saying, "We don't know that bitch" either. What she telling you?"

At that moment a souped-up car with three men inside pulled up along side the curb. Two men stepped out, both hurrying over to Shaved-head. One of the men held up a smart phone screen in front of Shaved-head, then leaned over to speak into his ear. Shaved-head's eyes narrowed in anger and the hand holding the gun came out of his pocket and dropped down by his side. "My man here tells me you ain't talking the truth. He says you are a private snoop." Shaved-head grabbed the smart phone and turned it so Toby could see. "Picture of you on your website."

Chagrined at underestimating the modern day underworld, Toby assessed the danger he was in: one man still in the car, three men on the street, at least one with a gun. These were bad odds for a fight even if he didn't have Erin to protect. The men had now fanned out in a semicircle, essentially blocking him in. He knew his only option was to try to talk his way out. Hoping that denigrating himself would show deference to the pimp he said, "Guess I'm too outdated and too stupid, thinking I could fool someone sharp like you, huh?" The eyes of Shaved-head relaxed slightly, but then the phone in his hand beeped, indicating a text message. He lifted the phone to read the text. Shaved-head's facial expression turned from anger to alarm.

Toby felt his stomach lurch. *Uh oh. This can only be bad news.*

Shaved-head yelled something at his men and all three began running toward the car. The speed at which they moved told Toby that the trouble was imminent. He quickly scanned the streets looking for whatever might be the cause for alarm. He saw a car with an automatic weapon poking out the back window coming right toward them. He shoved Erin into the alcove where Sydney had retreated and threw himself to the ground, covering his head with his hands. Toby had anticipated a spray of gunfire in his direction, but instead he heard tires screeching, men cursing, a deafening crash, followed by men crying out in distress.

Sydney, still in the darkened doorway, looked down at the phony bitch who had now crawled into the corner and covered her head with her hands. Other than terrified, the woman didn't seem to be badly hurt. She peeked out from around the corner of the doorway and assessed the mayhem. Shaved head and his gang were long gone. The big, black man was on the ground but didn't seem to be hurt, and the drive-by car had smashed into another car. Two men from the drive-by car were on the ground, undeniably out of commission. One of the men was whining about not being able to see.

Thinking it was a good time to exit, Sydney dropped her hornet spray back in her purse and took off.

Toby stayed low, crawling over to the doorway to find Erin. He glanced to his left and saw the woman they had been talking with moving quickly down the street. Erin, however, was frozen, scrunched in the corner of the doorway. Her scraped, bleeding knees were drawn to her chest, her eyes wide with fear, and her body trembling. Crouching in front of her Toby asked, "Are you hurt?" She didn't answer, just stared wide-eyed at him. In the distance he could hear sirens. *We have to get out of here now*, he thought. He started to move toward her, but she pushed herself back further into the corner, holding her hand up in a stopping motion. Speaking gently to her, he said, "Hey, Erin. It's me, Toby. Everything is going to be okay. I'm so sorry about all this. If you're not hurt, though, we need to get out of here. The cops are coming and you can't be found here."

Still wide-eyed and not moving she whispered, "All right," but she didn't move.

Guessing Erin was in shock, Toby said, "I'm just going to help you up. Okay?" She nodded yes. Toby reached out his hand to her, saying, "Give me your hand."

Erin looked at his hand for a few seconds, then finally put her hand in his. He took it and slowly standing, brought her up with him. The sirens were getting louder so Toby said, "I'm going to pick you up, okay?" She nodded her head yes.

He easily lifted her up in his arms and carried her down the street, walking around the first corner he came to. He spotted a bar a few yards ahead of him and carried her to the entrance, asking, "Can you can stand up?"

"I think so," she whispered.

He gently put her down. “I think you need a stiff drink.” Opening the door to the bar he told her, “I want you to take my arm.” Like a robot she did as he asked and he guided her inside and sat her down in a booth.

The low lighting of the bar didn’t succeed in covering up the squalid ambience. Erin, still trembling and in a trancelike state, wasn’t in any shape to notice. Toby, eyes now adjusted to the dark, looked around for a wait person and when he didn’t see anyone said, “I’m going to the bar to get us a drink. You okay?” She still had a vacant stare on her face but nodded yes, so he strode over to the bar, waiting only five-seconds before using a formidable voice to get the attention of the preoccupied bartender, who was leaning on his elbows staring down at the exposed, ample breasts of a rambling, middle-aged female juicer. “I need two double shots of vodka, pronto,” Toby demanded.

The bartender, choosing to ignore Toby’s urgency, didn’t realize his mistake until Toby stepped into his line of sight. Seeing the fiery expression on the face of the huge man in front of him, the bartender snapped to attention and produced the double shots of vodka with lightening speed. Toby brought the shots back to the table, placing one down in front of Erin, insisting, “Drink this.”

Still robotic-like, Erin picked up the glass and took a large swig, her eyes widening at the scouring taste of the cheap alcohol burning its way down her throat. She coughed several times before saying, “You bastard. You saved me from death back there only to poison me now with this vile shit?”

Toby breathed a sigh of relief. “Welcome back, Dr. Halloway.”

“Wow! I seemed to have zoned out. So, exactly what the hell happened back there?”

“Gangs settling their differences with a drive-by shooting is my guess.”

Shaking her head in disbelief, Erin slowly looked around the room, the shabby surroundings finally registering. She picked up the shot glass, asking, "You don't suppose this upscale establishment has some Tito's?"

"You're kidding, right?"

"Right," she answered, as she held up the shot glass of vodka. "Here's to surviving a gang war." She swallowed another mouthful of the liquor, her face scrunching up in disgust. "Whoa! I now know where the name firewater comes from."

"God, Erin. I'm so sorry about all this. I should never have involved you in my crazy scheme." Frowning and shaking his head in disgust, Toby continued, "We had a lead on Cunningham and then it ended with a gang war and I nearly got you killed."

"Don't be so hard on yourself. We did accomplish one mission."

"What's that?"

"I was literally thrown from my ivory tower when you shoved me into that doorway. I mean, there is nothing in any of my textbooks that prepared me for what just happened back there."

Toby narrowed his eyes at Erin, asking, "This breezy bravado you've got going—tell me you're not putting on an act. You know, trying to let me off the hook for being so irresponsible."

"Your first reaction was to protect me, Toby. I don't see how that could be seen as irresponsible."

"Yeah, well, it could have gone down very differently. We both could have been collateral damage. We got lucky somehow. After I shoved you, I hit the ground so I didn't see what caused the car with the automatic weapon to crash."

Erin closed her eyes, saying, "I'm remembering something...let me concentrate here. Okay, after you shoved me into the doorway, I crawled into the corner...the woman we were talking to was there...she was standing in front of me. I was scared witless but I have this vague image of the woman dropping something into her large handbag. Do you think she had a weapon? Maybe she was the one who saved us from being fired upon?"

"I can't say if she had a weapon but I'm positive there was no gunfire. Unless we find that woman again, we'll never know exactly how we got so lucky."

"Okay, now I'm remembering something else, something that I noticed before the drive-by car incident. We need to find this woman because she had this unusual pendant around her neck. I noticed it because it's identical to the pendant that juror Seven has been wearing in the courtroom. I mean, that doesn't sound like a random coincidence to me, especially because I heard her say she recognized Cunningham's photo."

"Let me get this straight. You're saying the hooker we were talking to is somehow linked to juror Seven?"

Erin shook her head in uncertainty. "I don't know exactly what I'm saying, except that I noticed that particular pendant from the courtroom and it's too unique for two very different people to be wearing it by coincidence."

"Your powers of observation are legendary, Erin. But you're sitting at least thirty feet away from juror Seven. How can you be sure the pendant you saw tonight is identical to the one Seven has been wearing?"

"I can't prove it, Toby, but my instinct says I'm right."

"People pay you the big bucks for those instincts, so I guess I'm inclined to believe you."

"Is there a way to find that woman again?"

"That's a tough one. We don't have anything at all to go on so I'd have to hang out around here, hoping to see her on the streets. But hanging around here after what just went down tonight is not a good idea."

"You don't have to convince me of that! So, finding her doesn't sound promising."

"No, it doesn't."

Sydney sat in her car, reviewing what had just happened. She was still a little shaky from the adrenaline that had poured into her body the minute she had spotted the automatic weapon in the window of the approaching car. Tonight she had, indeed, acted as a Light Warrior, not only hobbling the enemy but preventing two innocent people from getting hurt. So, what if her weapon had been a spray can instead of a gun? Hadn't it done the trick? She felt gratified by her quick-thinking, defensive actions, but she also was worried that the phony bitch had recognized her pendant, a fact that told her she had been right about the woman's working for the prosecution. The only way the woman could have seen Jane wearing the pendant was if she had been in the courtroom. Sydney hadn't even remembered she was wearing it tonight; that had been a mistake, especially since she had speculated the suspicious couple was acting undercover for the prosecution. Now she would have to make sure Jane no longer wore the pendant—and hope the woman, whoever she was, would forget about it after the trauma she'd just experienced. Anyway, what could the woman do if Jane didn't wear it anymore? Sydney didn't think the woman could ask Jane about it; after all Jane was a juror and the prosecution couldn't approach a juror.

Sydney checked the time and considered whether she had missed the opportunity to nab at least one of the women named by her street friends earlier at the coffee shop. Jane told her the defense would begin presenting its case on Monday. She had no idea how long the defense would take to present its case, but she needed every night she could get; it wasn't going to be easy to track down the strung-out woman or women who knew Cunningham.

She started the car and drove about a half mile to the decaying five-story building her friends had described. She parked so she could see the entrance and prepared to wait for several hours if necessary. What she needed right now was luck. About forty-five minutes into her wait, she spotted a short, white, middle-aged, potbellied man entering the building. A few minutes later a disheveled, bone-thin, Caucasian woman hurriedly left the same building. Sydney quickly got out of the car, locked it with her key fob and ran after the woman, easily catching up with her and calling out from behind, "Please, wait a moment."

The woman stopped and turned toward Sydney. She looked like a walking skeleton with sunken holes for eyes, limp, filthy hair, and track marks up and down her bruised, emaciated arms. "What do you want? I'm in a hurry," the skeleton snapped.

Sydney took a wad of bills from her pocket and held up the money she had grabbed from the large black man, saying, "I'm looking for somebody."

The skeleton suspiciously eyed the money, asking, "Yeah? Who would that be?"

Sydney took the photo of Cunningham out of her pocket and showed it to the woman. Skeleton glanced wide-eyed at the photo for only a second before turning and hurrying away.

"Wait," Sydney called after her. "There's more money to be had if you can help me."

Without stopping, the woman replied, "Yeah, how much money?"

Sydney caught up with her, "I've got five hundred in cash back in my car."

That stopped the forward motion of the skeleton-like woman. She turned back toward Sydney, asking, "Whadda you want with that man?"

"I need to know who he's buying from."

The woman's cadaverous eyes darted up and down the street in fear. "Get the hell outta here now," she hissed. "Otherwise, you gonna get your ass kicked or worse, asking fucking questions like that."

"Okay, I'll go. But you come with me. I'll take you where you need to go to buy your shit."

"You's a lying bitch. You ain't got no five hundred dollars and you's crazy if you think I'm going anywhere with you. I don't wanna be seen with you. Now get the hell away from me." She started off down the street again.

Sydney ran after her saying, "If you help me, I can help you and I can get help for your child."

Skeleton stopped in her tracks. She turned toward Sydney, her black holes narrowed in a crazed fury as she grabbed Sydney's arm, squeezing it tightly with her bony hand as she spat out, "I ain't got no child. Now leave me alone."

Sydney didn't flinch. She looked straight into the two black holes and gently said, "I think you do have a child and I think you know the man in the photo. I saw the look of panic on your face when I showed you the picture. This man is using you and your child, isn't he?"

Skeleton's shoulders slumped in defeat and she dropped her hold on Sydney as she asked, "Who the fuck are you anyway? You with the law?"

"No, I promise I'm not with the law. I'm a woman who used to work the streets. I know how drugs can control a person, can make them so desperate they hurt the only people who care about them."

"Fuck you, lady. I've heard that sob story before. But you don't know nothing about desperation and you gonna get me thrashed if you don't go. They have watchers, always knowing what I'm doing."

Sydney shoved the money into skeleton's hand. "Go to Connie's Coffee Cafe at nine this morning. I know they won't be watching you once you shoot up. My friend, Jane, will be there and I want you to meet her. She's twenty-eight now but when she was just six her druggie mother was desperate enough to pimp her to the same man in that photo. But Jane bit him when he tried to touch her, so he locked Jane in a closet and left her there. Jane's mom O.D.'d so she was locked in that closet for days before someone found her."

Tears leaked out from the deep holes that were skeleton's eyes as she sobbed, "If the law finds out what I've been doing, they'll take my kid away from a piece of shit like me. I'll never see her again."

"Just go to Connie's at nine this morning. I think there is a way you can keep them from taking your child away. Jane will tell you how." Sydney gently touched skeleton's hollowed out face and brushed away a tear, saying, "I know you love your little girl...Connie's at nine, okay?"

Skeleton lifted her bony hand up to grasp the hand Sydney had on her face. "I've never been touched nice like that...except by my kid. If you scamming me, I promise I'll kill you."

"And I'd deserve it. But I'm not lying to you. Connie's at nine, say it back to me," Sydney instructed.

"Connie's at nine," skeleton mumbled.

It was approaching six o'clock on a Saturday evening and RJ Holland, in a Polo shirt and slacks, was in his office, ostensibly going over his case file for the coming week, an unusual occurrence for the well-know purveyor of truth manipulation, who doggedly reserved his entire Saturday afternoon for golf. He had dressed for golf, had even teed off with his usual threesome, but by his forth bogey, he begged off, saying, "This Cunningham case has all my attention. I should get back to the office." Not a single, poor sport, wisecrack was made by the remaining threesome...well, that is, until later when the three men took great pleasure in maligning The Great One during their usual drinks at the club bar.

After leaving the golf course, RJ drove himself to his office. During the drive, he mulled over his pathetic golf game, puzzled by his lack of concentration. Once in his office, the reason for being there, to review his upcoming court strategy, had eluded him. Instead, he sat in front of his files, preoccupied with why his usual confidence to sway a jury in the direction he wanted had done a mysterious disappearing act in the last few days.

RJ Holland was no slouch. As he always did, he had worked himself and his two flunkies relentlessly in preparation for the trial, but it had always been his practice to pull back on the long hours during the actual trial, to trust his preparation and salesmanship. He knew that second-guessing himself *during* a trial was the worse thing he could do; it inevitably oozed out in his demeanor, leaving a nucleus of doubt behind for the jury to notice. In a case such as this one, a case with very incriminating circumstantial evidence, it was essential that he not shed even a microscopic germ of doubt. RJ believed that The First Commandment of the jury system, the presumed innocence until proven guilty, was a crock of shit. Humans were covertly programmed to believe that the prosecution, the guy in the white hat, the protectors of the people, would not charge an innocent person with a crime without good reason. Every defense attorney worth a grain of salt knew he started with the odds against him.

Yet here he was at the end of the first week of a major trial, second-guessing himself. He put his elbows on the huge desk in front of him, resting his head in his hands, thinking. From the very beginning he had known this case would be about circumstantial evidence, the kind of case in which he often and famously prevailed. So what had happened that had pulled the rug out from under him for the first time in his career? The list of mishaps was long, but setbacks and adversity were part of the game and had never before plagued him the way they were in this case.

As ridiculous as it was to entertain the possibility that it all started with the annoying Dr. Halloway and her preposterous remark about his cock, RJ could not get the woman out of his mind. He could not think of any woman in his entire life who had gotten under his skin the way she did. Working with such an aggressive shrew was enough on its own, but then she had served him up an additional humiliation by being right. Juror Seven was showing herself to be the problem Halloway had predicted. Had he been stupid enough to discount Halloway's concerns about Seven during the Voir Dire just because the woman so annoyed him? If so, that had been a big mistake, maybe even the reason for his current quandary. The background information he now had on Seven and the way she was behaving in the jury box indicated she would not easily bend to his cunning treatment of the upcoming witnesses or his carefully crafted summation.

The witnesses Saul Greene paraded in front of the jury on Friday were no surprise, yet he worried Greene was besting him in his hallowed temple, the sanctuary where he had reigned supreme. So he acted in desperation, appealing to Cunningham, pressuring him, even threatening him with failure if he didn't offer up an explanation for his being in the area—all to no avail.

The clients he defended often hid things from him, lying to him more often than not. Never before, however, had he gone against his ironclad policy of staying confident. This time he had stupidly demonstrated his vulnerability by shouting and threatening his own client, one more mistake to add to his growing list. And then Rose Cunningham had the audacity to twist the knife by refusing to return to court. What the hell was that about? He couldn't get any answers from anyone on that blunder. Was it simply that fate was against him; his long winning streak finally potentially ending? Had he been too arrogant, assuming no case was beyond his sleight of hand? Or had he simply taken on a bedeviled case...one that was hexed from the beginning? He slapped his hand hard on the desk. *Well, shit! I'm sitting here making the biggest mistake of all: I'm letting self-doubt become the pink elephant in the room. Ruminating about it is only making it worse.*

He swiveled his chair around, looking out through the huge picture window behind him. Seeing the view of the city, a city he had conquered, a city filled with people who paid him deference, a city where he was a household name, made him straighten up his shoulders and say out loud, "Get a grip. This isn't your first difficult case and it won't be your last. You'll prove yourself superior just like you always do." Then he stood up, walked over to the window and leaned in to it, putting his forehead against the glass as he gave himself a pep talk. *You're going to prevail as you always do. And tonight you're going to do what you planned: you're going to get laid.*

He had promised the seductive Caroline he would make up for the previous disappointing evening, the evening that had been interrupted by a call from the audacious Halloway woman who couldn't wait to give him the sordid background information on Seven. He looked at his watch, turned around and walked back to his desk, closing the file in front of him. Time to go home and dress for dinner. He was looking forward to tonight's date with Caroline, an evening that was sure to end with his ability to disprove Halloway's puny penis accusation. He was certain that a proper fuck was all it would take to get his confidence back on track.

Fortunately, RJ was able to put all his doubts behind him during dinner and turn on the charm, regaling the susceptible Caroline with courtroom stories of his hard-won victories. Predictably, Caroline listened with feigned rapture, pretending to understand complicated legal maneuvers, never asking questions for fear of showing her cluelessness and for fear of losing a ride on the magic carpet to wealth: a famously rich husband to transport her out of a pedestrian life. It was all a game to RJ, a game he knew he would win by simply ending it with Caroline in a few months. Finding gorgeous women who had been brought up believing they never needed to *worry their pretty little heads about it* (it meaning financial responsibility) was never a problem. Despite all the crap about women's liberation, there were still plenty of women who, as exceptionally winsome young girls, were schooled to believe that alluring sexuality was all it took to have what you wanted in life; nab the right man and you were set for life. RJ knew that most men were vulnerable to captivating female sexuality, but he prided himself on having learned his lesson; now he simply "caught and released." The dinners, like tonight, usually cost him around three hundred bucks, much less than a classy prostitute, so he felt his side of the scoreboard racked up points even if he was, in a manner of speaking, still paying for the sex.

However, the second half of tonight's game, the goal line, as RJ liked to think of it, ended in an unexpected play. His usually dependable, fully inflated "football" had somehow been drop-kicked into a dead zone, deflated and unplayable. Caroline had tried her best to reassure him that it was "nothing," but she succeeded only in further infuriating him. He finally screamed at her to get out and had called his driver to take her home. After she had dressed and run from the room in tears, R.J got out of bed and paced the room in a naked rage.

Although he was approaching sixty, impotency had never before fouled his game. He strode over to the full-length mirror in the corner of his room and stared at his naked body. Staring back at him was an ever-expanding waistline, showing the price he paid for the first half of the game. Worse, however, was his shriveled dick, which mocked him with a ghostly murmur, *puny, aren't I*?

He grabbed his shorts off the floor and hurriedly put them on. Then he headed downstairs to his library where he poured himself a double shot of twelve-year-old JohnnyWalker Black, neat. He swallowed a big slug and slammed the glass down on his ten-thousand-dollar desk, spilling some of the amber contents on the thousand dollar tooled leather inset. Then he picked up a three thousand dollar glass paperweight and hurled it across the room, howling, "This is all your fault, you bitch." The solid glass paperweight was undamaged, but a five-thousand dollar Lalique vase lay in shards.

What RJ didn't understand, what an achieving man who is used to getting his way would never understand, is that a turnover had happened in his own game. His playbook had been undermined by his own psyche. RJ had let Erin get under his skin and with that one act, he had also, unknowingly, let a kernel of self-doubt creep its way into his brain. Finding the soft, spongy material quite comfortable, the tiny germ of doubt would not be easily dislodged. Without his awareness RJ was experiencing a phase of the endowment effect, a psychological process that involves both winning and losing. It goes like this: human beings hate losing something they once had, so much so that the pain of losing outweighs the joy of winning. The usually unquestioning, narcissistic RJ Holland, king of the not-guilty-verdict, had become unconsciously preoccupied by the fear of losing his winning reputation. If he could have humbled himself to ask, Dr. Erin Halloway could have told him not only what his problem was, but how to get the doubt out of his mind. Of course, *The* RJ Holland would never demean himself by asking for help, especially from a woman, and certainly not the infuriating Dr. Erin Halloway. No, it was much easier, more self-appeasing to project the blame onto the doctor.

Finally noticing the shards of precious glass strewn about the room, RJ put his head in his hands, fantasizing how he might crush the brazen hussy who was responsible for his miserable state. A fleeting image entered his brain: he was bending the doctor over his huge desk, ripping off her panties, entering her from behind, and pounding her with his hugely engorged penis until he was satisfied. He quickly shook his head to dislodge the thought and swallowed another mouthful of scotch, now aware that his heart was pounding in his chest. He was angrier than he could ever remember, but even the egocentric RJ knew the image he had just conjured up was a dangerous sign of losing control. He finished off the scotch in one last swallow and headed upstairs, hoping the alcohol would numb him enough so he could get some sleep.

He managed only a few hours of restless sleep and spent Sunday morning moping about his huge house. He knew he was supposed to be preparing for his opening defense the next day, but concentrating on anything besides the events of the previous evening was beyond his grasp. By noon he was drunk and by two in the afternoon he was asleep with his head on his desk.

It never once occurred to him that the reason he had allowed Dr. Halloway to annoyingly skulk her way under his skin was because he was intrigued, even attracted to her. It didn't occur to him because being drawn to a woman whose strength came from her core was way too threatening to a man whose strength was superficial. No, acknowledging something as mutinous as this idea would shatter a womanizing man, the kind of man whose self-image was built on a flimsy house of cards, cards whose foundation depended upon denigrating women in a convoluted sham to cover up his own insecurities. Like Hitler scapegoated his insecurities on the Jews, a womanizing man scapegoats his insecurities on women. On the surface, RJ Holland appeared to be a powerful man. Look deep into his soul, however, and you will find a man of psychological fragility whose defenses operate on a rigid construct: failure is not an option. Unfortunately for RJ, his dam of psychological defense had sprung a leak, making him vulnerable to a trickle of uncertainty—and to the inevitability of the surge of doubt to follow if the leak was not plugged.

While RJ was wallowing in misery, his opposing counsel, Saul Greene, was taking pleasure in the recent events in his life. After months of a cloud hanging over his head, things were finally looking up. He was feeling confident, optimistic, and pleased with the way he was handling the trial. During the day on Saturday, he had spent several hours going over the draft of his summation. He would have to wait until RJ presented his case to finalize his remarks, but he was encouraged by the way things were going.

His one concern was juror Seven. She was an enigma and could still create a problem if she did the unexpected and held out for a not guilty verdict. He had no idea what had caused Rose Cunningham's disappearing act, but he knew that it worked in the prosecution's favor. As of the end of the day Friday, the defense had still not added Bradley Cunningham as a witness. Nor did the defense list any other witnesses who could explain why he was on Grover Street. Surprisingly, it appeared there would be no explanation by the defense of Cunningham's presence in the area of the hit and run. Absent any explanation, the jury would have to draw its own conclusion, a conclusion that Saul intended to influence in his summation.

While the trial appeared to be going in his favor, he was uncertain about how his relationship with Allan was going. He had met the man only a few days ago, had gone out to dinner and then back to Allan's place. It had been an evening of getting to know each other, of mutual sharing of histories, of philosophies, of politics, of religion, and, yes, of bodies. It had been a very enjoyable evening except for one thing. Saul was a little uneasy about Allan's vague description of his work; he would only say he worked for himself, was involved in "cyberspace security," and that he didn't like to talk about his work. Allan had received a phone call soon after they arrived back at Allan's condo from dinner. He had excused himself, taken his phone into his converted bedroom, closed the door on Saul, and been gone for fifteen minutes.

When Allan returned, he apologized to Saul but did not explain further, other than to say it was urgent and he couldn't ignore it. Saul had not pushed him on the topic at the time. Being a prosecutor for the state, however, he was suspicious by profession, which led him to wonder if Allan's unwillingness to discuss his work might mean it was quasi-legal. On the other hand, if Allan was involved in something fishy, it didn't make much sense that Allan had been the initiator. He had been the one to give Saul his phone number, clearly knowing that Saul was a state prosecutor, even commenting the first night they met about Cunningham's trial. Saul told himself he shouldn't be jumping to conclusions. He should remain open-minded for now, and go with the flow. He had immensely enjoyed another man's company, something he had not felt possible just weeks ago. Leapfrogging to judgements without evidence was premature and would only spoil the possibilities for a future with a smart, funny, charming man who might be a good match for him.

Saul awoke Sunday morning in Allan's bed to the smell of freshly brewing coffee. Allan was already up and Saul could hear noise coming from the kitchen. He put on his shorts, headed toward the bathroom, and then wandered into the kitchen where Allan stopped what he was doing to hand him a cup of steaming coffee. On the counter top were remnants of freshly squeezed oranges and broken egg shells. Two glasses of juice sat on the counter where Allan was now busily whipping up the eggs. He looked up as Saul walked into the room. "I was planning to cook us a Western omelette. You okay with the ham?"

"No problem," Saul replied, as he took a sip of the coffee. "Wow! This is marvelous coffee, strong, just the way I like it. You're spoiling me, you know."

"Not really. You should know that my cooking is not an attempt to spoil you or impress you. Cooking relaxes me, gives me a creative outlet, something more imaginative than machines. However, I only enjoy it if I have time. I don't like to feel pressured or obligated to do it. Bottom line? My cooking is erratic."

"In other words, don't develop expectations," Saul said, dryly.

Allan stopped beating the eggs and looked at Saul. "Guess I came on a little strong, huh?"

"A tad, yes."

"Okay, so I was being defensive." Allan looked away for a few moments before turning his attention back to Saul. "I guess what's going on is that I'm hoping this relationship has some kind of future and I'm a bit nervous about it. I think it is important to let you know who I am from the start. That way there are no surprises down the road."

If he had thought about his earlier pledge to go with the flow, Saul would have chosen to respond more encouragingly to the first part of Allan's comment, the part about a future relationship, but his prosecutorial proclivity automatically kicked in and he retorted with a challenge, "So, tell me, does knowing who you are include your work? Because it seems to me you have been intentionally vague about that."

Allan picked up his coffee, taking a sip before replying over the rim of his cup. "Yes, I'm vague about my work but it is only because my clients require anonymity. But I can tell from your suspicious demeanor you're wondering if what I do is legal."

"It has crossed my prosecutorial mind, yes."

"Well, if you bother to check me out, you'll find that years ago, when I was a pompous, egotistical kid, I got into trouble for being a hacker. A few years in federal prison quickly deflated my self-importance balloon. So, when I got out, I crossed to the other side. It took me years to build back my credibility, but I'm good at what I do and eventually I built a *legitimate* and very successful business."

"So, are you saying you're now a hacker for the good guys?"

Allan paused for a moment before saying, "Well, it would be more accurate to say I'm a security analyst for the *legal* guys."

"Legal guys, huh? As in The Patriot Act, I presume?"

"I hope you understand that I'm not at liberty to comment on that specifically, but what I can tell you is that some of my clients have nothing to do with the government."

"Hmm, *some* clients that aren't the government. I guess I can read between the lines here without your having to break any confidences."

"Look, Saul, I'll be honest. I felt something click when we met and I took a risk when I handed you my phone number, considering my past and knowing what you do for a living. I've learned the hard way the importance of trust, so, if it bothers you that I have a criminal record, if it is something you can't get past, then we need to end this relationship now."

Saul felt a a shot of apprehension flow through his body at the thought of ending it with Allan. He had promised himself he wouldn't push the issue of Allan's work, but that was exactly what he had just done. And now Allan was pulling back, not at all what he wanted. He needed to restore the damage he had done. "You're right," he replied. "Trust is essential in a relationship and I appreciate your honesty about your past. I, too, felt a click between us and I shouldn't have put you on the witness stand the way I just did. So, I apologize for that and will do my best *not* to act like a prosecutor when I want to ask you something."

"Fair enough." Allan picked up the egg mixture and returned to beating the eggs. "So, Saul, how do you like your eggs?"

It was after eleven in the morning when Saul left Allan's condo. His own apartment was a twenty minute drive and he headed in that direction, satisfied that he had successfully reset the original course of the relationship. About half way home, however, an unpleasant thought entered his mind, a sudden grain of uninvited suspicion that he couldn't banish, even as he was aware that he was invalidating the trust he had avowed earlier.

He altered his course and headed toward his office where he had access to data bases containing criminal records. He didn't know if his uneasy feelings about Allan were a remnant of his previous relationship with Richard, one that ended in such pain because of betrayal, or because, in his line of work, he was trained to be suspicious. Maybe it was both, but now he was wondering why Allan had suggested Saul do some checking on him. Did he bring up the background check so Saul would see that Allan was how he presented: an incredibly honest, straightforward guy? Or was it because he was one hell of a con? One thing was for certain, however, he wouldn't rest until he did the background check.

He now had to know whether the attractive cyber spy with an admitted criminal record might have some ulterior motive for handing a state prosecutor his phone number

When Sydney returned home in the early morning and told an anxiously awaiting Jane, what she had promised the skeleton of a woman, Jane freaked out. "I can't possibly be the one to meet with the woman. I'll fall apart and only frighten her."

"It has to be you. I could tell she related to your story. She's so frightened, I think you're the only person she might be willing to trust."

"But I won't know what to say. I'll just panic and ruin everything."

They had been sitting on the couch, but now Sydney stood up and looked down angrily at Jane.

"After all I went through last night," she yelled, I can't believe you're acting like such a spineless cripple. What the hell happened to the Light Warrior?"

Jane began crying, then sobbing, which then escalated into hyperventilation. This time Jane's histrionics only further infuriated Sydney.

"Get a fucking grip," she screamed. "You started all this. Now, when you're close to getting what you want, you play the helpless, pathetic card. I'm sick and tired of your paralysis when things get tough. So, if you don't get it together and do this, I'm out of here for good."

Jane, so stunned at the furious words coming from her only friend, immediately stopped crying. In all the years she had known Sydney, she had never threatened to abandon her. Life without her life-preserver friend was unimaginable. Jane closed her eyes and took five very deep breaths before replying, "You can't leave me, Syd. I'd die without you."

"Bullshit, Jane. You're being melodramatic and ridiculous. You're not six-years-old anymore, not helplessly locked in a closet, so stop acting like a frightened, defenseless child who can't do anything about her situation. You're a capable woman and you have to start acting like one."

Jane, shook her head no. "But I don't feel capable. I feel helpless and...and...ashamed."

Sydney's eyes narrowed in confusion. "Ashamed? Ashamed of what?" Sydney demanded.

"Of what I've done," Jane angrily screamed.

Sydney was taken aback. She had never heard Jane raise her voice in anger. Sensing some kind of breakthrough, Sydney, gently asked, "What do you mean what you've done?"

Jane started crying again, her whole body trembling.

Sydney gently repeated her question, "I don't get it. What exactly is it that you've done, Jane?"

"I k-k-killed my mother," Jane sobbed.

"What are you talking about? In the hypnosis session you said your mom died from an overdose of drugs. You were locked in the closet so it is not possible that you killed your mother, Jane."

"But...but...if I hadn't bitten that man, he wouldn't have locked me in the closet. I could have called for help. I could have saved her."

"Oh my God, Jane. All these years you've been blaming yourself for your mother's death?"

Jane, still violently shaking, sobbed, "Well, I didn't really realize it. Not until this very moment."

Sydney hurried into the kitchen and returned with a paper bag, handing it to Jane. "Breathe," she instructed.

Jane took the bag, covered her mouth with it, and breathed deeply. The crying and trembling slowly began to subside. When she took the bag away, she felt more in control. Jane stared off into the distance, remembering. "Mother told me to be nice to the man. But I wasn't nice. I bit him so hard he bled. If I'd just been nice like she told me, she wouldn't have died."

"No, Jane, you've got it wrong. The problem is you're still thinking like a six-year-old." Sydney took Jane's hand and pulled her up from the couch, leading her over to a hall mirror. "Look," she commanded. "Do you see a six-year-old?"

Jane stared at her reflection for a few moments before answering, "No. I see a grown woman, but I still feel responsible."

Sydney stood beside Jane so both reflections were in the mirror. "I want you to think about something for a minute."

"Okay," Jane said.

"What if it was *me* that was six? What if I had bitten a man who was trying to molest me? What if I had been locked in the closet? Would you blame me for causing my mother's death?"

Jane blinked her eyes several times, thinking. "No, I guess not. But you *never* did what you were told."

Sydney had to laugh. "Well, you're right about that. But that's not the point. The point is that a six-year-old is a child and shouldn't be expected to handle that kind of responsibility."

"But if I had been nice...just done what my mother asked..."

Exasperated, Sydney interrupted Jane, saying, "You're not getting it. So, let me put it this way. Let's say you're juror on a murder trial. Okay?

"Okay," Jane said hesitantly.

"The defendant is a six-year-old girl...."

Now it was Jane's turn to interrupt. "Well, that's impossible."

"Right. And why *is* that, Jane?"

"Okay, I'm getting it. We don't put children on trial because we don't hold them responsible."

"Great. Now look at yourself in the mirror again. You see an adult woman, right?"

"Yes."

"As an adult woman, would you say a six-year-old child was guilty of murder if she was locked in the closet by an adult—forced beyond her will to stay inside while her mother overdosed on the other side?"

"I guess not."

"So what happened all those years ago, no matter how awful, is not your fault. You didn't cause your mother to become an addict, you didn't bring that man to your place. All you did was try to protect yourself from being abused. For that you should be proud, not ashamed."

Jane continued to look at her reflection in the mirror. "I hear what you're saying but I think it might take a while to sink in. You know, a while before I can let go of feeling so ashamed."

"It's okay if it takes some time. However, you have to do something this morning, something I think will speed up your transformation process. This morning you have the opportunity to help another *blameles*s child before the situation gets worse than it already is."

Jane said, "All right, then. I'll do it for the child." Still looking at her reflection in the mirror, Jane mused. "I look like a Goddamn scarecrow. I should stop cutting my own hair."

Sydney laughed, "Brilliant idea. Which brings me to another step in your transformation that I think you should consider. I'm no shrink, but it now seems obvious that you also blame yourself for having been a cute kid. I'm guessing that you've been punishing yourself by intentionally downgrading your attractiveness."

"Well, I sure hadn't consciously thought about that, but maybe you're right. When this trial is over, I'm going to go shopping and I'm going to get a professional haircut."

"You go, girlfriend!"

Jane, her frayed nerves doing a jig in her stomach, arrived at Connie's ten minutes ahead of time. The coffee shop, open twenty-four hours, had only a few customers since most people who frequented the place were sleeping off their enslavement to illegal stimulants. The sleazy area and the grungy coffee shop only added to Jane's apprehension. To be polite, she ordered some food but when it arrived she just moved it around on the plate to have something to do. Fortunately, the waitress left her alone, not offering more coffee or inquiring about the uneaten food. By nine-fifteen, no one fitting the description Sydney had given her had entered the coffee shop and Jane's apprehension was approaching panic. Sydney had said to wait at least an hour, but her nerves were too raw to wait that long. Finally, at nine-twenty a disheveled, debilitated woman walked in the door. When Jane saw her, a foreboding mirage smacked her right in the gut, causing her to momentarily lose her grasp on reality. The emaciated woman was an apparition, a mirror image of her mother the way she looked the last time Jane had seen her alive.

The skeleton of a woman nervously looked around the room, gave Jane eye contact, turned around, and walked out. Seeing the woman exit was the only thing that brought Jane back to the present. She quickly stood up and ran after the woman, stopping her just outside the door to the coffee shop. "Please," Jane said. "Don't leave."

The woman turned back toward Jane, eyeing her suspiciously. "Why did you look at me that way?"

"I'm sorry if I scared you. For just a moment, I thought you were my mother."

The women's eyes narrowed even further. "Your mother? What crazy shit is that?"

"Please, come back inside. Let me buy you something to eat. I'll explain."

"You ain't with the law, right?"

"I promise I'm not with the law. I just want to ask you a few questions and then give you some choices."

"Those questions. They have something to do with the man in the picture your friend showed me?"

"Yes, but please come back inside. You look like you could use something to eat."

The woman's glazed-over eyes ran up and down Jane before saying, "I suppose I could use some food."

Jane opened the door to the restaurant and the woman hesitantly walked in. "Let's go back to my table," Jane said.

They took a seat opposite each other in the booth where Jane had been sitting. The skeleton of a woman eyed the cold plate full of food. "You didn't eat nothing," she said.

"No, I was too nervous to eat."

"You don't want it, I'll eat it," she said.

"No, no, that's okay. I'll get you some hot food." Jane looked around for the waitress but didn't see her. When she turned back to face the woman, she saw that she was in the process of devouring the two slices of cold bacon she had left on her plate. Jane pushed her plate in front of the woman, who immediately reached across the table and grabbed Jane's fork, shoveling the cold eggs and potatoes into her mouth, hardly chewing the food before she swallowed. The scene in front of her was so heartbreaking that the apprehension Jane had been nursing disappeared. Just then the waitress came out of the kitchen and Jane was able to catch her eye and signal her. When the waitress arrived at the table, she took no notice of the disheveled woman. In the same dreary manner as she had earlier, she took Jane's order for another of the same. Skeleton-woman kept eating, not bothering to look up from her plate of food the whole time the waitress was at the table. When she had scraped the last bit of food from the plate, her vacuous eyes looked up at Jane as she asked,"Why did you think I was your mother?"

Sydney had warned Jane that the woman would intuitively know if she was lying and instructed her to tell the truth and nothing but the truth. So Jane said, "My mother was a drug addict. The last time I saw her, twenty-two years ago, she looked like a mess, so thin and scruffy...just like you."

"Yeah, I ain't looking so good these days. The woman from last night told me your mother O.D.'d when you was six. Is that the truth?"

"Yes. I was in the room, locked in a closet."

"The man in the picture that woman showed me...he's the one that locked you in?"

"Yes, his name is Bradley Cunningham. Do you know him?"

"Why should I tell you anything? Talking could get me into plenty of trouble."

Jane reached into her purse and pulled out a folded newspaper clipping, holding it close to her chest, saying, "My name is Jane. What name can I call you?"

The woman hesitated before saying, "You can call me Lily."

"Okay then, Lily." Jane opened up the clipping, turning it toward Lily. "Did you know that Mr. Cunningham is on trial for felony hit and run?"

"Let me see that," Lily demanded, grabbing the clipping from Jane. She looked it over closely before saying, "Well, I'll be damn. I didn't know...don't read newspapers much."

"The law is trying to prove he hit a woman with his car and then left the scene."

Lily eyed Jane suspiciously, asking, "What's that got to do with me?"

"That's what we're trying to find out."

Lily screwed up her face in uncertainty, saying, "That other woman said she might be able to help me. What did she mean?"

"Well, if you have any information about this man that might pertain...I'm sorry. If you have information that might tell the law what the man was doing in the area where the woman was run down, they might be willing to trade you something for it."

"What do you mean trade?"

"You see, if you have information the law wants, then to get that information they might be willing to help you, maybe pay for rehab to get you off the drugs, for example."

Just then the waitress appeared with a new plate of food, setting it down on the table between the two women and disappearing without a word. Jane slid the plate toward Lily, who immediately began eating. With her mouth full of food, Lily asked, "What do you mean they *might* be willing? That doesn't sound too good. Ya know, I could get in plenty trouble talking to the law and then they could decide not to help me. Where would I be then, huh?"

"The other woman you met this morning...she says she will pay for a lawyer to help you. You see, Lily, the way it works is that *your* lawyer goes to the law, never mentions your name but tells the law you have information. If the law want to find out the information then they have to agree to a deal. But if they say no to the deal, then they have no idea who you are."

"I don't trust no lawyers. Why would a lawyer help me, anyway? And why would a stranger pay for it?"

"You trust a lawyer because they can go to jail if they don't do what they promise. And the woman you met earlier, well she wants to help you because it will help me."

"Hmm. Even if I did have information, I can't go into no rehab."

"Because of your child?"

Lily slammed her fork down on the table, hissing "Who says I have a child?"

"Look, Lily, I don't know for sure you have a child so I'm just telling you how it works *if* you did. So just listen to me and then you decide what you want to do. Okay?"

"I'm listening."

"If you have important information about this Cunningham man, information the law really wants, you can name your terms. In this case, you could make them promise not to take your child away from you. While you're in rehab they will take care of her...or him...and even let you see the child while you're in rehab. When you get out, the two of you can be together again."

"You make it sound easy. But I did rehab before and when I got out I couldn't get no job. I ended back on the streets, then back on drugs, only this time it just got worse and worse." Her eyes started tearing up. "Look at me! Now I'm not even fit for the streets. And I'm a terrible mo..." She cut herself off, the tears flowing freely now. "I get so desperate, I do awful things. Too awful to speak about."

"I know all about those awful things," Jane said, reaching across the table to touch Lily's scrawny hand. "My mother was desperate too and it eventually killed her, leaving me alone in the world. My friend and I want to help because...well, we want to be sure you don't end up like my mother and we want Cunningham to get what he deserves. Look, Lily, you can make the law promise to get you a job, even make them promise to train you for a job, providing you have information they want."

Pointing to the newspaper, she said, "Oh! I got information they want, all right. Stuff that would turn everything upside down. So, you set up that meeting with that lawyer person you said could make a deal. I'll decide what I want to do after I meet that lawyer."

"Okay, Great. How can I get in touch with you?"

"You can't. You give me a number where I can reach you. I'll call you later tonight."

"Lily, I promise nothing is going to happen to you if you don't call. So, whatever you decide, you should do it because you want to, not because you're afraid. Okay?"

"Girl, I don't know what it's like not to be afraid. My father slapped my mom and all us kids around as long as I can remember. Now I'm being slapped around by some asshole who gets me my drugs. If information is my way out of this shithole life I've dug for myself...well, you'll see. I'll call."

The first thing on Cunningham's mind early Saturday morning, after a few restless hours of sleep, was the nasty mess he was now calling *Debeck's debacle*; the man he once thought invincible he now thought of as a screw-up. However, fearing some sort of retribution, he decided to follow through on his promise of hiring a nurse. He didn't want any possibility of the transaction being traced back to him, however. So, making sure no reporters were following him, he drove to a coffee shop where he made the call for a nursing assistant from a pay phone. He used a phony name and told the nursing service he would messenger over the address and payment. Then he phoned a messenger service.

All the extra effort infuriated Cunningham, but he worried about repercussions from the injured Debeck if he did nothing to help. He waited at the coffee shop until the messenger arrived and then tipped a waitress ten bucks to give the messenger an envelope with the cash and Debeck's address. After the messenger left, Cunningham called Debeck's house to tell him a nursing assistant would be on the way. He wasn't surprised when he got Debeck's voice mail. He risked leaving a brief message, telling him a nurse was on the way and to be sure he immediately erased the message.

After the last phone call, he remained at the coffee shop drinking coffee and wondering how the once seasoned security chief had been bested by a young, apparently guileless, juror Seven. God damn that woman, anyway! Not only had she been giving him the evil eye from the jury box, but she had also somehow managed to put Debeck, a veteran miscreant, out of commission. Juror Seven was turning out to be more than just another thorn in his side, she was somehow defeating him at his own game of deception. On the surface she appeared to be a dingbat with nervous tics and a simpleton look that made you feel she could be easily exploited. Underneath the veneer, however, was a dangerous trickster, a con artist skilled enough to deceive even RJ. His supposedly unassailable defense attorney had not only missed the cues himself, but ignored the advice of the outrageously expensive jury consultant he had insisted Cunningham hire. Unless he did something about it this weekend, the witch of a woman would be back in the courtroom on Monday staring him down.

Juror Seven, however, was not the only problem he would be facing in the courtroom on Monday if he didn't take action today. There was also the matter of his conspicuously missing wife. Edgy from all the coffee he had consumed, he left the coffee shop and drove himself back home. He spent the whole trip trying to devise a way he could get Rose to forgive him and come back home. She wouldn't answer her cell phone and calling her parents' house had only resulted in having to talk to one or the other of her ridiculous parents, two people he found cloying with their scrupulous Bible quotations and their sanctimonious approach to "non believers." He'd been sucking-up to them for so long that the obsequiousness had become second nature. If he could just get this trial behind him, his life was going to change. He'd wait a while, until the media had moved on to another quarry, then he'd ditch his priggish, pious wife and her moralizing, holier-than-thou parents. This last thought, something he had never before let himself consider, gave him a surprising feeling of liberation which buoyed him for what he had to do: suck it up and do more of the fawning he'd perfected since he met Rose.

When he got home, he immediately went into his office and called his in-law's home. Rose's father answered and stiffly informed him that Rose was refusing to take his calls. Although, Cunningham had planned on being unctuous, the minute he heard her father's self-righteous tone, he almost lost his earlier resolve and, for a split-second, considered telling the man to go fuck himself. Fortunately, he was able to choke back the words. Instead he said, "Please tell Rose that I love her."

It was only nine o'clock in the morning when he hung up. This mockery of a trial had turned his obedient wife into a Judas. Her absence would be a void noticed by all the jurors, a silent message of character assassination that would wreak havoc on his already crumbling defense. Now that she was no longer his puppet, it would be worth whatever it cost him, which, of course, would be millions, to dump her for good. He might even leave town and start a new life, the idea of anonymity sounding sweet to him at the moment. But now was not the time to cast aside Rose and her family. Monday would be the day he needed his "devoted" wife back in the courtroom, the day RJ would be starting his defense. However, when the trial was all over then his life would be very different.

He paced his office floor as he thought about what he needed to do. He had all of today and tomorrow to come up with a plan for solving the numerous obstacles in his way. Now that Debeck was out of commission, he would have to find another way to remove Juror Seven. He would also have to find a way to get Rose back in the courtroom, and then he would have to find a way to appease his defense attorney, a man he had clearly alienated on Friday when he refused to explain why he was in such a questionable area at the time of the hit and run.

Since Rose was no longer responding to his declarations of love and long-term commitment, he realized he had something he could use as leverage: her passion for the children's foundation they had started. He sat down at his computer and wrote several drafts of a note before finally deciding that keeping it short and to the point would provide the best chance of its being read in its entirety. His final version read:

Rose: This trial, a travesty of justice, is ruining our wonderful past together and has the potential for destroying any possibility of our future happiness. I am not guilty of the hit and run. Nor am I guilty of your charges of homosexuality. I need you by my side Monday to show the jury that you believe the charges against me are false. If you won't do this because you believe in me, then do it for The Foundation. If you don't show up Monday morning, the future of The Foundation will be in jeopardy along with our marriage.

Your loving husband,
Bradley

Cunningham folded the note, put it in an envelope with Rose's name on the front, and phoned his driver, telling him to deliver the message to his in-law's home. After he hung up, he had a fleeting moment of hesitancy, realizing there was some chance the note could backfire. In the end, however, he decided such a bold move was shrewd. He had somehow lost his edge with Rose and felt his only option at this point was to remind his wife who called the shots. By the time he had finished the final draft of the note and sent it on its way, it was almost noon and he was surprisingly hungry. He wandered into the kitchen to see what his cook had left over the weekend for him to eat. He found a lasagna casserole, cut himself a large slice, and heated it in the microwave. Sitting down at the bar in the kitchen and waiting for the lasagna to reheat, he pondered his next step regarding juror Seven.

He had no idea who she was or where she lived, but Debeck did. The nursing service promised to have someone at Debeck's home by noon, so Cunningham decided he needed to speak with Debeck while he might, with any luck, be feeling somewhat appreciative.

He told his driver to take the day off after delivering the note to his in-laws. Finishing lunch, Cunningham dressed in casual clothes and drove himself to a pay phone. He dialed Debeck's home and was caught off guard when a strange male voice answered the phone. He almost hung up but then heard Debeck's voice in the background loudly asking who it was.

The male voice on the phone said, "Hello? Hello? Are you there?"

"Who are you?" Cunningham asked, in a low timbre, hoping to disguise his voice.

"Mr. Debeck had an accident. I'm assisting him. May I ask who you are?"

Cunningham realized he had assumed it would be a woman assistant. "Oh, well, I'm a friend. I'd like to speak with Mr. Debeck, please."

In the background he could hear Debeck again asking who it was. The male voice moved away from the phone, answering Debeck, "He says he's a friend but won't give me his name."

There was more background noise before Cunningham heard Debeck grumble into the phone, "Who is this?"

"It's me. I hope you got my earlier message and that you erased it."

"I heard it. And I hope you can appreciate that I'm still without sight, so I can't see to answer the Goddamn phone, much less erase a fucking message."

Bradley felt his heart accelerate with the thought of his voice remaining on Debeck's answer machine. "Well, tell the helper to erase it."

"Your concern for me is overwhelming," Debeck responded, dryly.

Bradley had to force himself to calm down, to remind himself he shouldn't expect Debeck to be in the best of moods. After all, he had been disabled, was in pain, and probably fuming about having been bested by a woman. "Look, I'm sorry about all this. I hired you some help. I'm doing what I can do without incriminating myself. Promise me, though, that you'll have the assistant erase the message."

"I'm not an idiot. I'll take care of it."

Inside, Cunningham wanted to laugh at that declaration. So far, the man hadn't taken care of anything and had succeeded only in ending up crippled. It would be stupid to remind the fuck-up he had twice failed, so he said,"I'll be sure you're compensated for all your trouble, but you understand I still need to take care of my original problem, so I need to know the woman's address."

"You're not thinking of taking care of the problem yourself, are you?"

"No, I just want to know where she lives."

"Her address is 190 Glencliff Ave. But Bradley, I think I should remind you not to underestimate the target, 'cause that bitch is straight out of a James Bond movie."

"That gives me an idea. You got the name of a good cyber spy—someone willing to keep quiet?"

"Yeah, I know a guy."

"Good, give me his name and number."

After ending the call with Debeck, Cunningham used the same pay phone to call the name Debeck had just given him. The man answered the phone on the third ring. Cunningham told him he needed all the information he could get on a nameless female living at a specific address and he was willing to pay whatever it cost to get the name and info by that evening.

"No problem," the man said. "It will cost you two grand upfront, cash."

"Hold on a minute." Cunningham opened his wallet to see how much cash he was carrying. He was short about six hundred. " Tell me where and I'll messenger the cash over within an hour."

The man asked, "You got something to write with?"

"No, but I'll remember."

"Okay, put the cash into an envelope and write the word, *Endeavor*, on it. Send it to 1103 Addison St. and drop it at the front desk. Now, where do I email what I get?"

" I don't want it sent electronically."

"Okay...but how you going to get it then? No one, and I mean no one I do work for comes to my place."

"Make hard copies, put them in an envelope and write...umm, write the name Sampson on it. Then call a messenger service and have them bring it to the northeast corner of Chase and Orange. Can you have it ready by seven tonight?"

"You want bank and tax records?"

Cunningham hadn't even thought that far. "Yeah, sure. I want whatever you can get."

"No problem, except I'm going out at six-thirty so I'll have to get it out by six."

"Six would be great. Give me an approximate time you think it would take for the messenger to get to Chase and Orange from your place."

"Hold on a sec...Goggle maps says it will take seventeen minutes...better add on ten to fifteen minutes since it's rush hour."

"All right, then. The address I want information on is 190 Glencliff Ave."

"I'm on it the minute the cash arrives...with an extra fifty for the messenger, right?"

"Yeah, yeah...I'll put in an extra fifty."

Cunningham hung up the phone feeling upbeat. He was confident that the information he just bought would somehow give him back the upper hand. No one knew better than he that everyone had skeletons in their closets. He would find something to use against the woman, something that would wipe that diabolical look off her face and bend her to his will.

Okay, he realized, so the first thing I have to do to get this plan going is messenger over the cash. He had to find a bank so he could get the extra six hundred plus money for the messenger service. He got back in his car and drove only a few blocks before finding an open branch of one of the banks where he had an account. Fortunately, across the street was a Seven-Eleven with a pay phone. It occurred to Cunningham that he hadn't used a pay phone in years and yet, in the last few days, he had used pay phones almost exclusively. He drove into the lot of the Seven-Eleven and entered the phone booth. Of course, there was no phone book so he had to call 411 to get the phone number of a messenger service. He instructed the service to send the driver to the bank across the street.

His picture had been on the front pages of the newspapers almost daily in the last few weeks so he walked into the convenience store, bought a pair of cheap sunglasses and a ball cap, and then drove across the street to the bank. He put on his disguise, such as it was, and went inside to a teller, withdrawing a thousand dollars and asking for the money to be put in an envelope. He wrote the Addison address on the envelope along with the word, *Endeavor,* inserted the necessary cash, and went out front to wait for the messenger service. The driver arrived in just under twenty minutes. Cunningham, still in ball cap and sunglasses, handed him the envelope with the address on it, paid the fee in cash, and sent the messenger on his way.

Being a victim was not in Cunningham's playbook, so finally taking action made him feel back on track and more in control of his fate. It was approaching two o'clock; he had about four hours before he needed to meet the messenger at Orange and Chase, plenty of time to come up with a way to take care of the next problem on his list: how he might mollify RJ. He drove himself back home, stretched out on the couch in his office to think about what he would tell RJ. Within minutes he was asleep. He awoke with a jerk, confused at first about where he was, then panicked when he remember he had to be somewhere. He looked at his watch: five-thirty-four. *Shit!* He jumped up, grabbed the ball cap and sunglasses, ran to his car, and sped out of his drive, accelerating through a yellow light before reminding himself he could not afford a ticket. *Shit, he had forgotten to watch for the media.* He didn't have time to mess with evasive action to avoid the media scoundrels, so he kept a close watch in his rearview mirror, relieved when he was certain he wasn't being followed. He arrived at the corner of Chase and Orange at a few minutes after six. There was no messenger car around. He parked his car and waited.

After about ten minutes, he began to get anxious. Had he been too impulsive, too rash? After all, he gave a man he didn't know two thousand dollars on just the say-so of Debeck, whom he had foolishly thought was bulletproof. All Cunningham knew about the cyber hacker he had hired was a name and phone number. After several more minutes of waiting and growing more anxious, Cunningham was sure he had been scammed. He decided he would wait ten more minutes and then leave. A little after six-thirty the messenger car showed up and Cunningham breathed a sigh of relief. Pulling the cap down over his face, he got out of his car and walked over to the driver's side of the messenger car. The window came down. "You have an envelope for Sampson?" Cunningham asked. The driver handed him the envelope and Cunningham gave him a five dollar tip.

Cunningham watched as the car drove away, and then slipped out the sheets of paper inside the envelope, fanning through them. *Jesus! It was scary what a computer hacker could steal.* He was glad he decided not to have the documents sent to him electronically where some hacker could do the same to him. He returned the papers to the envelope and got back into his car; he would take then home, study them, and hope something in this pilfered data would give him the edge he needed.

Once home, he quickly ate the dinner his cook had left for him and headed to his office to study the material on the woman who dressed like a Puritan but had the soul of the devil. He pulled out the first sheet of paper with the basic, personal information. Her name was Jane Nichols. She was twenty-eight years of age, single, and worked for the county in a water treatment lab. She rented her duplex on Glencliff, owned outright a red Honda Civic, had only one credit card, which she paid off each month, leaving her with absolutely no debt. Since she was serving as a juror, he wasn't surprised to discover she had never been in trouble with the law. *Could the woman who had given Debeck such trouble really be this mundane?*

He moved on to the next page where his cyber-thief had uncovered adoption records. Jane had been born to a woman named Tamara Romer; something about the name Romer nudged a memory for Cunningham. He went on to read that Nichols was the name given to her as a result of the adoption. Her birth name had been Bane, not Jane. *Come on...someone named their child Bane?* Then he realized it was the unusual name, Bane Romer, that was itching his memory. He looked at the date of the adoption: twenty-two years ago. The girl would have been between six or seven-years-old. The age where he....

Suddenly, a bombshell exploded in his brain and fear gripped him in the stomach. The papers he had been reading slipped out of his hand, falling all around him. In a knee-jerk response, he looked down at the scar on his hand and the memory became vivid: the six-year-old girl with the cruel name had bitten him so hard she had taken a small chunk out of his hand. He had used his shirttail to contain the bleeding then hurried to a pharmacy and bought some bandages. Being seen by a doctor had not been a choice...too many questions. Because of that decision, the bite had scarred badly. He had been beyond furious at the time and had never used the child again—never even thought about the fate of the girl from the moment he slammed and locked the closet door.

Impossible! The odds had to be enormous that the same brat who had bitten him would now be sitting on a jury where he was accused of a crime he didn't do. Cunningham jumped up."God damn it!" he screamed. "This trial is nothing but a cruel twist of fate?" He began pacing, wondering, maybe there really is a God. And He's being vengeful because I've rejected Him. He returned to his chair, leaning over with his head in his hands. Had it been preordained for him to stop and get out of his car when he saw the body, only to drive away without calling 911? He had never been one to believe in that sort of shit, but how else could you explain the coincidence of a grown-up Bane Romer now sitting in judgement of him?

That smug grin! Shit! She must know I'm the man who slapped her and locked her in the closet. Yet how could that be possible? A six-year-old child might be able to recall being locked in a closet, but how would it be feasible after all these years for such a young child to identify the person who put her there? He had been careful all these years, never using the same child more than several times and never a child older than six precisely because an older child might be able to later identify him.

Then he remembered the scar on his hand. *Oh, no! Not possible!* Surely she couldn't have noticed the scar and then remembered him. The cruel irony of such a thing happening...well, how could that be plausible? He shook his head, realizing he would never have any answers to the questions he was asking. He would just have to operate on the assumption that the improbable was possible.

So, being a man of action, he needed to have a plan rather than wallow in conjecture and self-pity, which would never get him out of his predicament. He lifted his head, gathered the papers from the floor, and looked through the remaining information for something he could use to gain some leverage. He dropped page after page on the floor as he read, shaking his head in disbelief. Nothing! It was all useless. Bane Romer, now, Jane Nichols, was a boring prude. The woman could not be blackmailed and trying to bribe her would likely end in a backlash, given the peculiar circumstances.

The only option seemed to be the original plan: to get her off the jury, only now the original plan needed to be tweaked. Jane Nichols needed to have a credible accident that would remove her not just from the jury but from the earth. The only villainous man he knew and could trust to keep quiet was out of commission. However, he now had her name and address and it seemed he would have to be the one to finish what Debeck had started. Monday he had to be back in court, so he only had the rest of the night and tomorrow to get rid of her.

He stood up from his desk and headed toward the liquor stash. He needed a specific plan and a drink would loosen his creativity. He poured himself a double scotch and began pacing. It would be safest for him to assume that she had told someone about their earlier connection. Therefore, a break-in, mugging, or shooting would be too suspicious; the last thing he needed now was to have anyone investigating him further. The only choice remaining was a plausible accident. He was a mechanical engineer, a brilliant one—or so his legacy went. Tampering with her car would be the simplest and the easiest; the tricky part would be getting access to the car without being seen. He would have to drive over to her home and wait until he was sure she was asleep. The cyber-thief had provided him with her license plate so there would be no mistaking her car. He swallowed the remaining alcohol and headed to the bedroom where he set the alarm for one A.M.

It was just before two in the morning when Cunningham first drove by the small duplex at 190 Glencliff. The neighborhood was dense with small homes, many duplexes and many without driveways, which meant residents had to vie for street parking. Jane's small home had a shed but not a garage. It did, however, have a driveway, but there was no red Honda Civic parked there. He drove around several blocks looking for the Civic but couldn't find it, his frustration mounting as he realized that his simple plan was becoming riskier and more complex than he anticipated. He would now have to find a place to park away from Jane's place, walk back to her duplex, find a hiding place where he could watch for her car; or he would have to come back later. He chose to circle the block, finally finding a space one block over. He then walked back to the duplex, avoiding the street lights. He found a place across the street where he could watch for the car but wouldn't be easily seen if he crouched in some bushes.

Jane's house was dark except for a dim light which seemed to be coming from one side of the house. He had been skulking in the bushes across the street from Jane's duplex for twenty very uncomfortable minutes when he concluded that this last minute plan required more patience and more willingness to tolerate discomfort than was within the capability of a man of his stature.

He was just about to walk back to his car when he noticed a woman walking on the opposite side of the street in his direction. He stepped back into the bushes and waited. As she got closer she passed under a street light and he could see that she had long hair and a stunning outline, her spike heels and short skirt accentuating enticing legs. She walked up the few stairs to the porch of 190 Glencliff and let herself in with a key. A light came on in the house and he could see the outline of the slim woman with the long hair behind the curtain that covered the front window. Then she disappeared.

Cunningham assumed the woman must be a roommate. If she was a roommate, however, why didn't she park in the driveway? Then it occurred to him she might be a lover. Jane Nichols certainly had a butch way about her with the short hair and unisex clothing. Debeck has said nothing about a roommate, but then Debeck had pretty much been insensible. He thought back to the material the cyber spy had given him on Jane, but there was nothing about her having a roommate.

After a few moments, he again saw a female shadowy figure behind the curtain, this time the woman had short, spiky hair. Well, he decided, it didn't matter to him who the attractive long-haired woman was. What mattered to him was that he had seen Jane, assuring him she was home. But where the fuck was the red Honda Civic? None of what he was seeing made any sense.

Maybe he had somehow missed the car the first time he drove around. The only thing he could think to do was to check again for the car by walking around the neighborhood. After searching around for twenty minutes, he still couldn't find the car. He didn't know what to do so he decided just to return home. He was in his car and about a mile from Jane's duplex when he saw a red Honda Civic. A coincidence, probably, but worth checking out. He stopped, backed up his car so he could see the license plate. Bingo! *What the hell was her car doing so far from her home?*

The car was on a commercial street and right under a light. All the shops were closed and there weren't that many cars on the road at this time of the morning, but it certainly wasn't the deserted driveway he had imagined. He thought about the risk he would be taking to tamper with the car when it was so observable and decided it was too dicey. Earlier, when he realized who juror Seven was, he had felt desperate. Out of panic, he had conceived a precarious plan that would have worked only under conditions in which the car was easily accessible and not observable. It would just be plain stupid to mess with the car parked where it was. Fuck it! He would have to go back to Debeck for help, paying him whatever it took. Meanwhile, he would have to face Jane

Nichols in the courtroom and pretend he didn't know a thing about who she really was. God! He hoped that by the end of the day tomorrow Debeck would be back in commission and feeling vengeful and greedy enough to tackle the she-devil again.

The double shot of firewater masquerading as vodka calmed Erin only for a short time before, feeling lightheaded and giddy from the combination of alcohol and adrenaline, she began a constant chatter about what just happened. Toby was amused by the animated, scattered thoughts that spilled out of the usually solemn Erin. She was rambling on and on about the woman with the pendant, speculating on the improbable coincidence and what it could mean. Then, as if someone turned down her dimmer, she began to fade, her words slowing and her eyelids rapidly blinking as she tried to keep herself awake. She nodded off twice before Toby came around to help her up from the booth. He put his arm around her waist and walked her to his car, fastening her into the seatbelt. By the time he was behind the wheel, she was asleep with her head on her chest.

She was still sleeping when he parked the car in front of her condo. He dug around inside her purse until he found her keys. Easily lifting her from the seat, he carried her up to her condo. With Erin still in his arms, he was maneuvering the keys and the locked door when she opened her eyes once, groggily asking, "Where am I?"

"You're in my arms in front of your condo."

"Hmm. Have we done the nasty?"

Toby laughed and was about to answer but Erin was already back into a deep sleep.

She awoke late in the morning to the sounds of a car crash, her heart racing as she bolted up in bed. It was only when she saw the familiar surroundings of her condo that she realized she had been dreaming, the memory of the previous night slowly coming back to her. She was shoeless but still wearing the short skirt and white stretch blouse. The bedspread was half pulled over her. She lay back down, going over in her mind what had happened early this morning on Grover Street: the woman with the pendant, the drive-by car with an automatic weapon hanging out of the window, the loud crash and, oh, yes, the awful vodka.

She vaguely remembered being in Toby's arms. Then her memory went blank, replaced by urgent messages from her bladder. She hurried out of bed into the bathroom to use the toilet. After peeing for what seemed an eternity, she got up and stood in front of the sink. What she saw in the mirror appalled her: eyes rimmed in black by smeared mascara and hair that looked like washed-up seaweed, matted and plastered to her head. This is what Toby must have seen last night. She flushed with embarrassment. *This was the remnants of agreeing to be dressed as a prostitute.*

She eliminated her *Rocky Horror Show* look with a shower, then bagged up the cheap clothes and threw them in the trash. She picked up the wig that now rested like a road kill on the floor by her bed and set it on her bedside table. Then she headed to the kitchen where she made a pot of strong coffee and a piece of whole wheat toast.

Thoughts of Toby returned as she munched on the toast and sipped her coffee. She was sure nothing sexual happened between them, but she had a warm, comfortable feeling at the fleeting memory of being in his capable arms. Would he be feeling the same? Probably not. He most likely would be doing a great deal of self-reprimanding for the way things turned out last night.

Then thoughts of the vampish woman with the pendant replaced thoughts of Toby. The pendant still nagged at her subconscious. Absurd as the impression was, something seemed familiar about the woman, especially the way she had touched the pendant. Erin had come to trust her well-honed instincts so she was confident the mystery would reveal itself soon. She would just have to let it percolate. She was about to pour herself another cup of coffee when her phone rang. She looked at the caller ID, smiled to herself, and answered, "Hello, Detective Parish."

"Hey. Hope I didn't wake you."

"No, I've been up for a while."

"I'm calling to make sure you're okay. It was a rough night I put you through."

"I'm fine but it appears that I flaked out on you at the end."

"Well, you did spiral down quickly. It's the other end of the adrenaline rush."

"I know there is such a thing as an adrenaline junkie, but after last night, I'm sure I won't be one of them. I've had enough excitement for a lifetime."

"I'm just glad you didn't get seriously hurt. It was a stupid idea, one that I really didn't think through because...well, I guess because I didn't want to just cancel our dinner and not get to spend time with you."

Erin was quiet several seconds before answering, "I guess I didn't think it through enough either—and for the same reason."

Erin heard a sigh of relief. "Well, okay, then, that's out of the way. How about I pick you up and treat you to brunch? I know a hotel where they have a Sunday morning buffet designed for a Hungry Man. I promise that, unlike both of last night's establishments, it's an upscale place. You can even wear the dress you bought that you didn't get to wear."

"Eating with you could be hazardous for my health, you know. A couple more meals like last night and I won't be able to get into the dress."

"You could always go naked and just watch me eat."

"In your dreams, big man."

"Hey! Have you been snooping in my dreams?"

"Very funny."

"You can skip the buffet and order from the menu. I'm sure they have a poached egg on dry toast. Yum...my mouth is already watering."

"Okay, okay, I get it. I'm sure I can find something I can eat that isn't guaranteed to bulge my waistline. By the way, I have Mitchell's wig. Did you take it off of me last night?"

"Nope. Just put you in the bed as is. Covered you with the bedspread."

"Well, I guess I threw it off in my sleep. It was on the floor this morning looking very much like a dead animal. He wants it back, right?"

"We'll drop it off after brunch. How about I pick you up in an hour?"

"Sounds good to me."

On Sunday morning Rose Cunningham read the first few lines of the note from her husband and began to wonder if she had acted in haste—until she came to the part about his threatening to withdraw support for the foundation. At first she was disbelieving, but by the third reading she was in tears. Furious, she crumbled the note into a ball and threw it across the room. How could he be so cruel? Everything she thought she knew about her husband of thirty-seven years had been shattered by recent revelations: his continued refusal to tell her what he had been doing on Grover Street, his unexplained motivation for staying in a sexless marriage, and now...well, now he was acting like Lucifer incarnate by threatening to destroy the one thing left she still valued. What an idiot she had been. For days, she had been agonizing over the nightmare that had become her life, but not once had it crossed her naive mind that Bradley would try to use the foundation as a threat to bend her to his will.

Well, she decided, the blackmail—yes, blackmail!—had backfired. Instead of doing what Bradley demanded, the note succeeded in firmly setting in concrete her new resolve to transform herself. Late last night, she had begun to retreat from her bravado, wondering if the sneaky plan she had concocted was too brazen, too full of deception for the normally unsuspicious, compliant, and submissive wife she had become. Then the note arrived!

Now she was angry and that anger fed her resolve; she was now more determined than ever to go through with the gutsy plan she had conceived the previous day.

During the height of her anger and new resolve, Bradley phoned the house yet again. For a split second, Rose considered taking the call just to tell him directly that his threat had backfired. On reflection, however, she realized it would be a mistake to have any kind of verbal confrontation with a man that malicious. He had chosen to play his most vindictive trump card and she wasn't folding, but she wasn't ready for him to know that yet. She needed a trump card of her own and her plan just might give her a higher card.

After refusing to take Bradley's call, Rose moved forward with her plan of yesterday. Knowing she was unsophisticated when it came to technology, she made a call to one of the foundation staff members she could trust. Even though she had little experience with being cryptic, she was able to ask the staff member for what she wanted without alarming her contact. Rose had no experience telling lies and after hanging up, she felt terrible about having made up a story to get the name of someone who could help her. She sat in front of the phone for five minutes before she got the nerve to call the name and number she had been given. Fortunately, the man she spoke with was polite and very businesslike, emboldening her determination to go through with her plan.

That evening she surprised her parents by sitting down at the dinner table with them, warning them, however, that they were not to ask her any questions about Bradley. The conversation at dinner had been strained but she had gotten through it. After dinner she returned to her room, reflecting on the day's events. Receiving the threatening note in the morning had been very distressing, but she gave herself credit for having decided to go ahead with her plan. She anticipated there would be many more unsavory times to come and she viewed this morning's ordeal, and her actions afterwards, as a test she had passed. For the first time in two nights, she was able to sleep.

DAY EIGHT

It was Monday morning and Rose knew Bradley would be in court, knew he wouldn't catch her when she returned to the house and put her bold plan into action. Still, being safe from discovery didn't mean she wasn't jittery, wasn't overwrought from the actions she was about to take. She was going against her nature and that made her feel dishonorable—on top of being disloyal. The alternative, however, was to continue to act blindly, to make decisions about her marriage based on speculation. Given that she no longer knew what Bradley was capable of, she needed facts not suppositions.

Since court started at nine, she waited until nine-thirty to drive herself back home. She let herself in with her key and went directly to the kitchen to talk with Miranda, the housekeeper and cook. She wanted to be sure Miranda would not tell her husband she had been in the house. She felt confident that Miranda would do as she asked since the two of them had always been close, whereas Bradley had never taken the time to get to know her as a person.

After obtaining Miranda's complicity, she went upstairs to her office and retrieved some papers from a file. Then she hurried downstairs, vacillating before entering her husband's private domain, a room she rarely entered because Bradley had made it plain from the time they had designed and built the house that the office was to be his solitary space. Like everything else about her marriage, she had not thought to question her husband about his need for a private space.

She had conceived of the plan yesterday when she remembered she had the combination to the safe in his office and that Bradley was clueless to this fact. She had been the one at home when the workmen had come to put in the safe. One of the men had given her the paperwork, including the combination. With her usual efficiency, she had made a copy of the paperwork and filed it away for safekeeping in her personal files. Bradley had been away on business and when he returned the safe was already installed and the original paperwork sealed in an envelope on his desk.

She took a deep breath and crossed the threshold, hesitating for only a moment in the middle of the room. She felt like a child disobeying a parent, a child worried about being punished if she got caught. Knowing the safe was located behind it, she studied the painting on the wall; her plan had so many uncertainties. Would the combination she held in her hand still work? Would the object she was after still be there all these years later? And if it was there, would it contain the suspected information? She continued to eye the picture hiding the wall safe, yet again going over in her mind the consequences and ramifications of knowing versus not knowing.

Enough! I'm here and I must not retreat.

She moved toward the safe, opened the picture, looked down at the numbers on the paper she had retrieved from her office and, with trembling fingers, began to dial the combination. Soon Rose was staring into the open safe: no papers, no money, no jewelry...only a small black box. She hesitated, her heart racing, her face flushed with foreboding, realizing she was at a crossroads that would likely change her life forever. However, she had to act quickly to ensure she had the box back in the safe by the time Bradley came home this afternoon. She closed her eyes and brought the image from yesterday to her mind, the one of herself in the shower when she had been determined to be brave and let go of the denial. She sucked in a deep breath and snatched the box from it's protecting cocoon. Quickly closing and re-locking the safe, she hurried out of the room. She grabbed her purse on the hall table, tucking the box inside the large bag as she rushed to the garage.

Her heart pounding in her chest, she drove out of the driveway and toward the address the man on the phone had given her. Her mind raced as she reflected on how she had come to this point: evading the privacy, stealing really, from her own husband.

She hadn't remembered she had the number to the safe until yesterday when she read the Bible verses before dumping the book in the trash. Something about the verses had caused a long ago repugnant happenstance to flash across her mind.

That evening, all those years ago, had been unusual. Bradley told Rose he wouldn't be home for dinner so, as she often did when her husband wasn't home for dinner, she had arranged to have dinner with her parents at their house. Just as they sat down to eat, however, Rose had started feeling shaky and the sight of the food made her nauseous. Her mother took her temperature and discovered Rose had a fever, so Rose had chosen not to have dinner and, instead, drove herself home, planning on going directly to bed. When she arrived home, she was quite surprised to find Bradley's Mercedes in the garage. At the time, she had thought that her husband might also be feeling ill. She entered the house and headed for the stairs, expecting he might already be in bed. Then she noticed the light was on in his office. Instead of being closed as it usually was, the door was slightly ajar. She walked in that direction and as she got closer, she could hear strange moaning sounds coming from inside. Was he also feeling ill? She moved closer to the office to check on him.

As she approached the barely open door, she could clearly hear the strange sounds coming from the room. She lifted her hand to knock, but then noticed through the door that her husband was sitting at his desk and looking at the computer. His hands were moving rapidly below the desk and an unnatural grimace was on his face, his body making rhythmic back and forth movements. Her first thought was that he might be having a feverish seizure, but before she could make a move, he let out a loud moaning, pleasure-like sigh, the likes of which Rose had never before heard. Then he lifted a balled up tissue from under the desk and placed it on top before leaning back in his chair with his eyes closed, a slight smile on his face.

Rose tightened her grip on the steering wheel as she now vividly remembered how she had stood transfixed in place, feeling intrusive and somehow terribly defiled just by watching the scene. Somewhere in the back of her mind she knew what her husband had been doing, but her conscious awareness of the actual name for the act wouldn't compute. Feeling confused and shamed, she had immediately turned and walked away. She had been halfway up the stairs when her brain registered: *masturbation*. A feeling of fury had caused her already feverish body to explode with an increased wave of heat. *How dare he*! Without thinking, she had turned around and headed back down to the office, intending to confront her husband with his sinful, repulsive, forbidden behavior. However, when she got to the door she stopped.

Confrontation! That's what she had been afraid of back then. She had no experience with the courage needed for confrontation. She must have intuitively known she didn't have the fortitude to challenge him, especially feeling as sick as she was. Through the crack in the door, she remembered seeing Bradley disconnect a black square box from the computer. She had watched in silence as he walked to the open wall safe and locked the box inside. Suddenly, she felt weak-kneed and thought she might faint on the spot.

She now remembered how her stomach had somersaulted and she had hurried upstairs to the bathroom where she repeatedly threw-up in the toilet. Weak from the vomiting and the disgusting scene she had witnessed, all she could manage to do was take some aspirin and crawl into bed. She never heard Bradley come upstairs to his room next to hers. She awoke several hours later to cold sweats and again took aspirin and sips of water. She lay in bed seemingly forever, shivering from both the fever and the vile scene she had witnessed.

The next two days she had been so miserable from the flu she didn't get out of bed. She remembered Bradley stopping in the doorway to ask how she was and explaining how he didn't want to take the chance of getting sick by coming into the room. The first time he stopped by, she was relieved he didn't come into the room. She didn't think she could stand being near him.

However, by the time she was feeling better, the memory of the disgusting incident had begun to fade. Then before she knew it, a week had gone by, then another. By that time, Rose knew that confrontation would be impossible; the bridge to cross had grown too expansive with each day she had failed to take a step.

Now, with the stolen box in her purse, she looked back on her choices all those years ago. They had been cowardly and different from the one she had just made and, while she was still anxious, she was glad she hadn't buried her head in the sand as she had back then. She now realized how convenient it had been to put to sleep the memory of that vile incident, a slumber brought on by the need not to know. Keeping the memory alive would have meant she would have to DO something about it. As she now uncomfortably admitted, she had deeply feared any change in the life she so coveted. The memory of the incident had not been erased completely, only tucked away in a vault in her unconscious. Apparently, it had been nudged and prodded out into the open from the stress of the trial and by Bradley's refusal to be truthful with her.

These turbulent thoughts were still on her mind as she parked the car a few buildings down from the address the man had given her. She got out of her car and walked back to the building, a modern condominium with a locked, glass front door. She pushed the doorbell to the man's apartment. Through the speaker a deep male voice asked, "Who is it?"

"It's me. The woman who called earlier. Geri Roosth gave me your name, remember?"

"Yes, certainly. When you hear the buzzer, pull on the door. Then take the elevator to the penthouse."

A few minutes later, Rose's shaking hand was pushing on a penthouse doorbell. She was nervous but determined to step over yet another threshold, one that would further her along on her new journey: an odyssey where grappling with her demons was the goal.

A pleasant-looking man in his mid-to-late thirties with dark curly hair opened the door. His casual dress, tan linen slacks and a deep blue polo shirt, showed off a fit body. Rose, her mouth dry from apprehension, swallowed and said, "Hi. You'll have to excuse me, but I'm a lot out of my league here. So, I'm a bit nervous."

"Come in, please," the man said, as he stepped aside.

Rose stepped into the his living area, immediately noticing the large sliding glass door leading to a deck with a dramatic view of the city. "How lovely," she said.

All business, he asked, "So how can I help you?"

Rose took the black metal box out of her purse. "I need copies of what's on here."

The man looked puzzled, saying, "You don't need someone like me to make copies off a hard drive."

"Okay, look, I can't go to anyone I know. What I'm doing...well, it has to be private. And while I'm not very sophisticated about computers, I'm pretty sure these are password protected and I need to know what's on them."

"I see. What you're saying is the drive doesn't belong to you."

"I'm not sure. You see, they were made by my...a family member."

"A family member, huh? Does this family member know you have them?"

"No. I took them out of a safe in my own home, one that I have a combination to. So, I didn't really break into the safe, you see?"

"Murky, grey area."

"Yes, I can understand that. However, I'm totally confident that my...my family member would never bring charges against me. To do so would mean the material would no longer be private."

"Well, as I told you on the phone, I don't take any work that means I'm breaking the law. I can likely get you the passwords but when I do, then I'll see the material. I only get a brief look, just enough to know I've broken the password, but if there is something I immediately see on the drive that is illegal, I'll have to report it."

"What about immoral? You don't have to report that, do you?"

"Hmm. Another grey area because immoral is a subjective thing. Sometimes there is a fine line between immoral and illegal."

"I'm not sure what you're saying."

"Example, child pornography is illegal while most adult pornography is legal, but would be judged immoral by many."

Rose had to think about this for a moment. She didn't know much of anything about legal versus illegal aspects of pornography. She was expecting there to be acts of homosexuality on the box. She did know homosexual acts, sinful as they were, were not illegal. Finally, she asked, "Give me a minute, okay?"

"Sure. I'll be over in the kitchen. You want some coffee?"

"No thanks, I'm fine." Rose walked over to the large glass doors, looking down on the only city she had ever really known. She realized she hadn't thought it all the way through. She vaguely accepted that the person who broke the password would have to know what was on the drive as he called it; it was the reason she had gone to a complete stranger. Now confronted with an actual person, the whole mess felt more sordid. Her husband's picture had been on the front pages of the papers for months and it was possible this man would recognize Bradley if he appeared on the screen. As his wife, she would suffer humiliation by association.

It wasn't too late to put the box back in the safe. But would she be able to live with not knowing the truth of who or what Bradley really was? Would she ever rest until she knew for sure? She opened the proverbial Pandora's box when she'd unwrapped all her years of denial. Could she put thirty-seven years of a sham marriage back in the denial safe where she had locked it up? Even if she tried, wouldn't she be doing what she resolved not to do: bury her head in the sand?

She turned around and walked toward the kitchen. The man was leaning against the counter drinking from a mug. She stared at him, thinking, *he was honest with me upfront so I'm going to trust that he will keep whatever he finds to himself.* "Okay, I've decided," she said. "How long will it take to find out what's on the drive?"

"Depends on how it's been protected."

"I was hoping to get it back in the safe by this afternoon."

"You haven't asked what it would cost."

"I don't care what it costs."

"Well, in that case, I might be able to do it in several hours. But I can't promise. I'd have to look at it."

"Can you look at it now?"

The man put his mug down on the counter. "Sure. I can do that."

Monday morning, the second week of the trial, and Erin was on alert for several important observations from which she intended to make deductions. Right away, she noticed that Rose Cunningham was not in the courtroom, an ominous sign for the defendant and a fact that would no doubt agitate RJ. Erin had not forgotten Rose's unusually assertive behavior on Thursday of last week, followed by her absence in the courtroom on Friday. It hadn't taken much deduction to figure out that something was amiss between Bradley and Rose, and whatever it was had obviously not been settled over the weekend.

Next on her list of observations was whether Jane Nichols was wearing the pendant? Erin was absolutely positive the pendant she had seen the mysterious woman wearing Saturday night was too distinctive and too similar to Jane's to be a coincidence. As certain as she was about her conclusion regarding the pendant, however, she had decided not to mention her conviction to RJ because he had made it clear that he was disinclined to listen to her hunches without definitive supporting data, a circumstance she found ironic since she was being paid to provide just such suppositions. As the jury filed in, Erin smiled to herself, glad she followed her intuition about not informing RJ; juror Seven was not wearing anything around her neck. Had she mentioned her conjecture to RJ, she would have looked foolish.

It was the defense team's turn to present their case and RJ had started by calling his automotive repair expert to the stand. Erin was carefully watching Jane, observing how the woman was obviously less nervous than at the beginning of the trial. Today, though, she seemed distracted by her own thoughts, often staring off into the distance as if something other than the trial was preoccupying her mind. Erin knew it was common for jurors' minds to wander to other things, especially if the witness's testimony was too complex, clinical, technical, or if the trial had been going on for weeks. The witness on the stand right now, however, was capturing the attention of all the jurors except Jane. Occasionally, Jane would look over at Cunningham, her eyes narrowing in intense concentration for a couple moments, as if she was trying to read his mind. Then she would return to her own thoughts.

Erin noticed that Cunningham continually stared straight ahead, refusing to give the jurors any eye contact. His demeanor was alarming; he seemed even more tense than he had at the end of last week. Instead of the neutral expression he had been instructed to assume, he, like Jane, appeared distracted by his own thoughts. His eyes were narrowed in concentration, his tight mouth in a glower. Whatever was on his mind was hurting his case because his expression made him look menacing.

Erin quickly scribbled a note to RJ to talk to Cunningham about his expression. She hesitated a few seconds before passing it to him, anticipating that her observation would be ignored. *Damn it, this is what I'm being paid for and I can't let him intimidate me.* She leaned forward handing the note to one of the Tweedles, who read it, looked over at Cunningham, and surprised Erin by nodding in agreement before passing it to RJ. RJ looked at the note, then at Cunningham, then leaned over and whispered into Cunningham's ear. The defendant turned toward Erin, narrowing his eyes in contempt before turning back toward the front of the courtroom, his face transformed into a neutral mask

Right before the lunch break, Erin received a text message from Toby, asking her to meet him for lunch at a local restaurant. She hoped that he had discovered more about the mysterious woman wearing the distinct pendant. They'd spent most of yesterday's brunch talking about what happened early Saturday morning, mulling over the shooting scene and comparing notes on what each could remember. Erin reminded Toby about the riddle concerning the pendant, speculating that the woman wearing it might somehow know Jane. Toby thought that possibility very unlikely. However, Toby's doubts didn't deter Erin from asking to see if he could find out anything more about the pendant-wearing woman.

Toby was already seated in a booth waiting for her when she arrived. She sat down opposite him, immediately asking, "Any luck with our mysterious woman?"

"Not hello, not how are you, not I'm glad to see you?"

"Sorry, but I can't get the idea out of my mind that Jane somehow knows the woman from Saturday morning."

"Hmm. I guess having a preternatural ability to observe details about people can be a drag sometimes, huh?"

"Since you're avoiding my question, I'm guessing you came up empty handed."

"Whoa! Take it easy, Erin. You're sounding like The Reverend on cross."

That remark gave Erin pause. She leaned back in the booth, sighing, "You're right. I am obsessed."

The waitress appeared and Erin ordered a small spinach salad without looking at the menu. Toby ordered a sixteen ounce T-bone with a double order of mashed potatoes. Erin started to say something about his unhealthy choice but then changed her mind; she was not his mother. Besides the man seemed to be all muscle despite his eating choices. When the waitress left, Toby leaned in over the table and said, "Even with your feathers ruffled over this mystery woman, you manage to look lovely today."

Erin smiled, saying, "Excellent way to distract me from my obsession."

"Well, it did get a smile out of you and your smiles are so bewitching."

"You're being very charming today, Toby. Makes me wonder why?"

Toby looked hurt, asking, "Are you always so suspicious of compliments?"

"Hmm. You're right again and I'm sorry. I am suspicious. It's a fault of mine from long ago when I lost my hearing and was teased and humiliated by kids my age...well, boys mostly. So, let's start again." Erin got up and walked a few steps away before turning around and coming back to the booth, taking a seat and smiling at Toby. "Hi," she said. "I'm thrilled you invited me to lunch."

Toby scowled. "Cut the niceties, lady. We've got business to conduct and we don't have a lot of time."

Erin laughed. "You're a hoot, you know that?"

"Now, if I was only as wise as an owl, I'd be set."

Erin shook her head in amusement. "Okay, Toby, enough banter. So, did you or did you not find anything out about the mysterious woman?"

"Unfortunately, her description fits many of the women in that neighborhood so we can't know for sure. However, I did find out that it's possible she's the same woman who regularly meets with some of the street girls in a coffee shop on Grover Street. I only got this information when I mentioned the oversized handbag. The waitress I paid, handsomely by the way, said she had no idea what the woman's name is, which is par for the course in a neighborhood where *don't ask don't tell* is the policy on all matters. The only identifier I could find is that the woman who visits the coffee shop tips extremely well—too well, I'm betting, to be a street girl."

"Well, that's very curious. If she's not a street girl, what was she doing hanging around Gover Street acting like one?"

"My thoughts exactly. If we had more time, I could stake out the coffee shop to see if she turns up. But that is such a hit or miss proposition."

"I guess it would be way too risky for you to covertly stake out Jane's home. You know, see if the woman turns up there."

Toby narrowed his eyes at Erin. "Why you devious devil!"

Erin feigned a surprised look, asking, "Whatever do you mean?"

"You know exactly what I mean. *Too* risky my ass. That's a dare."

"I'm offended you think I would do something that duplicitous."

"Bull shit!" Toby shook his head in dismay. "You know, if I got caught snooping around a juror's home, not only would I lose my license but I could go to jail for jury tampering."

"Let me see. Wasn't it just two days ago I was voicing similar reservations? If I remember correctly, you told me to quit whining. Or maybe you've conveniently forgotten now that the tables are turned."

"Touché."

"Look, Toby, all banter aside, I really don't want to put you at risk. So, how likely is it that you would get caught?"

"Hmm, if you had asked me three days ago, I would have been cavalier and overconfident, saying there was zero chance. After Saturday night, when I foolishly put you at risk? Well, now I would be more prudent and say there is always the chance of the unexpected."

"Okay, seriously then. I'm thinking this idea of mine is not worth the risk."

"So, you're saying you'll let go of this preoccupation with whether Jane and the pendant-wearing woman somehow know each other?"

"Wait just a second. I said nothing of the kind."

Just then the server arrived with their food. Erin looked at the two plates as the waitress placed them on the table. She shuttered inside. *What would it be like to cook for a man who could chow down that much food?*

Jane wasn't able to keep her mind on the proceedings in the courtroom because she was thinking about Lily. Sydney, who claimed to know a great deal about drug addiction, warned her not to get her hopes up about the unstable woman. For an addict to accept the lifeline Jane had promised, she would have to trust a stranger. And she would have to have the conviction that she could change her own life.

Long-term drug addicts, according to Sydney, were people with very low self-esteem. The self-destructive baggage attached to lack of worthiness was a major obstacle. Self-blame, hopelessness, mistrust, defeatism, were difficult hurdles to get over. For a person with low self-esteem, the initial use of drugs temporarily lifts the weight of the baggage, an irresistibly lighthearted feeling for someone carrying such a heavy load. Sydney told her that the brain's chemical hunger for this good feeling is so compelling, so demanding, so gripping that the guileless drug experimenter rapidly becomes a slave to the chemical cravings. Breaking free from the chemicals is a prolonged, arduous road that is rarely accomplished alone. The reason for this, Sydney claimed, was an inherent paradox. Self-worth was the key to recovery, yet, given their lack of worthiness, most addicts start their recoveries with the unconscious conviction: I don't have what it takes to make the formidable journey. With this conviction of failure as an underpinning, falling off the wagon is just too easy.

When Jane heard her roommate say all this about drug addicts, she immediately thought of herself. The experiences of this last week had made her aware of how much negative baggage she carried about her own coping ability. A few days ago she discovered her image of herself was built on a foundation of self-blame. No wonder she always felt like she would crumble at the slightest challenge. Probably, she decided, she would have ended up just like Lily if Sydney hadn't come into her life. Sydney didn't seem to have any problems with self-esteem or any of the other negative attributes, yet she had also been dealt a lousy hand as a child. What made the difference? Would she be more like Sydney if she could get past the self-blame? This last thought led her to look over at Cunningham. How much did this truly evil man contribute to who she had become?

Jane was also thinking about what Lily had said: she knew something about Cunningham, something shocking that would make a big difference in the trial. But Lily hadn't called and, according to Sydney, probably wouldn't. If she didn't call, it would be up to Jane to make sure Cunningham got punished. Would she really be able to stand up to the other jurors? She felt unsure of herself—just like she had felt for as long as she could remember.

Then an idea occurred to her; maybe she could pretend she was Sydney during the deliberations; she certainly knew her roommate very well. When she was wearing Sydney's wig and clothes to get in and out of the courthouse, she felt like a completely different person, and she noticed that people treated her differently, gave her more deference just because of the way she looked. She wondered if she had her hair done by a professional and dressed with more self-regard, would she feel more confident during the deliberations? It was something to think about anyway.

The lunch break finally arrived and by then Jane had talked herself into believing that Lily would never call. Still, once she was out in the hall, she checked her phone for messages.

When she saw she had a one, her heart seemed to thud in her chest. She nervously pressed the number to retrieve the message and listened: "It's me, Lily. I'll be at Connie's at seven tonight. You come first and tell that lawyer person you talked about to be there at seven-thirty."

Jane felt shaky. She had gotten what she hoped for, but now it meant she would have to be strong, have to be confident enough to persuade Lily to trust her. Her legs felt weak at the thought so she took a seat on the closest bench while she rummaged around in her purse for the phone number of the lawyer "friend" of Sydney's. She found it, took it out, and started dialing the number, her anxiety skyrocketing with each ring. *Damn it! Here I am facing another challenge, another test of my promised journey to feel better about myself and instead of feeling brave, I'm feeling like I'll crumble under the responsibility. Calm yourself! Breathe. Think positive. Hadn't she stuck it out on the jury? Hadn't she twice thwarted the man who had planned to harm her? Hadn't she survived talking with Lily?*

So, when the lawyer man answered on the fourth ring, she took a deep breath and without too much stammering, explained who she was and what she wanted. She was dumbfounded when the man said he was expecting her call and easily agreed to meet her at Connie's at seven-thirty. She told the man to look for a woman who would be dressed to look like Sydney. He told her to look for a man in his early fifties, grey hair with a soul patch and a gold hoop earring in his left ear.

She hung up the phone thinking how foolhardy she had been to make such a big deal out of a simple telephone call—how foolhardy she been all her life to turn every molehill into a mountain. It was now up to her to help Lily and to be sure Cunningham was punished for what he did to her. She felt a heavy responsibility to prevent further abuse as well. She closed her eyes and imagined herself confidently talking with Lily and the lawyer. When she opened her eyes, she said aloud, "I can do this."

Only when he received the note passed to him from the jury consultant had Cunningham forced himself back to the present. He'd been caught doing something very hazardous to his already shaky case: letting his face show the devious plots that were gyrating in his mind. The trial was taking more of a toll on him than he could ever have imagined. It felt like he hadn't slept in weeks and his thoughts the last few days were often incoherent and reckless. He had even considered risking it all by tampering with a juror's car.

Of course, he would never have predicted that Rose would desert him just when he needed her the most. And the Jane Nichols catastrophe? Well, that had been an inconceivable fluke, a blow beyond his worst nightmare, an adversity that could only be overcome one way: she could not be allowed to stay on the jury. Last week he had been angry at her for the contemptible looks she had given him, but all that had changed. His anger had transmuted into fear for his survival, which meant drastic action had to happen soon. No matter how good a defense RJ mustered, Jane Nichols would ensure that, at the very least, they would have a hung jury, an outcome that meant he would have to go through the torture of another trial. He'd always seen himself as a survivor, but now he wasn't sure he could keep himself together if he had to endure another trial. The only positive factor in this whole mess was that there was no way Jane could ever prove he was the man who had locked her in the closet. Having a scar on his hand would never hold water as proof of anything after all these years.

Late yesterday, Cunningham had finally smartened up and bought a throwaway cell phone at WalMart. At the lunch break, he excused himself from meeting with RJ. Instead, he called the injured Debeck, who answered on the third ring.

"It's me. I'm calling to see how you're doing. I'm on one of those throwaway phones."

"Man, I was so out of it when you showed up. By the way, thanks for hiring that assistant. I don't know what I would have done without him."

"I'm sorry you got hurt and I'm hoping you're angry enough with the woman to finish the job—at triple rates, of course."

"Uh...when you say finish, what exactly do you mean?"

"I mean an end to the problem forever."

"End, huh? After what she did to me, it would be my pleasure."

"If her demise is at all suspicious, I'd be the first person they'd suspect. Even with an iron-clad alibi like being in court, they would be checking to see if I hired someone, which would easily lead to you."

"That makes things much more complicated. I mean I could try to get to her car, cause her to have an accident like I originally planned, but I can't be sure she'd die."

"Yeah, I've thought about that."

Debeck snickered, "Don't suppose you'd want to go for a hit and run?"

"Believe me, I've thought about that too, but it would be like throwing a T-bone to the media hounds. They'd be gnawing on the irony...and me until there was nothing left."

"I was such a mess when you came to my house, I didn't tell you that I was watching for her at the end of court on Friday, but I didn't see her leave the courthouse, nor did I see her car leave the parking lot. That's how I ended up at her home later. That bitch was just waiting for me, like she knew I was coming. She could have easily blinded me if she hadn't called 911 right away. The stuff she sprayed in my eyes is illegal to use on humans, but I'm sure she knew I wouldn't be able to press charges."

"Well, I can tell you she was sitting in the jury box all day Friday, so if you didn't see her leave, she purposely snuck out somehow. Combine that with your thinking she was expecting you Friday night, and I'm sure it means she's on to me. She'll be on the lookout for any more threats."

"I guess that means we need to come up with something she won't be expecting."

"I've been running options through my mind for days. Here's the plan I've come up with."

"You've got my attention."

"I had someone do some digging on her while you were laid up. So, I know something about her past. She was born to a drug addicted mother and was abused as a child and then adopted later by an older couple. So, I'm thinking unstable person...ergo suicide would not be such a stretch. She'd have to leave a note saying the trial was too much pressure."

"Hmm. What method are you thinking?"

"Get her in the bathtub, slit a wrist."

"That could be dicey. She's got a roommate we'd have to deal with."

"Yeah, I know and that puzzles me as the info I got didn't mention anything about a roommate. It does make it more complicated. You'll have to get to her when the roommate isn't home. Unfortunately, I don't have much time. The trial may go to the jury by the end of the week."

"Since she's on to my following her, I'm thinking the best plan would be for me to be in her house when she comes home from court. She won't be expecting me to be in the house. Of course, all this is predicated on the roommate's not being there."

"I like it. If the roommate's not there, go for it."

It was now one o'clock and with each minute she waited in the man's living room to learn if he could break the password to the drive, Rose's uncertainty grew; her anxiety mounted in proportion. How could she ever have ever thought she had the guts to go through with her plan? What was she going to do with the information if it confirmed what she suspected? A stronger, more malicious person might use the information to blackmail

Bradley into funding the foundation. Despite her promises to herself to change, however, she knew she would never be unprincipled enough to blackmail her husband. Only a few minutes ago, she had resolved to no longer live with denial, but now she wasn't so sure what she would gain this late in the game. The crippling doubts circling in her head were giving her a terrible headache. Tears of exasperation and indecisiveness started leaking from her eyes.

She looked around the apartment for a tissue, spotted a box on the counter in the kitchen and walked over to take one. She pulled several tissues from the box, wiped her eyes, and then noticed a business card that was sitting near the tissue box. The name on the card didn't register at first, but then suddenly it did, startling her so that she automatically picked it up to be sure she had seen what she thought. She quickly placed the card back on the counter, her previous anxiety now reaching paranoia proportions. *What in the world was this man doing with Saul Greene's business card?* Was someone purposely messing with her sanity? Suddenly, she felt too weak to stand. She grabbed onto the counter to keep her legs from collapsing under her. The man's voice startled her, "Are you all right?"

"No, I feel faint."

"Here, let me help you." The man walked over to her, took her arm by the elbow, and guided her over to the sofa, helping her to sit her down. "Lower your head between your legs," he gently urged. The man then moved to the kitchen to get a glass of water.

Rose did as he suggested and immediately began to feel less lightheaded. She carefully sat back up. The man was standing over her with a glass. She looked him straight in the eyes, saying, "You never asked my name."

Extending the glass toward her, he said, "Here, drink this." She took the glass from him and drank half of it. He continued, "My clients' names aren't important, unless, as I told you, I find I'm dealing with something illegal."

"Do you know who I am?"

"Yes."

Rose narrowed her eyes at him. "And how is it that you know me?"

"Your picture's been in the paper."

"Is that the only way you know me?"

"Yes."

"Are you being honest with me?"

"Yes, why do you ask?"

Rose wasn't sure if she was being smart to ask, but she felt she had to see what he would say. "What is Saul Greene's business card doing on your counter?"

"Oh, I see," he replied. "He's the prosecutor in your husband's trial and you think what?"

"I think it's too much of a coincidence. And I think you didn't answer my question. So, what is his card doing on your counter?"

"I can see how you would be suspicious, but I can assure you I didn't know who you were when you called. You do remember that you called me. I did not initiate this meeting."

"Yes, I guess that's true. But you still haven't answered my question."

"No, until five minutes ago it wasn't relevant."

"What's that supposed to mean?"

"I was able to break the password."

Rose felt her heart skip a beat. "And?"

"So, I don't know, of course, what you thought was on the drive, but I am fairly certain it isn't what you thought."

"Why is that?"

"Because what's on them is illegal and you probably wouldn't have brought them to me."

Rose slumped back on the couch, letting her head fall into her hands. "On, God, I don't know if I want to find out. I thought it was homosexual pornography. But that's not illegal is it?"

"No, it's not."

Rose lifted up her head, letting out a big sigh, "Well, if it isn't pornography, I don't know what to think."

"I didn't say it wasn't pornography."

"Look, you're being cryptic and it's giving me more of a headache than I already have."

"I'm sorry, but this is a delicate matter. You see, it's not up to me to decide if you want to know what's on the drive. I told you up front I would have to report illegal material and I will report this, but whether you want to know or not is your decision."

"Well, it seems to me that if it's illegal, I'll find out anyway. And I'm thinking I'd rather not be hit by surprise later. At least this way I'll have some time to prepare for the inevitable repercussions."

"Look, Mrs. Cunningham, I'm not sure this is the right time and place for you to find out. I think it might be better if you were with someone who could be there for you. I have the password now so you can open them if and when you want."

"From what you're saying it's got to be awful."

"I won't lie to you. It will be shocking and most likely repugnant."

Rose, letting his words sink in, started to cry. "I'm scared and I don't know what I want to do. My whole life is falling apart. All I know for sure is that I have to get that drive back in the safe soon," she sobbed.

When Jane arrived home she was so excited about Lily's call, she woke up Sydney to tell her the plan was working. Sydney reassured her that her lawyer friend could be trusted to keep everything confidential. Later, still in the outfit she had been using to disguise herself to travel to and from court, Jane left for Connie's.

She arrived early and sat down in a booth where she could watch the door. She almost didn't recognize Lily when she walked into Connie's a few minutes after seven. Her long, straight blonde hair had been washed and combed and she was wearing a floral print sun dress that was belted at the waist. She was still thin as a rail with dark circles under her eyes but she no longer resembled the walking dead. Jane stood up, raising a hand as a signal to Lily. Lily narrowed her eyes in suspicion before heading over to the booth where Jane was sitting. Suspiciously, Lily said, "I thought that other woman was coming. The one who Cunningham locked in the closet."

"It's me, Jane. I'm just dressed like the other woman because I shouldn't be seen here...you know, because of the trial."

"Hmm, I was strung out the time I talked to the other woman, but I'd swear you look just like her. So, is that lawyer dude coming?"

Jane, unsure herself whether the lawyer would show, could only answer, "I talked to him earlier today and he said he would be here. By the way, Lily, you look very nice."

"Yeah, well, once upon a time I cleaned up pretty good."

"Why don't you sit down? If you're hungry I can get you something to eat."

Lily hesitated but finally scooted onto the bench seat across from Jane.

"What would you like to eat?" Jane asked, handing her the menu.

Lily took the menu, opened it for a few seconds, then closed it and placed it on the table. "I'm hungry but I'm too nervous to eat anything. I shouldn't be here anyway. I still don't get what's in this for you."

"Cunningham's been preying on little girls for at least twenty-two years that I know of and maybe much longer. Now you and I have a chance to make him stop by getting him locked up so he can't harm any more children."

"How do I know you were really one of the little girls he used? You say you're wearing a disguise because of the trial, but I don't know 'bout that. You could be pulling a con job on me. You wearing a wire?"

"No, I'm not wearing a wire and I'm not conning you, but I don't have any proof Cunningham tried to abuse me other than the scar I left on his hand when I bit him. That's the reason I need *your* help. However, I know how difficult it is to trust anyone." Jane's heart beat like a drum as she said, "I won't be happy about it, but if you need to back out, I'll understand."

Lily started to cry, saying, "I don't know what to do. If you're telling the truth about trading information, this could be the only ticket for me and my kid out of this shit hole life I've made for myself. I know I can't do it on my own 'cause I've tried and failed too many times. Each time I fail I just end up deeper and deeper into the shit. Look at me now! I can't even be trusted not to pimp.... Shit! I am such a fucking loser."

Jane reached a hand across the table, touching Lily gently on her hand. Lily started to pull her hand away and then stopped, letting Jane's hand stay on hers. "I can tell you're scared," said Jane. "Believe me, Lily, I know what it means to be afraid all the time."

Lily used a paper napkin to dry her eyes. "My name's not Lily. It's Tisha. So, okay, I guess I gotta do this now when I'm not strung out. But I'll only talk to the lawyer man on one condition."

Jane smiled, hoping that Lily's giving up her real name meant that she was beginning to trust her. She kept her hand on top of Tisha's. "Okay, *Tisha*. Tell me. What's the one condition?"

Tisha pulled her hand away and stared hard at Jane before leaning toward her and declaring, "You gotta be the one to take care of my little girl for me while I'm in rehab. It's the only way I'll talk."

Stunned, Jane reflexively gasped, feeling a stab of fear pierce her heart and clutch at her gut. *Please, don't let me fall apart now*! She knew she had to keep breathing or she would go over the edge. Closing her eyes she took several deep breaths. When she opened them, Tisha was sliding out of the booth.

"Wait!" Jane cried. "Please, I...I just needed a moment to take in what you are asking."

Tisha remained standing looking down at Jane. "You want my help—that's the condition. My little girl...well, being with me is bad, but she's not gonna go into foster care 'cause, believe me, I personally know how that can fuck you up. Besides, I know I won't ever get her back once she's in the system, even if I get clean. I've fucked up too many times for a judge to give me a another chance. If you're telling me the truth about what happened to you, then you're the best person to look after her while I kick my habit."

"Well, Tisha, now it's my turn not to know what to do. Honestly, I don't know the first thing about taking care of a child. I don't even have any nieces or nephews. Besides, I'm on the jury. If you named me to look after her, it would look very suspicious. I'm not sure but I might even go to jail if the law finds out I know you."

"I don't care. That's my condition. Promise me that or I'm outta here."

Just then a middle-aged man with grey hair and a soul patch walked in the door and looked around. Jane, relieved by the presence of the lawyer, stood up and raised her hand toward him; he nodded and walked toward the booth.

Tisha reached across to Jane and grabbed her by the shoulders, desperately asking, "You promise you'll take my girl?"

Jane looked into Tisha's eyes, pleading,"Please, Tisha, just stay and hear what he has to say. Then we can decide what to do about your little girl."

The man reached the booth and stared hard at Jane. Then he extended his hand, saying, "I'm Jason Vermillion." Jane shook his hand while the man continued to stare, adding, "You told me you'd be dressed like Sydney but, well...you two look like twins."

"Yes, I guess we do, but I'm Jane and this is...." Jane looked at Tisha, not sure of what name to use.

Tisha glanced at the man, saying, "I'm not telling you my name until I hear what you have to say."

The man smiled, replying, "No problem."

Jane sat back down, moving over to make room for the man. "Please, sit down."

Vermillion slid into the seat next to Jane and Tisha sat back down across from them. The waitress came over after the three were seated, asking for orders. Jane asked for hot tea and a piece of pie, Vermillion ordered a cup of coffee, and Tisha, despite her earlier declaration of nervousness, ordered a hamburger and fries. After the waitress left, Vermillion looked at the frail, unnamed woman and said, "So, I understand you have some important information about a man who is currently on trial. I also understand you want something in exchange for that information."

Tisha narrowed her eyes at him, saying, "First thing I want is no bullshit."

Vermillion nodded. "Fair enough. No bullshit. To begin with, as of this minute, both of you are my clients, which means whatever either of you says is confidential. No one hears what you tell me unless you give your permission." Pointing at Tisha, he continued, "If you talk to me and then change your mind, it's over. I'll leave here and no one will ever know what you told me."

Tisha was quiet for a moment before asking, "You mean if I tell you something about the man on trial and then I tell you not to tell anyone, you won't tell?"

"Not only won't tell but can't tell."

"How do I know you're telling the truth?"

"Good question. There is no way for me to prove it this minute, but it's the law. You could look it up if you want to. It's against the law to break that confidentiality rule so, you see, I could lose my license to practice."

"I don't trust the police."

Vermillion shook his head, saying, "Well, I can't make you trust anyone. Trusting is a leap of faith, a decision you have to make on your own. But I will tell you a lawyer is *not* the same as the police. Please understand, if I become your lawyer, then I'm on your side *against* the police, or in this case, the prosecutor."

Lily stared hard at Vermillion. "Hmm. Okay, so, how will I be sure I get what I ask for?"

"Well, it's a cat and mouse game. You tell me what you know and what you want in exchange for what you know, then I give the prosecution just a little taste of what information you have, just enough so they have a reason to be curious. You know, so they want to know more. Then they have to agree to your terms to get more."

"And I don't got to be there, right? You do this for me?"

"Well, you don't have to be there when I whet their appetites, but if they agree to your terms, it's likely you will have to tell them in person what you know."

"Do I gotta testify in court?"

"Well, that depends on what information you have. If it's information that implicates Cunningham...I'm sorry, information that may help the prosecution get a guilty verdict, then you would have to testify in court."

"I'm not saying it is, but what if what I know would show he didn't hit that woman?"

Vermillion widened his eyes in surprise. "Well, now that is a whole new story. I thought...."

Jane interrupted, saying, "Mr. Vermillion, you've got to hear the whole story to understand why Tis....why she has information the prosecution would want."

"Okay, then," he said. "Let's hear what you have to say."

Tisha looked back and forth between Jane and Vermillion before finally saying,

"Well, shit. I guess I'm not ever gonna get a chance like this again. So, I'm gonna tell you what I want. Then maybe we'll talk about what I know."

Vermillion listened to Tisha's conditions and then said, "Okay, I'm going to be honest here. I think we'll be okay on all of what you're asking except specifying Jane as your daughter's temporary guardian. That could be a tough one."

Tisha shook her head. " All's I know is that I'm not letting them put my little girl in foster care."

Vermillion narrowed his eyes in thought before saying, "I won't lie to you. My guess is that your little girl would have to go into Protective Service for a short time, enough time for Cunningham's current trial to end and get you into rehab. Then Jane could come into the picture."

"I don't want nothing to do with them fucking Protective Service people. I know what can happen 'cause it happened to me already. *Protective* my ass. My foster father raped me silly."

Vermillion frowned, replying, "Well, I can certainly understand why you don't trust them, but all I can do is reassure you that I'll get the prosecution's promises in writing and I'll stay on them until they do what you ask."

"Well, shit," replied Tisha. She looked back and forth between Jane and Vermillion, saying, "Seems like I have to trust some lawyer dude I don't even know or I have to walk away."

Jane looked pleadingly at Tisha, saying, "You know what your life will be like if you walk away. But if you stay and talk to Mr. Vermillion, at least you and your little girl may have a chance at a new start."

It was now four in the afternoon and Toby was perched high on a long ladder leaning up against a tree. Although he was a devoted cat lover, he was not on the ladder to rescue one of his furry friends. Instead, he was busy pretending to be a tree trimmer, a ploy he sometimes used because there were few other stakeout possibilities for a black man the size of Toby Parish. Especially if the stakeout was in a mostly white neighborhood. The scrunching-down-in-a-car option didn't work for a six-foot-five, two-hundred-fifty pound man. Toby had rented a pickup truck with a long ladder attached to the top and secured his well-used phony, magnetic tree trimming signs to the sides.

Dressed in jeans, a denim shirt, heavy work boots, leather gloves, and protective eye wear, Toby's observation point was across the street and several houses down from Jane's duplex. He had the appropriate tools hanging from a pocket belt and a not-so-appropriate miniature, high-powered, telescopic camera stuffed in one pocket of the tool belt. He had been up on the ladder for forty-five minutes, the last forty of which he spent wondering how he had let Erin manipulate him into such a quasi-legal escapade.

He was in the process of listening to his better judgement, which told him to come down from his perch, when he spotted a short, heavyset man with thick grey hair walking down the same side of the street where Toby was roosted. The man was carrying a large shopping bag. Toby watched as the man slowed when he reached Jane's duplex, giving it more than a cursory glance before moving on. Lifting his eye shields to his forehead and pulling his camera out of its pouch, Toby caught the man in his high-powered lens; something about his full head of grey hair didn't seem right. *A wig, maybe?* The man stopped walking when he was only a few feet from Toby's ladder and took his cell phone out of his pocket. He was so close Toby could have heard the conversation, except the man didn't say anything. Then he snapped his phone shut, gave Toby, who had quickly returned the camera to his belt, a brief upward glance. He then looked toward the pickup truck and back at Toby before turning around and heading back in the direction he had come.

Toby watched the man cross the street toward Jane's house and then again took out his camera. Through the high-powered lens, Toby could easily see the thick-haired man as he looked both ways on Jane's block before heading down the paved side of her duplex toward the back.

Distressed by what he had just witnessed, Toby decided to investigate. He had only descended two rungs when he noticed a slender, well-built woman with long, dark hair coming around the corner and walking down the street toward him. She was dressed in tight-fitting, cropped jeans, a body-hugging T-shirt, and three inch heels. He stopped his descent to take out his camera, capturing the familiar, alluring woman in his lens and firing off multiple shots as she came closer to him and then turned, walking up the sidewalk to the front door of Jane's duplex and taking out a key from a large bag, using it to open the door.

Well, I'll be damned. Erin was right. Things were getting curiouser and curiouser: a wig-wearing man sneaking around Jane's duplex and a street hooker with a key to Jane's home. Time to check out these strange happenings.

Toby debated the risk of following the grey-haired man. If the man came back toward the front of the house, along the same walkway, they might just meet up. What then? However, his curiosity got the better of him. He finished his climb down the ladder, crossed the street, and, as quietly as possible for a man his size, followed the other man's path down the side of Jane's house, stopping when he recognized a small item just under the frame of a window. He snatched the item, a listening device, off the house and slipped it into his pocket.

Hmm. Obviously, someone besides Erin was wanting to know more about the puzzling goings on of the not-so-plain-Jane. Could it be the prosecution that was snooping?

Toby continued along the paved concrete side of the house, stopping before he came to the corner to listen for movement. Then he heard the phone ringing inside Jane's house and he risked peeking around the corner. The thick-haired man was about five feet away, leaning against the back of the house with his back toward Toby, a cell phone to his ear. Toby counted three rings and watched as the man closed his phone; the ringing stopped. Then the man started to turn in Toby's direction.

Knowing he couldn't be caught near Jane's home, Toby acted instinctively. He withdrew his head and waited only moments before the man came around the corner and met a surprise: a quick, solid face-punch. The man's eyes rolled upwards and he dropped his bag before going down on his knees and falling forward, landing hard, face down, on the concrete. Toby waited a few seconds to be sure the man was unconscious and then turned him over. The fake hair had slid backwards, partially exposing a bald head; a latex nose piece was also askew. Toby removed the wig completely and then peeled off the fake nose to reveal the real squashed, off-centered nose that was now oozing blood. He quickly took several close-up photos of the unconscious man. Then he searched the man's pockets looking for some ID. but came up empty-handed.

Acutely aware of the need not to be caught—no matter who the man was or what he was up to—Toby reached into the man's pocket and confiscated his phone. He also grabbed the shopping bag before hurrying back down the side of the house toward the front. He slowed as he came out from between the duplex and the next house and calmly strolled back to his truck.

Opening the shopping bag he found a Tyvek coverall, a package of razor blades, and, strangely, a gas mask. *What the hell?*

Toby threw the shopping bag in the back seat of his truck, took his camera out of his tool belt and put the belt beside the shopping bag, locking both in the truck before strolling back toward Jane's duplex. Knowing he only had a few minutes before someone in the neighborhood might become suspicious, he put the camera in his shirt pocket and crouched behind a car opposite Jane's duplex where he could see the walkway between the two homes. He pretended to be inspecting the back tire of the car while he waited.

Fortunately, it took only minutes before the downed man came around. Toby removed his camera from his pocket and watched through the lens as the man on the ground pushed himself to a sitting position, still obviously dazed and confused. Still drowsy, the man looked around for a few moments to orient himself before reaching up to touch his nose. Then he seemed to realize where he was, his face transforming into panic as he searched around for the shopping bag. When he didn't find it, he grabbed the latex nose and wig and stood up, holding on to the side of the house for stability, failing to notice the bloody hand print he left on the side of the house. Toby snapped more pictures as the man continued stumbling forward toward the front of the house, stopping to look for the listening device under the window. He threw his hands up in frustration when he didn't find it. Then he searched the ground before shaking his head in dismay and moving toward the street. Before emerging from between the two homes, he peeked out to look up and down the street. Seeing no one, he rapidly walked, head down, in the direction from which he had originally come.

After the man was several houses away, he shoved the wig and the fake nose up under his armpit and used his hand to again wipe his bloody nose. He smeared the blood onto his pants before reaching into his pants pocket. Muddled, the man patted his other pocket before shaking his head in irritation. Then he quickened his pace and as he approached the intersection, turned the corner and continued walking. Toby's view of the man was now blocked by the houses. He had no idea who the man was, but he was now sure he hadn't been sent by the prosecution. Razor blades and a gas mask meant someone was intent on inflicting serious damage, not just gather information. Another thing he was sure of: having been caught red-handed, the man wouldn't return anytime soon. Toby decided to follow the man and hurried toward the corner where the man had turned before disappearing.

From the intersection, Toby could see the stocky man fumbling around in his pockets for the keys to a car. Finally finding them, he opened the door and bent down to get in when he suddenly grabbed his stomach with one hand and the door jamb with the other. Then the man suddenly took several steps backwards into the street.

It was at this point that Toby saw the fast moving SUV come around the corner just a few feet from him. The driver, a young woman, had a cell phone to her ear. Instinctively, Toby anticipated the accident about to happen; he yelled out to the staggering man. Unfortunately, the man was now engrossed in giving up the contents of his stomach and didn't look up. The breakes on the SUV squealed loudly, but the car couldn't stop in time, slamming into the puking man, throwing him in the air and into the open door of his own car. Toby quickly moved forward until he could see beyond the SUV. The woman was bending over the man who was sprawled like a broken doll on the asphalt. The grey wig was now lying like roadkill a few feet away. The distraught young woman was rocking and wailing, "Oh, my God! Oh, my God! Someone call 911! I think he's alive! Please, someone help!"

Several people had come out of their houses with phones to their ears and one man was rushing over to the wailing woman and injured man.

Knowing there was nothing he could do at this point to help, Toby turned and walked rapidly back to his truck. Sirens wailed as he removed the ladder from the tree and secured it to the truck. He looked down the street to see an EMT vehicle with flashing lights, followed by a firetruck. *Whoever he was, the gas mask toting man wouldn't be back anytime soon, if ever.*

Back in his truck, Toby drove for a mile before pulling over to the curb to text Erin, asking her to meet him at his office in thirty minutes. Before he drove off again, he mulled over what had just happened and who the devious man might be—or had been? The man's real nose was distinctive, one that had obviously been broken several times. Something about the nose was ringing familiar bells in Toby's head. Where/how did he know the man he had decked? The flattened nose was such a distinguishing characteristic. He heard more sirens and a police car sped by. Then a flash of memory came to him.

Police!

Before his PI days, Toby had worked for a bail bondsman and often dealt with the police. That's how he knew the unlucky scoundrel! He was a former policeman, a bad apple noted for rough tactics. He thought he remembered something about the man being let go for excessive brutality charges. *What the hell was the man's name?*

It wasn't coming to him, even though he did remember the two of them had once had a brief skirmish over something, Toby couldn't remember what. It had been so many years ago and he had no idea what had happened to the man after he left the police force. Obviously, the jerk was still up to no good. Toby was sure he could show the pictures he had just taken to his contacts in law enforcement, confident some of the old timers would have the name for him in no time.

Back at his office, Toby went right to the computer, downloading all the pictures he had just taken. He quickly emailed several close-ups of the flat-nosed man to three of his law enforcement contacts who could be trusted to keep his inquiry confidential. Until he knew more, he was hesitant to let Erin know about the snooping man. Her priority was the identity of the brunette. Telling her about the man would only stir-up more questions than answers at this point. He had just finished organizing the pictures of the brunette when Erin arrived.

He motioned her over to the computer, pulling up the other chair, saying, "Your intuition was right. Take a look at these."

She took a seat next to Toby, engrossed as the shots of the brunette cycled through a slideshow. After the last picture, Erin leaned back in her chair, saying, "Wow! Okay, so I *was* right. This woman does know Jane. Hmm. There is something else bugging me about this woman. Some message my brain is giving me...." Erin pointed at the screen, continuing, "I've seen the woman before somewhere. I mean besides Saturday night. It's just that I can't put my finger on it. Maybe if I look through the pictures again something will click."

After letting the pictures cycle through a second time she said, "Damn, the familiar thing is not coming to me now. I guess I'll just have to let it percolate and see what happens. I noticed the woman has a key to Jane's house. They must be roommates, don't you think?"

"At the very least they know each other well. If this woman is turning tricks with men...well, she's not likely to be Jane's lover. Although, I guess you can never be sure about that."

"I wouldn't think they're lovers. I can't see Jane being that friendly with a hooker. It just doesn't fit her profile. Think about it. Jane tests water samples for a living. Can you imagine anything more tedious or unadventurous? Besides, I'm convinced that Jane has a bonafide Schizoid Personality Disorder, which certainly doesn't fit with having a prostitute for a friend."

"Wait a minute! You're saying Jane's schizophrenic?"

"No, no, I said *schizoid*, not schizophrenic. They sound similar but they're different kinds of disorders. Schizoid means an individual has certain severe dysfunctional personality characteristics, usually stemming from a history of severe childhood trauma. A Schizoid Personality type doesn't lose contact with reality or have delusions or hallucinations like a schizophrenic. However, a person with the disorder deeply mistrusts everyone, which means Jane would have trouble maintaining relationships; she would be a loner. It would be highly unusual for a Schizoid Personality to have a roommate—at least for any length of time. Also, a person with the disorder has severe trust issues and fears intimacy. Additionally, they go out of their way to avoid anything unfamiliar."

"If that's the case, I wonder why she didn't find an excuse to get out of jury duty?"

"Good question and one I've been asking myself. Though, what's bothering me more is our running into Jane's acquaintance on Grover Street. I don't buy a coincidence. You see, I'm always reading in mystery books that good detectives don't believe in coincidences. What about you?"

Toby beamed, "You read detective novels, do you?"

Erin looked over at Toby with a big grin, saying, "Love 'em, but right now we've got our own real-time mystery. And we have a big problem as well."

"What big problem?"

"Well, since this woman knows Jane, she could accuse us of jury tampering. After all, we showed a friend of a juror a picture of the defendant and we were asking questions about him. If this roommate, or whatever she is, somehow figures out you and I are working for the defense...."

"Shit! I forgot about showing her Cunningham's picture."

"Yeah, me too—until just now. It's a potential serious hiccup."

Erin stood up and began pacing. "Can you believe any of this? I mean, none of it's making any sense. Obviously, the brunette was hanging out on a street known for harboring prostitutes, but she's different from the other street girls, classier, less desperate. I get the feeling it isn't her regular hang out. So, what was she doing there?"

"I don't know, but I agree with you. I don't think our running into her was a coincidence."

"One thing for sure, if you're not a regular on Grover, you'd have to be one intrepid woman to go down there on a Saturday night." Erin smiled and pointed to herself, adding, "Or an inexperienced, gullible one like me."

Toby winced. "That was my bad, remember?"

"Water under the bridge. It's bugging me, however, that I'm just not getting any meaningful read on this woman. Maybe you can do some of that magic stuff you do on the computer? You know, check the address and see if Jane has a roommate. A telephone or utility bill, or something. If we know her name, then I'm sure you could pull the rabbit we need out of your computer hat."

She turned to Toby, asking, "So, can you do your computer voodoo?"

"Sure. You want to wait while I give it a go—or should I call you later?"

"How about I go out and get us something to eat while you do your wizardry?"

"Hey! I don't remember ever turning down an invitation for food."

With a serious expression, Erin replied, "Okay, then. I'll go get us a couple of salads."

Toby eyed Erin, saying, "The deal you offered was work in exchange for food. Salad isn't real food."

Erin laughed. "I didn't think you'd go for the salad. How about I get us a pizza?"

"Now that's food. Make *mine* a sausage and pepperoni, large with extra cheese. None of that gourmet crap with the stinky cheese and fancy sauce."

"You have a favorite place near here?"

"Absolutely. There is a takeout place called DeLeone's, about a quarter mile east from here, on the same side of the street. No need for drinks. I have both hard and soft in the fridge."

Erin picked up her purse, saying,"I'm off then." She pointed to the computer, directing, "Get to work, do your magic. I'll be back in less than an hour."

When Erin returned forty-five minutes later with the food, she was surprised to find the ordinarily unflappable Toby ruffled by his inability to find a single lead on the roommate hunch. Jane Nichols was the only name on any of the bills being sent to the house, so all of their efforts to ferret out the name of the mystery woman had led to a dead end. With no other leads to check out and the pizza getting cold, they sat down to eat.

Having counted on Toby to solve the enigma, Erin was frustrated and dejected by the dead end, so much so that she pushed aside the minestrone soup she had bought for herself and reached across the desk and tried to grab a slice of Toby's pizza. He caught her hand in mid air, saying, "No way! This is mine. You had your chance to get one for yourself but, no, you decided to go healthy. Now you want to steal from me."

"Healthy was okay when I was sure you would find out something. Now I'm craving seriously self-destructive food to go with the frustration I'm feeling. There's a connection, you know."

"No, I didn't know, but I'm sure you're going to tell me, right?"

"Yes, I am. It's called emotional eating, a strong desire for comfort food when you feel disappointed and discouraged. You see, frustration lowers self-control and right now my will power is as dead as our efforts. So, pretty please, may I have a slice of your pizza? I'll even trade my soup."

"Oh, all right, go ahead and take one. I would never want to be accused of depriving you of comfort."

Erin reached over and picked up a slice. She was taking a big bite when Toby's computer dinged, signaling he had an email. Suspecting it might be something on the scoundrel, Toby turned toward his computer to take a look, warning Erin, "One slice. I'm watching you."

The email was from one of the contacts to whom he had sent the pictures of the ex-policeman. When Toby read the name of the man, the memories began to tumble to the front of his brain. Of course! Daniel Debeck. The man had been an amoral asshole, causing enemies to sprout as quickly as weeds. Toby had been one of many men Debeck had crossed the wrong way, as indicated by the scathing description written in the email from his contact.

However, it was the last sentence that really got Toby's attention: 'The last I heard, Debeck was employed as head of security by the corporation formerly owned by Bradley Cunningham.'

I'll be damned. Debeck has to be Cunningham's man.

Considering the contents of the shopping bag Toby had snatched from Debeck, he had been sent there not just to snoop but to do serious damage. Now what? Toby wondered. *I wasn't supposed to be anywhere near Jane's house so telling RJ presents weighty problems.*

He was deep in thought when he was brought back to the present by Erin's question, "What's on that computer that's got you looking so troubled?"

Toby told her the whole story about Debeck's being at Jane's duplex, about decking him, and about the man getting hit by a car. Then he told her about the connection he had just discovered between Cunningham and Debeck.

Erin was so unnerved by the unscrupulous nature of the man she had been hired to help defend, that she mindlessly ate a second slice of pizza. Cunningham had made her uncomfortable from the minute she met him. Her job, however, was to read the jury, not the defendant, then to feed the juror reading to whoever employed her. She had stepped outside her professional boundaries when she suggested to Toby that he do a little sideline snooping. As a result of her meddling, she was now in over her head, struggling with her conscience. What should she do with what she knew?

Toby was in a similar battle with his own conscience. He had snooped around on his own dime and discovered extremely disturbing information. Apparently, Jane's life was at stake. He'd been hired by RJ to find evidence that would absolve a man *accused* of a crime. Now he knew that man to be a reprobate, a man who would likely stop at nothing to be proven innocent.

Toby had tried to reassure Erin that Debeck had been hurt badly, maybe even killed, and wouldn't be able to hurt Jane. And he told her he felt confident Cunningham couldn't get a replacement on short notice. So, in the end, she and Toby decided to wait one more day to see how the trial was going. If they got lucky, their decision not to tell anyone what they knew would be made moot by the trial's outcome.

Later that night, as Erin was trying to sleep, her mind would not let go of the situation she had gotten herself into. She worried that postponing any action was just a cowardly way to avoid dealing with her own culpability. She reviewed over and over in her mind the messy state of affairs she had created. By two A. M., she knew the debate going on in her head would never let her sleep. Giving in to the relentless neurons firing in her head, she fought back with a Xanax, knowing the chemicals in the drug would overpower her buzzing neurons. As the drug she had taken began to calm the electrical storm in her brain, a flash of unrelated insight wrestled its way into the cocktail of her brain activity.

Strangely, the insight had nothing to do with the moral dilemma that had kept her awake; rather it dealt with her earlier quandary about the mysterious brunette. She looked at the clock, sighed deeply. *I guess there is no sleep for inquiring minds who have to know.*

She dragged herself out of bed and headed to her office, where she again pulled out her Diagnostic and Statistical Manual on psychological disorders. This time she flipped to a completely different section of the book. After less than a minute of reading, she realized she had gotten it wrong the first time she had consulted the manual. If what she was now reading was the correct fit, and she was confident it was, she had the answer to the motives behind the mysterious brunette being on Grover Street. And an answer to the relationship between the brunette and Jane.

After Saturday night's sexual debacle, RJ moped around the house all Sunday morning. His feeling of abject despair began to permeate his body like lava seeping downhill into every crevice. He started in on the booze around noon. By one P.M. he was asleep with his head on his office desk. He woke around five with a mouth dry as cotton, a pain in his right eye that felt like a nail was being hammered into it, and a pinched nerve on the left side of his neck that felt as though a vise was gripping the nerve.

As he turned his neck in an attempt to relieve the imagined vise, his eyes settled on the shattered vase he had destroyed. The sight of the once valuable fragments suddenly jolted him out of his self-pity. He was no Humpty-Dumpty and if he didn't pull himself together, he would be useless in the courtroom, as worthless as the broken pieces that lay scattered in front of him. He reached for the phone to call the massage therapist he often used, making her an offer she couldn't refuse even on a Sunday:

three hundred dollars to immediately come to his home and work on him for an hour and a half.

Three hours later his body felt functional again. The first half hour of the massage he had done nothing but silently chastise himself for being weak enough to fall into such despair. As the therapist began working out the knots in his body, however, he began to relax and switch gears, reminding himself of his many years of hard work that had brought him such success in business —and, fuck it! the bedroom. *One* incidence of impotency was not a pattern. When this trial was over and he had prevailed, he would get back to his previous unfaltering sexual performance. Besides, he acknowledged, there was always Viagra. After the massage therapist left, he ate a light supper and spent the rest of the evening going over his defense strategy for the next day. Feeling confident he had his game back, he slept well that night.

Monday morning brought a new optimism. Just walking into the courtroom, an arena where he reigned supreme, gave his returning confidence an additional boost. So, by the end of the first day of the defense's case, RJ Holland had completely recouped his aplomb. He'd put his expert CSI automotive witness on the stand and, if he said so himself, (which he did) he had been a virtuoso in the way he had questioned the witness. Complete with a Power Point presentation explaining how it was impossible for the damage to Cunningham's car to be caused by hitting a human body, RJ believed his expert had creamed the prosecution's automotive expert. Tomorrow he would be calling two witnesses to testify that Manny Islas, the newspaper delivery guy who claimed to have seen Cunningham leaning over the body, was not the upstanding citizen that the prosecution claimed.

Monday's testimony had gone so well that RJ was now much less concerned about the absence of an explanation for Cunningham's presence in the Grover Street area. After all, the defense only needed to prove reasonable doubt and his expert witness that day had started the ball rolling. There remained, however, two bumps that might impede the momentum he was gathering for the rest of the week. Juror Seven, of course, was one and the other was how distracted Cunningham had been that morning.

At the end of the day, he took Cunningham aside, asking, "What was going on with you this morning? You were giving the jury the impression that this trial was about somebody else."

Annoyed, Cunningham flippantly replied, "Okay, so I was distracted for a while. But I fixed it. It won't happen again."

Not wanting to have a repeat of last Friday's confrontation, RJ contained his irritation. "Good. Because we are picking up momentum and I don't want anything to slow us down."

"I get it, RJ. Look, I have something I need to do right now. So, just get me out of here; don't stop to talk to the media, okay?"

Like a plug being pulled out of a basin full of water, the buoyant feelings drained from RJ. He had been brilliant today and he was due his shine time in the big top of the media carnival waiting outside. Between clinched teeth, he said, "Not answering the media's questions after today's victory would only garner suspicion and negative speculation. It's important we don't look like we have something to hide."

"Then be quick about it. I don't want you posturing for those blood hounds."

RJ, now furious, responded by ignoring his client's demand, heading straight for the waiting reporters. He was posturing for the press when Cunningham suddenly pushed past him and moved toward the waiting car and driver. Stunned, RJ stopped talking midstream, blinked in disbelief, and watched in rage as the crowd of reporters turned to follow the accused celebrity, leaving RJ with nothing to do but follow his client to the car.

Fuming, RJ climbed in next to Cunningham, who had already leaned over and told the driver to take him to his own car. When Cunningham leaned back, RJ, spat out, "That was foolish what you did back there."

"It doesn't matter," Cunningham sighed.

"Of course it matters," RJ's shouted. "The posturing matters a great deal. How many times have I told you that we need to have public opinion on our side. Your good image is crucial to the outcome."

Cunningham was furious. *How many times have I told you?* Never accustomed to scolding from anyone, the billionaire lost it. "Fuck you and fuck my image!" he exploded. "Don't you get it? It's all useless if juror Seven stays!"

The stunned RJ put a hand up, saying, "Calm down, Bradley. You know we've had Seven in our sights from the beginning. I can handle her, I'm sure."

"Handle her? You have no fucking idea what you're dealing with," Cunningham screamed."

"What the hell is that supposed to mean?" RJ roared back.

Suddenly, Cunningham realized how foolish he had been to lose it; now he was trapped. He stared out the window without answering RJ, thinking about the backlash of losing his temper. He couldn't tell RJ about his past encounter with Seven, and his loose lips a minute ago had aroused RJ's suspicions, something that could later come back to haunt him if his plan to eliminate Jane Nichols from this world succeeded.

RJ put his hand firmly on Cunningham's shoulder, saying, "Look, Bradley, I need to know what you're talking about. If you know something about Seven I don't know..."

Cunningham backpedaled, saying, "Forget it. I'm overreacting and I'm sorry. It's just the stress is getting to me. You were great today and I'm grateful. I know I'm in good hands, RJ."

Saul Greene was also reflecting on the first day of the defense's case. The testimony of the defense's CSI automotive expert witness had been solid as a rock; he had not been able to budge him one iota on cross. Anticipating tomorrow to be equally difficult, Saul called his team together to strategize at the end of the day. He knew that tomorrow the credibility of the prosecution's eyewitness, Mr. Islas, would come under scrutiny and his team was now gathered in the conference room for what promised to be a long after-court session.

They had been engrossed in various possible scenarios of what RJ would be presenting tomorrow for several hours. Expecting to be there for some time, the group had ordered takeout. The food had just arrived when Saul received a text message from Allan: *Urgent. Please call ASAP.* The urgent part of the message seemed odd, so Saul excused himself and went out in the hall to call Allan. Allan answered immediately saying,"Hey, sorry my text was so cryptic, but it's important I talk with you."

"I'm in with my team. What's so urgent?" Saul asked.

"It's a bit tricky. I've come across some information that may be relevant to your current case."

Saul remained quiet for a moment, thinking. *Had his suspicions about Allan been correct?* Cautiously, he answered, "Okay, you've got my attention."

"You're at your office, right?"

"Yes."

"I'm going to bring it over to you now, okay?"

"Wait a minute. Give me something more. Is this information good news or bad for our case?"

"It's not for me to say."

"Why so cryptic?"

"Look, I'm sorry but it's not something I can talk about over the phone. You need to *see* what I have. At this time of day, I'm thinking maybe it will take me about a half hour to get to your office."

"Hmm. All right, then. If I can't pry even a morsel out of you, I guess I'll deal with it when you get here."

The call left Saul disconcerted and with a shadowy feeling of dread. It was only yesterday morning that he had questioned the way he and Allan had met. He'd gone to the office to check out Allan's story and found nothing that could confirm or deny his concerns. After combing his database sources, Saul concluded that Allan seemed to be who he said he was: a rehabilitated and transformed felon. Now, however, he was claiming to have something on Cunningham. Even without knowing what it was, the coincidence was dubious and Saul's suspicions from yesterday quickly resurfaced. Was he a plant of some sort? He wouldn't put the tactic past RJ. Saul knew he had to be very careful.

He returned to his team and tried to direct his focus on the current agenda: speculating about what the two defense witnesses would be saying tomorrow. The team was deep in discussion by the time Allan knocked on the door. Saul excused himself to go into the hallway to meet Allan. It was awkward for him to see a new lover, especially one he wasn't sure he trusted, standing in his work place. Shaking hands with the man he had recently slept with didn't seem right, so he tried a bit of humor, saying, "Hey, you certainly know how to *arouse* a guy's interest."

Allan briefly smiled but quickly returned to a grim demeanor, replying, "Can we go somewhere private?"

"Sure, my office is just down the hall." Saul turned and walked toward the room; Allan followed right behind him. Once inside the office, Saul said, "Okay, Allan, I'm beginning to lose patience with all this intrigue. What is it that you need for me to see? And how did *you* come by whatever it is?"

Allan reached into his jacket pocket and withdrew three discs, which he offered to Saul. "These are copies off a hard drive."

Saul, uncertain about taking possession of questionable evidence, narrowed his eyes but did not take the discs. "I'm assuming you know what's on them or you wouldn't be here."

Allan lowered the discs to his side. "They were password protected, which is how I got involved, and, yes, I've opened them briefly. The password is written on a piece of paper inside the case."

"Hmm. You said on the phone that this has to do with Cunningham. So, are you going to tell me who it was that asked you to break the password?"

"My client didn't give me permission to do that. My client did, however, give me permission to tell you that the originals are in a safe in Cunningham's home office."

"This is all very suspect, Allan. I only met you a week ago and now you're in my office with information on a trial in progress."

"It's an unlikely coincidence, I agree. But it is what it is, Saul. I'm giving you these discs because what's on them is illegal and I no longer deal with anything criminal."

Saul stood still, uncertain of what to do. Finally he said, "Okay, then, I guess I need to see what's on them."

Allan handed the discs to Saul, saying, "I understand that my involvement in this seems suspicious, but I can't change that. I had no idea what would be on them when my client asked me to open them. When you see what's on the discs, you'll know why I had to turn them over to you. I can only hope this doesn't change the direction of where you and I were headed."

"I don't know what to say about any of this, especially about our future. Let me get through this trial and then I'll give you a call."

Allan was quiet for a moment before saying, "Our backgrounds and our work make us an unlikely pair. Still, I find myself already very attached to the possibility of us. I hope you decide to give us a chance."

"I agree we are an improbable couple." Saul smiled and then put a hand on Allan's shoulder, saying, "However, improbable doesn't mean impossible. I'll call you later."

After Allan left, Saul stuck his head in the door of the conference room. The group had just about devoured the food when Saul said, "I need to check something out. Better hand me that last sandwich before you pigs eat it all. I'll be back in a few minutes."

He returned to his office, grabbed a bottle of water, sat down in his chair, and slipped one of the discs into his computer. He typed in the password written on the note Allan had given him and unwrapped his sandwich, taking a bite before leaning back in his chair. When he saw the first images fill his computer screen, his eyes widened in disbelief, just before he choked on the food in his mouth.

After coughing up some of the sandwich which had nearly asphyxiated him, Saul took a big slug of water. To be safe, he put the remaining part of the sandwich on the table, watching as the disturbing images on the screen continued to unnerve him. After only twenty-five seconds of watching, he couldn't take it any more. He pushed his rolling chair away from the computer and jumped up, yelling, "Jesus Christ! This is a fucking bombshell. What the hell am I supposed to do with this?"

He began pacing the room, thinking: My God, if this filthy shit belongs to Cunningham, it could explain what he was doing on Grover Street that morning. However, the disgusting child pornography he had just witness didn't prove one way or the other whether Cunningham was involved in the hit and run. The scandalous material on the discs was an entirely different case. He pounded his desk, screaming out loud, "Fuck! Fuck! Fuck!"

He began pacing again, talking out loud to himself. "Okay, Allan said his client told him the original discs were at Cunningham's home. So, I'd have to get a search warrant to prove the discs belonged to him. But, damn it, I only have Allan's say so. If I'm being suckered, I could make a food of myself and completely screw up the hit and run charges against him."

Lost in a miasma of confusion and turmoil, he was startled by a knock on the door. He walked over to the door and jerked it opened. A member of his team was standing there with a look of concern on her face. "Are you okay? I mean we could hear you yelling all the way in the conference room."

"No! I'm not fucking okay!"

The woman jumped back, stammering, “I’m sorry, can I help?”

Suddenly, Saul was at a loss. He had no proof the discs belonged to Cunningham, so bringing his team in on this would only derail their focus and his. “It’s not your fault or your problem so, no, you can’t help. Please go back to the conference room. I’ll be there in a few minutes.”

Saul realized how abrupt he had been when he saw the surprised and wounded look on the woman’s face. He held up his hand. “Wait a minute. Forgive me. I’m out of line here,” he said. “I wish the team could help but the timing...anyway, I’m sorry I was so curt. I’ll join you guys in a few minutes, okay?”

“If you say so,” she said hesitantly, as she turned and headed back down the hall.

Saul removed the disk from his computer and put a second one in. Similar images popped-up on the screen. His stomach was lurching at the sights, so he ejected the second disk and then locked the three discs in the safe in his office. He threw the rest of his sandwich in the trash and marched back to the conference room, where he had to force himself to stay focused on the strategy for tomorrow’s cross examination.

The team called it quits a little after nine. Saul returned to his office where he sat at his desk and stared at his safe, thinking about what the images on the discs meant. Since he had nothing to go on other than Allan’s word, he would be risking a lot if he acted on this new evidence. A revered man such as Cunningham...well, his being convicted of a hit and run was one thing. But for the community to find out that their esteemed philanthropist was into child pornography, well, that was a whole new ballgame, a game with serious repercussions. There would be a media uproar, possibly with himself at the center. Did he want to be the catalyst for such mayhem?

Even if Saul won the hit and run case, RJ would appeal, which meant a possibly dangerous sicko would be out on bail. Just as he decided it was useless to ponder the various scenarios because he would never be able to get a warrant based only on Allan's say-so, his cell phone rang.

Saul didn't recognize the number but decided to answer it. "This is Saul Greene."

"Hello, Saul. This is Jason Vermillion. I don't think we've ever met. I'm an attorney and we need to talk. I've got a client who has information on the defendant you're currently prosecuting on the hit and run and she wants to make a trade."

What the hell? More complications?

"A trade? What kind of trade?"

"Sorry, Greene, not on the phone. We need to talk in person. I can be at your office in twenty minutes."

Saul was at a loss and feeling very overwhelmed. "Look, Vermillion, it's been a long day and I'm in no mood for games. You'd better not be wasting my time."

"Oh, I promise I won't be wasting your time. On the contrary, I'm one hundred precent sure what my client has to offer will *make your day*."

Hanging up, Saul continued to stare at his safe where he would swear the discs were glowing red hot. He drummed his fingers on his desk, thinking, *I've heard of this guy, Vermillion...what other nerve-wracking, eleventh-hour intrigue is going to be thrown at me*?

Twenty-three stomach churning minutes later, Jason Vermillion was sitting across from Saul. Although he and Jason had not crossed paths before, he knew why the man was nicknamed Vermillion The Chameleon. On the outside the man had a nerdy veneer and a polite, quiet demeanor. Underneath, however, his reputation as a shrewd, persistent arbitrator was well known.

Vermillion got right to the point. "I have a client who says she was with Cunningham in his car the morning of the hit and run. According to her, he didn't hit the woman. My client says the woman was already in the road when Cunningham's car got there. He stopped to check on her, found her dead, and drove off."

Saul was nonplussed. "Wait just a minute here! I don't get what's going down. Why are you coming to me instead of the defense with supposed proof of innocence?"

"Simple. Because the witness's testimony would implicate Cunningham in a different criminal act."

When Saul heard Jason's last statement, he concluded that Vermillion's client was likely a prostitute. However, it still didn't make any sense why Vermillion had come to the prosecution with information that would prove Cunningham innocent.

Saul said, "You're talking prostitution, right? Come on, Jason, you've got to know there is no way the state would drop the hit and run charges to prosecute Cunningham for the lesser crime of prostitution. Especially not now when our case is looking good."

"Right, Saul. We're talking prostitution but not the kind you're thinking."

"What the hell? I told you no games, Vermillion."

"Yes, I know I'm being vague, but my client won't say more unless you agree to her demands."

"This is totally absurd. You haven't given me any reason to consider demands."

"What have you got to lose by listening?" Vermillion gave Saul a sly smile, "You'll find an answer to your question about why you instead of the defense."

"What I've got to lose is sleep, but go ahead...I'll nibble." Saul leaned back in his chair and put his feet up on the desk with his hands behind his head.

"Okay, so here's what she's demanding. She wants the State to pay for rehab to kick her drug habit and, after she gets clean, she wants job training and a guaranteed job. Most importantly, there's to be no prosecuting her for child sexual exploitation..."

When Saul heard the demand, *no prosecution for child sexual exploitation*, a flash of revelation caused his feet to come off his desk as he bolted upright in his chair.

Jason put up his hand. "Hold on! There's more. She also wants therapy for her six-year old daughter and a guarantee that the State won't take her daughter away from her."

Saul was now getting it, the pieces of the puzzle finally falling into place: the discs filled with child pornography combined with the involvement of a six-year old girl made it clear why Vermillion was in *his* office rather than RJ's. Now Saul understood why Cunningham had refused, during interrogation, to explain what he was doing in the area the night of the hit and run. Vermillion wasn't referencing mere prostitution as Cunningham's criminal act, he was alluding to felony sexual abuse of a minor. The earlier unease about the mayhem that would result if he charged Cunningham with possession of child pornography skyrocketed.

Saul knew he had to proceed with caution. With as much composure as he could muster, he said, "Okay, Jason, I'm getting why you're here instead of going to the defense. But I'm sure you realize a drug-addicted prostitute is not a believable witness. Especially one that's making excessive demands in return for her testimony."

The same sly smile crossed Vermillion's face. "Of course, but what about a six-year-old girl picking Cunningham's picture out of a group of photos?"

This last statement did away with Saul's attempt at composure. "The mother's agreed to this?" he asked with skepticism.

"Yes, provided you agree to her demands."

Well, damn. The hit and run charge would look trivial in comparison to what Jason was offering.

Saul needed time to think about all the repercussions involved in such a high profile, unsavory case. He shook his head, "I don't know, Jason. This is a tough one. You're asking me not only to ignore the crime the mother has committed but to essentially reward her."

"Well, I'm sure she won't feel rewarded as she goes through rehab. But that's beside the point." Again the crafty smile, as Vermillion added, "You're stalling and we both know it. The State gets a pedophile off the streets and stops a child from being abused in exchange for rehabilitating a mother? It's a no brainer, Saul."

"Maybe. In any case, you know I can't make this decision without talking to the DA. So, I'll have to get back to you."

"Of course." Vermillion reached across the desk to shake Saul's hand, saying, "I'm confident we can do business together and both come out winners. The only loser will be a sexual predator."

After Vermillion left the room, Saul began to rehash the ramifications of Vermillion's offer. He knew the combination of the mother's testimony and the little girl's picking out Cunningham's picture would be enough probable cause to get a warrant to search Cunningham's home. Finding the drive, along with the mother's testimony and the child's ID, would be enough to charge Cunningham with felony child abuse. Of course, it would also mean dropping the hit and run charges.

What really bothered him, though, was the appearance of the discs—showing up just hours before Vermillion; a coincidence like that just didn't seem possible. Suspicions about Allan resurfaced yet again. Then a larger, more ominous scenario began to emerge in Saul's mind. What if all of this was Cunningham's doing, an elaborate scheme to get the prosecution to drop the charges?

Whoa! What if he was being set up? What if Allan's *unidentified* client was Cunningham and Vermillion's *unidentified* female client was a phony, a prostitute paid by Cunningham? What if the State barged into Cunningham's home and found nothing? Oh, man! What if there was no little girl? Cunningham would go free and Saul Greene would look like a fool, his career in shambles.

Saul stood up and started pacing again, thinking through his dire conjectures. *Wait!* His suspicions of Allan were causing him to go off the deep end. The scenarios he just conjured up couldn't be possible if the little girl identified Cunningham before the search. Okay, Okay, he would hear what the mother has to say. Then they would be sure the child existed and was willing to look at pictures. If she picks Cunningham out, only then will we get the search warrant. If we find the discs, then and only then, will we drop the hit and run charges and slap him with new charges.

Saul picked up his phone and dialed his boss. She answered with, "At this time of the night it usually means bad news. What have you got?"

Shortly after the stroke of midnight, the DA, Saul, and his team, having seen as much as they could stomach of the discs, sat across the conference room table from Vermillion as he again listed the demands his client wanted in exchange for her testimony. The room was eerily quiet after he finished. Before anyone could say a word, Vermillion offered to go out in the hall while they discussed their decision.

After fifteen minutes they called him back in.

DAY NINE

When he hadn't heard from DeBeck by midnight, Cunningham had gone into panic mode and, using his pay-as-you-go phone, began calling the man every hour. Each time he got a voice mail, his rage and helplessness grew. By four in the morning Cunningham was sure that Debeck had flaked out on him. Had the bitch thwarted him yet again? He was beginning to rethink it was all preordained. He was a puppet in his own life. Believing he was ruined, he dragged himself upstairs to bed; sheer exhaustion was responsible for a mere two hours of sleep.

He opened his eyes to daylight. Victimization and self-pity were unchartered territory for him and now, in the light of day, he felt ashamed of last night's self-indulgence. He sat on the side of the bed with his head in his hands, thinking about how he had let himself drift so far from the determined man who had built an empire. Resolved to reconnect with that steadfast part of himself, he dragged his sleep-deprived body into the bathroom, swallowed two Tylenols, and stepped into the shower, turning the water as hot as he could tolerate.

By the time he was being driven to court, Cunningham had left the despair behind and replaced it with a list of reasons to be optimistic. It was still possible that Debeck had a good reason he hadn't called and that his nemesis, Jane Nichols, would be a no-show today—due to a little problem called death by suicide. He smiled at the thought. With Jane gone and an alternate in her place, RJ's efforts could turn the tide.

Despite his tiff with RJ after court yesterday, the man *had* indeed performed well on Monday and today was RJ's opportunity to attack the damaging testimony of Manny Islas, the one eyewitness. RJ had reassured him that after he was finished with the Mr. Islas, the jury would have reasonable doubt his word could be trusted.

At eight-ten on the morning of day nine, Saul Greene, with two detectives by his side, were sitting at the table in his conference room. Opposite Greene were Mr. Vermillion and his extremely jumpy client, Tisha. Tisha's daughter, Megan, was by her mother's side, coloring in a color book. Sitting next to Megan was a uniformed, female police officer with a stack of photos on the table in front of her.

At nine A.M., the courtroom was thrown into complete disarray when the DA showed up in Saul's place and explained to the judge that Mr. Greene was attending to an important matter regarding the trial and was expected back for the afternoon session. RJ strongly objected to the DA taking Saul's place and asked for a side bar where he requested that the judge see the parties in chambers, insisting that the prosecution needed to justify the unexpected turn of events. The judge, unsettled by the sudden monkey wrench, scolded the DA for the highly irregular maneuver, but overruled RJ's objection and sent the two attorneys back to work.

At five minutes after nine, the jury was called in. Cunningham, silently swearing when he saw Jane Nichols enter the room, felt bile rush into his stomach. It mattered little to him that Saul Greene was absent; as long as his nemesis remained in the jury box, he was doomed. He now knew he had to come up with a Plan B.; no way that woman could remain alive.

At nine-ten, a thwarted but ever tenacious RJ, called his first witness. Cunningham remained absorbed in his treacherous thoughts, even as his defense counsel masterfully questioned the credibility of the only eye witness.

At nine-thirty, Dr. Halloway passed another warning note to one of the Tweedles about Cunningham's demeanor. The note was handed to RJ after his first witness left the stand. RJ, seated and waiting for the next witness to be called, read the note and whispered a reprimand to the defendant. Cunningham gave RJ a perfunctory nod and returned to his conniving, preoccupied thoughts on how to get rid of Seven.

A fuming RJ, doing his very best not to let his mutinous client disrupt his momentum, stood and called his next witness. Then, like the hungry vulture he was famous for being, he used the witness to further pick apart the flesh of Manny Islas.

At ten-fifteen, while RJ was skillfully ripping apart the prosecution's main witness, Saul Greene was having his search warrant signed by a judge. Moments later, Saul, hoping his speculation was right, made a telephone call to the person he now concluded had brought the incriminating evidence to Allan. His heart raced as he waited for Rose Cunningham to answer.

At ten-fifty, with the warrant in his hand and the two detectives from the morning's meeting by his side, Saul rang the doorbell at the home of Bradley Cunningham. An expectant, but nevertheless weepy and extremely shaken Rose Cunningham opened the door and stepped aside. With great effort just to remain standing, she led the group to her husband's office, pointed to the wall safe, handed Saul a slip of paper with the combination, and promptly fainted. Fortunately, on her way down, she was caught by one of the detectives.

At eleven-forty-five, the judge called for an early lunch recess.

At twelve-seventeen P.M., Erin, her salad Nicoise untouched, was attempting to convince Toby that her latest theory on the relationship between Jane Nichols and the mysterious brunette was credible. Toby, dubious that such a thing was possible, kept shaking his head in doubt as he listened to the wild tale Erin was spinning. His disbelief, however, did not hinder his ability to devour his entire plate of fried onion rings and fried calamari.

At one P.M., the judge called the court to order and looked questioningly over his glasses at the now reinstalled Saul Greene. Saul did not disappoint; before RJ could call his next witness, Saul rose to speak. "Your Honor, I know this is highly irregular, but the prosecution has recently come into new evidence..."

RJ shot to his feet, shouting, "I object! I know nothing about this so-called new evidence."

The judge summoned the two attorneys to a side bar. He gave Saul a stern look before scolding him, "Mr. Greene, you know damn well that if this evidence is inculpatory, Mr. Holland should have been informed."

"Of course, Your Honor. The evidence, however, is exculpatory."

Taken aback, the judge said, "I don't know what you're up to Mr. Greene but it better be worth the disruption." He paused before saying, "Okay, I'll hear what you have to say." He gave a nod to RJ, saying, "I'm overruling the objection..."

RJ, astounded, insisted, "But Your honor..."

The judge put up his hand, palm forward, saying, "I've made my ruling, counselor. However, since this is highly irregular I'm going to have the jury removed."

At one-ten, the judge sent the two attorneys back to their tables and announced that he was removing the jury. The courtroom erupted in curious murmurs at the judge's pronouncement. Cunningham, finally coming out of his malicious reverie when the judge announced the removal of the jury, leaned over to an obviously fuming RJ, asking, "What's going on?"

Under his breath RJ rasped, "Weren't you paying attention? Greene's claiming to have new evidence and I have the sickening feeling that whatever it is that you've been withholding from me is about to come back and bite you in the butt."

At one-fifteen, the jury box had been cleared and Saul Greene spoke in a loud and clear voice to an eerily silent courtroom, "Your, Honor, the State, based on new eyewitness evidence, wishes to drop the charges."

The courtroom erupted in pandemonium, the media almost causing a stampede as they pulled out their cell phones and pushed through the crowds to be the first to get the story back to their newsrooms.

When Greene's words finally registered in his mind, Cunningham's heart hammered with a foreboding thud. *Could it be possible that the prosecution had found the one person who could testify to his innocence?*

At one-twenty, the incredulous judge, finally reinstating order in what was left of his courtroom, had no choice but to dismiss the defendant. Within seconds of the dismissal, Saul and his team were hurrying out of the courtroom through a side door.

At one-twenty-two, trying to absorb what this unforeseen turn of events meant to him, a stunned RJ, was still sitting in the courtroom, his brain calculating his next move. He had never had a case where the prosecution dropped the charges during the trial. A high-profile case with a not guilty verdict would have been another feather in his cap, but this? Could there be some payoff in these events for him? With the media bloodsuckers waiting outside, he would have to quickly decide how to spin this new circumstance to his advantage. *Incompetent prosecutor...innocent all along, blah, blah.* He looked over at his duplicitous client; the man was looking disconsolate when he should have been joyous. Leaning into his client, RJ sarcastically whispered "Why is it you don't look so good, Bradley? Didn't you just hear that you're free to go?"

Cunningham, fearing that the prosecution had somehow located the prostitute who had been with him in the car, was deep in a crisis stratagem and didn't answer his attorney. Instead, he was constructing Plan C., a plan that involved readying his private jet for a trip to a country that didn't extradite. He pulled his cell phone from his pocket and turned it on; the second he was alone he would call his pilot. Thank God he had moved most of his assets off shore when he sold the company. He calculated that the prosecution would need a few days to put together a case; by then he would be long gone. Rose had already deserted him and forfeiting the million dollar bail meant nothing.

He grabbed RJ's shoulder and demanded, "I need to get out of here, now! And I'm not going out the front. Absolutely no media, do you hear me?"

RJ was in no mood for a deceitful, ungrateful, client. He firmly removed Cunningham's hand, saying, "I'm fed up with your secretive, recalcitrant behavior. You better tell me what's going on, Bradley, and you better tell me now or I'm washing my hands of you."

Cunningham returned the threat, saying, "Didn't *you* hear the judge? I'm a free man. So, what do I need you for anyway? Just get me past the media and I'll be out of your life forever."

"Jesus, Bradley! Have you lost your fucking mind? You've been cleared of the charges. Now is the time to restore your image with the media."

"On the contrary. I'm finally going to do the only sane thing I should have done months ago. Now, if you want the rest of the money I owe you, you'll show me the back way out of here and keep the media away."

Dumbfounded, RJ shook his head but packed up his briefcase. Turning to the Tweedles, he told them they were to meet him in the conference room in twenty minutes. Then he turned and dismissed Erin, telling her he would be in touch. Shaking his head at Cunningham he said, "You have no idea how bad running away from this outcome will look." He then led Cunningham out the side door.

At one-twenty-five, the tension in the deliberation room where the jurors were waiting was palpable. They all knew that being removed from the courtroom meant something was amiss, but only juror Seven knew what shit was about to hit the fan. Moments later the bailiff entered the room, profusely thanked the jurors and the two alternates for their service, and told them they were dismissed for good.

The perplexed group found it disorienting to be suddenly cut loose from something that had absorbed so much of their lives, something that had been weighty and worthy of so much attention. The majority agreed that it felt wrong not to have some kind of closure. Five of the members, unwilling to let it go, decided to wander over to a nearby bar to see if there was anything on television about what had happened. The remaining members, minus one, decided there was nothing to be done except to go back to their lives.

Juror Seven knew that she would never go back to the life she had been leading. As the jurors headed out of the building, Jane Nichols hung back, waiting. When the others were outside the courthouse, she turned in the opposite direction and walked toward the side exit of the courtroom.

At one-twenty-eight, RJ and Cunningham stepped into the hallway and came face to face with Saul Greene and two detectives. One of the detectives stepped forward and announced, "Bradley Cunningham, you're under arrest for felony child sexual abuse."

RJ, so astounded by the words he was hearing, dropped his briefcase on the floor, the loud noise reverberating through-out the hallway. *Felony child abuse? Holy shit!* Now it made sense why Cunningham had repeatedly refused to tell him what he was doing on Grover Street that morning. RJ bent down and picked up his briefcase. Then he stood up and faced Cunningham, giving him a Machiavellian smile before mockingly asking,"What was it you were saying a moment ago about not needing me?"

RJ's snide remark was completely missed by Cunningham whose heart had constricted in his chest, leaving him lightheaded, ashen-faced, breathless, and weak-kneed. The phone slid from his hand and his legs became so wobbly he was forced to reach out a hand to hold onto the wall to keep from falling. As his hand touched the wall, his eyes traveled several yards behind the three people in front of him and settled on a little girl pointing a finger in his direction; she was whispering something to the female police officer holding her hand. The last thing his eyes caught sight of before he (and the world as he knew it) collapsed, was the steely face of a triumphant Jane Nichols as she walked up behind the little girl.

Rose Cunningham had not slept since she left Allan's apartment and returned the drive to her husband's safe. It had taken her hours of mental anguish to grasp the reality of what was to follow after Allan turned over to Saul the disc copies he had made. Even in her anguished state, the irony of what was about to happen had not escaped her: she would be the one responsible for seeing her husband put behind bars. When she was at Allan's, it had taken every bit of her resolve to stay faithful to her earlier promise to stop burying her head in the sand. So, when Saul Greene called her that morning, she knew she would do the right thing, even though it would be the most difficult decision she would ever make.

It was now noon on Tuesday and Rose Cunningham, alone since Saul and the detectives had left, was curled in a fetal position on her bed. Plagued by the realization that there was not a single event in the entirety of her princess-like life that would serve to guide her through the chaos ahead of her, she came to one conclusion: she couldn't manage the shame.

Before he left, Saul asked her if there was anyone he could call to come stay with her. She lied, saying she would be all right; the truth was she would never be *right* again. For over thirty years, she, her parents, her church friends, and the world had thought of Bradley as saintly. The ugly truth—that he was an evil, amoral, despicable fraud—well, how could she ever face anyone again? How could she explain that she didn't know about his sexual deviance without revealing she was a virgin? Besides, virginity would be no excuse in the mind of anyone...and it would make her out to be a freak. No one would look at her the same, no matter what she did.

She opened the crumpled business card in her right hand, the card that Saul Greene had slipped her on his way out the door. He had leaned over and whispered, "Call this woman, she's a friend, a female RJ. She can help you through this."

But what could a lawyer do to help her except to make sure she was taken care of financially? Getting her money would do nothing to help with the shame. How could she ever run a children's foundation with the community knowing it had been funded by a child molester? Everyone would realize, as she now did, that the foundation had been a brilliant way to cover-up Bradley's true nature. The foundation, which had done so much good, would go down with Bradley, just as she was going down.

She pushed herself up and sat on the edge of the bed until she thought she might be able to stand up, letting go of the business card in her right hand. If floated to the floor. Then she staggered into the bathroom and opened the medicine cabinet, taking down the bottle of Tylenol PM and upending it in her left hand. She wondered if the thirty-plus pills left in the bottle was enough to do the trick. She filled a glass of water and began swallowing the pills a few at a time. When none were left, she slowly walked back to her bed and crawled under the covers. Waiting for it all to end, she felt some peace for the first time in days; she had done the right thing by ratting out her sicko husband. Just before she drifted off, she heard the doorbell ring, then some loud pounding on the door before all awareness faded.

After Cunningham had been dismissed, Erin, who was as stunned as everyone else, immediately called Toby, asking him to meet her at her condo. They spent almost an hour speculating on the new evidence that had caused the prosecution to drop the charges. Erin was convinced that it had something to do with the connection between the mystery brunette and Jane Nichols. She was unable to persuade Toby, however, that her speculation was even possible.

It was later that evening when Erin heard on the evening news that Cunningham had been re-arrested on sexual abuse charges that the last piece of the puzzle finally fell into place. If she was right about her latest conclusion on Jane's diagnosis, it now made sense to her why juror Seven had been so taken aback that very first day in the courtroom. Jane wasn't being reminded of someone in her past who hurt her; *she had just come face to face with her own perpetrator.* It had to be Cunningham who locked Jane in the closet. Admittedly, the odds against a coincidence like that were enormous, but Erin was sure that is exactly what did happen. After listening to the news on television, Erin reached for the phone to call Toby; it rang before she could make the call.

"I didn't see this coming," Toby said when she answered.

"I was close, but just a little off target. "Maybe if I had correctly diagnosed Jane the first time, I could have hit the bullseye."

DAY TEN

Jane Nichols awoke Wednesday morning with an unfamiliar feeling plaguing her. The routine of her life, once a source of comforting escape, now seemed dull, unimaginative and, well...a cop out. For almost ten years she had hidden herself away in a ghost town of a lab, an isolated, non-confrontational environment that served the purpose of avoiding the expectations of others. She hadn't made friends and avoided dating for the same reason. In the last nine days, however, so much had happened in her cocooned life that, for the first time she could remember, she questioned her protective shield of isolation. Hadn't her decision to be on the jury been about wanting to stop running away from the obstacles that life inevitably threw in front of her? And hadn't she succeeded? If she returned to her old life, wouldn't everything she accomplished during the trial go to waste? As she dressed, she thought about all the possibilities in front of her if she continued to be the Light Warrior that Sydney claimed she could be.

Vermillion told her he would know more about Megan's situation by the weekend. If the lawyer was able to pull it off, to get her appointed Megan's guardian until Tisha could stand on her own feet...well, she'd have to be stable enough to take care of the child. And that would mean much hard work ahead of her. She would have to change from the fragile, gutless person she had been to a strong, independent person. It would require conscious effort and hard work. She decided she would begin that effort when she got home that afternoon by telling Sydney she had agreed to take care of Megan.

As she drove to work she thought about all the ways she had prevailed in the last nine days. She had subdued her anxiety long enough to get on the jury. She had looked Cunningham directly in the eyes without crumbling, thwarted a physical attack, disguised herself as Sydney to get to and from court without being harmed, and twice summoned the courage to talk with Tisha. All her actions had caused the downfall of a powerful but depraved man, a man who had locked her in a closet and walked away without a hint of remorse. Admittedly, she couldn't have overcome all the challenges without Sydney's help. However, if she was to change, to be less fearful, she would have to stop turning to Sydney every time she faced a stumbling block. Just like her insulated, unchallenging work, running to Sydney had been an easy way out, a way to avoid taking on difficult obstacles and making decisions. What she had recently accomplished these last two weeks, though, was a damn good beginning of a new journey, a rite of passage to a different kind of life, a life without constant fear.

She now understood that shame and guilt were responsible for her blocked memories surrounding the events of her mother's death. All these years, she unconsciously blamed herself for her mom's death; the guilt and shame, even though unconscious, had caused her to be a fearful person. She would have to keep reminding herself that it wasn't her fault that her mother was a drug addict, an addict so desperate she would sell her own child for a fix, an addict just like Tisha.

This last thought shot a stabbing pain into her gut, so powerful that she had to pull over to the side of the road. She leaned her head on the steering wheel and sobbed. Something awful must have happened to her mother to cause her to do something as desperate as pimp her daughter. All these years she had been blocking out the realization that her real mother was a sick degenerate; blocking it out because it hurt so much to acknowledge it. The truth was that her mother was incapable of love; no wonder she felt unloved and unwanted. Jane cried even harder when she realized she would never know what had caused her mother to do something so awful. She beat her hands on the steering wheel at the frustration and hopelessness of never knowing the answers. Eventually, it seemed her body could produce no more tears.

She thought about Megan, a child of only six, the same age she had been when she had refused to bend to the will of the despicable stranger. She remembered what Sydney had asked her: would you blame the child? Of course it wasn't Megan's fault that Tisha was a drug addict. Yet, she had been blaming herself for her mother's self-destructive decisions. She didn't need Sydney to tell her that the important thing was to rid herself of the guilt—because holding on to the guilt meant holding on to the blame and the fear.

She lifted her head from the steering wheel and began to breathe. What would Sydney tell her? Be a warrior...think about the future instead of the past; the past can't be changed. She sat up straight and squared her shoulders. Because of her, Tisha, unlike her own mother, had a chance for redemption and Megan had the opportunity to be loved instead of used.

Thinking about the future brought her full circle: ten minutes ago she was listing her accomplishments, then she had slipped back into self-pity. Now she was in a place where she could choose not to give in to regret and sorrow. She could choose to embark on a new life of self-determination rather than passivity.

Countless adopted children had researched their backgrounds, many finding their own parents. Why couldn't she do the same? Her adoptive mother had told her that her biological mother and father were dead and that she had no living relatives. It had never occurred to her to question what she had been told. Maybe she did have a sister or other relative? Mustering the deepest breath she could, she vowed out loud: "I'm a Light Warrior, fearless and indestructible!"

While Jane was declaring a new way of dealing with her life, Erin was sitting next to Toby as he turned on his computer and brought up his file on Jane Nichols. No longer worried about jury tampering, Erin had requested the name and phone number of Jane's aunt. She had thought long and hard about whether intervening in the life of Jane Nichols was the right thing to do.

The trial was over and her professional role had officially ended. But unofficially? Did she have a responsibility to do something with the information she had? Or was Jane's life really none of her business? In the end she decided that doing nothing was cowardly and couldn't possibly be the right thing to do.

When she asked Toby last night if he would help her, he had said yes without giving her any grief. Now, however, with the phone number glaring at them on the screen, he questioned her. "Okay, I'm playing devils's advocate. Are you sure you want to disturb the dust bunnies that have been under her bed for so many years?"

"It just seems wrong to do nothing. I mean we have this information about Jane...information I'm sure she doesn't have...and we couldn't use it when she was a juror. Now we can use it and I think it could dramatically change the lives of two people who don't know the other one exists. So, I think it's right I share it with Jane. Maybe she will choose to do nothing, but then at least she will have made the choice."

"Being a private detective, I'll argue that my experience with sharing this kind of information is a toss of the coin. Yes, it can be liberating, but it can also be shattering. Predicting which outcome has been something I never mastered."

"I concede that the outcome is a gamble. However, I still think it should be Jane's choice. If I don't tell her, then she doesn't have the option. Admittedly, it's a liberal point of view, like Pro Choice when it comes to abortion. I'm not saying I personally would ever choose to have an abortion, but I think I should have the legal choice. Now that the trial is over, telling Jane she has an aunt is perfectly legal, right?"

"Well, now that you bring up the legal issues...you do realize, if your theory about Cunningham being her perp is right, she committed a crime by not taking herself off the jury? First hand knowledge of the defendant requires you to excuse yourself."

"We don't know that she knew. Maybe she repressed the memory. That happens in trauma all the time. But what a question! If a memory is unconscious is it known?" Then Erin looked Toby straight in the eye and said, "But even if she did consciously know, considering the man and the circumstances, I've decided my lips are sealed on that possibility."

"It could be argued that by keeping quiet you are committing a crime of omission. And I guess that goes for me as well."

"Yes, I've thought about that. When it comes to right or wrong, however, there are rarely absolutes, at least in my mind. I always consider the circumstances. The hit and run charges have been dropped, so the purpose of ratting her out on the issue of the trial entirely escapes me. We'll never know if Jane did something illegal. But even if she did—considering what new charges have been brought against Cunningham—well, does it matter?

"I take it you're certain Cunningham is guilty of the new charges."

"Well, I'm convinced that he traumatized Jane when she was little...that he was the one who locked her in that closet. So, yes, I think he's guilty of at least that."

"What is it that has convinced you of that scenario?"

Erin pointed at the computer, asking, "Could you bring up the photos of the brunette entering Jane's home?"

Toby gave her a questioning look but started typing and clicking until the slideshow of pictures began cycling on the screen. Erin tapped her fingernail at the woman on the screen, saying, "My conviction has to do with my theory on the connection between the brunette and Jane."

Toby shook his head in disbelief. "That theory? Well, let me just say that I'm not convinced about that one. It's just too weird, too out there."

"Yes, it is far-fetched. But I did some research. Excuse my bad pun, but the jury is still out on the possibility that I'm right."

"So, what exactly is your plan?"

"I'm going to confront Jane about it...right after I tell her she has an aunt."

"Well, if your theory turns out to be correct, you should write a book about it. It would make a hell of a sci-fi."

"Yeah, well, just remember truth is often stranger than fiction."

At the same time Erin and Toby were discussing the merits of telling Jane she had an aunt, RJ Holland was giving a press conference outside his office. When the TV cameras were in place and the mayhem finally subsided, he read from a prepared statement.

As you know, attorney-client communication is privileged. However, I am able to tell you a few truths. First, I always believed Mr. Cunningham to be not guilty of the hit and run and I felt sure we would have won our case if the charges had not been dropped. Second, I am as completely astounded as everyone else at the announcement of the new charges. Third, I will not be representing him on these new charges. Thank you for your attention.

The crowd of reporters began yelling questions but RJ turned and walked into his building without answering. He rode the elevator to his office with the Tweedles beside him. Not a word was spoken. He stepped off the elevator, walked rapidly into his office, passed his secretary without acknowledging her, and closed the door. He sat down at his desk and picked up the volume of new messages his secretary had left for him. Most of them were from the media, which he carefully put aside. One message, from another client with an impending trial, did not surprise him: sorry, but the negative publicity would hurt his case and he was already in negotiations with another attorney. The man was also asking for half of his fifty-thousand dollar retainer back.

Fuck him, thought RJ. No way he was giving the money back. Thinking about the money reminded him that the asshole

Cunningham still owed him two-hundred-thousand dollars. Considering what happened yesterday, he doubted the man would voluntarily hand over the money, so it was likely he would have to eat the outstanding debt. Taking legal action to collect would only serve to keep him associated with the God damn leper.

He glanced at the other messages on his desk. Another client was fleeing as well. RJ swiveled his chair around and looked out on the city below as he pondered how to be proactive. Then he stood up, left his office, and marched over to the open doorway of Tweedle Dee. "Come with me," he demanded. Dee immediately jumped up and followed him as he walked into the office of Tweedle Dum.

RJ began to pace, saying, "I want you two to research every attorney for the past ten years who has defended a child molester. I want to know what happened to the career—and the personal life—of any defense lawyer associated in any way with the molester."

"Are you thinking you might take Cunningham's case?" asked an astounded Dum.

"Absolutely not! But I need to know what to expect, because it's already clear I'm being caught in the collateral damage of this stink. When you finish with the child molester stuff, I want you to find me a high profile pro bono case...you know, damage control to replace the bad smell that surrounds me."

"Smart thinking," Dee said.

"Drop whatever else you're working on and bring me everything you guys get by three today."

"Yes, sir," Dee and Dum said in unison.

Once he left the room, Dee looked over at Dum and shook his head, saying, "I'm sending out resumes today."

"Man! I'm with you. The Reverend is caught in a sinkhole the size of Mars. No way I'm going down with him."

"You got that right!"

On the way back to his office, RJ decided the best thing he could do right now was to take a break from the events of the last twenty-four hours. He again checked his cell phone for the message he had been waiting for since last night. After the embarrassing night with Caroline, he had called a woman he knew would jump at the opportunity to be wined and dined by the famous RJ Holland; he had been right. The woman was aflutter, practically jumping into the phone when he asked her out. They agreed to meet on Friday night after the trial ended. Last night he called her and left a message to move the date up to tonight. It was disturbing that she had yet to return his call; no woman he had ever courted had failed to return his call.

God dammit! The fallout from Cunningham was apparently going to foul his already shaky sex life as well. The notion gave him a shiver of apprehension—immediately followed by the image of Dr. Erin Halloway. *God Damn I hate that woman. At least I don't have to see her vexing face again.*

He approached his secretary's desk. She nervously looked up, expecting one of his outbursts of rapid-fire orders. Instead he calmly said, "Send Dr. Halloway the rest of what we owe her, but *do not* follow up with the standard note of thanks. And if she calls for any reason, I'm not available."

His secretary did her best to hide her surprise at his calmness—and her curiosity at his *no thank you note* demand. "Yes, Mr. Holland," she replied obediently. She turned to her computer, brought up the electronic banking screen, and sent off a check. Looking around the office to be sure no one was watching, she then pulled her resume up on the screen. She was sure it needed a bit of tweaking before she began sending it out. The HMS Reverend was sinking and she wanted to get off before it went under for good.

While Erin and Toby were discussing the merits of telling Jane Nichols she had an aunt, and while RJ was giving his press conference, Rose Cunningham was waking up in a hospital psychiatric ward. Her eyes opened to a petite, middle-aged Asian woman sitting in a chair by her bedside. The woman said. "Hello, Rose."

Still groggy and quite confused, Rose asked, "Who are you?"

"My name is Amanda Chin. I'm a psychotherapist."

Rose slowly pushed herself to a sitting position and looked around the room. "Is this a hospital?"

"Yes, it is."

Then the memories began to flood Rose's mind. She cried, "Oh, no! The last I remember I was in my bedroom and I never wanted to wake up. What happened? How did I get here?"

"The police found you and brought you here."

"The police? What were the police doing in my home?"

"They were there to secure it. To be sure nothing else was taken out of it."

Rose sank back into the pillows, tears now easily flowing. "Why couldn't I just have died? It would have been so much easier."

Amanda leaned forward, taking Rose's hand, saying, "Faced with overwhelming hopelessness, Rose, death often seems more appealing than life."

Rose withdrew her hand and reached for a tissue on the table by her bed. Wiping the tears from her eyes, she said, "Obviously, you know who I am. I'm sure the whole damn world now knows who I am! So....what was your name again?"

"Dr. Amanda Chin."

"So, Dr. Chin..."

"Please, call me Amanda."

"So, Amanda, tell me honestly. If your husband of thirty-seven years turned out to be a degenerate child molester, would you want to face the world?"

"No, I wouldn't."

Rose gave Amanda a suspicious look. "So, you're saying you would have tried to kill yourself?"

"You asked for honesty, so I'd have to say I don't know what I would do, Rose. I do know I would feel overpowering shame."

Hearing these words brought another onslaught of tears from Rose. After several minutes of sobbing and fists full of tissues, Rose finally quieted. "You have no idea," she finally said.

"You're right. I can't know exactly what you're feeling. Though I do know that an attempt at suicide means you feel there is no one in your life to whom you can turn, no one who understands what you're going through. That's why I'm here."

Rose's face tightened into a look of worry. "Has anyone in my family been told I'm here?"

"Yes, your parents were called. They're in the waiting area down the hall. Father Clement is with them."

Rose waved her hand in front of her, saying, "No! No! I don't want to see my parents and I certainly don't want to see Father Clement."

"Okay, Rose. You don't have to see them, but you understand, of course, they are concerned. Is there anything you would like me to tell them?"

"Yes, tell them all that God is a fraud."

"God is a fraud? That's a sweeping, dismissive sentiment."

Rose turned her head away from Amanda and stared out into space. After a while, she turned back and looked straight at Amanda, her eyes filled with tears again. "If I had learned to depend more on myself rather than expecting God to *always be there for me*, I wouldn't be in this miserable situation."

Amanda leaned forward in her chair, replying, "I'm guessing, from the fact that you tried to kill yourself, you decided it's too late to learn how to depend on yourself."

"A few days ago I thought I might be able to...but that was before I found out I was naive enough to have been married to a monster for thirty-seven years. No one will believe I didn't know something was very wrong."

"I believe it."

"You're just saying that because you're supposed to."

"Actually, I'm saying that because I know something about pedophiles. I know how deceptive and scheming they can be. Your husband didn't just fool you; he duped everyone who knew him."

"Yes, but everyone didn't live with him and I did." Rose dropped her head to her chest, tears again leaking from her eyes.

Amanda said nothing and after almost a minute of silence, Rose lifted her head, saying, "You must want to know how it's possible a wife doesn't know her husband is a sexual pervert."

"All I want right now is for you to trust me, Rose. I want you to believe that you can tell me anything, that I won't judge you, and that I will keep what you tell me confidential."

Rose looked away again for several moments. Keeping her eyes averted, she murmured, "I didn't know because I'm a pathetic person. I'm sixty-two years old and I'm still a virgin." When Amanda stayed silent, Rose turned her head back toward the therapist and continued, "I've lived my entire married life in denial because it was easier than admitting I'm a sexual freak."

When Rose saw that Amanda's expression remained neutral, she continued, "When I was growing up, sex was a taboo topic in my home and the nuns in my school terrified me with their dire warnings of *out-of-wedlock* pregnancy. The scriptures commanded virginity until marriage. So I was a virgin when I got engaged and didn't know I had a sexual problem until I went for a premarital exam. The doctor couldn't do the exam. He said I had some sexual problem...I don't even remember what he called it. He told me it could be fixed and that I needed to see a sex therapist. I went once and quit because I was...well, I'm not sure exactly why I quit. At least I knew I couldn't keep it from the man I was about to marry. So, when I told Bradley about what the doctor said, he promised me it would resolve itself after marriage...but it didn't and Bradley never once brought it up. Because I was so ashamed, it was easy to convince myself Bradley loved me so much that he accepted me as I was." Rose shook her head back and forth in distaste. "Now I know he chose me because, with my problem, I would never confront him about the lack of sex." Her head dropped to her chest again as she sobbed, "I've been such a fool."

Amanda scooted forward in her chair, saying, "Look at me, Rose." Rose shook her head no. In a more commanding voice, Amanda said, "Look at me, Rose."

Rose kept her eyes downcast.

Amanda, gently lifting Rose's chin until their eyes met, said, "It's not too late to learn to depend on yourself. If you give up now, Bradley will have destroyed yet another life. It is time for his path of destruction to stop."

Rose collapsed back on her pillow. "But I don't know how to face the world."

"Forget about the world. What you need now is to learn how to face yourself. The shame has to stop. I can help you get rid of the shame."

"No. I don't think that's possible."

"I promise you it *is* possible, but it will take some time."

Again, Rose shook her head no. "Sorry, but I can't picture it. Besides, even if what you say is true, how am I supposed to live while I'm supposedly getting past the shame? The media is going to stalk me for the juicy details, they'll dig and dig...those voyeurs will never leave me alone. I'll have to check myself into some nut house so I don't have to face the world."

Amanda reached into her pocket and withdrew the crumpled business card that Rose had dropped on the floor and held it out to Rose. "The police found this by your bed. Look, Rose, I know this woman and I'm sure she can help by being your spokesperson, as well as protecting you legally. Why not let her be the one, for now, to deal with what you're calling *the world*. Right now all you need to deal with is retrieving your self respect."

"Self respect? I'll never be able to look in the mirror again."

"Rose, it's not hopeless. People do recover from sexual scandals. How about Hilary Clinton and Monica Lewinsky, for example? They got more media coverage than you will ever get and Hilary came close to becoming our president."

Amanda lifted the business card toward Rose.

Rose narrowed her eyes in thought and then reached for the card. She took it and studied it for a few seconds. Then she lifted her head saying, "Spokesperson, huh? I hadn't thought of that. It would be such a relief to let someone else deal with the hounds. She could be my own personal Gloria Allred." Rose turned toward Amanda with a slight smile, "Hilary Clinton, huh?" She tapped on the business card and then asked, "So, Amanda, how much do you think she could get me for a book contract?"

Amanda laughed. "I like it, Rose. Humor is always a good place to start."

Saul Greene stood in front of the TV monitor in his office watching RJ give his spin to the press and thinking, no matter what he says, he won't be having an easy time of it for months, if ever. When RJ turned to go inside his building, Saul turned off the TV, admitting to himself that he had been a roundabout winner on this case. The suspicious timing and circumstances of Tisha coming forward, still made him very nervous. If Cunningham decided to fight these new charges, his defense investigators would be undoubtably poking around, asking how Saul learned about the pornography.

From the moment he opened the discs he realized he was exposed to both a personal and professional conflict. Without the graphic visuals on the discs, however, the testimony of Tisha, a drug addicted low-life, would have been vulnerable, but how he came to *know* about the discs also made him vulnerable. He shuddered at the image of Allan being forced to testify on the stand, forced to admit he had a sexual relationship with Saul. The press would suck on that one like a hungry baby on a bottle. With his private life front page news, his career would crumble like a sand cookie. A second image resulted in a more intense shudder: he was sitting in a sleazy bar next to RJ commiserating over ruined careers.

So, how was it that Rose Cunningham had chosen Allan to hack into the discs? The whole series of events still seemed way too convenient. Meeting Allan and then the appearance of the discs within a week just didn't seem kosher. Without concrete evidence to prove that Allan wasn't legit, Saul was left to decide for himself how he wanted to proceed, both with the new case against Cunningham and with the new relationship with Allan. One thing for sure, if he wanted to explore the romantic relationship, he would have to remove himself as the prosecutor in any case against Cunningham.

When he had been given the hit and run case against the well-known Bradley Cunningham, he thought he had *the* case that would make his career. The high profile trial he had just finished, even with it's unexpected outcome, would pale in comparison to a prominent philanthropist being charged with pedophilia. When it came to a heinous crime, pedophilia trumped most all others at provoking the outraged absorption of the public and, thus, the media. The entire world would be watching if this one came to trial. It would be as big as the Sandusky spectacle.

Saul sat at his desk with his head in hands, his uncertain destiny heavy in his heart. Even if he recused himself as prosecutor on any new case involving Cunningham, there seemed to be no way he could prevent a defense attorney from finding out that he had received the discs from the man with whom he had a sexual relationship.

All of these dire considerations were whirling around in his mind when his secretary buzzed him. He sighed, lifted his head, and pushed the intercom. Her voice said, "Saul, I think you might want to talk with this caller. She claims she has some firsthand information about Cunningham and his sexual preferences."

Saul perked up. "Please tell me you don't think she's a crank. Maybe a crack head looking for some attention...or to make a deal of some kind."

"No, I don't. She called earlier and I grilled her for information and told her to call me back in an hour. Then I called around and her story checks out. She's a recovered addict whose daughter, only seven at the time, died four years ago. She's been sober ever since the daughter's death and has had a steady job now for three years. She says she never told anyone about what happened because she was so ashamed. When Cunningham was charged, however, she says she knew it was time to tell her story."

Saul's heart accelerated, thinking this could be too good to be true. "Okay, then. This should be interesting."

"Her name is Betty Niesen. Before I put her on, though, you need to know I had another call while I was checking out Betty's story. This new woman says her name is Sonya Beiging and she's claiming to have been one of Bradley's victims about sixteen years ago. I'll be checking her story out right after I put you through to Betty."

"Hot damn! It sounds like what happened with the priests...and Sandusky as well. The victim's shame keeps them quiet against a supposed saint until one person somehow develops the courage to go public."

"Exactly what I was thinking."

"You know, if these women's stories check out, Cunningham may just decide not to go to trial. After all, look what happened to Sandusky."

In the split second before Betty's Niesen's shaky voice came on the line, Saul allowed himself a selfish and comforting thought: if true, the testimony of these woman would likely solve the relationship dilemma he was having regarding Allan.

Despite her earlier resolve, the rest of the day Erin held a debate with herself about the wisdom of approaching Jane. Would she be stirring up emotions that would he harmful to Jane? It was now four o'clock and she was sitting, immobilized by doubt, in her car across the street from Jane Nichols's duplex. Twenty minutes ago she had seen Jane go into her home, but she couldn't get herself to move. She was staring ahead, deep in conflictual thought, when a tapping noise startled her. She looked over her shoulder to find Jane's face outside her car window. Erin immediately realized that her indecision had provoked a decision. She cracked her car door and Jane moved backwards so Erin could get out.

With more bravado than she felt, Jane said, "I don't know who you are but I recognize you from the courtroom. What are you doing staking out my home?"

"I am not staking...wait, I'm being defensive. Let me start over. My name is Erin Halloway. I *was* the jury consultant for the defense and I'm parked out here because I have information—it's information I was uncertain I should tell you."

"What kind of information?"

"It could be life-changing. Is there someplace we could go to talk?"

"I'm not going anywhere with you until I know what you want."

"Look, Jane, I understand why you would be skeptical. It's part of why I couldn't make up my mind about telling you. But I don't think this is a good place to talk."

Jane took a step backwards. "Well, I'm not inviting a suspicious stranger working for the defense inside my home if that's what you're thinking."

"No, of course not. And I'm no longer working for the defense. Is there someplace close by, a public place where you would feel more comfortable?"

Jane held up a hand, displaying a cell phone. "You haven't yet convinced me why I shouldn't just call the police."

Erin shook her head no, gently replying, "You're not going to call the police, Jane."

A bolt of anxiety struck at Jane's heart. The woman was calling her bluff; she must know about what she had done. Her bold decision to confront the woman now seemed more than foolish, but she felt frozen with uncertainty. What information did the woman have? Was she here to make her pay for the revenge she had extracted?

Seeing Jane's agitated reaction, Erin realized she had unintentionally pushed the fragile woman too far. She would have to do something to relieve some of Jane's mounting anxiety if she wanted Jane to talk with her. In a calming voice she said, "I promise I'm not here to make things difficult, Jane. Just let me tell you a little of what I know. Then you decide if you want to hear more."

Narrowing her eyes, Jane waited a few anxious seconds before saying. "Okay, go ahead."

"My job, what I'm paid to do, is to study jurors during trials, to predict what they're thinking and feeling. From day one I noticed you had an excessively negative reaction to Mr. Cunningham. So, I had our investigator research your background..."

"Wait a minute! That can't be legal."

"Well, yes it is as long as we follow the rules about jury tampering."

"It's legal to invade my privacy?"

"What we found is public information but, again, let me reassure you I'm not here to use the information against you."

Jane was frightened into silence. *She'd been found out. The woman must know what she and Sydney had done?* Her breathing became rapid and shallow, the familiar signs of an anxiety attack coming on.

Erin took a small step forward saying, "Please Jane, don't be afraid. I was hoping we could sit down and talk but it's obvious you don't trust me. So let me just quickly say that I'm here to tell you that you have an aunt living in another state. She's your biological mother's sister."

Jane stood there in disbelief, trying to shift gears while her accelerating heart pounded in her body. Despite her earlier reflections about having a possible family member, what the woman just said was so unexpected, so contrary to what she was thinking, that she was momentarily dumbfounded. After a few overwhelming moments she asked, "Let me get this right. You're saying I have an aunt who's alive?"

"Yes, she lives in another state."

Jane, now lightheaded and trembling asked, "How could this be possible when I was told I had no living relatives?"

Erin stepped closer to Jane, saying, "You've lost all the color in your face. I knew I shouldn't have told you this unless you were sitting down. Will you let me help you to my car?"

Weak-kneed and dizzy, Jane conceded, "Yeah, okay."

Erin took Jane's elbow and helped her walk the few feet to the car, placing her in the driver's seat. A pale, shaky Jane looked up at Erin, saying, "This is not what I was expecting."

"I anticipated it would be a shock, which is why I was so uncertain about telling you. It will help if you breathe slowly and deeply,"

Jane took some deep breaths and then gave Erin a weak smile before saying, "You sound just like Sydney."

Impulsively, Erin couldn't resist the opening, "Yes, Sydney...she's the woman with the long brown hair. Your roommate, right? I wanted to talk to you about her as well."

After the shocking news about having an aunt, hearing that the woman also knew about Sydney was too much. Jane put her head in her hands and began to cry.

Erin, admonishing herself, thought, *shit...I am so screwing this up.* She put a hand on Jane's back, saying. "I'm so sorry, Jane. This is not what I intended. Can we please go somewhere to talk? There are things I need to tell you and this is just not the best place."

Lifting her head, Jane said, "I guess you're right about that." Wiping the tears from her eyes with her hand, Jane took several very deep breaths and said, “There’s a Starbuck’s about a mile from here. Why don’t you follow me there?”

“Maybe it’s not a good idea for you to drive right now.”

“Well, it’s not that far and I’m certainly not getting in some stranger’s car, a stranger who claims to have personal information about me that I don’t even know about.”

“I could call a cab for you.”

Suddenly, Jane’s entire demeanor changed. She lifted her shoulders and sat upright, no longer seeming fearful. “No, I’m better now and I can drive. Just let me get my keys.”

Five minutes later they were sitting across from each other at an outside table at the coffeehouse. Jane appeared much calmer, asking, “I was so nervous back at the house that I don’t remember your name.”

“Erin Halloway. Call me Erin, please.”

“So, okay, Erin, now that you’ve got my attention would you please start at the beginning?”

“Sure. Like I said, I am a jury consultant. The attorney for the defense hired me to watch the reactions of the jury and to feed him information to help him win the case. The first day I noticed your strong reaction to the defendant...”

Jane put her hand out, palm forward,“Wait a minute. You’ve got to know how unnerving it is to hear that you’ve been psyched out without your permission. Jurors agree to be impartial, they don’t agree to being analyzed. Who and what gives you the right to muck around undisclosed in people’s private lives?”

Erin was taken aback. Ten minutes ago, Jane was an anxious, cowering woman who could barely keep it together and now Erin was sitting across from a confrontational woman who was attempting to put her on the defensive. She felt sure she was getting a glimpse of something that few people ever knowingly experience. Mesmerized, she wanted to see more and knew she had to be careful not to blow it. Cautiously, she replied, “Well, I can see how it would be upsetting to find out someone has been studying you.”

"Please, no psychological empathy tricks. You're evading my question, so I gotta ask, why that is?" Before Erin could answer, Jane, demanded, "By the way, do you have some ID? I want to be sure you are who you say you are."

Erin was amused. *How ironic. Jane Nichols is challenging my identity.* Nevertheless, she complied, reaching into her purse for her driver's license and handing it over. Jane studied it for a few moments, then looked up at Erin and studied her before handing it back. Erin took the license, placed it back in her purse, and then looked Jane straight in the eye, saying, "You're right. No one gave me permission to analyze you. Still, it's legal and it's what I do. Some of my conclusions about you concerned me, so I asked our investigator to research your past."

Jane shook her head no. "Research? What bullshit! You stuck your nose where it didn't belong. You've got some nerve, lady. How do you sleep at night?"

Fascinating. Mousy, timid Jane had metamorphosed into a combative woman, assuring Erin that her theory about Jane Nichols had to be right. Deciding she no longer needed to be cautious, Erin replied, "I find it very revealing that you're more interested in putting me on the defensive than you are in hearing what I discovered about your past."

"My past is none of your business."

"I don't think Jane would be saying that."

"What the hell is that supposed to mean?"

"Just what I said. I think Jane *would* want to know about her past. It's her imaginary roommate who would do what you're doing—protecting Jane—doing her best to keep anyone or anything from potentially hurting Jane."

Jane stood up and leaned over into Erin's face, snapping at her, "You're insane. You stay away from us, you hear?"

Jane turned to leave but Erin quickly responded, "Us?"

Jane spun around, asking, "What did you say?"

"You said *us*. I'm looking at Jane but it's her imaginary friend who's talking to me right now." When the woman didn't walk away, Erin hurried on, "It's called Dissociative Identity Disorder; *one* person, *two* distinct personalities. The stronger personality steps in for Jane whenever Jane is too terrified to deal with reality. It's a rare psychological response to severe childhood trauma." Erin reached into her purse and pulled out the photos of the brunette going into the duplex. She slid the photos toward the woman. "While Jane's roommate looks and acts totally different from Jane, the two personalities have some identical mannerisms."

Jane glanced at the photos. After a few moments she sat back down, glaring at Erin. "How very clever of you."

"Not really. Turns out I got it wrong at first. But then last Saturday night on Grover Street, I noticed you were wearing the same pendant Jane wore in the courtroom. That's when I first started to be suspicious. It took me a while but I eventually came to realize that Jane invented you years ago when she felt she couldn't cope. Jane had to have felt so helpless and afraid that she conjured up an alter ego just to survive. She worships you because you're the part of her that's not afraid."

When Jane didn't argue, Erin continued. "In most cases, the stronger personality *knowingly* plays along, while the weaker personality remains blind, truly believing they are two separate people."

Jane's eyes narrowed in consideration but she didn't answer. Instead she kept her steely eyes fixed on Erin.

"I'm sure it was you who somehow caused the car to crash," Erin continued. "You saved my life, as well as that of the man who was with me, so I want to thank you for that."

With a sly smile, Jane said, "You mean you *owe* me for that."

Erin returned the sly smile, "Exactly what Sydney, but not Jane, would say." She fished around in her purse and came up with a business card; she placed it on top of the photos. "Here's my card. It has the name and phone number of your aunt on the back. There is also a name and phone number of a therapist who specializes in Dissociative Disorders. Since Jane's consciousness doesn't allow her to acknowledge she has another personality, she won't know we had this conversation. It will be up to you to tell her about the information on the card. However, since you exist for her benefit, I feel confident you'll do what's best for her."

Jane picked up the card, turned it over, and studied it before looking up at Erin, the cunning grin still on her face. "It's been fun while it lasted. But you're right. It's always been Jane who's the Scaredy Cat. When she made the decision, against my advice, to be a juror, I knew she was ready for a change, that she wanted to face her demons, although she could never have anticipated she would be facing the actual demon. Anyway, given how Jane, alone, managed to outwit Cunningham, maybe it is time for us to merge. Besides, maybe the aunt can answer some of the questions gnawing inside Jane about our messed-up mom. I don't suspect the answers will be pretty, but knowing will help Jane get on with her life without me."

"Does that mean you're going to tell Jane that you exist within her?"

Standing, Jane picked up the card, snapping it twice with her thumb and forefinger before leaning down toward Erin. "It's been riveting meeting you, Erin." She then stood up and slid the card into her pocket before continuing, "However, if you're honestly here to help Jane, this is the end of it. Remember, you owe me. Which means neither Jane, nor I, will be seeing you again—or anyone who had anything to do with the trial, right?"

"If you're asking me if I'll rat Jane out for jury misconduct if she doesn't get help, the answer is no. Jane's been through enough and I believe in this case that revenge is not only sweet but deserved. So, I'm butting out and leaving it up to you. You have my card, though, and I sincerely hope you'll contact me if you think I can be of help."

Jane turned to go, saying over her shoulder, "Ta-ta, doctor." As she retreated, she began skipping and singing, "We're off the see the wizard, the wonderful wizard of Oz."

Erin, shaking her head in wonderment, watched her leave. *Such a ballsy woman. If she wasn't a figment of Jane's tortured mind, I would like to have her as a friend.* She was still watching Jane retreat when the ring of her cell phone startled her. She looked at the caller ID and answered,"Hey, Toby. I had a feeling it was you."

"Well, duh. No secret I was snared by your scheme to confront Jane. So, give it up. Is she or isn't she?"

"How about I spill the beans over drinks at my place?"

"No way I'm waiting any longer. You sprung the trap when you told me you were going to talk with Jane. I've been locked in nail biting suspense and I need to be released from the snare."

Erin laughed. "Okay, okay. I'll throw you a crumb. Here's the deal. I was right about the dissociative diagnosis, but if you want to know the juicy details, you'll have to come over."

"Right about the multiple personalities? Well, I'll be damned. Who but you would have thunk it? Have you ever considered being a consultant for a PI? I could sure use somebody whose power of observation borders on the occult. As a team, we couldn't be beat."

"Hmm. Intriguing offer. Working for you would sure beat working for assholes like RJ. Don't know if you could afford me, though."

"Well, there's that. But there is also working *with* me, fifty-fifty partners."

"That's a temping offer worthy of discussion. Meet me at my place in thirty?"

"Bells on my toes and all that."

After ending the call, Erin returned to thinking about the rarity of what she had just experienced. She knew that even with therapy, merging two personalities was a long shot. Still, she couldn't help being intrigued by the potential of a consolidated Jane/Sydney. Her next thought surprised her.

Could she could keep her promise to butt out?

AUTHOR'S NOTE: Jane Nichols and Rose and Bradley Cunningham are fictional characters. The description of the behaviors and origin of their emotional and sexual problems, however, are based on composites of real-life people with whom I spent many therapy hours.

FURTHER INFORMATION

National Hotlines on sexual child abuse;

http://www.childhelp.org/pages/hotline-home

http://www.childhelp.org/

Etiology and Treatment Of Pediophilia:

http://neuroanthropology.net/2010/05/10/inside-the-mind-of-a-pedophile/

http://www.stopfamilyviolence.org/info/child-sexual-abuse/the-science-of-child-sexual-abuse

http://dynamic.uoregon.edu/%7Ejjf/articles/dpf04.pdf

28701287R00182

Made in the USA
Lexington, KY
28 December 2013